# The Girl Who Got Revenge

## MARNIE RICHES

**avon.**

Published by AVON
A Division of HarperCollins*Publishers* Ltd
1 London Bridge Street
London SE1 9GF

www.harpercollins.co.uk

First published in Great Britain by
HarperCollins*Publishers* 2018

1

Marnie Riches asserts the moral right to
be identified as the author of this work

A catalogue record for this book
is available from the British Library

ISBN: 978-0-00-828508-1

Set in Minion Pro by Palimpsest Book Production Limited,
Falkirk, Stirlingshire

Printed and bound by CPI Group (UK) Ltd, Croydon, CR0 4YY

This book is dedicated to the memory of my cousin, Beverley Thorpe, whose light shone brightly but faded far too soon.

# PROLOGUE

## *Amsterdam, the house of Brechtus Bruin, 2 October*

Brechtus Bruin was not aware that the kitchen clock ticking away on the wall was counting down the last few minutes of his ninety-five years. His movements had slowed of late, and now his complexion was noticeably wan and waxy. Perhaps he was finally feeling the poison in his bones that rainy morning. He must surely have been wondering that his shaking, liver-spotted hands wouldn't obey his still-sharp brain, telling him to pour the coffee.

'Here, Brechtus. Let me help you. Please.'

His guest had been sitting at a worn Formica table in that homely place, waiting. He had been drinking in the familiar scene of the cramped kitchen with its sticky, terracotta-painted walls. Savouring the stale scent of cakes that had been baked decades ago by Brechtus's long-dead wife. Now, he stood to take the kettle from the old man.

'You sit down. I've got this. Honestly.'

'I don't like people fussing,' Brechtus said, wiping the sweat from his poorly shaven upper lip. 'I don't know what's wrong with me. I've not been feeling myself. You know?' His breath came short. His Adam's apple lurched up and down inside his haggard

1

old neck. 'Not just my bad back. More than that. I feel ...' He pursed his deeply pruned lips together and frowned. 'Wrong. Horrible, in fact.'

Brechtus Bruin fixed his guest with the dulled irises of a dead man walking. There was fear and confusion in those bloodshot eyes; eyes that had seen almost a century of life. Even at his grand age, it was clear that he didn't want to go. But any minute now, one of the greatest heroes of Amsterdam's WWII resistance would be nothing more than an obituary in *de Volkskrant*.

Slipping a little extra Demerol and OxyContin into the old man's coffee cup, he hoped that the taste wouldn't be bitter enough to put him off one final swig.

'There you go, Brechtus,' he said, setting the mug down on the table. 'Drink it while it's hot. Maybe you're just coming down with something. There's an awful lot of bugs going round at the moment.'

The coffee sloshed around as the old man raised the mug to his mouth with an unsteady hand. His thin arms barely looked capable of holding even this meagre weight.

*Go on, drink it,* the guest thought. *Let's finish this.*

He savoured the sight as Brechtus Bruin gulped down the hot contents, grimacing and belching as he set the cup back down.

'I think maybe the milk was off,' he said.

Still, the clock ticked. Even closer to the end, now. Tick. Tick. Tick.

Brechtus's pallor was the first indication that the medication had started to do its work. Then, the sheen of sweat on the old man's face grew suddenly slicker, giving him a waxy look, as though he were preserved in formaldehyde. One side of his face started to sag in a strange palsy. The old man's eyes widened.

'I feel ...'

2

He tried to speak, but it was as if the poisonous cocktail was paralysing his vocal chords.

'Help. Oh.'

Brechtus Bruin's guest watched with amusement as the elderly war hero clutched at his chest and inhaled deeply, raggedly.

'I don't—'

'What is it, Brechtus?'

With his other grey, gnarled hand – already blue at the fingertips – the old man grasped at the tablecloth, tugging at it as though the fabric were his mortal coil and he was holding on for dear life. Everything that had been placed on the table fell with him and the cloth, clattering to the floor. Broken china everywhere; coffee spattered across the varnished cork tiles like the victim's blood from a well-aimed headshot in a shoot-'em-up movie. Finally, still gasping pointlessly for air like a determined goldfish flipped out of its tank, Brechtus lay on the floor, limbs splayed in improbable directions. Pleading in the old man's eyes said he didn't want to leave this life.

Did he suspect? Did he realise that this friend of old, a guest in his home, had committed the ultimate act of betrayal?

It was too late. When his eyes had glazed over, the guest knew that his latest victim was dead. To be certain, he squatted low, pulling the fabric of his shirt aside to reveal the small tattoo of a lion on the aged, freckled skin of his shoulder. The lion wore a crown and carried a sword. It was flanked by the letter S and the number 5.

He checked for a pulse.

Nothing.

Whistling to himself, he started to wipe the place down of fingerprints, careful to pick up from the floor the shattered remains of the coffee cup that he had drunk from, disposing of them in a small plastic freezer bag that he had brought in case of exactly this kind of accident. What a shame that the silly old bastard had made such a mess on his way out of that overlong, sanctimonious life. He pinched his nose against the smell of death, already rising from the body. Tiptoed over the spilled coffee to ensure he left no footprints.

Turning back to survey the scene, he decided that this termination had been well executed. On to the next one. By the time Brechtus Bruin's body would be found, he would be sufficiently far away to evade suspicion. The method of killing was flawless. And most important of all, he thought, as he pulled the door to the house closed, he was certain that Brechtus Bruin had suffered in the last few weeks of his life.

What a cheering thought. He smiled and was gone.

# CHAPTER 1

## *Amsterdam, Van den Bergen's apartment, 3 October*

The sound of someone closing a cupboard door in the kitchen was the reason for George's wakefulness. Her body taut beneath the duvet, she listened carefully. Held her breath until the only sounds she could hear were the rushing of blood through her ears and the intruder. The cutlery drawer was being opened. The rattle of metal told her something was being removed. Heavy footsteps of a man.

Throwing the duvet aside, she leaped out of bed. In an instinctual choice between fight or flight, George opted for the former, grabbing a tin of Elnett hairspray from the dressing table as she exited the bedroom.

'Bastard!' she yelled, sprinting towards the kitchen and the source of the noise. She held the can of hairspray aloft, ready to press the button and blind this cheeky burgling wanker.

The tall, prematurely white-haired man who had been stooped over the worktop spun around with his hands above his head. His gaunt, wan face contorted into a look of pure surprise. 'It's me, for Christ's sake!'

With her heart thundering inside her chest, George froze in the middle of the living room, staring at her opponent through the large hatch to the kitchen. She glanced at the clock on the wall.

'It's four in the morning. What the hell are you doing out of bed?' She set the hairspray down on the battered old coffee table, her hand shaking with adrenalin. Her voice wavered with slowly subsiding fear. 'I thought you were a burglar.'

Van den Bergen shook his head and smiled grimly. He clutched at his stomach. 'In my own apartment?' Belching quietly, his brow furrowed. 'It's my stomach. I just couldn't sleep. I could taste the acid spurting onto my goddamned tongue.'

George padded into the kitchen and put her arms around her lover. His grey, baggy T-shirt smelled of washing powder, but as she stood on tiptoe and nestled her face into his neck, she drank in the scent of his warm skin beneath. 'Poor you,' she said. 'Honestly, Paul. You've got to demand that your doc sends you to a specialist. You're at the surgery every five bloody minutes, but the shit she's prescribing isn't working.'

Van den Bergen kissed the top of her head and moved away from her. 'I don't want a gastroscopy. I've heard it's grim, like having drains rodded. I wish they'd give me a PET scan, and then I'd know, once and for all.' The low rumble of his voice had taken on a hoarse edge over the past few months. He closed his eyes and curved his six foot five frame into a stoop, as though his long spine had been replaced by nothing more than a pipe cleaner.

Picking up the large brown bottle from the worktop, George read the blurb and raised an eyebrow. She sucked her teeth. Scratched at her scalp and shook out the wild curls of her afro. Irritated by this anxious man who overthought everything. But genuinely fearful for him, this time. 'I'm sick of your bullshit. Every five minutes, you're moaning at me that you're coming down with a spot of terminal this and deadly that.'

'I think I might have throat cancer, George. I mean it. Have some sympathy for an old fart. The longer I live, the more likely it is that something's going to get me.' This tormented, difficult bastard of a chief inspector, whom she loved so much, rubbed his stomach. 'Maybe it's stomach cancer. Can you get stomach cancer?'

George slammed the bottle of antacid down. She switched from his native Dutch to her native English. 'For God's sake, man. Get it fucking sorted. You demand Dyno-Rod or a scan or some shit, or me and you are going to tangle! I can't keep getting woken up in the middle of the night. If it's not your stomach, it's the job. It's bad enough back at Aunty Sharon's with Letitia up 'til all hours and then stinking in bed 'til midday, Aunty Sharon not getting home from work until three in the morning, and then Dad getting up when she comes in because his body clock's buggered.'

'I can't help it! This is what you get when you fall for a man twenty years your senior.'

George waved her hand dismissively at his mention of their age gap. It hadn't mattered when they'd met almost a decade ago and she'd been a twenty-year-old Erasmus student, and it didn't matter now. 'When I come to Amsterdam, I need to get my kip. I'm a criminologist, Paul. I spend my days with murderous mental cases in draughty prisons – when I'm not scrapping for funding or teaching snot-nosed first-year students. My life's stressful as hell. This is where I decompress, yeah?' She switched back to Dutch. 'I've got nowhere else I can relax – until you commit to getting a mortgage with me, so I've got a home I can call my own … And I don't care if it's here or London or in Cambridge. Whatever. But don't think you can keep wriggling out of that conversation, mister.' She wagged her finger at him. Still sour that Van den Bergen had refused to be drawn on the subject of the bricks-and-mortar commitment George so desperately sought since her brush with death in Central America. 'It's time we put down roots together! Anyway, until you get your shit together so I can stop this nomadic, long-distance romance crap, your place is my happy place. I need some peace and quiet. Not you, wandering round like a spectre, swigging from a family-sized bottle of Gaviscon in the early hours.' She poked him in the stomach, careful to avoid the long line of scar tissue that bulged beneath the fabric of his top – a permanent aide-memoire of the mortal danger a job like his put him in – put both of them in. 'And for a hypochondriac, you're a total failure. You need to man up, get to the doc's and insist that she doesn't fob you off. I can't have you dying on me, Paul. Sort it out!'

Her lover belched and grimaced. He rolled his eyes up to the bank of spotlights that she had recently scrubbed free of cooking grease, accumulated from those occasions when Van den Bergen had been bothered to cook – badly. 'You've got the cheek to talk to me about peace and quiet, with your family? There's no escaping their noise, even from the other side of the North Sea, thanks to them Skyping you every five minutes!' He grabbed her around the middle and pulled her close. 'Anyway, you're exaggerating. This is the first time in ages that I've woken you up.' He ran his long fingers gently along the sides of her unfettered breasts. 'And there was once a time when you were happy to be disturbed in the middle of the night.'

He was smiling now, though the mirth didn't quite reach his eyes. George could see that he was suffering. Nevertheless, Van den Bergen lifted her off the ground as though she were a doll, amidst her shrieked protests, and carried her into the bedroom. They had just begun to enjoy a passionate kiss, only slightly marred by the aniseed taste of his antacid medicine and the knowledge that Van den Bergen's heart wasn't entirely in it, when the mobile phone on his nightstand started to buzz.

'Oh, you're joking,' George said, rolling his long frame off her. 'See?'

'Who the hell is it at this time in the morning?' Van den Bergen asked, rummaging for his glasses among the pile of pill packets and gardening manuals. He held the folded spectacles up to his eyes and scowled at the phone's screen. 'Bloody Maarten Minks.' He pressed the answer button and lifted the phone to his ear. 'Morning, Maarten. Isn't it a little early—?'

Gathering the duvet around her like a cocoon, George could hear Van den Bergen's boss, the commissioner, on the other end. His voice sounded squeaky and overexcited. Demanding dickhead. She guessed he liked nothing more than to lord it over his ageing subordinate at an unsociable hour.

'Yes. Okay. Straightaway. I'll call you with an update.' Van den Bergen nodded and hung up, exhaling heavily.

'What is it?' George asked, stifling a yawn.

'Port of Amsterdam,' he said. 'Customs have found a truck full of suffocating Syrians, and guess who's been tasked with investigating!'

'Trafficked?'

'What do you think?'

'How many?' George wiped the sleep from her eyes.

Van den Bergen was already on his feet, pulling on the weekend's jeans, which were only slightly muddy from a trip to his Sloterdijkermeer allotment. 'Fifty-odd. Minks has got his knickers in a twist. He's under pressure to stem the tide of refugees coming into the city. The burghers of Amsterdam are happy to throw money at Syrian charities but they're not overly pleased at the thought of hundreds of them arriving in cargo trucks to shit on their highly polished Oud Zuid doorsteps.'

'Hypocrites,' George said. 'It's the same in the UK. Most of the people you speak to are sympathetic about what's being done to those poor bastards. Bombed by the Russians. Bent over by Daesh. Shat on by Assad. But nearly half the nation voted for Brexit, mainly to keep immigrants out, so somebody's telling fibs.' She padded back to the kitchen and switched on the kettle. As she prepared a flask of coffee for Van den Bergen, she thought about her own father, currently holed up in South East London with her mother, from whom he was estranged, and her long-suffering Aunty Sharon. With his Spanish passport, would he be sent packing back to his country of origin, unable to rebuild the relationship with his long-lost daughter properly?

Screwing the lid closed on the flask, she eyed the printout of the ticket to Torremolinos that she'd propped behind Van den Bergen's peppermint teabags. Ten days, descending en masse on the three-star Sol hotel of Letitia's choice, at Letitia's insistence, with the sea-facing rooms that Letitia had stipulated. George in with her cousin, Tinesha. Her Dad in with cousin Patrice. Mommie Dearest, bunking up with poor old Aunty Sharon, where she'd undoubtedly hog all the wardrobe space – ''Cos I gotta look my best if I'm not well with my pulmonaries. I gotta make that rarseclart know what he's been missing all these years, innit?' Not long now. George could almost smell the rum and Coke by the pool and the melange of coconut sun cream scents from Thomson's least intrepid travellers.

When Van den Bergen took his flask and kissed her goodbye, his phone was welded to his ear yet again. A grim expression on his handsome face and his thick shock of prematurely white hair seeming cold blue in the dawn light.

'And one of them's died?' he asked. Presumably it was Minks on the other end. 'Oxygen deprivation?' A pause. He snatched a bag of crisps and the key to his Mercedes from the console table in the hall. 'Dysentery?! Ugh. What a way to go in a confined space. How old?'

His brow furrowed. He pulled the door closed.

George could still hear him speaking in low, rumbling tones on the landing. 'Twelve? Jesus. Poor little sod. Okay. I'm on it.'

10

# CHAPTER 2

## *Port of Amsterdam, later*

'How come the truck was intercepted here?' Van den Bergen asked Elvis, his voice almost whipped away entirely by the stiff dockside wind and swallowed by the sobs of those Syrian refugees who were yet to be assessed by paramedics and ferried to hospital. He blinked hard at the sight of this desperate diaspora, sitting on the pavement, wrapped in tinfoil blankets, with blood-pressure cuffs strapped to their arms and oxygen monitors clamped on their fingers. 'Seems a weird place for the driver to have come. It's all logistics and exporter head-quarters in this bit of the port.'

He studied the heavy goods vehicle, which had been cordoned off with police tape by the uniforms. On the side of the truck's battered burgundy container, the livery of a produce company, Groenten Den Bosch B.V., had been emblazoned in yellow. It looked no different from any other cargo vehicle carrying greenhouse-grown unseasonable fruit and vegetables to the UK and beyond.

'Apparently the port authority cops were heading this way after they'd been to investigate a break-in over there ...' Elvis gesticulated towards some grey industrial sheds in the distance that bruised the watery landscape with their utilitarian bulk.

11

It looked exactly like the place the junior detective had almost met an untimely end at the hands of the Rotterdam Silencer's men. Small wonder that he was shivering, his shoulders hunched inside his leather jacket, a pinched look to his face. 'It was a chance discovery,' he said, his eyes darting furtively over to the wharf-side warehouse behind them. The scar around his neck was still livid, though he'd covered it up today with a scarf. The quiff and mutton-chop sideburns that had earned him his nickname may have been replaced by a stylish cut and better clothes, but Van den Bergen's protégé looked positively vulnerable these days.

'Are you eating right?' Van den Bergen asked, scratching his nose with the edge of his notebook.

'What? What's that got to do with a truckload of trafficked Syrians?'

Van den Bergen coughed awkwardly, wondering how to dress his fatherly concern up as idle curiosity. It wouldn't do to let Elvis know that he cared … Would it? 'Nothing. You just look …'

'I've been going to the gym.' He patted his newly flat stomach.

'Oh. It's just … what with you being garrotted and left for dead and—'

'Can we just not, boss?' Elvis smiled weakly and pulled his jacket closed against the wind. 'Anyway, the driver was trying to turn around, can you believe it? Who the hell tries to do a three-point turn with a heavy goods vehicle on a road like this?! When they pulled over to ask him what the hell he was doing, the guy freaked, jumped out of his cab and tried to run away. That's when they opened up the back and found all these poor bastards inside.'

Van den Bergen belched stomach acid into his mouth and swallowed it back down with a grimace. Wondered how Elvis felt about the black body bag that lay on a gurney by the roadside, having been found inside one himself on the brink of death. He walked over to the gurney.

'Give me some space,' he told the uniform – a young lad who looked like he was barely out of cadet school. 'Let me see her.'

Breathing in deeply, he slowly unzipped the bag to reveal the pale face of the girl inside. Were it not for the blue tinge to her lips and the general grey hue to skin that had certainly been olive in life, she could almost be sleeping. One of the sobbing women who sat on the pavement leaped up and made for him. Tears streamed down her red face. She shrieked something at Van den Bergen – words that he didn't comprehend, though he understood her anguish perfectly. Bitter, biting grief needed no interpreter. One of the other women pulled the girl's mother back before two uniformed officers could restrain her.

Thinking of his granddaughter, Van den Bergen's viscera tightened. He ground his molars together. Turned to the uniform. 'How many of the refugees are critical?'

The lad touched the brim of his hat respectfully. Visibly gulped. 'Twenty have gone off with the first lot of ambulances,' he said. 'They were in the worst shape. The rest …'

He inclined his head to the remaining ragtag band of chancers sitting on the pavement: about two-dozen men in dusty, cheap suits or hoodies and jeans, yellowed at the knees. They looked like they had stepped straight from a war zone into the truck. The half dozen or so women wore jeans and tunics for the most part – full-length, loose-fitting dark dresses on the older ones. All had their heads covered, though they had oxygen masks fitted to their faces. The remainder were children, ranging from about five years old to young teens, dressed in bright colours. Van den Bergen was struck by how ordinary they all looked. He berated himself for having expected them all to appear like Middle Eastern stereotypes instead of electricians, nurses, teachers, lecturers: people who had simply had enough of certain death in their homeland and had decided to take their chances on possible death in the back of a heavy goods vehicle.

'Make sure they get whatever they need while they're waiting,' Van den Bergen said, swallowing hard and clenching his fist around his pen. 'If the paramedics say they can eat and drink, arrange it. Good policing is about more than just arresting bad guys. Speaking of which, where's the driver?'

The uniform pointed to a squad car that had been parked at an unlikely angle across the street, forming part of the roadblock. 'He refuses to speak. My sergeant's about to take him in for questioning. You'll want to sit in on the interview, right?'

The squad car's engine started up. The reverse lights came on, and the vehicle started to roll back slowly. In Van den Bergen's peripheral vision, he caught sight again of the body bag that contained the little girl. Her keening mother was now being tended to by a paramedic. A corrosive force stronger than stomach acid welled up inside him. Pushing the uniformed lad aside, Van den Bergen took long strides towards the brightly liveried *politie* squad car. He wrenched open the passenger door and held up his large hand. Flashed his ID. Fixed the female sergeant with a stern and unflinching gaze. 'Stop the car,' he said. Pushing the central locking button on the console, he unlocked the car's doors. Then he leaped over the bonnet to the driver's side and opened the rear door. Without pausing to take a look at the greasy-haired trucker, he grabbed the handcuffed man by the scruff of his neck and pulled him out of the car.

'Who are you working for?' he yelled at him.

The trucker was a middle-aged man with a bloated, red face and veined nose that spoke to high blood pressure and too much whisky. Puffy beneath the eyes. He stank of stale cigarettes

14

and fried food. A dark band of grease described the collar of his blue sweatshirt, ending in a V above his sternum. This didn't strike Van den Bergen as a scrupulous or discerning man who might be bothered where the money for his alcohol might come from.

'No comment. I want a solicitor,' the man said, holding Van den Bergen's gaze. 'You just manhandled me out of that car. That's police brutality.'

'You ran, didn't you? When the port cops pulled you over, you ran, you piece of shit. A kid's dead on the back of your actions.' He pushed the trucker hard in the shoulder – a family man's rage taking over his professional sensibilities.

By the time the trucker had stretched his cuffed hands down towards his baggy jeans, Van den Bergen was too late to realise he was aiming for his pocket. With determined fingers, the man pulled out a white object.

'Boss! Watch out!' Elvis yelled, sprinting towards them.

What was it? A note? An envelope? Van den Bergen didn't have time to put on the glasses that hung on the end of a chain around his neck to work out what the trucker had armed himself with.

'Stay back!' the man shouted, wide-eyed. Spittle had gathered at the corners of his mouth, putting Van den Bergen in mind of a crazed bull. 'I'll open it. I will. And you'll all be fucked.'

'Take it easy!' Elvis said, holding his hands high.

Trying to make sense of the situation, Van den Bergen's fingers crept slowly towards the gun in its holster, strapped to his body. 'Whoa!' he said. 'What have you got there?'

'Let me go, or I'll throw this shit everywhere!'

'What shit?'

Van den Bergen took a step closer, poised to draw his service weapon.

'Anthrax.'

# CHAPTER 3

## *Van den Bergen's apartment, a short while later*

Peering dolefully at the side of Van den Bergen's wardrobe that she commandeered whenever she stayed, George saw only a phalanx of drab: nothing but washed-out jeans, black long-sleeved tops and her old purple cardigan, which was still going, despite the holes in the elbows.

'How you going to wear any of that shit to the pool?' Letitia screeched through the laptop's monitor.

George closed her eyes and bit her lip. The joys of Skype, bringing her over-opinionated mother, who was currently sprawled on Aunty Sharon's sofa in South East London, straight into her lover's bedroom in Amsterdam. There was Letitia's round face – no make-up yet today, and the recently sewn-in ombré hair extensions made her look more like a spooked lion than Beyoncé – grimacing at the collection of casual wear.

'I ain't going to no fancy tapas bars with you dressed like a builder, lady.' Pointing with her talons, which were green today. Head rolling indignantly from shoulder to shoulder. 'Them tops is a fucking embarrassment. Sort it out! Get down the shops. Or don't they have shops in Holland?'

'I'm skint,' George said, angling the laptop's camera away

16

from the contents of the wardrobe. 'I'm saving for a deposit, remember?'

'Skint, my arse. All that fancy shit you do for the university and that old lanky Dutch bastard you call a boyfriend has got you on the payroll over there?' Her mother sucked her teeth, snatched up a packet of cigarettes from the coffee table and lit up with a dramatic flourish. She blew her first lungful of smoke towards her screen, clearly aiming for George's image. 'Your Aunty Shaz's gaff not good enough for you?'

'Maybe I want to get away from you.'

The words had burst their way out before George had had chance to filter them. Damn it! She'd made a pact with herself not to rub her ailing mother up the wrong way, especially as Letitia had nearly lost her life prematurely at the hands of the Rotterdam Silencer himself.

And there was her father, edging his way into the frame and waving timidly. The last thing she wanted was for him to think she was planning to get away from him when they had only just been reunited after decades apart.

'Not you, Dad!' she said – in Spanish, for his ears only. 'When I get my own place, you'll always be welcome. There will be a bed for you, anytime. I meant Madam Gobshite. I need to put some distance between me and her when I'm in the UK.'

Her father looked at the monitor with warm brown eyes. A wry smile softening a face that was still somewhat haggard after his ordeal, though his cheeks had begun to plump up, presumably thanks to Aunty Shaz's incredible cooking. George's stomach rumbled at the thought. Jerk chicken. Rice and peas. Goat curry. Bun. *Jesus, I've got to learn to cook.*

'Don't worry, my love. I'd worked that out,' he said.

But suddenly, Letitia's grimace blocked up the picture. 'Hey! Don't you be thinking I don't know you're having a pop at me, you cheeky lickle rarseclart.'

Her mother snapped her fingers at the camera, and even with the breadth of the North Sea between them, George winced inwardly at the castigatory gesture. She knew she was in the wrong for bitching so blatantly in front of her, and felt instantly guilty for it. Wouldn't let on to that horrible old cow, though.

'My internet's down,' she said, slamming the lid of her laptop shut. Ending a conversation that had quickly soured – though she had been trying her hardest to keep it sweet.

Glancing at the clock, she just registered the fact that it was gone 11 a.m. and she still hadn't heard from Van den Bergen when her phone rang. It was Marie on the other end.

'What's up?' she asked. 'Has he forgotten his reading glasses again?'

But Marie's voice was thin and stringy, stretched to its limit with angst. 'The boss has been rushed to hospital. You'd better come quick.'

The taxi seemed to drive too slowly down the s100, though George could see from the driver's speedometer that he was flooring it.

'Please hurry!' she said, reaching forward to grab the man's shoulder. She withdrew her hand when she spied the navy jumper full of dandruff.

They took a sharp right off the motorway and left the canal, speeding down Rhijnspoorplein. The clusters of high-rise office blocks blurred into the less densely built-up dual carriageway of Wibautstraat. A tram approached from the left and the lights were changing.

'Put your foot down!' she shouted.

'No way, missy. Sit tight. I'm not going to kill us both to save thirty seconds.'

The driver eyeballed her through the rear-view mirror. She could see from the stern promontory of his brow that he wasn't

18

going to yield. In sullen silence, she sat with folded arms, imagining Van den Bergen breathing his last in the high-dependency unit. Marie, being Marie, hadn't gone into any great detail and had hung up all too quickly. George ruminated on what gut-wrenching drama might greet her when the taxi finally swung into Eerste Oosterparkstraat.

The brutalist mid-century-modern block of the hospital sprawled on their left.

'Drop me here.' George thrust money at the taxi driver and sprinted into the Onze Lieve Vrouw Gasthuis, arriving at the information desk with a tight chest. 'I'm looking for Chief Inspector Paul van den Bergen,' she wheezed, determining to quit the clandestine cigarettes she was still snatching when nobody was watching.

The receptionist looked her up and down. The smile didn't quite reach her eyes as she gave George the ward location and reminded her that it wasn't currently visiting time.

When George arrived on the specialist heart ward, she found Van den Bergen's bed empty. Grabbing a passing male nurse by the arm, she was dimly aware of tears pricking the backs of her eyes. She shivered with icy dread. 'Where's the patient? Where's Paul van den Bergen?' she asked. 'I'm his partner. *Please* tell me he hasn't—'

The male nurse looked down at her hand with a disapproving expression. He gently withdrew his arm from her grip and patted her knuckles sympathetically.

'Don't worry,' the nurse said. 'He's not dead. He's too busy grumbling about the "service", like we're some kind of hotel and not a hospital. He wouldn't believe the doctor when he was told he hadn't had a heart attack.'

George shook her head. 'I don't understand.'

'He's on the guts ward. Stomach, bowels and liver.'

With a thundering heartbeat and unsure what to expect, George finally found her lover, looking pale and ruffled in a bed, surrounded by patients who looked far worse than he did, wired up to rather more than a simple blood-pressure cuff and oxygen monitor. She glimpsed the stickers from an earlier ECG on his chest.

'Jesus, Paul! Marie called and told me you'd been *rushed* in here. She put the fear of God into me. What the hell's going on? You look like shit.'

Van den Bergen sighed heavily and bypassed her lips to give her a cheek that was rough with iron-filings stubble.

'Not on the lips. My tongue's like a fur coat. You wouldn't believe what they did to me, George. It was inhumane.' He reached out to caress her face but pulled his finger free of the oxygen cuff, sending the machine's alarm into overdrive. 'I thought I'd had a heart attack.'

George pulled up a chair to his bedside. 'Why are you on the guts ward if you're not dying? Have you been poisoned?'

Van den Bergen's sharp grey eyes seemed to focus on something far away that George couldn't see. 'There was this truck full of trafficked refugees. A little girl had died.' His hooded lids closed, the lines around his eyes tightening. 'One minute, I'm trying to get some information out of the bastard of a driver, next minute, he's pulling an envelope out of his pocket. I don't know how the hell he did it, the sneaky, agile bastard. He was cuffed!'

'What was in the envelope?' George took his hand and gently put the oxygen monitor back on the end of his finger.

'It was full of powder.' His eyes opened and locked with George's, the ghost of fear still evident in pupils that had shrunk to pinpricks. 'Anthrax, he said. He threw the stuff all over me.' Van den Bergen swallowed hard. The digital beep of his pulse sped up. 'I thought I was a goner, George.'

Backing away slightly at the thought of contamination, George inhaled sharply. 'And was it? Anthrax, I mean?'

He shook his head. 'Talcum powder, apparently. But I didn't know that at the time. I felt this unbelievable griping pain in my chest and I just hit the deck. I have a vague memory of medics in biohazard suits and breathing apparatus crawling all over the place. Maybe they tested the powder on site. I have no idea.' He exhaled heavily. 'Obviously, it was a hoax.' He ran a shaking shovel of a hand through the white thatch of his hair. 'Maybe the arsehole had been using it to blackmail the refugees. How else, as a lone operator, could you get a large group of poorly treated people to be compliant on a long journey?'

'Easier to conceal than a gun,' George said, suddenly flushing hot as anger engulfed her on behalf of the dead little girl. She imagined the child, sick, terrified and whimpering for help as some moron of a driver threatened her with poison. She pushed the thought aside. For now. 'But never mind all that. Why did you collapse?' She stood and poured Van den Bergen a glass of water. Proffered it to him.

He sipped and winced. Belched audibly. 'Panic. I thought I'd had a heart attack, but it wasn't. It was bloody stomach acid, would you believe it? They gave me a gastroscopy.'

George threw her head back and laughed. 'At last! About bloody time! And?'

Van den Bergen growled, pushed the glass back towards her and threw the flimsy hospital covers off the bed.

'Where you going, old man?' George asked in English, standing quickly so that the blood rushed to her head.

As he began to rummage in the cabinet beside his bed, George could see that the invalid had been replaced once again by a chief inspector. He pulled out the clothes he had been wearing that morning and plonked them onto the bed. Dark trousers and a plain blue shirt. He stripped off the ugly fawn-coloured support stockings that covered his long, long legs. 'Gastroscopies are no laughing matter,' he said, taking out his size thirteens – gleaming from George's ministrations with shoe polish. He made a spitting noise like a cat with a fur ball stuck in its throat. 'They shoved a hosepipe down me. A damned hosepipe! With a camera on the end. And I was awake.'

Taking his arm, George tried to usher him back into bed. 'Look. Give it up, will you? They clearly think you need observation, so why the hell are you trying to escape?'

'I want to question the owner of Groenten Den Bosch. That's the livery on the side of the truck. There's a girl dead and maybe more on their last legs because of some profiteering bastard who thinks human beings are interchangeable with exported goods. Maybe it's this Den Bosch guy. Maybe he gets twelve-year-old girls mixed up with capsicums and courgettes.'

'Paul!'

'Well, I'm not going to find out why the Port of Amsterdam's latest cargo is the dead and dying from the war-torn Middle East unless I get out of here.'

George snatched up his clothes and held them to her chest. 'You're my priority. You're the one I love. The girl's dead and we'll catch whoever did this to her. But she *can* wait until tomorrow.'

Van den Bergen grabbed the garments back and hastily started to pull his trousers on. Yanked the ECG stickers off his chest, grimacing only slightly when they tugged at the scar tissue that ran from his sternum to his abdomen. 'I've got a granddaughter, George. This can't wait. And I've not had a heart attack.' He dropped the hospital gown to the floor and pulled his shirt on over the wiry musculature of his torso. 'I've got a hiatus hernia. A bad one. But—'

'So you're *not* about to die on me?' George asked as she appraised him. He was still in decent shape for a man of fifty, thanks to all that gardening. She licked her lips and winked. 'Good. The banks won't turn you down for a mortgage then.'

Her pointed remark was met with a disdainful harrumph.

Van den Bergen pulled a blister pack of painkillers from his jacket pocket and swallowed two with some water. 'You can sit here feeling concerned for me, like a mother I don't need, banging on about getting a place together *yet again*, or you can come and help me. I'm about to do what I always do, Georgina.'

'Which is?' George raised an eyebrow and folded her arms. Irritated by his inferring that she had morphed from red-hot lover into some suffocating, clucky guardian. That she was nagging him.

'Fight for the wronged. Get justice for the innocent dead.' He fastened the metal links of his chunky watch and hooked his reading glasses on their chain around his neck. 'Well? Are you coming?'

## CHAPTER 4

# North Holland farmland near Nieuw-Vennep, Den Bosch farm, later still

'It's pretty deserted for a big enterprise,' Van den Bergen said. 'I don't like it.' His voice was even hoarser than usual, George noted. Though his right hand was hidden inside his coat, poised to draw his service weapon, he had wrapped his left hand around the base of his neck.

'You look knackered, old man,' George said, wishing the difficult sod had sent Elvis or Marie to check the provenance of the truck.

The slight stoop in Van den Bergen's shoulders said everything, but he merely pursed his lips and stalked off towards the red steel door of the Den Bosch reception.

Casting an eye over the utilitarian grouping of brick buildings with their corrugated-iron roofs, George could see that there was not a single light at any of the windows. Nothing to see beyond them apart from acres and acres of the Dutch flatland. To the left, the polders had been neatly planted with crops or were festooned with row upon row of grey polytunnels that shone like fat silk worms in the dim sunlight. They snaked away into the distance, their uniformity punctuated only by the inky stripes of dykes. To the right, the horizon was broken by a veritable crystal palace of greenhouses. The place gave her the creeps.

'Wait for me!' Crunching the gravel of the courtyard beneath her new Doc Marten boots, she watched Van den Bergen try the handle.

'It's locked,' he said, taking a few steps backwards. Still rubbing his neck. He approached one of the windows and peered inside. 'Elvis said he couldn't get the owner on the phone, either.'

'Look, Paul. I think you should go home and leave this to the others. You've just been in hospital, for Christ's sake! I'm worried about you.'

Waving her away, he took long strides around the side of the reception building. Jogging after him, George wanted to drag him by the sleeve of his raincoat back to his Mercedes. But this was Van den Bergen, and she knew he took stubborn to a whole new level.

'There *is* someone here!' he said, gesticulating at a pimped-up Jeep, an old Renault and two Luton vans bearing the company's insignia, all parked up by the bins.

'Maybe they're in the fields,' George said.

The wind had started to blow across the expanse of green, flattening the leaves that sprouted in neat rows. She clutched her duffel coat closed against the chill, wistfully thinking that a rum-fuelled family bust-up by the pool in Torremolinos would be infinitely preferable to a bleak afternoon in the agricultural dead centre of the Netherlands. She was just about to suggest they call for backup when a man exited one of the giant greenhouses, carrying a tray of seedlings. He caught sight of them and frowned. Started walking towards them. He moved at a brisk pace and wore jeans and a sweatshirt that were covered in mud at the knees and on the belly.

'Can I help you?' he asked. There was a bright glint when he spoke. Braces?

George couldn't place the man's accent. He wasn't an Amsterdamer. But she could tell from his confident stance that he was at least the manager, if not the boss. There was something about the confrontational tone of his voice; this wasn't someone who took orders. He was big, too. A wall of a man with a thick bush of greying hair that looked like an overgrown buzz cut.

'I'm looking for Frederik den Bosch,' Van den Bergen said, blocking the path.

'Who wants him?'

'I do.' Van den Bergen withdrew a battered business card but was careful to give the sapling-carrying man-mountain a flash of his service weapon, strapped to the side of his body. He stuck the card between two swaying plants. 'Chief Inspector Paul van den Bergen. Where might I find Den Bosch?'

'You're looking at him.' He grinned widely, displaying a perfect set of gold teeth.

Following the proprietor into the main office building, George took in her surroundings, trying to get the measure of Den Bosch. The place was cold and dark, despite the whitewashed brick of the wall. It was cluttered with vintage furniture – more charity shop than antique-dealer cool. It felt damp and smelled of moss and mildew. An earthy, utilitarian place. Den Bosch set the tray of saplings down on the draining board of a sink in a kitchenette area at the far end.

'Coffee?' he shouted. 'Biscuits?'

George's stomach rumbled.

'Milk, no sugar,' she said.

'Not for me.' Van den Bergen glowered at her and started to flick through his notepad, perching his glasses on the end of his nose. 'Let's get to the point, Mr Den Bosch. One of your trucks was pulled over this morning at the Port of Amsterdam.' He read out the number plate, watching as Den Bosch's eyes narrowed. 'It was found to contain just over fifty trafficked Syrians, all suffering from dysentery and on the brink of suffocation. Several are now critically ill in hospital from oxygen deprivation and dehydration. One – a girl of twelve – died. The driver tried to escape by pretending to throw anthrax in my face. What do you have to say about that?'

As Van den Bergen sat back in a saggy old armchair that was positioned by the beat-up horseshoe of a reception desk – almost certainly a relic from the 1980s – George walked over to the sink. Den Bosch was stirring the instant coffees too quickly, sloshing dark brown liquid onto the yellow Formica worktop. He plopped in thick evaporated milk from a bottle that looked like it had seen fresher days.

Turning to face Van den Bergen, Den Bosch shrugged. 'I reported that truck as stolen the other day. Didn't you know?' He treated them yet again to that bullion smile, eyebrows framing an expression of apparent confusion. 'Jesus. I can't believe some scumbag was using it to smuggle Arabs. But at least they were smuggling them *out* of the country, eh?'

'Come again?' George said, snatching up her coffee and eyeing the chip in the mug with distaste. She threw the coffee down the sink. Stood too close to Den Bosch. 'Sorry. Just remembered I'm allergic to coffee.'

Her gaze travelled down his tracksuit top to his forearms. She caught a glimpse of colour on his skin, though he yanked the fabric over his wrists so quickly that she wondered if she had imagined it.

'Arabs,' he said. 'ISIS and all that. They come over here but all they want to do is blow innocent Dutch citizens up and contaminate our fair northern land with their Muslim bullshit. Knocking up our women to make brown babies.' Pointedly looking George up and down, he thrust a packet of biscuits towards her. 'Chocky bicky?'

Taking several steps backwards, she sucked her teeth at him.

Decided to spare him the insults in her mother's patois. An ignorant shitehawk like that wouldn't understand it anyway.

'Dr McKenzie,' Van den Bergen said. 'Why don't you go and wait for me in the car?'

George nodded. But as she left the down-at-heel offices, she heard Den Bosch reiterate that the truck had been stolen.

'The Netherlands is a world gone mad,' Den Bosch said. 'There's so many foreigners running round, making tons of cash from criminal activities and not paying taxes ... They come over here and bleed us dry. You want to think twice before you come and interrogate a legitimate businessman like me over my truck and a bunch of illegals, Mr Van den Bergen. Why don't you save your police harassment for those terrorist bastards?'

In the luxurious cocoon of Van den Bergen's car, George got the special cloth and the antibacterial spray from the glove compartment and started to wipe down the dashboard and polish the dial display and gearstick with a fervour bordering on frenzy. *Cheeky chocky bicky bastard.*

'What do you think of him?' Van den Bergen asked some ten minutes later as he lowered himself into the driver's seat and slammed the door with a thunk.

'Scumbag, of course,' she said.

'Do you think he's a people trafficker? God knows you've met enough of them in your line of work.'

She eyed the deepening creases on either side of Van den Bergen's mouth and traced the lines gently with her little finger. 'You tell me, Paul. What do people traffickers look like? The Duke? The Rotterdam Silencer? Or a sprout-growing lout?'

As they pulled out of the courtyard, she glanced back to the reception building. Den Bosch was standing in the doorway, staring straight at her. He pulled up his sleeves, and George was certain she glimpsed a swastika among the complicated designs that covered his forearms in sleeves of ink.

## CHAPTER 5

# Amsterdam, Van den Bergen's doctor's surgery, 4 October

The display beeped, flashing up the name of the next patient in red digital letters. But it wasn't 'Paul v. d. Bergen'. Instead, an Indonesian woman snatched up her bag with a harried look on her face and marched briskly from the waiting room to the doctors' surgeries beyond. She certainly didn't look that bloody ill.

Van den Bergen clutched at his throat as a hot jet of acid spurted upwards into his gullet. He exhaled heavily, all thoughts of the Syrian refugees and the racist produce farmer pushed to the back of his mind while the prospect of throat cancer took precedence. Yet again. Rising from his uncomfortable chair, he approached the reception desk.

'Am I next?' he asked the bouffant-haired woman behind the counter. He spoke mainly to the wart on her chin – though he tried not to.

She checked her computer screen. 'Sorry. Doctor's running late this morning. There's two in first and then you.'

Leaning forward, he tried to invoke an air of secrecy between them. 'I might have … throat cancer.'

He expected her to rearrange her disappointing features

into a look of sympathy or horror, but the receptionist's impassive expression didn't alter.

'Two more and then you're in.' She smiled, revealing teeth like a horse. 'There's a new magazine about cars knocking around on one of the tables.' As if that was any compensation for being made to wait when he was almost certain that his slow, painful demise had already begun inside his burning throat. Just because the gastroscopy hadn't found cancer yesterday didn't mean it hadn't conquered his healthy cells today.

Sitting back down, Van den Bergen folded his long right leg over his left. Thought about deep-vein thrombosis and uncrossed them swiftly. Sitting opposite him was a beautiful blonde young mother, wrestling with a yowling and stout-looking toddler, whose chubby little fists, when he wasn't clutching his ear, pounded her repeatedly on the shoulder. The fraught scene put him in mind of his own daughter, Tamara, and his granddaughter, Eva. Ah, parenthood. All the joys of making another human being with your own DNA, but the crippling burden of worrying if they'll make it to adulthood and fearing what kind of person they might become. He was silently thankful that Tamara hadn't turned out a nagging, self-obsessed harridan like her mother, Andrea. His daughter had inherited his quiet stoicism, but had he passed on his weak genes? Would she too possibly be prone to the Big C that had taken his father; definitely destined for digestive rebellion and constant anxiety?

Batting the thought away, he turned his attention to an old, old man two seats along, who was gazing blankly ahead. Though the man was smartly dressed in a tailored dark jacket that didn't quite match his navy gabardine trousers, the ring of unkempt white hair around his bald head lent him an air of institutional neglect. Given the rash of freckles on his hairless pate and the translucence of his deeply furrowed skin that revealed the blue web of veins beneath, he couldn't have been far off a century. The old guy didn't look too good. He lolled in his chair, his pale face sweaty under the unforgiving strip light of the waiting room. Van den Bergen watched with growing concern as saliva started to spool out of his mouth onto his smart trousers. The angry toddler had fallen silent and suddenly all that was audible above the thrum of electricity from the lights was the man's rapid, shallow breathing. His colour changed to a sickly grey.

'Sir! Are you okay?' Van den Bergen asked.

The elderly patient didn't respond. His eyes had taken on a vacant glaze. Water began to drip from the seat. Van den Bergen realised the man was urinating.

'Help!' he shouted, lurching from his chair and propping up the old man just as he started to tumble forward. His own hands were shaking; a prickling sensation as the blood drained from his own face. 'Come quickly! This man is very ill.' Craning his neck to locate the receptionist, he saw nothing but the blonde mother, edging away with her child in her arms, covering the toddler's eyes. His heart thudded violently against his ribcage.

Alone with the dying man, unable to decide in his panic if he should try to administer mouth-to-mouth or not, Van den Bergen was relieved when his own doctor ran from the consulting rooms to the scene of the emergency. She knelt by the old man's side, feeling for a pulse.

'Inneke!' she called towards reception, with the calm tone of a medical professional. Smoothed her hijab at her temples as though this were nothing more than a routine examination. 'Bring the defibrillator, please.'

Finally, the receptionist emerged from behind her desk, carrying the life-saving equipment. Van den Bergen was ushered aside as they manoeuvred the old man gently to the floor and the doctor started to work on him.

The panic rose further inside Van den Bergen along with

his stomach acid, encasing his chest in an iron grip. The old guy's colour was all but gone now. He knew that those eyes, now bloodshot and deadened like cod in a fisherman's catch, were no longer seeing. It was too late. The doctor administered CPR for a little while longer while the receptionist used a pump to simulate mouth-to-mouth. But after a minute they both stood and stepped away from the lifeless figure on the floor, who had only hours earlier clearly made the decision to wear a smart jacket today. The old man, and all his memories and stories and loves from a long, long lifetime, had gone.

In the men's toilets, Van den Bergen leaned against the mirror above the sink and wept quietly. Drying his eyes, he surveyed his reflection and saw an ageing man. Having a lover twenty years his junior was not going to save him from the rapid physical decline and the premature death that was almost certainly lying in wait for him just around the corner.

Dialling George's number, he just wanted to hear her reassuring voice.

'What's wrong?' she asked. The sounds of a tannoy announcement and the beep of the supermarket checkout were audible in the background.

'I've just seen a man die. Right in front of me in the surgery.' He wrapped his free hand around the base of his neck, feeling for the place where the stomach acid was almost certainly eroding the healthy tissue of his gullet. Cellular changes. That's what Google had suggested. The feeling of constantly being strangled and a worsening hoarseness of the sufferer's voice. None of it boded well.

'Oh shit,' George said absently. 'Sorry about that. But you're a cop! You see dead people all the time. How come you're so cut up? Have you been crying, Paul?'

'No.' He looked at his bleary eyes in the mirror, still shining with tears. 'It's just ... he died right in front of me. It's different from work. They're already dead and part of a crime scene. This was so sad and unexpected.'

She didn't understand. And why would she? George had her foibles, but a constant nagging fear of the end wasn't one of them. And she was young, with both parents still living. She'd never known what it was to create life, or to accompany one to the very bitter end.

Finishing the call and splashing his face with water, he returned to the waiting room to find the dead man covered by a blanket, being wheeled away on a gurney by paramedics who had arrived on the scene too late. A janitor was already mopping up the old man's urine, as if he had never been there. With several of the other witnesses dabbing at their eyes with tissues, the funereal mood was normalised only by the shrill noise of the blonde woman's squalling child.

'Well, he wasn't registered with this surgery,' the receptionist told the others, who had gathered around her as though she were Jesus's own earthly mouthpiece, disseminating the Word of God to the mortal believers. She patted her hair grandly and folded her arms. 'Obviously I can't tell you more because of patient confidentiality.'

'Oh, go on,' the blonde woman said. 'We need to know.'

The receptionist glanced over her shoulder and then leaned in with an air of secrecy. As she started to speak in hushed tones, Van den Bergen's phone buzzed. A text from Minks.

'What's the latest on Den Bosch?'

He was torn. Answer Minks's query about an investigation that was currently the last thing on his mind, or find out more about the old man? But his decision was made for him when the digital display beeped at him, showing his name in bright red letters.

Taking his seat at the side of the doctor's desk, he placed a hand over his spasming stomach.

'Who was he?' he asked. 'How come he was left in such a bad way in the waiting room?'

His doctor shook her head. She buttoned the jacket of her smart trouser suit and closed her eyes like an indulgent parent. 'Now, Paul. You know I can't share those details with you.'

'But I'm a cop.'

'I'll know more when he's been looked over by Marianne de Koninck, but given his age and the fact that he popped in here as an emergency patient, he was just a very elderly, poorly gentleman who took a turn for the worse in our waiting room. Death comes to us all.' She adjusted the clip in her hijab and smiled. 'Now. I've had the results of your gastroscopy.' With narrowed eyes, she scrutinised her computer screen. 'Hiatus hernia.'

'I already know that. Will I need an operation? You know, before it gives me throat cancer.' Van den Bergen put his right leg over his left knee and started to bounce his foot up and down, up and down.

The doctor smiled. 'Thirty per cent of over-fifties have this condition. It's very common. I'm going to up your antacids. Give you a stronger proton-pump inhibitor. We need to keep that acid under control. But you must stop worrying about throat cancer, Paul. Nothing untoward was found in the investigative procedure.'

'Can't you fix it?'

'Do you really want your ribcage sawn open and your stomach taken out? Because that's what the operation entails. Haven't you had enough trauma to that area?' She pointed to the place where he had been carved from sternum to abdomen by the Butcher in a previous case.

He shook his head.

'Well then.' She handed him a prescription. 'Take these twice a day. Have you cut out spice, alcohol and anything acidic from your diet?'

'Yes,' he lied. 'Do these antacids have any nasty long-term side effects?'

'Stop waiting to die, Paul.'

In the persistent drizzle outside the doctor's surgery, Van den Bergen tried to force the memory of the old man's unseeing eyes from his mind. Tried to stop worrying if he'd been frightened at the end. Had he had children who wouldn't know where their father was? Had he been frustrated that he was breathing his last among uncaring strangers? Perhaps he'd felt relieved that his long life was finally over.

*Enough!*

He dialled Marie's number. She picked up straightaway.

'What have you got on Den Bosch?' he asked.

On the other end, he could hear Marie crunching. Crisps, in all likelihood. 'The guy's got a clean record. I checked out his story. Apparently the heavy goods vehicle *had* been reported as stolen the day before port police intercepted it.'

'And Den Bosch's whereabouts over the last few days?'

Marie cleared her throat and started to speak, sounding like she was picking food from her molars. 'Get this, boss. He was at some right-wing political rally at the time the heavy goods vehicle was stolen.'

Van den Bergen nodded, remembering what George had said about the swastika tattoos on the guy's forearms. 'Go on.'

'I've had a look through his social media accounts. There's not much, to be fair, but he's connected on Facebook to some known neo-Nazi bullies who align themselves with the far right. They're always showing up in press photos where the anti-racist lefties clash with supporters of Geert Wilders and his Party for Freedom.'

'And his business records?'

'Clean as a whistle. Den Bosch produce exports, mainly to British supermarkets. Courgettes. Peppers. The usual greenhouse produce. It's a thriving concern. He's worth a few million, from what I can see from his accounts. I haven't met him, boss, but on paper it looks like he's legit. An unpleasant type, maybe, but pays his taxes, bought the local church a new roof and funds a youth group in the village where his farm is located. You said he keeps those tattoos covered with long sleeves?'

'A man who keeps his fascism as a weekend hobby!' Van den Bergen said, chuckling.

'Why would a neo-Nazi, who's well off on paper, at least, traffick Syrians into European countries?' Marie asked. 'Surely that's the last thing he wants. And he certainly doesn't need the money.'

'Anything more on the driver?'

He started to walk towards the car, fingering the folded prescription in his coat pocket. More poison in his system. Hadn't he read somewhere that prolonged use of proton-pump inhibitors made you more susceptible to osteoporosis? What did that mean for a man who was six foot five? Would a degenerative disease affect the tall worse than the short? There was so much more of him to crumble, after all.

'Elvis has questioned the driver again, boss. He's still refusing to talk. He won't even give us his name. Won't have legal representation. Nothing. It's as though the guy doesn't exist and nobody has come forward to his rescue. It's a no-hoper of a case.'

'With a dead twelve-year-old? There's no way I'm letting this go. Not on my damned watch.' Unlocking the car, he folded his long frame into the driver's seat. 'Where does Den Bosch live?'

'In De Pijp. I'll text over his address.'

'A multimillionaire living in a shithole like that? I don't buy it.'

'It's an up-and-coming area,' Marie said.

'Up and coming means ethnically mixed and full of lefty

trendies,' Van den Bergen said, gunning the car towards the nearest pharmacy. 'Why the hell would someone like Frederik Den Bosch live in anything other than a white, conservative enclave?'

He rang off, sensing there was considerably more to the owner of Groenten Den Bosch than was immediately apparent. Calling George, he cut through her concerned chatter with a simple instruction: 'Get ready. I'll pick you up in an hour. We're going to De Pijp.'

But first, he planned to take a little detour to the morgue.

# CHAPTER 6

## *Van den Bergen's apartment, later*

'Fucking arseholes.'

George read the email yet again. The first time, she had digested its contents, open-mouthed and with a thudding heartbeat. She'd had that horrible feeling of dread she'd known on many an occasion, where all the blood drained from her skin, leaving her numb. The second time, she'd read it with a degree of disbelief, thinking there must have been a mistake. She had even called the entitled limp-dick who had signed off on the decision. Perhaps he'd accidentally emailed her instead of some other poor sod, who had put their heart and soul into a piece of work for an entire year or more and who had been looking forward to their travails coming to fruition in print. But no. There had been no error. Now, she reread the curt missive and felt only white-hot fury.

From: Timothy.Fitzmaurice@potestasbooks.co.uk
To: Georgina.McKenzie@cam.ac.uk
Subject: Forthcoming publication of 'Heavy Traffick'

Dear Dr McKenzie,
I regret to inform you that, owing to a change in publishing priorities at Potestas Books, we have had to

look again at our list for the forthcoming year and have come to the conclusion that your detailed study of 'The traffick of women through Europe, and modern sexual slavery' is no longer a good fit with our other titles. I am afraid your excellent criminological tome will have to find another home.

With all best wishes,

Timothy L Fitzmaurice MA Oxon

Grinding her molars together, George shook her head violently, tempted to pick up the laptop and hurl it through Van den Bergen's French doors, onto the balcony. But what good would it do? This was the precarious life of a criminologist, she knew: reliant on her university teaching post to maintain her status and publication prospects as an academic; reliant on publication to secure funding; reliant on funding to continue her research work in prisons. She was just another arse-kissing PhD, trying to make a name for herself in a world where you had to stick your fingers in as many pies as possible to make ends meet, always preparing for them to get burned when you were inevitably kicked from grace into the fires of unemployable hell by some senior academic.

'Bastards! I know exactly what's going on here,' she shouted at the glowing screen. 'Same shit, different day. She-Who-Must-Be-Obeyed, twisting the knife.'

Making herself a foul-tasting coffee, using some granules from the bottom of a jar that had seen better days, she logged onto her UK online bank account. Checked the balance: £367.92. And no payday pending, thanks to her own personal academic puppet-master, Sally Wright, who had cut George's strings after she'd flouted her demands once too often. Controlling bitch.

Feeling disgusted with herself, she logged out, imagining all the things she would say to that duplicitous cow when she next saw her. *Do you get off on abusing your position of power, you hatchet-faced old bag? Is this what you had in mind when you signed up to being my mentor and protector? Fucking black-balling the black girl? Rescinding her tenure, leaving her potless, shamed and out in the cold?*

In her mind's eye, she was standing in Sally Wright's office in St John's College in Cambridge, shoving the cup of tea back onto her desk, leaving behind a spatter pattern that psychologists might interpret as pure disgust in liquid form. Except Professor Shitbag All-Wrong was now the vice chancellor of the university and was invincible before all but God and her close cousin, Satan.

She clicked the iPlayer link to the breakfast show on which her saviour-turned-nemesis had recently appeared. There she was, with her ridiculous blunt-cut fringe and short bob and those daft red cat's-eye glasses that only someone thirty years younger with infinitely better bone structure could really carry off.

'Of course, writing this *Sunday Times* bestseller about the legendary, enigmatic Duke was a dream piece of research. I'm so glad the layman has embraced the story of this seemingly respectable peer of the realm, who was in actual fact a people and drug trafficker at the head of an international web of deceit.' Professor Plagiarism had toyed with her big red beads with those nicotine-stained fingers that looked like lumps of amber, grinning inanely with newly whitened teeth at the show's blonde host, whom George knew Sally hated for nothing more than cultural snobbery reasons.

'Bitch!' George yelled at the buffering screen. 'Ruinous, treacherous bag!' Unwelcome tears started to well in the corners of her eyes. She definitely needed this holiday.

Just as George was contemplating a sneaky cigarette, remembering she had hidden an emergency pack of Silk Cut behind the cleaning products under Van den Bergen's sink, a Skype alert popped up on her monitor, informing her that Letitia the Dragon demanded an audience.

'What the bloody hell do you want?' George asked, wiping the first rogue tear away hastily.

'You crying? What you crying for?' A lo-res Letitia the Dragon exhaled a plume of blue and yellow cigarette smoke towards the webcam on Aunty Sharon's PC. 'That miserable old bastard you call a boyfriend dumped you again so's he can spend time with his precious "girls"?' A raised eyebrow. Her head at a sassy angle that spelled cynicism.

Steeling herself to show no reaction, George stared down at the coasters on the battered coffee table, lining them up in a perfectly parallel row along the edge of the tabletop.

'Or is it some case that's got him all fired up and now he's pissing in your chips? Or some ailment? Eh?' Letitia stared into the webcam, making George feel as though her innermost thoughts were being excavated at the determined and brutal hand of a tomb raider. Letitia the Dragon was examining her talons, now painted with stars and stripes; studded with tiny diamanté.

'It's nothing to do with Paul. Paul and me are fine,' George lied, conjuring the memory that played on repeat in her mind's eye: Van den Bergen jettisoning their date night, only hours after her touchdown at Schiphol airport, in favour of driving down to Tamara's because Numb-Nuts was playing a gig and Tamara fancied a little help with baby bath time from Opa. George swallowed hard. *Distract the Dragon. Tell her about Sally Wright.* But she was reluctant to betray the betrayer, since she knew Letitia would love nothing more than hearing George malign the very woman who had enabled her to escape the clutches of a toxic narcissist of a mother and her dead-end life on the dead-end streets of a South East London shithole. 'I've got PMT. That's it. And I'm skint.'

Letitia threw her fat head back and started to laugh. All

heaving bosom in some gruesome draped polyester number – from Primark, by the looks. Fashion that loved the thin, young and long-limbed, but was rather less forgiving of the chubby possessor of a G cup. 'Do us a favour, girl. The rum and Coke's all on you once we hit Torremolinos.' She cast a glance to someone just out of the frame. 'Ain't that right, Shaz? Drinks on her, innit? With her fancy book ting and that.'

There was giggling in the background as Aunty Sharon appeared in front of the camera, the flesh of her sturdy arm wobbling as she stirred something in a mixing bowl. 'Take no notice of her, darling. What's the matter? Tell your Aunty Shaz.'

George tutted dolefully. Wondering if her family knowing the truth – at least in part – would be quite that bad. 'Things have gone a bit tits up on the work front, if I'm honest.'

'You paying your fair share of the holidays, though!' her mother said, pointing at her with one of those Uncle Sam talons.

'Yeah, yeah,' George said, contemplating the modest balance in her account and the £500 she owed Aunty Sharon. Van den Bergen would surely lend her the rest. Wouldn't he? 'But my publisher has pulled out of the next book. And if I don't publish every year, my funders won't look kindly on me …' She chewed her bottom lip, knowing she'd already said too much, but feeling the words pushing for release. 'And if I can't get funding, I won't get my tenure renewed at St John's.'

'What the fuck does that mean? What hoity-toity bullshit you coming out with now?' Letitia asked, flicking her ash into the palm of her left hand.

Aunty Sharon approached the camera and budged her sister out of the way on the well-worn old sofa. A look of alarm on her kind, unadorned face. She clutched at her mixing bowl as though it were a baby. 'You gonna get the push, love?'

Though she tried desperately to hold them back, the rogue tears burst forth, and George could only submit to a bout of racking sobs. 'I've already been given the push, Aunty Shaz. The Peterhulme Trust rejected my proposal for a new study.'

As Aunty Sharon reached out to stroke George's image on her screen, Letitia elbowed her sister out of the way. 'You need to come home is what you need to do, girl. Get your shit together. Get a proper bloody job. Not this arty-farty bollocks that white witch got you doing. Sally fucking Wright. Where's Professor Fucking Do-Gooder when your shit's hitting the fan, eh?' She narrowed those eyes, the curling holiday false eyelashes obscuring the true intent behind them. 'Or maybe she's stirring the shit because you wouldn't toe the line. Is that it? Am I right?' She sucked her teeth loud and long, having nailed the truth of the situation. 'Oh yeah. I see this now. And there's you, flying across the North Sea every five minutes to service the Jolly Green Giant's needs so you've not got a nicker to your name.' She snapped her fingers and folded her arms triumphantly. 'Bending over for Sally Wright. Blowing off Van der Twat and still no sign of commitment.' She broke into patois. 'Yu caan tun duck off a nest. Know what I mean? You ain't going nowhere. You need to change your shit up, Ella.'

'Don't call me Ella. You know I hate it.'

'She's right, George,' Aunty Sharon said, muscling her way back into the frame. 'You letting people walk all over you, darling. But never mind.' She started to beat her cake mixture anew, a look of grim determination on her face. Her towering confection of silk scarf and hair extensions shook with the effort. 'This break will do you good. Tinesha's coming home this afternoon. Patrice has even put his Nikes through the wash, can you believe it? And your dad ...' She glanced at Letitia. Her concerned frown was almost imperceptible. 'Well, let's just say some of that paella and sangria will fatten him up. You'll be with your own, love. Give you time to mull things over, like. I can always get you a job with me behind the bar at Skin Licks, if you like.'

George swallowed hard at the thought of doling out vodka tonics to dirty old men at the Soho titty bar where she had once cleaned. Sticky glasses, stale booze and sodden beermats. *Sod that.* 'Nah. You're all right, Aunty Shaz. I'll work it out.'

'You need to be with your family for a bit,' Letitia said. 'Blood's thicker than water, innit?'

Nodding, George glanced down at her phone. Noticed a text from Van den Bergen and absently started to read it. Felt the tears evaporate away as the fire lit within her again.

> 'Home late. Nipping to Tamara's first, then got a few people to interview. Don't wait up.'

Was this it? Life with a policeman? A life sentence, trapped in a situation where Van den Bergen's 'girls' always came first. And plans for their future together always came last. Perhaps Letitia, Queen of Shit-Stirrers, was right. Maybe it was time to change her shit up.

'Listen,' she said, studying the unlikely twosome of her homely, long-suffering aunt and her slowly dying glamour puss of a mother, with her sickle-cell anaemia and pulmonary hypertension and her Lambert & Butlers. 'I'm gonna finish packing. I'll see you tomorrow morning at Gatwick.'

Faking a smile, she severed the connection to her family and flopped back into the sagging second-hand sofa, like a deflating blow-up doll who serviced everybody's needs but her own. With work-worn hands, she fingered the cashmere throw that she'd bought for Van den Bergen to cover the well-worn chintzy upholstery. Swallowing a sob, she savoured the memories of both her mother and her father having slept there, eschewing the uncomfortable guest bed. Her mother had been lured away and abducted by a psychopath. Her father, recovering after years of slave labour, had been unwittingly working

44

for the same psychopath in the Coba Cartel. Happy families happened to other people, she mused, picking off the bobbles where the cashmere had started to pill.

And then there was the spectre of her own recent memory, having spent the night on the sofa only the previous Saturday after an argument with her ill-tempered lover. She allowed the loneliness to engulf her. Wept. Imagined the warmth of the Spanish sun on her skin and the barbed tongue of her mother as she sipped rum and passed harsh judgement on the pasty Thomson travellers that weren't part of their noisy extended clan.

But then, her phone rang. Van den Bergen was on the other end, sounding flustered.

'You won't believe what happened to me today,' he said. 'And I've just come from the mortuary. Honestly, George. I've stumbled across something crazy.'

'Yeah?' she said, chewing the inside of her cheek. 'Well you can tell it to Tamara, can't you? I'm going on holiday.'

'No! You can't. That's why I'm calling. I need your help. I'm not going to Tamara's now. I'll tell you when I get back. I'm on my way—'

'Paul! No!' she said. But it was too late. He'd hung up, pronouncing the death of her holiday plans whether she liked it or not.

# CHAPTER 7

## *Amsterdam, mortuary, later still*

White walls. Stainless steel slab. Greying corpse. George hated the mortuary. And yet, here she was, with Marianne de Koninck staring at the side of her head, waiting for signs of weakness, no doubt.

'I wanted you to see this,' Van den Bergen said, beckoning her close.

'Not the sort of date night I had in mind.' George clutched her inadequate cardigan closed against the cold. It was always chilly down there.

He turned to the head of forensic pathology and nodded. 'Tell her, Marianne!'

The tall pathologist took her place at the side of the old man's body, spreading ribs that had already been sawn down the middle. George grimaced at the sight of the dark cavity where his heart had been, feeling deep-seated sadness that all the old man had done, thought and felt during his lifetime, had been reduced to composite body parts, like a puzzle made from spoiling flesh. There was his heart on the scales. There was his brain on a dissecting table. Here was his stomach, being carefully lifted out of the abdominal cavity like a bad caesarean birth. De Koninck reopened the foul-smelling stomach and pointed with a latex-gloved finger to the clearly visible remnants of a small white tablet.

'Arnold van Blanken. Ninety-five,' she began. 'Amsterdamer, born and bred, who was apparently visiting a friend in a different neighbourhood when he felt ill. I understand he registered at the surgery as a temporary emergency patient. When he came in here, as I told Paul last night, I took one look at him and presumed it was natural causes. A worn-out heart giving up.'

'He just died in front of me,' Van den Bergen said to nobody in particular, staring at the florid post-mortem colours in the old man's face. 'I had to get closure, I suppose. My doc wouldn't tell me anything. That's why I came. And I'm glad I did.'

'Well, he looks ancient,' George said. 'Is that medication inside his stomach?' She shrugged. 'Surely there's nothing weird about old guys taking tablets for this, that and the other.'

De Koninck stood straight, towering above George, looking austere and unforgiving in her white coat beneath the bright mortuary lights. The prominent veins in her masculine hands gave her away as the athletic type. Her punishing regime of tennis or hockey or whatever the fuck she did outside work had stripped away any softness to the woman's face. She was all long Patrician limbs and skinny, shapely legs beneath those scrubs and the lab coat, unlike George's bone-crushing tree-trunks. The pathologist had no arse to her name, though. Those blonde, northern European types never had any booty to speak of.

'It's cisapride,' De Koninck said, 'twenty-milligram tablets, which is normally prescribed four times per day for those with gastro-oesophageal reflux disease. I sent it off to the toxicologist overnight to get it analysed. There were *four* tablets, half-digested just like this one. Too high a dose in one go.' She rummaged inside the upper end of the stomach and showed George a scene of coagulated gore, muscle and connective tissue that made little visual sense. 'Van Blanken had a hiatus hernia. See where the stomach is protruding into the gullet?'

'Like me, George!' Van den Bergen said, his voice a shade higher than his usual low rumble. 'Listen to this!'

Barely able to believe she was passing up a trip to Torremolinos to look at the dead body of a man who'd had more than his fair share of life, George folded her arms and put her weight on one foot. Tapping the tiled morgue floor with her steel-toe-capped Doc Martens. She rolled her eyes. 'You've got staff for this, Paul. Put me on the payroll, or I'm off to catch a late flight to Malaga.' She checked her watch. '*My* family needs *me*.'

'Listen!' Van den Bergen placed a hand on her shoulder.

Marianne de Koninck raised an eyebrow and snapped off her gloves, throwing them into a biohazard bin. She sat down in front of her computer. 'When I found the hiatus hernia, I wasn't surprised that Mr Van Blanken should be taking cisapride, which is an antacid medication. But four twenty-milligram tablets at once? That's dangerously high.'

'Senility?' George asked. 'If you're meant to take one four times per day, is it not feasible he got mixed up and took four instead? It's easy to be forgetful, even at my age.'

'No.' De Koninck scrolled through a report. 'I've had his medical records sent over, and it seems his GP, a Dr Saif Abadi, had prescribed abnormally high doses of the medication, which is weird. You could say it's professionally negligent at the very least. The Americans have taken their version of cisapride – Propulsid – off the market entirely. One of the dodgy side effects is that it's widely known to put patients at risk of something called Long QT Syndrome.'

'What?'

'It's a rare condition where a delayed repolarisation of the heart, following a heartbeat, increases the risk of something called Torsades des Pointes.' She shook her head disapprovingly at George's blank expression.

'Do you want to tell me all about the foibles of drug mules or poor mental health among the female prison population?' Now it was George's turn to shake her head. 'No? So, why the hell should I understand about bloody Marquis de Sade or whatever it is you just mentioned?'

'Georgina!' Van den Bergen said.

But George had had enough. 'Look. Why am I here? What's so fascinating about poor Arnold damned van Blanken and his dicky ticker?'

De Koninck pursed her lips, the nostrils of her narrow Dutch nose flaring. 'Torsades des Pointes is an irregular heart-beat originating from the ventricles. It can lead to fainting and sudden death due to ventricular fibrillation. It basically brings on heart failure.'

'And his GP intentionally put him on an unnecessarily high dose,' Van den Bergen said, reaching into his pocket and withdrawing a pack of tablets that said 'Omeprazole' on the side. 'I was worried that my own doc had prescribed the same killer meds.'

*Well*, thought George, *that explains the previous night's tossing and turning in bed.*

'*Potentially* killer,' De Koninck said, smoothing her expensively streaked urchin cut behind her ears. 'Normally, it's a very safe drug.'

'So, the old man was wantonly poisoned,' George said.

'And that's the least of it,' Van den Bergen said, approaching the corpse and pointing to his neck. He beckoned her over with a nod of his head. 'See this tattoo?'

Not wishing to get too close, George craned her neck to see a tiny inking of a lion that had faded presumably from black to navy blue over time. The lion wore a crown and carried a sword. 'I wonder what the S and the 5 stand for?' She sniffed and took a step back. 'Looks like a prison tattoo. Ink and a needle. Something really old school.'

Van den Bergen raised an eyebrow and treated her to a wry smile. Was he being patronising about her turn of phrase? Or was she overreacting because she was already so mad at him?

'Well,' he said, grabbing surreptitiously at his throat, 'Marianne has had more than one old guy in here lately who's died of a meds-induced heart attack and sported one of these tattoos.'

Breathing in sharply, all the cynicism and defensive, studied boredom fell away from George like a layer of dead skin, revealing the questioning machine of her intellect and curiosity beneath. 'Really?' She unfolded her arms and looked again at the tattoo. 'You got photos?'

'What do you think?' De Koninck said, taking a file from her desk and opening it to reveal post-mortem shots of another old man. 'Brechtus Bruin. Another ninety-five-year-old. I did his autopsy a week ago. He'd been taking Demerol and OxyContin as prescription painkillers. And guess what he died from?'

'Heart attack,' George said.

De Koninck nodded, raising both finely plucked eyebrows with a wry smile. 'You guessed it.'

George studied the shots of Brechtus Bruin's neck, feeling the hairs rise on the back of her own. 'The same tattoo! Marie's going to have a field day searching for the background to this on the internet.' She was undeterred by the sight of the lifeless nonagenarian in the pictures. It was far easier than cosying up to the discoloured, slowly decomposing neck of the actual corpse before her.

'Both Bruin and Van Blanken had the same superficial cause of death and the same tattoo,' Van den Bergen said, peering over her shoulder at the regal lion. 'There's a definite link.'

The pathologist switched tabs on her computer screen to another report. She scanned the notes, tapping the screen.

'Though Brechtus Bruin took ill at home, so there were no witnesses. As I understand it from the ambulance team who brought him in to me, he'd been lying dead in his house, undiscovered, for several days before his neighbour realised he wasn't picking up his grocery deliveries. But the painkillers he was taking are also notorious for causing heart attacks in the frail in high doses.'

George ran through the implications in silence. 'Are you sure it's not all just conjecture and coincidence? The tattoos and heart attacks, I mean. Or do you think you've got a Harold Shipman-style serial killer of oldies running riot in the city?' She bit her lip in horrified anticipation.

Van den Bergen turned to her with a grim smile. 'Worse than that. I think we've got someone who's clearly targeting just one specific group of old men. We need to find out why and we need to find out who else is on the hit list. And you're closer than you know with that Shipman analogy, Georgina. Both of these men were prescribed these meds by the same GP, and I don't like it one bit.'

George let out a long, low whistle. Suddenly, she didn't give a hoot about abandoning a bickering Letitia, her father and Aunty Sharon and her brood to a three-star poolside with only a partial view of the freezing cold Med. She thought about her ailing bank balance, and grinned. 'Think you can use a free-lance criminologist on the usual day rate?'

# CHAPTER 8

## *Amsterdam, police headquarters, 9 October*

'Where are you with the illegal immigrant situation?' Maarten Minks asked, sitting bolt upright, as though the chief of police had personally rammed a pointy-ended paperweight up his young commissioner's rectum. Minks was flushed. He was only ever red in the face when he was wetting his big boy pants with excitement over a development in a case or if he had been given a dressing-down.

Suspecting the latter, Van den Bergen folded his arms over the maelstrom of griping wind and acid indigestion that raged in his beleaguered stomach. He sighed. 'Frederik den Bosch is an unpleasant character with some really disgusting views, but you can't arrest a man for that unless he acts on them. And his record is squeaky clean. His claim that the lorry containing the Syrians was stolen checks out. He called in a theft in a couple of days before the find. Uniforms went and took a statement from his office manager, and Den Bosch contacted his insurers soon afterwards.'

'Was it stolen from the yard?' Minks asked, smoothing the leather padded arms on his captain's chair. 'Surely an international exporter with acreage like that has got decent security. A guard? Dogs? Cameras?'

Van den Bergen nodded, wondering if he should mention the two old men and their suspicious deaths. But with a little girl dead, the Syrian refugee case was a murder investigation that warranted his full attention. If Minks got wind of the two nonagenarians with their mysterious tattoos, the overzealous stickler for rules would cry conflict of interest and immediately pass the case on to one of the other senior detectives. No way was Van den Bergen willing to let that happen. Especially since Arnold van Blanken had breathed his last only a few feet from where he had been uselessly sitting in the doctor's surgery.

'Marie has the CCTV footage from Den Bosch's premises and has yet to find anything.' He rubbed his stomach and belched quietly, trying to picture the inside of his ulcerated gullet.

'You seem distracted, Paul. Is there anything you'd like to share with me? Are you ...' He leaned forward. '*Well*?' Minks cocked his head in the semi-concerned fashion of a careerist who often practised being human in front of a mirror.

'What kind of a question is that?' Van den Bergen asked, straightening in his seat until, thanks to his long torso, he could see the top of Minks's head. Thinning hair, since he'd whipped Kamphuis's old job from under Van den Bergen's nose.

'A suspected heart attack and collapse at the scene of an arrest?' Minks examined his perfectly clean fingernails. Clearly, the man was not a gardener. He failed to make eye contact with Van den Bergen. 'Seems your little adventure in Mexico has knocked the stuffing out of you.'

'I brought down the Rotterdam Silencer, and not for the first time!' Van den Bergen could feel irritation itching its way up his neck. He regarded his superior officer with some cynicism. The smug arsehole was showing signs of turning into his predecessor. 'I think *you* might find it physically testing to have anthrax thrown in your face.'

Minks's eyes narrowed. He touched the stiff Eton collar on his shirt. 'It wasn't anthrax.'

'I didn't know that at the time, did I?'

The silence between them made the air feel too thick to breathe. Finally, Van den Bergen relented and spoke.

'I've put Dr McKenzie on the payroll. She's an expert in trafficking of all sorts.'

'For Christ's sake, Paul! I'm trying to keep departmental costs down. Not let them spiral out of control, and all because you want to play the generous sugar daddy with your girlfriend. Why the hell can't you co-opt some junior detective from another station? McKenzie's expensive.'

Van den Bergen closed his eyes momentarily and swallowed down the scorching poker of bile that lanced its way up his oesophagus. 'Dr McKenzie is a specialist consultant. Even if I didn't have a relationship with her outside of the workplace, I'd still hire her. Pay peanuts, get monkeys.'

'I've studied your expenditure. It's gone through the roof in the last few years.' There it was. Spreadsheet King had been getting his rocks off after hours with a five-knuckle shuffle over some ancient Excel files.

'The world's a bad place, Maarten, and every year it gets worse. Ten years ago, we didn't have half the violent trafficking-related crime that we have now in the city. Or at least we weren't aware of it. You want me to keep solving cases? Then I need the right people. Georgina has come in on our most complex and dangerous cases – multiple murders and organised criminal networks that have had international reach. Can you think of a single one that my team didn't solve?' He folded his arms triumphantly. 'She's got a criminologist's insight – something that we lack. Dirk and Marie are the best officers I've ever had working for me, but there's a limit to what—'

Minks balled his fist, clearly ready to thump the table. His wrinkle-free face seemed even tauter than usual. 'My priority is to crack down on crime committed by immigrants, Paul. Many influential Amsterdamers are not happy with the city being over-run by ISIS bastards, masquerading as refugees from these far-flung, bombed-out shitholes. The great and the good of Amsterdam are taxpayers, Chief Inspector! They're our bloody bosses!'

Listening to the alt-right bilge that Minks was spouting from between those too-tight lips of his, Van den Bergen was suddenly tempted to take the bottle of Gaviscon from his raincoat pocket and neutralise the commissioner's acidic mouth with it. But he knew this edict had come from on high. It was in the papers daily: panic, prejudice and paranoia.

'I'm not getting into a political point-scoring contest, Maarten,' he said, standing abruptly. 'That's why I'm not sitting on your side of the desk. I'm a policeman. I put the bad guys behind bars. Let me find the bastard who landed a bunch of vulnerable people in hospital and killed a twelve-year-old. If I say I need Dr McKenzie's help, just pay the invoices, will you? There's a good lad.'

Minks scowled at him. Van den Bergen could practically hear the potential responses that were being tried for size in his mind. But he merely gripped the desk, his fingernails turning bright pink; white at the tips.

'You got a mandate to keep illegal immigrants out of the city? Let me find the trafficker that's bringing them here.' *And whoever's bumping off those poor old sods with the tattooed necks*, he thought, already walking through the door.

Flinging himself into his desk chair, Van den Bergen growled when the lever mechanism that allowed him to adjust the height of the seat gave way, dropping him to only inches above the floor.

'Damn thing!'

On the other side of the cubicle, he could hear Elvis sniggering.

'Have you been pissing about with my chair?'

'No, boss. Do you want me to show you how you adjust it … again?'

'Get your jacket on, smart-arse.'

Elvis appeared, red-faced, from behind the partition, which was covered with photos of the Den Bosch truck, its beleaguered occupants, the driver and their prime suspect – Frederik den Bosch himself.

'Sorry, I didn't mean—'

Van den Bergen merely pulled on his raincoat. 'De Pijp.'

'Den Bosch's home turf? Nothing came of the door to doors,' Elvis said, buttoning his leather jacket. 'Me and Marie knocked every single neighbour up within a quarter of a mile radius. Most weren't even keen to open the door to us, let alone say anything about the man down the street.'

Tossing the key to his Mercedes into Elvis's hands, Van den Bergen took a final slurp of his now-cold coffee. 'Wait for me in the car. Anyone who seemed overly reluctant to talk about their charming tattooed neighbour … they're the ones who will have the most interesting tales to tell. You mark my words.'

Striding with apparent purpose down the corridor, though everything was still tender from the gastroscopy, he entered the fug of Marie's dedicated IT suite. She was sitting with her back to him, sucking on the ends of her fingers, an empty packet of paprika-flavoured Bugles on the desk by her keyboard.

'I'm going to tell George to stop bringing you those from England,' he said. 'She's enabling you and it's wrong. Too much salt in the diet can lead—'

'I'm a big girl, boss.' Marie gave him a watery smile, watching as the gust of wind that Van den Bergen had brought in with him wafted the crisp packet into the air. It drifted to the floor like a misshapen parachute, landing softly amid the flotsam and jetsam of Marie's previous snack attacks. She regarded it impassively, scratching at the new spot that had appeared on her cheekbone – the same size and milky hue as the cultured pearls in her ears. 'Now, what can I do for you?'

'Did you find anything at all from Den Bosch's CCTV footage?'

'No. I've gone through backups from the last three weeks and there's nothing that could disprove what he's said. The heavy goods vehicle in question shows up several times per week, gets loaded up, heads off with the produce. Then, after the theft is reported, you don't see it again.'

'And the driver?'

'Definitely not the same man the port police arrested. The usual driver is a young guy in his early thirties, blond and overweight.'

Van den Bergen scratched at his stubble. 'The bastard with the anthrax was in his fifties and dark-haired. If Den Bosch is somehow in the frame, maybe he's not mixing his legitimate staff with his dodgy hired help.' He closed the door to her room quietly. Approached her desk. 'Listen, there's something else I want you to look into.'

Marie hooked her red hair behind her ear and smiled knowingly. 'Oh, here we go. Are you trying to get something below Minks's radar?'

Grimacing, Van den Bergen reached into his trouser pocket and took out a USB stick. 'Check out the photos on here.' He cleared his throat, desperately trying to shake off the sensation that something was blocking his airway. 'Two old guys, dead, with identical tattoos on their necks.'

Plugging the USB stick into her PC, Marie uploaded the files. Morgue photos of Arnold van Blanken and Brechtus Bruin filled the monitor screen. With a flurry of mouse clicks in rapid succession, she zoomed in to reveal the crowned lions, flanked by the S and 5. 'Never seen that design before.'

'Neither have I,' Van den Bergen said. 'That's why I want you to look into it. We've got two guys – both ninety-five and both registered to the same doctors' surgery – who have died within days of one another.'

'Coincidence? Serendipity?' she asked. Opening her desk drawer, she pulled out a bar of chocolate. 'At ninety-five, I bet they were feeling bloody smug that they'd made it to such old bones or else just waiting for God.' She peered thoughtfully at the photo of the smiling baby boy by her keyboard. 'Not everyone's lucky enough to make it to such old bones.'

Had a glassy film suddenly appeared on her eyes? Van den Bergen couldn't be sure. He lifted his hand, ready to pat her supportively on the shoulder, but realised that perhaps she didn't want to dredge up the subject of cot death and loss over a bar of Verkade creamy milk.

'Both had been prescribed wrong doses of medication by their doctor, leading to death from heart failure. Same GP. Do me a favour, will you? Can you also do a little digging into Dr Saif Abadi's patient list and see who's died recently – elderly people and those suffering cardiac arrest or sudden death. In fact, pull the register of deaths and make a list of everyone who's keeled over in similar circumstances. It wouldn't be the first time someone's decided to start bumping off the old and vulnerable.'

'If that's what's happened,' Marie added.

'Yes. If. Oh, and don't breathe a word about this to anyone until I know more. Okay? Minks is giving me heat about the refugee case.'

'Has anyone even reported suspected foul play with these old men?'

He shook his head. 'George is going to help me make discreet enquiries. I have a hunch … and I can't let it go.'

Snapping her chocolate in two, Marie treated him to a yellow-toothed smile. 'Leave it with me, boss.'

# CHAPTER 9

## *Amsterdam, the home of Kaars Verhagen, 10 October*

'You know …' The old bastard wheezed fitfully, collapsing back into his wheelchair by the kitchen window. The timorous morning sun shone on his face, making the papery crumple of skin look almost translucent.

He imagined he could see through the network of blue veins to the bones beneath. Not long now till the blood would slow to a standstill, thickening and turning black.

'The problem with life is you've got to die sometime.' There was a volley of barking coughs. He sat in silence while the filthy old liar coughed up gobs of blood-streaked phlegm into a handkerchief. 'Even at my age, you're never ready for death.' More wheezing, as if the speech had sucked all the air out of those decayed lungs, leaving nothing but the vacuum of thwarted instinct behind.

'That's why it's important you take your medication, Kaars. Come on.' He moved over towards the wheelchair and took the prongs from the oxygen tubing out of the old man's nose. 'Don't worry. I'll hook you back up in a second. Take the pills.' The hiss and grind of the oxygen machine droned on in the background: the monotonous soundtrack to the quiet drama that was about to unfold. He dropped the tablets into that shaking, liver-spotted hand – the hairs on the back of it the only indication that this ancient man had ever enjoyed a prime.

Kaars Verhagen struggled to swallow down the medicine with the tepid water. Perhaps he'd choke to death! That wouldn't do.

'Come on now, Kaars,' he said, banging the old man on the back. 'Don't choke. That defeats the object!' He grabbed the glass of water impatiently from Kaars's trembling hand and forced the pathetic old fart to sip again. 'That's right!' he said, keeping his voice concerned and calm. 'Just swallow.'

Finally, with the pills safely in his stomach, Kaars turned to him. Rail-thin now, even his appreciative smile looked like an effort. 'I know I'm a goner,' he said. 'But I appreciate the treatment on the side. They'd written me off at the hospital. Too frail for experimental trials or extra chemo, they said.' His words were swallowed by another big choking bout of coughing. His milky eyes looked fit to burst from his skull. 'When you get to my grand age, they think you've had more than your three score and ten. Way more. They won't fight for you. But *you've* fought for me.' Tears came, then. He held his scrawny arms out, expecting a hug. It was only fair to reciprocate.

'There, there. It's the least I could do. A man like you could have another ten years of life. More! You've always had the constitution of a horse. You all did. Amazing, when you think how many never even made it to adulthood.'

Patting his back and breaking free of the hug, Kaars waved him away. His colour had started to wane. The sheen of sweat indicated that the final super-high dose of anthracycline was taking effect. Surprised that the duplicitous bastard had struggled on thus far, he said a silent prayer that sheer exhaustion or kidney failure wouldn't take him first. It had to be his heart. Had to. It was the only way.

The old man started to cough violently again, dry-heaving when the cough finally subsided. 'I must get Cornelia round. This damn building work needs finishing before I die,' he said. 'I'm worried she'll be left with a mess.' Their eyes locked. The old man's were pleading. 'If she needs some moral support, or help with the builders, you'll pitch in, won't you? Promise me you won't leave her to tackle all that alone. I need to know there's a man around I can trust. You've become that man.'

'I'm just at the end of a phone.'

It was a non-committal response, and that was all the old fart would get from him. Why should he let the fucker die with a mind free from care?

Kaars Verhagen grimaced. He was pointing at some half-built stud wall, the skeleton timbers describing a new doorway wide enough to accommodate his wheelchair. Though he opened his mouth to speak, the words did not come. Now, he was gasping for air. Clutching at his arm and frowning, as though something had occurred to him that was just beyond his comprehension.

'I feel …'

Falling from his wheelchair to the floor, Kaars curled up into a ball. With that bald head – hair only just growing back after months of chemotherapy and radiation treatment – he looked like a foetal bird inside an egg. Gasping. Moaning.

Good. Causing pain was a definite bonus. But he was certain it was happening. This was it.

'Are you okay, Kaars?' he asked, amused by the hollow intent of his words.

The old man stretched out a thin arm towards him, clearly begging for help. The mucus in the back of his throat rattled. His breath was shallow, almost imperceptible. His eyes clouded over.

Pushing the old man's pyjama collar aside, revealing the lion tattoo as he did so, he checked that his work here had been successful. Sure enough, no blood flowed beneath his fingertips as he felt for a pulse. Kaars Verhagen was gone.

Wiping the place down for prints was easy, though he had to be extra vigilant that he left no footprints in the dust. The unfinished building work coated everything in a persistent layer of grime. A quick scatter of the debris that had been left behind in a dustpan would soon sort that. Leaving was a consideration, though. This was a busy area. Not like the others. Would he be seen?

No. He was the grey man.

Pulling his average and unremarkable raincoat closed against the wind and drizzle, he unfurled his average and unremarkable black umbrella and walked away at an unremarkable speed into the dank morning.

# CHAPTER 10

## *Amsterdam, Den Bosch's house in De Pijp, later*

'No answer,' Van den Bergen said, peering through the letterbox. 'He's not at his business premises. Not at home. Shit. Where the hell is he?' For good measure, he thumped on the front door a fourth time. The paintwork was surprisingly shoddy for a man with company finances as robust as Den Bosch's.

Elvis placed a placatory hand on his arm. 'We can come back, boss.' His nose was red and his eyes were watering against the stiff wind. 'In fact, without a warrant, we've got no option.'

Van den Bergen batted him away. 'Are you patronising your superior officer?'

Smiling. Elvis was bloody smiling. He was all Zen since he'd discovered the joys of love and a second chance at living.

'No. But there's no point sweating it. He could be anywhere. We know next to nothing about him. He puts hardly anything on Facebook and he's not on any of the other social media sites. There's no way of proving he's got anything to do with the trafficked Syrians.' He dug his hands deeper inside his leather jacket and scanned the street. 'We're grasping at straws.'

'We're being thorough. In a case without leads, we have nowhere else to go.'

Two flamboyantly dressed students ambled by, chatting too animatedly about someone called Kenny who'd drunk so much that he'd puked in some girl's mouth. Van den Bergen thought about his baby granddaughter and shuddered at the thought that, one day, some chump might vomit into her mouth in some student fleapit of a bar in De Pijp. Across the way, two women clad in burkas scurried into a run-down house, glancing over their shoulders. One was carrying a large tartan shopper – the kind Van den Bergen had seen people fill with washing. The other clutched at bulging bags. Neither were old.

'Excuse me, ladies!' he shouted to them, trying to keep the friendliness in his voice and the weariness out of it.

But they had already slammed the door.

'Oh,' he said. 'Like that, eh?'

Approaching, he rang the bell several times, but there was no answer. It was as if he had merely imagined them.

'I told you,' Elvis said, peering up at the dirt-streaked windows. The pointing between the bricks was crumbling and the gutter near the roof on the three-storey building was cracked and coming away from the facade. 'Me and Marie had the same thing. Nobody wants to talk round here.'

'But it's supposed to be trendy and vibrant, these days.' Van den Bergen cast an appraising eye over the café that was several doors down from Den Bosch's house. The windows were steamy. The lights were on. The sound of chatter and laughter spilled onto the busy street as three young men bundled out, wrapping themselves with scarves against the biting autumnal air. Business was booming in De Pijp. 'Bohemian, and all that crap. I expected the people here to be more talkative. Let's keep going.'

Together, they worked their way down the street, knocking on doors only to be met by twitching net curtains or vehement denials – from the neighbours who did deign to open their doors – that they knew Den Bosch at all. Helpfully unhelpful, often in pidgin Dutch and in several different accents. The air was heady with the smells of cooking from Africa, Asia and the Middle East. Van den Bergen could also smell bullshit very strongly indeed.

'Are you telling me that not a single soul knows a successful businessman like Den Bosch on a busy street like this?' he asked Elvis as they entered the welcoming warmth of the Wakker/Lekker café – its name a claim that its fare could both wake you up and be delicious. Van den Bergen yawned and his stomach growled. The smell of coffee and cake wafted around him like a timely greeting. 'Den Bosch's name is emblazoned on the side of those giant bloody trucks.'

'Yeah. But you'd only see those on the motorways and at the docks, boss. Not locally. I'd never notice one in a million years unless I was looking for it specifically.'

Donning his reading glasses, Van den Bergen looked longingly at the lemon cake, remembered that anything acidic was a no-no for hiatus hernia sufferers. And there was the small matter of being on duty.

'Just a koffie verkeerd please,' he said to the woman behind the counter.

She looked at him blankly, forcing him to reappraise the menu, which only had the café's offerings in Italian.

'Latte. I mean a latte.' Then he remembered that anything high in fat was discouraged too. Damn it. 'With skimmed milk.' He swallowed. Patted his stomach. 'I've got a hiatus hernia.'

He removed his glasses and treated the woman to a half-smile that was more of a grimace. Why the hell had he just shared that detail with her? Perhaps because the doc had said that thirty per cent of all over-fifties were afflicted, and she looked well over fifty. Maybe he was just looking for a connection with someone who understood.

She laughed, hooking her no-nonsense grey bob behind

her ears. 'Me too, lovey. Me too. Haven't we all? I'm a martyr to mine!'

Hope surged inside him for the first time in days. But in his pocket, the blister pack of super-strength antacids he was forced to pop twice per day reminded him that there was little to be happy about. His body was crumbling. And then, the memory of Arnold van Blanken, expiring on the waiting room floor, returned, snuffing out every emotion except frustration. Here he was, saddled with the murder of a trafficked girl that he couldn't solve; unable officially to investigate the murders of several old men that perhaps he could.

'Do you know anything about Frederik Den Bosch?' he asked, pointing to the lemon cake and indicating that she should serve him up a slice of it after all.

Her friendly smile soured into mean, thin lips. 'The farmer? Mr High and Mighty?'

Van den Bergen placed his coins carefully on the counter. 'Not keen?'

She kept her voice low. Leaned in so that the rest of her clientele couldn't eavesdrop. 'He's selfish. He always takes my parking space with that ridiculous Jeep of his and he obviously doesn't give a hoot that I'm much older than him. It's not like he doesn't know I've got arthritis in my knees. We had a conversation about it years ago. Big turd.'

Sensing that the café owner was rather enjoying offloading about her neighbour, Van den Bergen showed her his ID. Winked conspiratorially. 'Go on. My colleague and I are both very interested in Mr Den Bosch. Anything you say may be of help to our investigation.'

The woman glanced at the group of young people who were enjoying croissants and hot drinks by the window. She turned back to Van den Bergen and beckoned him and Elvis into the back room.

In a space that was otherwise stacked high with boxes and

cluttered with shabby, broken seating that had reached the end of its useful life, she gestured that they should sit on beat-up armchairs, arranged in a sociable group. Wakker/Lekker's proprietor was a woman who liked to hold court on a regular basis, Van den Bergen assessed.

She wiped her hands on her flowery apron, her face flushed. 'Why are you investigating him? Can you tell me?'

Clearing his throat, Van den Bergen considered his words carefully, sensing that this might be a woman prone to hyperbole and conjecture. 'One of Mr Den Bosch's trucks was stolen and I'm afraid the port police found cargo on board that shouldn't have been there. We're trying to find out more about Den Bosch, and why his truck might have been used to commit some very serious crimes.'

'Drugs!' Her eyes brightened. 'Was it drugs?'

'No. Please, Mevrouw. Tell me if there's anything else you know about Frederik Den Bosch. His other neighbours seem reluctant to speak to us, but I can tell you're a fine, upstanding Dutch citizen.'

She nodded vociferously. 'I am. You bet. But *he's* not, that overgrown ferret. Everyone thinks he's a pillar of the community, but what he's doing with those houses is wrong.'

'What houses?' Van den Bergen had already opened his notebook and was poised to write. At his side, Elvis sat silently observing the woman's body language.

'Didn't you know? He owns three houses on this street alone, and about five on the next. Stuffs them to the rafters with immigrants. It's a disgrace.'

'Oh?'

She closed her eyes. 'Rammed in there like shrink-wrapped sausages. That's why they won't talk to you. They're all afraid. And he lets his properties go to rack and ruin. Have you seen the state of them? All bust guttering and filthy windows. Slum landlord – that's what Den Bosch is. And they're all illegals, I reckon.'

'Why? What makes you say that?'

Shrugging, she splayed her fingers and examined her spotless short nails. 'They're shifty. They don't speak Dutch. I live above my café, see. I can see them when they arrive in the middle of the night. They don't bring anything more than a small case or a rucksack. And I may have dodgy knees and a hiatus hernia, but I've got an excellent memory for people's faces. So I can tell the new ones, even by the light of the street lamp.'

Van den Bergen wrote furiously in his notepad, sensing that here was something to go on. 'How frequently do new people arrive?'

She cocked her head thoughtfully. Glanced through the open doorway to check no other customers were standing at the counter. 'Every few weeks. You get men. Women with children. All sorts. They all come from those Muslim countries. I know that because of the way the women dress. They're always wearing those burka things, or have got their heads covered, at least.' Rubbing her knees, she tried to glimpse what he was writing. 'All I know is that he must have thirty living in each house. It's not on, you know. It's unsanitary. And they leave rubbish strewn on the street. The bins are overflowing every week with stinking nappies.' She wrinkled her nose. 'You want to talk to environmental health about that, you know. He wants locking up, he does. Expecting the rest of us respectable residents to put up with that mess. And the people in there! Imagine kiddies having to live in that filth and with all those strange men! It's not right.'

With the addresses of the houses safely recorded in his notepad, Van den Bergen made a second attempt at encouraging the reluctant residents to speak out about their enigmatic neighbour.

'Jesus Christ!' he said, as yet another hijab-clad woman

refused to come to the door. He looked up at her as she shouted something in Arabic through the cracked glass of her first-floor window. 'This is sending my acid into overdrive.' He swallowed down the foul taste in his mouth.

Elvis stepped away from the front door, where he had been peering through the letterbox. 'Let's give it up, boss. Try one of the houses on another street and maybe come back later. See if Den Bosch shows. He won't dare refuse to talk to us.'

Driving only one street away, so that he could keep his car within sight, Van den Bergen sighed heavily. Tried to get into a tight space and failed. Ended up at the wrong end of a long road.

'Ever wish you'd just stayed in bed? Or at least did another job?' he said, pointing his fob at the Mercedes and arming the alarm. He thought fleetingly and fondly of retirement, then remembered that he wanted to be the opposite of old Arnold van Blanken. He needed to be a working man, in his prime for as long as possible.

Elvis chuckled softly. 'My mother's dead. I nearly checked out in the spring, thanks to one trafficking bastard. I often think about doing something boring and safe, but this job is all I know.'

'I guess it's just me, then,' Van den Bergen said, eyeing a group of youths who were hanging around too close to his car for comfort. He could see that they were scoping him out. Debating whether to pre-empt a clash and tell them to move along, he jumped when he felt a hand on his back.

'Watch your car, mister?' a shrill voice said.

Turning, he saw a small boy of about ten, dressed in a tunic and trousers that gave him away as Syrian, maybe, or Afghan. Van den Bergen stooped low so that they were face to face. The boy's breakfast was still visible at the corners of his mouth.

'Why aren't you in school, young man?'

'Ten euros to watch it. I'll keep it safe, I promise.' His Dutch was fluent but his Amsterdam accent was laced heavily with Middle Eastern flat vowels and clipped intonation.

Van den Bergen's knees cracked as he crouched. He could see childish mischief in those shining dark eyes. 'What's your name?'

'Not telling you, am I?' The boy grinned, revealing adult teeth awkwardly pushing the milk teeth aside. One incisor was growing outwards, almost horizontally, poking through the boy's full-lipped smile. 'Go on, then. Ten euros. It's a good price.'

Reaching for his wallet, Van den Bergen wondered how much a boy who never went to school, but who had been around long enough to pick up the regional accent, might know about a local landlord. 'Here's five for now. I'll give you the other five later.'

The boy made to snatch the money, but Van den Bergen drew himself to his full height and held the cash at a height impossible for the kid to reach. 'First, though, tell me if you've ever heard of a man called Frederik den Bosch.' He waved the five-euro note close. Withdrew it. Felt bad for teasing.

'That'll cost you more.' The boy glanced over at the group of youths. One of them shouted to him in their native tongue. Definitely an Arabic dialect. There was a clear connection between them.

'Tell you what, I'll give you twenty if you tell me what you know about Mr Den Bosch. And you won't have to share the extra ten with those bigger boys. It'll be our secret.'

The boy stole a surreptitious glance over at the older boys and nodded. 'Give me the extra ten now. Behind the car, where they can't see.'

'Information first.'

Sighing, the boy began. 'Den Bosch is nasty. He owns the house where I live.' As they progressed slowly down the street, it was clear he walked with a pronounced limp.

71

'Can we go there?'

'Not while my brothers are watching.'

'Where are you from?'

'Syria. Lots of us are from there.'

'How did you get to Amsterdam?'

'Are you a cop?'

Should he tell this astute child? He didn't want to risk the kid clamming up. 'Tell me more about Den Bosch. It's him I'm interested in. Why is he nasty?'

'He charges everyone in our house too much money, and my mother says it's dangerous. Also, I don't like his tattoos.'

The mention of tattoos piqued Van den Bergen's curiosity. He exchanged a glance with Elvis. 'What kind are they?'

The boy wrinkled his nose. 'They're scary. He's covered in them, all up his arms. Skulls and symbols and demons. My uncle heard that Den Bosch goes to big gatherings where other men say horrible things about Muslims and immigrants like us. Marches that are on TV. That kind of thing. Uncle Jabril says that's why he treats us so badly. He wants our money but he doesn't like us. Den Bosch is nothing but a racist Kufar.'

Clearing his throat, Van den Bergen wondered how he could get the boy to say more about his arrival on Dutch shores without spooking him. Wary of offering him more money lest it be construed as coercion, he relied simply on a little boy's innate need to brag. 'I bet you were really brave when you came over from Syria, weren't you?'

The grin told him everything. 'Yes. My uncle says I'm brave enough to have fought with the rebels.'

'I've seen boys like you on TV. Sailing the high seas on rickety ships and nearly drowning. Is that what you did? Did you sail across the Mediterranean?'

The boy chuckled. 'Oh no. I can't swim.' He pulled up the left leg of his baggy trousers to reveal a deep, florid dent in his calf muscle. 'I was hit by a big chunk of brick when I was little. A bomb went off at our school. It means I can't do much sport.'

'What about flying, then? Did you come on a plane?'

Shaking his head, the boy said, 'No. I might have a bad leg but I'm as good as any grown man. I looked after my mum and my big brother when they got sick in the truck.'

'You came in a truck? Maybe like the ones Den Bosch has.'

The boy clasped a hand over his mouth and glared at Van den Bergen as though his indiscretion were his fault. Snatching the money from his hand, the boy fled between the cars and disappeared down an alleyway with an uneven gait but impressive speed.

'Shall we go after him, boss?'

Van den Bergen felt the corner of his mouth twitch upwards involuntarily. 'Yes. We could give it a go. Let's see where he—'

Poised to sprint after the boy, he stopped short when his phone rang shrilly in his pocket. It was the ringtone for Marianne de Koninck, who only ever called when something dire had landed on her mortuary slab.

'Van den Bergen. Speak!'

'There's been another,' she said. 'Another old man. Heart attack. Tattoo. The lot.'

# CHAPTER 11

## *Amsterdam, Oud Zuid, Kaars Verhagen's house, 12 October*

Staring up at the brass plate on the door of the elegant town-house in Oud Zuid, watching her breath steam on the air, George thought wistfully about her family, who were undoubtedly now all sprawled by the pool in Torremolinos.

'I could be swigging rum and Coke in the sun, you know,' she said, glancing up at Van den Bergen. But he wasn't listening. He was burping quietly and rehearsing his opening gambit. 'And bouncing some young Spanish waiter off the walls of my hotel room,' she added. No reaction.

Footsteps behind the door, click-clacking on wooden flooring, by the sounds. Van den Bergen cleared his throat, fixing what approximated to a friendly, open smile on his face. All the anxiety surrounding his health and the candle perpetually burned at both ends, thanks to his job and his new grandfatherly responsibilities, seemed to have etched their way into his skin as permanent souvenirs of a life hard-led. In spite of her frustrations, George found she felt some sympathy for the contrary old fart. As the multiple locks on the other side of the door were undone, she squeezed his hand fleetingly.

Planted a kiss on his knuckles, then faced forward, releasing him and shoving her hands in her pockets.

'Can I help you?' the woman said. She had only opened the door a fraction. Her voice was hoarse and timorous, her eyes red-rimmed. Her hair was dishevelled and greasy. George had her pegged as the grieving daughter.

Van den Bergen showed his ID. 'Chief Inspector Paul van den Bergen. This is my colleague, Dr Georgina McKenzie. We're here about Mr Kaars Verhagen. And you are?'

'Cornelia. Cornelia Verhagen. This is my father's house. Was.' Tears welled in her eyes and her lower lip began to tremble. 'You'd better come in.'

Inside, the double-fronted house smelled of plaster dust and new timber. But George caught a whiff of a medicinal top note and stale urine coming from the downstairs toilet as they passed from the hallway to a study that faced onto the quiet street. Packing boxes were strewn about, half-filled with books. Here, the air was mustier, heavy with decades of memories. Cornelia Verhagen gestured for them to sit on the old leather sofa, which squeaked beneath their weight.

'Sorry for your loss,' George said.

Cornelia blew her nose loudly, nodding as if quiet acceptance was all that was left. 'Thank you. My father was very old and very ill. I knew he had to go someday, but it still came as a shock.' Her voice started to break. She tapped her chest as if trying to encourage a breaking heart to keep beating. 'Silly, really. Sorry.'

'No need to apologise, Mevrouw.' Van den Bergen leaned forward, resting his elbows on his knees. The furrows in his brow gave him an air of solemnity and respect.

'It's Doctor. Not Mrs.'

'Sorry. I know from my own father's death that even when you know it's coming, it still hurts like hell.'

Cornelia frowned. Wiped her nose with a pristine white handkerchief. 'My father died of natural causes. A heart attack, in the end. Hardly surprising given the months and months of treatment and trials he endured. So why did they order a post-mortem and why are you here? There's not a problem, is there?' She sat up straight. Folded her arms over her bosom. 'I wasn't with him at the end, you know. I was at work. I teach. Anyone will tell you where I was all day.' Alarm registered on her pinched features. 'But I did find him in the evening.' She looked to George, presumably for womanly understanding. 'You know what it's like with parents. I always go round just before bed to check on him and make him some tea. It looked like he'd passed away when he was having his morning coffee. Nothing untoward whatsoever.'

George watched with interest as the daughter's body language changed from naked grief to frightened defensiveness. Van den Bergen held his hand aloft in a placatory gesture.

'Nobody's accusing you of anything. And I know you can vouch for your whereabouts at the time of your father's death. But the fact is, there have been a few recent deaths of very elderly gentlemen – all aged ninety-five, in fact. They've all suffered heart failure, despite having no previous weakness in that department. And they all had the same tattoo on their necks.' He removed a close-up photo of Verhagen's neck from his notebook.

Gasping, Kaars Verhagen's only child took the photograph and studied the discreet lion with its crown and sword. Bit her lip. A tear tracked its way down her cheek. 'That's him!'

'Yes,' George said. 'But it could just as easily be one of the other elderly men. They all had the same mark in the same place, hidden by their shirt collars.'

Van den Bergen took the photograph back, slotting it into his notebook. 'I watched another of the men die in a doctor's waiting room. Arnold van Blanken. Have you heard the name before?'

Cornelia's eyes widened. 'Yes,' she said almost inaudibly. 'He was one of my father's oldest friends. They grew up together. Don't tell me he's also passed on!'

'I'm afraid so. There are three dead old men in total, all with the same tattoo, including your father.'

George felt cynicism start to nibble away at her sympathy. 'How come your dad didn't mention Van Blanken's death, if they were so close and you saw him every day?'

'Well, as it happens, I hadn't actually been over for a week.' Cornelia started to wring the handkerchief between skinny fingers. 'I am entitled to a break. I went away.' Racking sobs took George by surprise as the woman's shoulders started to heave up and down.

Guilt. She knew it when she saw it. But guilty of what? George looked over at Van den Bergen and wondered if he was thinking along similar lines: that perhaps this poorly dressed, modestly salaried teacher had grown sick of waiting for her inheritance and had somehow conspired with her father's GP to bring about the end and that shower of pennies from heaven sooner, rather than later. Now, she was making out to all and sundry that she had always been the dutiful daughter and that her father's passing was a loss of biblical proportions. But then, that wouldn't explain away the other old men's demises.

'How well did you know your dad's GP?' George asked.

'Very well,' Cornelia said. 'Well, reasonably so.' She swallowed back down her gushing words, as if she'd let slip too much. 'I liaised with Dr Abadi over Dad's treatment. Took him to the doctors' on a regular basis. That kind of thing. He's been looking after my father for the last fifteen or so years. They got on. Why?'

Van den Bergen scribbled in his notepad. 'Would it surprise

you to know that Abadi was the GP for all three of the men who died? All tattooed in the same way. All reliant on the same medical professional. All dying of heart attacks. That's why I'm here, Dr Verhagen. As fishy goes, this is one hell of a big bag of battered kabeljouw. The entire stocks of the North Sea couldn't match it.'

George watched, rapt, as Cornelia rose from her father's easy chair – markedly more worn than the leather sofa – which still bore the greasy doily where his head had presumably rested. She strode over to a box on the wooden floor, crouched down and started to rummage through the contents. After a moment, she produced a battered leather photo album, its leaves edged in gold. With a glimmer of a satisfied smile playing on her lips, and tears in her eyes, she stood. Flipped through several pages of old black and white photos, reverentially lifting the protective parchment that covered each leaf. Finally, she held the album out, open at a page displaying one large black and white photo, professionally taken, by the look of it. Beneath it was written, in a beautiful cursive hand, '*Dagelijkse Amsterdammer* krant, Kerstmis 1939.'

'Look at this photo from the old local paper, the *Daily Amsterdamer*. They were full of triumph and hope for the future. Fresh out of school. They'd set up some kind of support for the poor who were freezing and going hungry. Handing out blankets and free meals. It was apparently a humdinger of a winter. Even Hitler had to shelve his plans to invade France because it was so darned cold. Anyway, these fellows were celebrated as local heroes. That's why they were in the paper. Now they're all gone.' She shook her head, as if in disbelief that the five young men who smiled out from the image should be merely a footnote in history.

'I take it your father's among these men?' Van den Bergen gently took the album from her.

George stood on her tiptoes to absorb the detail of the

portrait from close quarters. All of the men were wrapped in thick woollen sweaters. One of them – a tall lad with fair hair, a prominent chin and a pinched nose – bore a clear resemblance to Cornelia. 'Is this your dad?'

'Yes.' Cornelia ran a finger tenderly over the monochrome image. 'And these are his best friends. Brechtus Bruin, Arnold van Blanken, Hendrik van Eden and Ed Sijpesteijn.'

Van den Bergen breathed in sharply. 'Brechtus Bruin and Arnold van Blanken also died—'

'From heart attacks. Yes, you said. And so did Hendrik van Eden, earlier in the year,' Cornelia said.

'A *fourth*?' Surprise on Van den Bergen's face. 'I didn't— Was Abadi his GP?'

She shrugged. 'How should I know?'

'What about Ed?' George asked, feeling that the number of young men was somehow significant to this case – if it was a case.

'My father's first cousin. He went missing during the war years,' she said. 'Everyone assumed he'd been shot by a Nazi; that he'd been found out.'

'What do you mean?' George asked. 'What had he been doing?'

Flicking to a page further into the album, Cornelia drummed her index finger on another photo of the young men, all posing topless with their fists raised like boxers. Each man inclined his neck to the camera's lens, revealing their identical lion tattoos. Crown, sword, the letter S and the number 5.

'*They* were the five!' George said, feeling her pulse quicken.

'Yes. De Strijdkrachten Vijf,' Cornelia said, smiling sadly. 'S5 for short – the self-titled "Force of Five". They gained a reputation in the city for being the most fearless resistance fighters.' She flicked to another photo of the young men, standing with about ten other people – four of them women. They posed as a group in a forest, all carrying rifles. Kaars

Verhagen was grinning from behind an anti-tank gun. All were wearing ragged, baggy suits and overcoats.

'That's some serious-looking hardware,' George said, whistling softly through her teeth. Her gaze moved from the heavy-duty weaponry to their attire. There, she spotted the resistance armbands that they wore. 'Oranje,' she said. The crowned, sword-wielding lion was visible, superimposed onto the Dutch flag. The stripes of the flag were hard to make out in the black and white photos, though the lion was crisp and clear. 'So they were all the same age. All reached their nineties.'

'Ninety-five,' Cornelia said, nodding. 'Celebrated as the city's finest sons throughout their adult lives, and deservedly so. All except poor Ed. Who knows what end he met?'

Van den Bergen cleared his throat and rose from the sofa. 'May I take a look around?' Methodically, he prowled the length of the large study, and then moved into the hallway and beyond, examining the half-finished building work, where a wall had been removed here and a doorway expanded there.

With Cornelia dogging his footsteps, still holding the album, Van den Bergen stopped short at the single bed – still unmade – in a dining room that had been partially converted into a bedroom. He turned to the doorway that led to the kitchen. 'He died in the kitchen, didn't he?'

'Yes. That's where I found him. He was on the floor by the little breakfast table. He'd fallen out of his wheelchair.'

George watched Van den Bergen, imagining him as a large bloodhound on the trail of some deadly intrigue. She turned to Cornelia, who placed the photo album on the dining table and closed it reverentially. 'Looks like your old dad had grand plans. He certainly didn't have death on his mind when he started all this.' She waved her hand to describe the sprawling warren of half-renovated rooms.

'He started the work a couple of years ago. Dad had been in a wheelchair whenever he went out for a good month or two. He managed on sticks indoors. His arthritis was finally getting the better of him, or so we thought. The house has always been a jumble of rooms and narrow doorways. Obviously, there's a lot of steep stairs for an infirm man to contend with, and suddenly, he's confined to the ground floor. He decided he'd have this level reconfigured so it's a bit more open-plan, and all the doorways widened to accommodate the wheelchair.'

'Fiercely independent, I'll bet. I've got a mother a bit like that. You say black; she says white just for the hell of it.'

Cornelia nodded. 'Dad was never giving up, despite being in his nineties. Except it turned out his arthritis hadn't been playing up at all. He went to Dr Abadi with other symptoms, and when they gave him a few scans, they realised he had secondary cancer in his bones. Took us all completely by surprise.'

Van den Bergen coughed and pointedly stared out of the window. Hand around his neck as though he were trying to placate some malignancy that hid in his throat.

'That's when the building work halted,' Cornelia said. 'It's just stayed like this all that time. Dad was so worn out by the treatment that he didn't want the builders banging and making a mess around him. Mind you, that hasn't stopped the dust getting everywhere constantly.'

George scrutinised Cornelia with narrowed eyes, wondering what sort of a woman she was. 'You didn't get it finished for him, then? Looks a bit dangerous and uncomfortable to me.' She felt instantly guilty for judging this bereaved woman. There were plenty of things she refused to do for Letitia the Dragon. Accompanying her on holiday was just one.

Cornelia shook her head. 'He just wanted it to be left. He said he'd do it when he was better. Didn't want any fuss.'

They moved back to the study at the front of the house. While Van den Bergen asked some additional questions about

Kaars Verhagen's regular friends and acquaintances, his state of mind shortly before his death, George stole out of the room and took a look at the kitchen, keen to see where the old man had breathed his last … not that she anticipated there being any clue remaining as to how he had spent his final hour.

Returning through the dining-room-cum-bedroom to the hallway, she was struck by the sizeable length of blank wall between the doors of the dining room and living room, which didn't seem to correspond to any kind of chimney breast or alcove in either room.

'Weird,' she muttered, moving back and forth between the rooms to see if she could solve this architectural puzzle. All those years spent living and working at St John's College in Cambridge had taught George that old buildings could hide many a surprise. 'What quirky shit's going on here?' she muttered in English, tap-tapping on the blank wall. It sounded solid enough. But then she extended her efforts into the dining room, tapping until she reached a tall rosewood sideboard that supported integrated shelving above it. It was stacked with books. Except the books seemed to be stuck to the shelves. Looking down at the wooden floor, she spied scuffmarks that described an arc. 'Someone's been playing silly buggers with the furniture.'

Trying her hardest not to attract the attention of Cornelia Verhagen, who was still deep in conversation with Van den Bergen in the study, George pulled the hefty piece of furniture out, following the trajectory that had clearly been used time and again by someone else. Behind the sideboard, she found a door painted the same colour as the walls, with only a recess for a handle. It had been cunningly crafted – easily missed by the casual observer.

Pulling the door open, the blood rushing in her ears so she could no longer hear the low rumble of Van den Bergen's voice, George sneezed as the stale air of a poorly ventilated room billowed out to greet her. A secret room.

'Paul! Have you got a minute?' she asked.

The curious space pulled her inexorably inside, as if it had been waiting for decades to be discovered. The floorboards squeaked. Her breath was loud. Not a stick of furniture. Not a photo or painting on the wall. And yet, George sensed that the room had a story to tell. And there, above her in the murk, was a light.

'What the hell are you doing?' Cornelia asked, the tone of her voice so sharp, George felt her every consonant as a scratch. She fumbled for something on the wall and switched on the light. Too bright. It was a bare bulb, shining on a room full of nothing. 'How dare you rifle through my father's house without permission? Or a warrant!'

George swung around abruptly, hand on hip, pretending moral authority, though she knew that she and Van den Bergen didn't have any jurisdiction over Cornelia Verhagen whatsoever. There was no case at all – yet. They were merely acting on Van den Bergen's conviction that there was no such thing as coincidence, and his suspicion that something was decidedly amiss. 'Er, excuse me, but aren't we talking about the probable murder of four friends? Elderly they might have been, but murder is murder, lovey.'

Van den Bergen stood beneath the unforgiving light, his white hair almost glowing – a beacon in its own right. 'Jesus,' he whispered. 'I've heard about secret rooms like this in old houses.'

'Dad wanted it all knocked through,' Cornelia said. 'There's nothing to see here. It's just a box room. So if you don't mind, let's go. I think it's time you left.'

But as George retreated, she stood on a loose floorboard that cracked, rather than creaked, beneath her boots. A hollow sound. Crouching, she swallowed down disgust at the thick layer of dust and grime that covered the wood, digging her fingernail between the planks. Levering the rotten pine board up was easy. When she saw what lay beneath, she gasped.

'An old journal!' she said, reading the neat hand that proclaimed this was the diary of Rivka Zemel. She took the green, canvas-backed book out.

'Give that to me!' Cornelia shouted, grabbing at the book. A scuffle ensued where the bereaved daughter trod heavily on George's foot and yanked at the book so hard, trying to prise it free of George's grip, that she thumped her inadvertently in the arm.

But George held the book steadfastly to her chest. 'Look, I appreciate you're grieving, but back the hell off, lady,' she said in English.

'Dr McKenzie! Dr Verhagen!' Van den Bergen laid a hand on the women's shoulders. 'Please!' He gently manoeuvred them apart. Turned to Cornelia, with a placatory softness to his voice. 'I'm afraid we're going to have to take the book. Old men keep long-forgotten secrets and something about this room and this book has my policeman's senses tingling. It might turn out to be evidence in a murder case. We'll return it as soon as we're done with it. I promise.'

Nodding, Cornelia wiped an angry tear away. 'Okay. I don't know what came over me.'

'There's nothing that frustrates and angers more than death. Don't be too hard on yourself. If there's been foul play, we'll uncover it.'

Outside, George turned to Van den Bergen and beamed. 'Looks like I've just found myself some new bedtime reading.'

# CHAPTER 12

## *Van den Bergen's apartment, later*

The TV was overly loud, niggling George to the point where she noticed everything that was wrong in the room: the misaligned coaster; the scuffs on the coffee table; the messy fringing on Van den Bergen's rug; and the place on his jaw where he'd missed with the razor.

'Jesus! Do you have to have that on so high?' Wriggling, George tried and failed to get comfortable on this sofa she hadn't chosen in this apartment that wasn't hers.

At her side, Van den Bergen was slouched with his trousers unzipped, holding a bowl of blueberries on a belly that was full from a tasteless yet solid dinner of risotto. He shovelled them in whilst watching a platinum blonde, perma-tanned anchor-woman on NPO 1 news reel off a list of misdemeanours that had taken place downtown that afternoon. From the corner of her eye, George could see her gesturing to some blurry live footage that was being beamed from the epicentre of the upheaval.

'As you can see, the right-wing protestors who align them-selves with Geert Wilders' VVD party have been throwing bricks at the anti-racist movement. The clashes that have been raging over the last couple of hours having been both shocking and violent …'

George slapped the arm of the sofa. 'Are you bloody deaf, old man?' Standing abruptly, she turned away from the images on the TV of angry shorn youths and bloodstained, weeping white kids with dreadlocks. Studiously ignoring the fat talking head and token 'immigrant community leader' now being interviewed in the studio about racial tension. 'Turn the fucking thing down!'

Tutting, Van den Bergen hiked the volume by a couple of notches. 'Sorry. What?'

'Childish bastard!'

'Either I'm old or I'm childish. Which is it, Dr McKenzie?'

'You tell me. You're sitting there with a glazed expression on your face. Are you even listening to that shit?'

'If you must know, I'm thinking about how I can investigate the deaths of those old men without Minks taking the case off me. And I'm wondering how I can get Den Bosch's tenants to speak to me about their shifty landlord. Multitasking. See? You're not the only one can do that.' He treated her to a grin and winked.

'Most of the time, you're not even home,' she said. 'You're working or at Tamara's, playing Action fucking Opa. When you are here, you're a million miles away. What happened to our passion? Our togetherness? Grandfatherhood has changed you. I feel lonely, Paul. And I'm not even in my own space!'

But he was staring at the box, frowning. Clearly deep in thought once again.

Sucking her teeth in her lover's direction, George took Rivka Zemel's diary and repaired to the relative peace of the spare room. She heard Van den Bergen's voice drifting in from the living room: 'Maybe this community leader guy on the TV can help …'

Closing the door, she plumped the pillows on the spare bed,

careful to turn the dusty side down so that there was only pristine bedding between her and the headboard. Imagining dust motes and germ spores hanging in the air, waiting to colonise her lungs, she cracked the window open. Finally made herself comfortable on the creaking bed, making a mental note to clean the room in the morning.

'Come on then, Rivka Zemel,' she said, opening the green diary and running her finger over the yellowed pages and blue-black ink. It was in Dutch, written in an old-fashioned, looping, sloping hand. 'Let's see what you've got to say. What part did you play in Kaars Verhagen's life and why did your story end up buried beneath the floorboards?'

The first entry was dated Monday, 5 February 1940.

*Yesterday was my birthday. I hadn't really been looking forward to it at all, because of what's been going on. Everybody says that if Germany invades France and the Netherlands, we'll be made to wear stars like the Polish. The papers say Jews over there are getting arrested if they forget to put on their special armbands. Mainly, though, the news is full of speculation about there being war with Germany. Papa's very afraid for us all – especially Shmuel, because he's always so ill and can't stick up for himself. Kaars says the Germans are deluded if they think they can simply walk into Amsterdam and take over!*

*I'm trying not to think about it. I just get on with my work. Anyway, even though I had to polish the silverware – deathly dull and goes on forever – my birthday turned out to be much better than anticipated! I brought in a cake that Mama had baked to celebrate during my break. Famke made coffee and we were just about to sit down with Jan in the scullery when the Verhagens came downstairs and presented me with a gift! It was a beautiful hairbrush, made from ivory, I think. Mr Verhagen said it had come*

*from the tusk of a giant elephant he had hunted as a much*
*younger man on the Gold Coast of Africa. Fancy that! Ed*
*was there too, looking terribly handsome, as ever. He said*
*the brush would be perfect for taming my curls.*

*The Verhagens are good people. I feel lucky to have got*
*this job, though Mama keeps warning me not to get too*
*attached. I'm sure she thinks I have feelings for Kaars. He*
*is rather dashing and great fun to be around. She doesn't*
*realise, however, that his cousin Ed is the apple of my eye.*
*I realise he's not Jewish and that he's from a wealthy family,*
*so there's no way we could ever be together. He probably*
*doesn't even like me in that manner.*

The diary entry ended abruptly with a sentence that had been
written and then scribbled out with such determination that
George couldn't read it. She remembered back to her own teen
years – some ten years ago now – and the intensity of emotion
that had ruled her every waking moment. Most of her sleeping
ones, too. She smiled at the thought that there should be some
kind of a connection between Rivka Zemel from 1940 and
Georgina McKenzie of the twenty-first century.

But then, she remembered that her own teen years had
been a dysfunctional fiasco of intimidation, incarceration
and incursions of the council-estate kind. Not so similar.
Rivka Zemel's mother had baked her a birthday cake. George
had been lucky if Letitia had even bought her a shit card and
a past-its-sell-by-date chocolate bar from the cheap shop.
What fate had befallen this hopeful Jewish girl? And what
light could this diary shed on the life and secrets of the
Verhagen family?

She delved further into the dairy's musty pages, feeling like
a voyeur as she read how Rivka's feelings for Ed Sijpesteijn
developed apace, and how he apparently cared for her, using
his friendship with Kaars as a ruse to drop in regularly on this

self-deprecating, unassuming housemaid, making her laugh with jokes about the idiot Germans.

'Poor dim bastard,' George said, feeling certain that this simple love story would inevitably veer down a sinister path at some point. Wondering if Rivka's words were somehow connected with the mysterious deaths of four nonagenarians.

She flicked forward to 25 May 1940.

*Bombs were dropping for days on Rotterdam, and apparently the city is now in ruins. The Germans were determined to invade our beloved country and they have! What I can't believe is that the government gave in so quickly and accepted Nazi occupation. Kaars and Ed were here just now and they think it is a cowardly disgrace. They've resolved to band together with some of their other pals – Brechtus, Arnold and Hendrik – to trip the Germans up whenever they get the chance. Apparently, there's already a resistance movement gathering strength in secret. I think they knew this invasion was inevitable.*

*Famke and I went into town today to buy some food. We had no idea that German tanks were actually rolling into Amsterdam, so we got caught up in the ranks of onlookers. The Nazis seem to have brought out the worst in Amsterdamers. I was horrified to see people cheering them on! You never really see things like that in Waterlooplein, where the Jewish Quarter is, but then, I suppose that's because we're all Jews. Yet even where the Verhagens live, I've never witnessed any unpleasant bullying or name-calling personally. Famke said there are a lot of Nazi sympathisers around who are excited to have the weight of the German army behind us in war. There's already talk of them rounding up and arresting German Jews who had escaped to the Netherlands. What will happen to my family if they start to single out Jews in*

*Amsterdam? Mama hopes that good old Dutch common sense will prevail, but Papa isn't so sure. Only time will tell.*

Feeling sleepy, George pushed herself to continue reading, keen to discover how the German occupation of Amsterdam had shaped the life of a young Jewish maid, and if this journal would reveal more of the five young men who were now all gone. As Rivka wrote of her burgeoning love for Ed, George felt as though she were watching an old black and white film of a packed train with excited holidaymakers on board, heading full pelt for an unfinished bridge over a ravine. It was heartbreaking to read, and yet, she wanted to know what sort of people the missing Ed Sijpesteijn and the possibly murdered Kaars Verhagen, Arnold van Blanken, Brechtus Bruin and Hendrik van Eden were.

*3 October 1941*

*The Nazis are pretending that they're the best thing to happen to the Netherlands. They talk about us like we're Germany's favourite Aryan cousin. Everything has been carrying on as normal at the Verhagen house. I work hard and Famke is pleased that I'm learning to cook under her tutelage. Maybe when she retires as the housekeeper in the next few years, I'll be able to take over her job. Papa says not to hold my breath, though. He's been saving up to get us safe passage to England, but Shmuel is too poorly with his chest at the moment to leave the house. Mama says he should be in a sanatorium, but there's no question of that happening right now.*

*The newspapers are full of the triumphs of the Fatherland. Now that Hitler has defeated Stalin and his Soviets in battle and Russia's burning, the Nazis are boasting that the war is practically won. Yesterday evening, Kaars, Ed and the others appeared just as I was about to go home after a long day. They gathered in the scullery to tell us the latest news from the resistance meeting in the country. Apparently, the Germans have marched into Kiev and have shot thousands and thousands of Jews dead. Mr Verhagen says he thinks that tale is far-fetched, but Papa also heard tell of it from old Kramarov, the barber. Mr Kramarov's aunt was still living in Kiev, even though the rest of the family left in the Twenties to come and live over here. Tragically, she and two of his cousins were shot dead and their bodies, along with everyone else's, pushed off a cliff. A third cousin managed to escape and was smuggled by kind non-Jewish folk to Amsterdam in a grain truck. If he says it happened, it must be true.*

*Ed is such a brave sort. He says he will fight to the death to defend our family. Hendrik was boasting that his sniping skills are so refined that he could kill an entire battalion of Nazis with one packet of bullets. He also says he'd make the best spy and that he has infiltrated some Nazi sympathisers – whatever that means – so that he can pass on information about the Germans to the rest of the freedom fighters. Kaars says he's the organiser of the band of five, as it's always the Verhagen house where the boys meet. Arnold and Brechtus are obsessed with tactics. They're the ones always trying to second-guess what the Allied forces are going to do next to thwart the Germans. Brechtus is really good at making radio equipment. He says if he can cobble together some kind of eavesdropping device, he'll be able to listen in on the Nazis' communiqués and feed the information back to the English. Arnold speaks German, so he's going to help translate. What a band of excellent souls they are! I said we'd have to come up with a code name for them.*

George tried to make out a list of slogans and names that

Rivka had thought up, but all had been scribbled out. All except one: De Strijdkrachten Vijf – the Force of Five. Next to it, she had doodled the sword-bearing, crown-wearing lion that appeared on their Oranje armbands. She'd added an S on the left and a 5 on the right.

'Aha!' George said, patting the diary with a smile. 'So *you're* responsible for the design of those tattoos!'

Tempted to call it a night, George was just about to close the diary and return to her cantankerous lover on the sofa when she scanned the next entry. Her pulse quickened as Rivka wrote…

*Just when I thought that things might remain as they are in Amsterdam, this morning has been dreadful. There's talk of the SS stepping up their activities to make the Netherlands more like Germany, but I didn't expect this. It was early. Mama was making breakfast. Papa and Shmuel were at the synagogue for morning prayers before he went to work and Shmuel went to school. Mama and I were chatting about a new dress she is making me when there was a loud knock at the front door. It was more of a violent thump and I could hear shouting – no Dutch voice that I recognised. The fear that gripped me made me shake with cold as Mama went to answer the door.*

'George! George! Have you been listening to a word I've been saying?'

Still holding her breath, George was jolted out of Rivka's story by the sound and sight of Van den Bergen looming over her, demanding a reaction. The pupils of his grey eyes were black pools of feverish enthusiasm.

'What is it?'

'Marie's just called,' he said. 'I'd asked her to go through the wills and financial records of the Force of Five.'

'And?' George closed the diary, stroking its cover with her index finger. Promising Rivka that she would be back.

'I'm bringing Abadi in for questioning. Right now! They left him money, George. If it turns out he's another Shipman and is bumping off the old men on his books for pennies from heaven, we're going to have another death on our hands if we don't act fast.'

# CHAPTER 13

# Amsterdam, police headquarters, 17 October

'How can you explain this?' Van den Bergen asked, pushing the stapled sheaf of printouts across the table towards Abadi.

In the interview room, which had already taken on the cabbagey fug of Marie, George was seated at the very end of the bolted-down, battered table, observing this unassuming middle-aged doctor. Abadi wore conservative slacks, a V-neck jumper over a crisp white shirt, open at the collar, and had stubble that attested to a long day in the surgery. His hair was starting to thin, though George was certain he must dye it black, since there was no grey to be seen. It was the only obvious sign of vanity in an otherwise unobtrusive-looking, diminutive man whose accent barely hinted at his Middle Eastern origins. Was it possible that this guy was a serial murderer of elderly patients?

Abadi took his tortoiseshell glasses from the case on the table with trembling hands. Pushed them up his nose and started to leaf through the papers. 'I don't know what these documents are. Why are you showing them to me? Lawyers?' He examined the headed paper, clearly seeing but not reading in his barely concealed panic.

*This doesn't look like some hardened criminal or con man to me*, George thought. But she knew better than that as a criminologist – especially given some of the cases she had helped Van den Bergen to solve. The worst predators were almost always the least obvious and most intelligent of suspects. She opened up a stapler and started to run her finger over the chunks of staples so that they formed an unbroken phalanx. Watching. Half-thinking about Rivka Zemel's adulation of the Force of Five. Wondering how it had all panned out and knowing that four of the men, at least, had made it to old, old bones. Had Dr Saif Abadi deliberately composed the ending of their fascinating and epic stories?

Marie rotated the pearls in her ears, fixing the suspect with her stark blue eyes. 'You know exactly what these are, Dr Abadi, because they've been read out to you by the solicitors who drafted them, haven't they?' Her voice was small but retained a certain steel to it. Though Marie didn't look like much, George knew she was far from a pushover.

Abadi shifted in his seat. Swallowed hard. 'Have I?'

'Stop flirting, Dr Abadi,' Van den Bergen said. 'This interview tore me away from some very important health-maintenance involving a bowl of blueberries and ten millilitres of Gaviscon. Now, my detective here has asked you about these legal documents. Why don't you explain to us all how you came to be named in the wills of Brechtus Bruin, Kaars Verhagen and Arnold van Blanken.'

George considered the hundreds of prison inmates she'd interviewed as part of her academic research; the women she'd been banged up with as a girl when she'd fallen foul of the law, thanks to an almighty administrative cock-up and one ailing detective. Most of them either denied, denied, denied or wore their crimes like an extravagant tattoo to be feared and revered. As Abadi wiped the sheen of sweat from his upper lip and blinked hard behind the thick lenses of those glasses, she wondered which kind he would be if he turned out to be guilty. A denier or a boaster?

'You look like a man who's been caught with his fingers in the till, Dr Abadi,' George said, leaning forward to make eye contact with him.

He shook his head. 'No. It's coincidence, that's all.' His placatory half-smile faltered.

'What's coincidence?' Van den Bergen asked.

'The money. The fact that they were my patients. I turned it down, you know!'

Marie pushed a sheaf of bank statements towards him. 'But it still managed to turn up in your account, didn't it?'

The doctor opened and closed his mouth, but no explanation was forthcoming. He looked at George with pleading in his eyes. Then, it was as if his fear switched off, replaced by exasperation. 'The sums were hardly massive! A couple of thousand here and there. I've told the families I'm returning it or donating it to charity. It's a gross conflict of interest.'

'Yes. It is,' Van den Bergen said. He leaned back in his chair, drumming a pencil against his teeth until Abadi's lower left eyelid started to flicker. 'And what about the manner in which the men died, Dr Abadi? All ninety-five years old. Hendrik van Eden was the first. We haven't yet been able to get hold of his will. Were you in that as well, I wonder? Then, a month later, Bruin and Van Blanken within days of one another. Now Kaars Verhagen. Poor Kaars. Left for days, undiscovered and slowly spoiling on his kitchen floor.'

'I can't believe you're insinuating that a respectable man of my standing would murder his patients for a few thousand euros. For God's sake! As jumping to conclusions goes, that's … that's nothing short of appalling.' He toyed with the cuff of his shirt. Buttoning. Unbuttoning. Buttoning. Clearly agitated. 'Hasn't it occurred to you that perhaps my patients were just expressing gratitude in some small way for over a decade of dedicated service? These are men I respected and tried my best for. For old guys who became socially isolated once their mobility started to go, you could say that they saw me as a friend. I liked them! They were heroes. The sort of men this city needs *today*! Men who didn't turn their backs on their kinsmen just because they believed in a different god and maybe their faces didn't fit with an idealised notion of ... Dutchness.'

Van den Bergen thumped the table. 'Don't mistake the Dutch police for a bunch of idiots, Abadi. We've got your bank statements. It doesn't take an economist to work out that you're a shocking financial manager. You must be the only doctor I've ever heard of who's got such a hefty overdraft.'

Abadi's lips thinned to a line. He studied Van den Bergen's stern face, blinking rapidly. 'You're adding two and two and making five. I give almost every penny that I earn to Syrian charities that provide shelter and food for those who have lost everything in the war. Have you arrested me for caring about refugees who are fleeing Assad's bombs and Daesh's brutality?'

'No. I'm investigating the suspicious deaths of old men who were prescribed medication in doses that killed.' Plucking his reading glasses from their chain and perching them on the end of his nose, Van den Bergen read extracts of Marianne de Koninck's post-mortem reports aloud. She speculated that the men's heart failures had been caused by the regular ingestion of drugs that were notoriously dangerous and in fatal quantities. 'What have you got to say to that?' Van den Bergen asked, looking pointedly over the tops of his lenses at Abadi.

From an evidence baggie, Marie produced several bottles and packets of tablets. She lined them up on the table in front of the doctor, reading out the contents and dosage instructions that had been printed on the pharmacy labels.

George strained to catch a whiff of bullshit on the stale air, above the bouquet of Marie's armpits. The evident surprise and ensuing confusion in Abadi's face was unexpected.

He shook his head. His voice cracked. 'I didn't prescribe any of that!'

'Well, who did then?'

He shrugged. 'There was nothing wrong with their medications. I knew those men's health records inside out. And I'm fastidious about dosage and suitability when I prescribe.'

Van den Bergen held a tub of tablets that had belonged to Brechtus Bruin in the air, twirling the label in front of Abadi. 'You never prescribed this?'

'No! I absolutely did not. I swear to God. Check the surgery records!' He took the tub from Van den Bergen, reading the label in silence. Tutted. 'Our patients don't even use that pharmacy normally. They use the place two doors down. Who the hell would trek all the way across town to get their tablets if they've got a twenty-four-hour pharmacy on the surgery's doorstep? Especially the infirm! If you were terminally ill and in a wheelchair, like Kaars Verhagen, would you go out of your way to get your tablets?'

Exhaling heavily through flared nostrils, Van den Bergen folded his arms and regarded his earnest suspect. George watched the two men staring each other down. She exchanged a glance with Marie, trying to read her mind to see what she thought of this unprepossessing general practitioner.

'Nowadays, you can get whatever you want off the internet,' Abadi said, pulling his cuffs smartly down. 'Family doctors have no jurisdiction over what patients get online from places like Eastern Europe and China. There's a global market for anything. Legal or illegal! And there's the very real possibility that my patients were seeing another doctor. At their age, they'd all been careful to get really comprehensive insurance. Check their insurance details! Or maybe they were paying someone in cash. Who knows? But I'm telling you – I give you my word – that I didn't prescribe those meds. Look into it! Phone the dispensing pharmacy.'

'I can check, boss,' Marie said to Van den Bergen.

'Can I go, then?' Abadi asked. 'My wife's expecting me. I don't like to leave her home alone with our young son. She'll be worried.'

'We've got you for forty-eight hours,' Van den Bergen said. 'Your wife will have to cope until we've made some further enquiries.'

As he and Marie gathered their paperwork, nodding to the uniform who waited in the corner to take Abadi back to his holding cell, George studied the disappointed expression on the doctor's tired and waxy-looking face. She considered what he'd said about his charitable proclivities and interest in Syrian refugees. Rivka Zemel prodded at George's conscience, bringing the dead twelve-year-old girl who had been carried from the back of the Den Bosch truck to the forefront of her mind. *Don't let the girl in the body bag down,* Rivka said. George could almost picture them both. The teenage maid from the Forties standing next to the grey-faced child who had dared to hope for a new life; a life her parents had sacrificed everything to give her. Different circumstances. Different era. But just another desperate young girl relying on the mercy of those around her to save her from war and a terrible fate.

Wasn't George one of the lucky ones, having escaped her own hellish youth in an urban warzone of a rather different kind? Didn't that make her somehow responsible to seek justice for those girls who had fallen, when the very people they'd depended on had steered them down a dangerous path, pushing them over the precipice? She felt a tugging sensation in her chest.

There had to be a way to infiltrate the guarded and silent ranks of Amsterdam's illegal immigrants. She felt certain they held answers that would help bring to book the twelve-year-old's traffickers.

'Hey, Dr Abadi. Before they cart you off,' she said, 'you're active in your community, right? Tell me, do you have much of a hands-on relationship with new refugees coming into Amsterdam?'

'What do you mean?'

'Syrians. The trafficked ones.'

# CHAPTER 14

## *Den Bosch's house in De Pijp,*
## *then a mosque near Bijlmer, later*

Elvis couldn't help but think he'd drawn the short straw, given that Van den Bergen and Marie were tucked up warm and dry in the police station. Yet, here he was, squatting at the bottom of Frederik den Bosch's garden in the drizzle and twilight of the early evening, peering into the suspect's rear lounge window using an uncomfortably heavy and unwieldy long-range camera lens. He thought wistfully of the dinner he'd been meant to have with Arne – a romantic dinner for two at a fine restaurant that Arne had refused to name, booked as a surprise to commemorate their having been together for six months. As he peered through the magnifying lens of the camera, Elvis worked his way through a list of possible eateries that he would now not visit.

'Bloody Frederik den Bosch. You owe me a night out, you ugly bastard.'

With his legs cramping beneath him, he watched carefully, praying the surveillance stint would pay off somehow. But the back room had been in darkness all day. Den Bosch had not yet returned home or else was restricting his movements to the front of the house. If only he could have watched the front, spying from some neighbour's window.

'Should have got a damned warrant and just forced them to open up.'

Glancing up at the adjoining houses on either side, Elvis glimpsed domestic scenes: on one side, a trendy-looking couple cooked something together – the man chopping, the woman stirring the contents of a wok. They laughed at some shared joke. On the other side, a woman was supervising three small children, eating at an undersized table. Middle-class urbanites who had recently moved to the increasingly gentrified area, Elvis assessed. He wondered what they made of the man who lived alone – according to the electoral and utility records – in a shabby, run-down property, where the garden was strewn with car and motorcycle parts, the broken patio furniture thick with green algae-like growth. The flotsam and jetsam seemed to grow like rotten-smelling weeds among the tall grass. The only sign that the garden was ever used was a large ashtray close to the back door, full to the brim with yellowed water and disintegrating cigarette butts. Not the sort of outdoor space Elvis would have expected from a professional horticulturalist.

He thought of his own father: a builder, when he had been alive, who couldn't bear to do any DIY at home, much to his mother's chagrin. He'd preferred them all to live in a tumble-down dump of a house than to take his work home with him. The kitchen had taken ten years to fit. The new central heating system that had been partially installed when Elvis was ten had never quite heated up more than three inches of bathwater at a time.

In the fading light, Elvis chuckled to himself, then felt a sharp pang of grief as he remembered his long-suffering mother. So frail at the end, thanks to the Parkinson's. He touched the base of his neck, running his finger along the groove of the scar from where he had been garrotted. For all his loss and pain, he considered how lucky he had been. Unlike the poor bastards in the back of that Den Bosch truck.

'Come on, you tit. Give me something to go on.'

As if Den Bosch had heard his plea, warm light suddenly shone from the room at the back of the house. From his vantage point, hidden behind an overgrown, sodden bush, Elvis could see that the room was furnished as a kind of sitting-room-cum-study. He zoomed in, using the camera's lens to see the detail. There was Frederik den Bosch, rolling up his shirtsleeves and sitting at a desk by the window. He started up a PC, swigging from a can of beer. Behind him, Elvis could see bookshelves. It was impossible to read what was written on the spines of the books, or to catch a glimpse of what appeared on the computer monitor. But in a glazed cabinet next to the shelves, Elvis could clearly see a collection of war memorabilia that somehow didn't surprise him at all. He shivered at the sight of Nazi Wehrmacht helmets bearing the swastika, placed in a row of three; an SS officer's hat, complete with its skull-and-crossbones badging at the front; a bust of Hitler, perhaps in bronze; an assortment of medals pinned to a framed board, as though a butterfly collector had been given the wrong brief.

'Jesus. I might have known,' he muttered softly, clicking the shutter on the camera to capture the unsavoury montage.

What else would this cripplingly uncomfortable surveillance session uncover about Den Bosch? How was it even relevant that this grower of vegetables clearly hated anyone who wasn't white and Christian?

For an hour, Den Bosch did nothing more than drink beer and sit at his computer. Once, he left the room, returning minutes later with a pizza on a plate. The irony of a fascist who was happy to eat foreign food was not lost on Elvis. He wondered how Den Bosch felt about anyone who wasn't heterosexual.

Wishing he could go home to Arne, Elvis downloaded some of the images to his phone and emailed them to Van den Bergen.

'Is this enough, boss? Can't see the point in hanging around.'

A short while later, as Den Bosch began to masturbate in front of his computer, Elvis received the curt reply.

'Stay on it. See what he does at night.'

'Wanking!' Elvis told the screen. 'That's what he does.'

By nine o'clock, he could no longer feel anything from the knees down but had taken a good number of photos of Den Bosch's study. Sick and tired of being cooped up in the cold and wet with only his sombre memories and wistful longing for home as company, Elvis made the decision that it was now dark enough to go back to the car and watch from the front, unnoticed by Den Bosch or his neighbours.

'Crappy damned job,' he said, climbing with an unpleasant, freezing squelch into the driver's seat of the pool car. The floor of the passenger side was littered with the remnants of hastily eaten sandwiches and snacks. Peanuts caught down the side of the seats. The windows steamed up immediately. Wiping the greasy glass, Elvis was just about to call his boyfriend when Den Bosch's door opened. Almost completely unrecognisable, the normally dapper Den Bosch was dressed in ripped jeans and a T-shirt sporting the South African three-legged swastika, a symbol normally wielded on flags by pro-Apartheid Afrikaners. On his feet, he wore ten-hole Doc Marten boots with red laces – the kind Elvis knew were favoured by British neo-Nazis. On a grim night like this, Den Bosch had opted for a plain black zip-up hoodie, rather than a coat. Hardly dressed for a date or a quiet night in the local pub.

Starting the engine of the pool car and putting his windscreen demisters on, Elvis was nonplussed to see Den Bosch crossing the road. Coming towards him on foot. Had he been spotted? Bending down as though he were reaching into the glove compartment, with his heart thundering so violently that he wondered if it would pound its way clean out of his body, Elvis waited. He clenched his eyes shut, expecting a thump on the steamy window. When the confrontation didn't materialise, he sat up abruptly. Dizzy from the sudden movement after hours spent in wet clothing on an empty stomach.

He watched through the slowly demisting rear window as Den Bosch banged on the front door of one of the run-down properties he owned. Light flooded the street as the door was answered. Elvis could see that Den Bosch's body language was aggressive and confrontational. Momentarily, he disappeared inside. Would he be there for hours? No. He emerged some minutes later, clutching a bulky envelope, which he slid into the back pocket of his jeans.

For the next half hour, Den Bosch zigzagged his way along the street, picking up envelopes at every house. From his limited vantage point in the pool car, Elvis could see that the tenants were frightened by this man.

He thumbed out an update to Van den Bergen:

'Rent day. Who the hell collects rent in a neo-Nazi get-up from a pile of terrified refugees? Prick.'

Wondering if this was simply Den Bosch's modus operandi as a landlord and assuming he would go home when the collection was complete, Elvis was surprised when Den Bosch didn't return to his own house. By now, he had transferred his fat envelopes, presumably stuffed with cash, into an Albert Heijn bag. He eschewed his pimped-up Jeep and climbed instead into a Volkswagen Passat – a strange choice of car for a single, childless man, and yet cleverly unobtrusive, befitting a man who spent his days being outwardly respectable and his nights masturbating at his computer while surrounded by Nazi memorabilia.

'Where are you going, you shifty little ball sack?'

Careful to keep tucked in a few cars behind, Elvis followed the Passat out of town along the A2, a road studded on either side with industrial units and car dealerships. The landscape changed from redbrick city-centre familiarity in the quirky nineteenth-century streets of De Pijp to a schizophrenic mid-century suburb made up of open green spaces, studded with brutalist concrete apartment blocks. Gone were the independently owned boutiques, trendy bars and bijou eateries that felt like a logical expansion of this glorious Venice of the North that Elvis called home. They had been replaced by graffiti and low-grade shops-full-of-shit, Asian and African minimarts and fast-food joints.

Den Bosch slowed, pulling in to park on a busy road, at the end of which loomed a giant mosque. Its white stone glowed in the dark; its minarets, stretching nobly heavenwards, beyond the rail-viaduct that bisected the night sky with blunt force. It gave the impression of some Persian palace having been plucked from a hot, distant land and dumped at the edge of a dual carriageway in some Wizard of Oz-style chicanery.

'What the hell's going on here?' Elvis muttered, watching Den Bosch hasten towards a hundred- maybe two-hundred-strong crowd of white men. Already parked up, he climbed out of the car, his damp clothing sticking to him, and followed Den Bosch into the fray.

The throng had gathered outside the mosque, bellowing obscenities, chanting and carrying white placards and fluttering banners. Some carried swastika flags, their shorthand for hatred, waving them at the TV cameras that had gathered to film the mob. Many of the larger banners looked to have been professionally produced, with PEGIDA slogans, telling whoever would listen that Patriotic Europeans Against the Islamisation of the

West wanted all Muslims out – no mosques, no halal, no sharia, no Koran.

The crowd was made up predominantly of men, all dressed in dark, casual clothing like Den Bosch. Several of the jeering men, deep in the heart of the crowd, were wearing fluffy pig hats. Their childish garb with its provocative message seemed at odds with the reverential way in which they carried the Dutch flag. Elvis trembled from top to toe as he marked Den Bosch's steps into the heart of the jeering mass. He couldn't recall a time when he had ever felt so alien amongst his own species. Would they sniff him out as a lefty liberal interloper?

From a safe distance, he watched Den Bosch fist-bumping and exchanging overly butch embraces with several of the men. Observed as he handed the supermarket bag full of cash to a much older protestor, unremarkably clad in a dark anorak.

*He's funding this crap!* Elvis thought. *If he's handing money over, he's close to the top of this shower of bastards.*

Trying to keep eyes on Den Bosch proved difficult. He moved swiftly towards the mosque, stopping only now and then to shake hands with some of the others – clearly popular and well known in these brutish circles. Distracted by the gruesome and tasteless sight of slaughtered pigs lying open-mouthed on the ground only metres from the entrance to the house of worship, Elvis almost lost sight of Den Bosch entirely. But there he was!

'Hey, you!' a protestor shouted at him, clamping Elvis's shoulder in an iron grip. The giant of a man had blue swastikas, iron crosses and other Nazi iconography tattooed over his entire bald head and neck.

Elvis balked. Smiled. Thought his heart was going to give out. He clocked a placard in the distance and bellowed its sentiment straight into the terrifying giant's face. 'Go home, rapefugees!'

The giant faltered. Drew his cannonball of a fist back, poised to punch some part of Elvis into next week. But suddenly, it was as though the sun had come out. 'Good lad!' the giant said, grinning. 'I thought you looked like a bit of a poof with that gelled hair and those disco-togs.' He punched him in the shoulder as a gesture of solidarity, and Elvis stumbled backwards from the force. 'Yeah. Go home, rapefugees! Fuck those krimigrants!' Laughter then, that came on like a hurricane, forcing Elvis further into the crowd.

'Aaargh!' He found himself cocooned in orange. What was this bullshit? Extracting himself from his wrapping, he realised he'd barrelled headlong into an orange flag, ironically bearing the same black lion as had been tattooed on Van den Bergen's mystery old-timers' necks. On it was also emblazoned 'PEGIDA Nederland'.

'Watch it, mate!' a wiry, weaselly-looking Nazi yelled, spitting with every consonant.

Making his apologies, almost drunk on fear, Elvis realised he'd lost Den Bosch. And there, only metres from the TV cameras on the opposite side of the road, were the anti-racists. Big men, mainly. Some black. Some white. A lot of brown. Some ferocious-looking white women with dreadlocked hair or beanie hats. All tooled up with rainbow flags and 'Fuck Racisme' T-shirts, their stern faces told a tale of anger and violent intent that belied the tree-hugging 'Queers Against Islamophobia' banners. A fight was a fight after all for the serial brawlers on both sides, and this was a Thursday night with very little on the television.

'Not good. Not good,' Elvis muttered, desperately trying to see his way through the fug of testosterone and adrenalin. 'This is going to kick off. Any minute.'

He was caught between two tribes: his liberal kinsfolk on one side; Hitler's genetic offcuts on the other. He had to find Den Bosch or get out of there. And fast.

Suddenly, Elvis heard the roar of engines and the squeal of a loud hailer. 'Break it up! Go home or you'll be arrested,' shouted the police's voice of reason. Or was it? The arrival of the cops seemed to throw a match on this already flammable pile of dead wood.

'Flatten the hippy, lefty bastards, lads!' the tattooed giant screamed by way of a battle cry.

With no means of escaping, Elvis found himself being pushed towards the police and the anti-racists beyond them. Memories flashing by of being trapped in mosh pits at rock gigs as a teen, where taking the punches and enduring a good trampling was inevitable. Dread roiled around his empty gut.

'Shit! Shit! No!'

He couldn't flash his badge among this lot of psychopaths. It would be suicide. But wait! Was that Den Bosch he glimpsed right by one of the mosque minarets? Disappearing around the corner. What was the sneaky bastard up to now?

Elvis harnessed the determination to get away from this rabble and pushed against the tide of muscle and hatred. He broke free like a drowning man finally finding which way the surface lies – just in time to see Den Bosch disappearing through a side door, beckoned in by a middle-aged man with a large beard, mosque hat and salwar kameez. Instantly recognisable as the imam Abdullah al Haq, thanks to several recent TV news appearances.

Elvis stopped as Den Bosch peered through the murky streetlight in his direction, then followed as he turned away. Caught the two men shaking hands. 'What the bloody hell is going on here?'

## CHAPTER 15

# *Van den Bergen's apartment, 18 October*

Aware of the noise, George opened one eye to check the time on her bedside clock. The digital display read 05:30. *Jesus. It's still night-time.* A floorboard creaked. The sound of a drawer sliding open. She rolled over abruptly. Van den Bergen was standing by his chest of drawers in his pants.

'Where are you off this early?' she asked, watching as he rummaged inside for a clean shirt and pulled it on hastily over his scarred torso. 'The allotment? You're not going to the allotment in a smart work shirt, are you?' She propped herself on one elbow, scratching at her tangle of black curls. Rubbed her nose and sneezed. The bedroom would need dusting with a damp cloth. Again.

'Tamara's,' he said. No hint of a smile. Just a look of mild panic – the kind he got when he was summoned for Opa duties. Action Gramps on a mission. George knew it well.

'Oh yeah? You said you were taking me out for breakfast. We were going to have a proper conversation about me and you … and the future. Remember?' Two bloody minutes of wakefulness and already George could feel her blood simmering.

Van den Bergen donned his reading glasses and buttoned

his cuffs. Fiddling and faddling in haste. 'Andrea was supposed to take Eva this morning while Tamara goes for a job interview.' He pulled his trousers over his long legs and sat on the end of the bed to tackle his socks. 'You know what a waste of space Numb-Nuts is. God forbid he should get off his lazy arse and get a proper job. Like I did.'

Lurching out of the warmth of the bedclothes, George embraced Van den Bergen from behind. Felt the curvature of his long spine against her chest. 'You've got the weight of the world on your shoulders.' She kissed his freshly shaved cheek, drinking in the smell of shower gel, deodorant and toothpaste. Aware of her own early morning breath, she backed away, sitting cross-legged on the bed in her T-shirt and knickers. He didn't look round. 'You're spreading yourself too thinly, Paul.'

'I've only got one granddaughter,' he said, tugging his socks up.

'But you're treating Eva like your own child, stepping in where her parents should be doing the hard graft.' Malcontent wriggled inside her like an unwelcome parasite. George knew exactly which emotion it was feeding off. She felt like a petulant child. But thought of how readily the people around her took her for granted, sidelined or betrayed her in order to fulfil their own petty ambitions. Danny. Letitia. Sally Wright … 'You've done your time! You gave up your dreams to bring home the bread and play dutiful daddy.'

'I never would have made much of an artist, anyway.'

'Bullshit. You gave your entire future to Tamara when she was born. And you're still giving it! Now it's time for you to invest more in *your* life. In us. What about us, Paul? Do we not matter anymore?'

Finally, Van den Bergen turned to her, surveying her with his body at an awkward angle, as though he didn't think her query warranted a straight response. 'I'll not be long,' he said.

'So you can't even commit to an answer?'

'You never wanted formalised commitment before. Why now?' He rose from the bed. Donned the watch she'd bought him. 'You're just feeling insecure, Georgina.'

'Fuck you.' She lay back down and threw the duvet over herself. Turned away from Van den Bergen. Silently, she hoped that he would at least approach the bed and plant a placatory kiss on her cheek. A hand of solidarity on her shoulder. Anything to show he cared and that she mattered.

'You've lost your job in the UK. Your family situation is more chaotic than ever. I get it. You want to settle down, finally. Didn't I say you would?' He chuckled, the sanctimonious bastard, but stayed on his side of the bedroom. No kiss. No hand on the shoulder.

'I'll see you later,' she said, not bothering to hide the sulk in her voice. 'I'm going to read more of Rivka Zemel's diary. I'll report back if I find anything untoward or interesting, Chief Inspector. Enjoy babysitting. *Opa.*'

Closing her eyes, she could hear him taking his suit jacket from its hanger in the wardrobe. Maybe his granddaughter would hawk up all over him. It would serve him right. *Dad, can you just pop over? Dad, can you help with bath time? Dad, can you lend me and Willem a thousand euros? Dad. Dad. Fucking Dad.* Every time his kidult of a spoiled, entitled daughter called, he went running. He never refused her. Never. He just couldn't or wouldn't see that Tamara had turned over the last few years into her spoiled, demanding, selfish cow of a mother, Andrea. Now the baby had conferred even more power on her. And what did George have?

'Do me a favour, will you?' he asked.

Had he even picked up on her pointed tone or use of Opa? No. *Insensitive arse-wipe.*

'What?'

'If I'm not back by 11 a.m., can you and Marie interview Dr Baumgartner? He's the—'

112

'The owner of the practice where Abadi works. Yes. I know. Fine. Give Eva a kiss from me.'

George bit back the sarcasm that was infusing itself on the tip of her tongue. It wasn't the baby's fault that her grandfather was being a spineless twat.

With Van den Bergen gone, George found she couldn't get back to sleep. Now was an ideal opportunity to venture further into Rivka Zemel's world to find out more about how life had inevitably taken a turn for the tragic for her. George was certain that this tale would not have a happy ending. She thought of the idealistic young love that was developing on the pages of Rivka's diary between her and Ed Sijpesteijn. Swallowed hard to quash the pain and disappointment that the cynical arrangement she and Van den Bergen had stoked up within her.

'Oh, fuck Van den Bergen! Come on, George. Earn your money, seeing how that's all he seems to think you're good for.'

Picking up where she had left off, she discovered who had thumped with such aggression on the Zemels' front door...

*I have to say, when Mama opened up, I feared the worst. I honestly thought the SS had come for us. Some Dutch Jewish men had been arrested not so very long ago and tensions have been growing in the city. The local authorities put up signs months ago, ring-fencing the Jewish quarter, as though we're animals to be penned into a restricted area. A few of the parks bear notices saying Jews are forbidden entry, which is horrid. I used to love strolling in the Vondelpark with Mama, Papa and Shmuel when there was nothing else to do on a Sabbath.*

*Hendrik's new girlfriend, Anna Groen, says she has an uncle and an aunt in Poland who wrote recently, saying that all the Jews there are being made to wear a yellow* badge, marking them out in public as such. So, imagine my relief when the insistent knock at the door turned out to be our neighbour Mr Wolff. He broke the news that Shmuel can no longer attend the local school but must attend a new special school for Jewish children only. Ed says it's something called 'segregation'. I say it's outrageous! Shmuel has so many friends in his class. For a boy who really suffers with his health, seeing his schoolmates is the only thing that gets him to leave the house some days. When he was little, Mama home-schooled him, but he got so lonely. I really don't think it's fair. How long before I'm not allowed to work in a gentile household? What will we do for money then? Papa already had to sign his business over to his non-Jewish business partner. That was a whole year ago, and we've been struggling for money ever since, though Mr Van den Broek says he's being fair.

Anyway, my time at the Verhagen house is the only thing that keeps me from despair these days. When Ed comes over, we snatch some time alone in the scullery (only when Famke's out on errands, of course). We hold hands and talk about how we will be together after the war. I think the other Sijpesteijns are not nearly as keen on Jews as Ed. His parents are really quite formal and conservative. You'd never believe Mr Verhagen and Mrs Sijpesteijn are siblings! Mrs Sijpesteijn, who occasionally drops round on her own to discuss 'family matters' with Mr Verhagen, is a po-faced old bat, if ever I met one. She still wears ankle-length skirts like they wore in 1910, for a start! I don't doubt it is to hide her horrid, swollen ankles. She looks the type to have swollen ankles.

When I bring her coffee and cake, she sneers at me and always finds something unpleasant to say about the wrinkles in my stockings or the dry skin on my hands. I often catch her deliberately dropping crumbs and putting her cup directly *on the table, leaving a ring, knowing that I will have to clean up after her. Airs and graces, as if she's the Queen! And she never, ever laughs. Small wonder, then, that Ed seems to think the Jews' clannish love of family, colourful use of Yiddish, dry humour and, of course, our good old chicken soup and kneidlach are quite the thing. I wonder if Her Royal Highness, with her mean-spirited Calvinist sensibilities, who almost certainly regards the Nazis as an efficient, bureaucratic machine to be admired (that's what Ed said), realises that her son is a free-spirited resistance fighter?*

Pausing to make a coffee, George contemplated the modern Dutch people. She recognised the irony in the Netherlands historically being a liberal haven for the world's vulnerable people – now, more than ever. And yet, weren't the likes of the PEGIDA supporters and the rising alt-right the antithesis of that reputation? How very like the po-faced, apparently anti-Semitic Mrs Sijpesteijn the contemporary conservative Dutch were, George assessed.

'Fucking hypocrites,' she said, settling down for another few pages. Skimming forward, she sighed deeply as she came across the next major change in Rivka's life.

*17 July 1942*
*The winter was so hard, and though the canals were frozen solid, my family and the other Jews of Amsterdam couldn't even enjoy skating on them. Imagine that! Unsurprisingly, everyone has been filled with joy to see the trees come into bud once again. Papa has been hopeful that the Germans are starting to lose their power, especially after failing to defeat the Soviets thanks to the dreadfully cold weather. Germany has joined forces with Italy and Japan, but the United States has stepped into the fray, making everything suddenly possible.*

Mama has always maintained that we should have gone to England or else followed Uncle Joost to New York when we had the chance. When the German army started to falter, though, Papa started saying that she shouldn't be so pessimistic. By his reckoning, if the British and Americans gain the upper hand and the Soviets keep fending off the Nazi advance, the Germans will be crushed and we'll all be able to get back to normal, soon. When they're gone, we Jews will be able to ride the trams again and go shopping in the mornings, like normal people!

Famke's not exactly happy that I can't help her anymore if she has to run errands in the afternoon. Really, she should be grateful that I still work here at all. Jews aren't supposed to visit non-Jews in their homes these days. And when I stay late to darn the Verhagens' clothes, I'm being incredibly daring, I suppose. The eight o'clock curfew is nonsense. Mama and Papa shout at me for staying out, but how am I to have any life at all if I can't be at the Verhagen house in the evening when the boys are all together?

The last few days have been great fun, I have to admit. Summer is in full swing. Hendrik's girlfriend accompanies him whenever he comes over for a Force of Five meeting. She sings the most beautiful songs for us. I'm not officially allowed out at night, of course, but Anna, who's only two years older than me, is a chanteuse in a fine restaurant on the Keizersgracht. She sings for the SS officers, and says some of them are terribly charming and dapper. I can't say I feel that comfortable when she comes out with things like that, but if Hendrik's happy that she's trustworthy, then so be it. Anna is awfully beautiful, with gleaming blonde hair and bright red lips. Just like Marlene Dietrich! She really has cheered the Verhagen house up.

The thing is, Anna had just offered to dye my hair blonde

*– to give Ed and me an opportunity to sneak into the Vondelpark together – when everyone in the Jewish Quarter was issued with an order to wear a yellow Star of David badge. No chance of blending in now. It really feels like the final straw. It's bad enough to be quarantined in our own little ghetto (as Papa says), but now I feel so embarrassed to have 'Jood' written on my chest – labelled like a piece of meat in a butcher's shop window. People gawp at us. When Rebbetzin Meijers was caught not wearing hers by an SS officer, she was beaten about the head with his pistol. Poor old lady! But I suppose we should be grateful. Apparently they've just deported all the Jews in Eisenach, Germany, saying they're going to be resettled in Bełżec in the east, but everyone has worked out what that means. Hard labour, and then … who knows what?*

*Last week, Brechtus intercepted a German telegram that said some Dutch Jews were going to be called up for 'work duty'. Sure enough – and this is far worse than wearing the silly old yellow star. It's also the reason for Papa's change of heart – Shmuel and Papa had letters this morning saying they had to register for work. Papa is now saying this is it. This is where it all goes horribly wrong. He doesn't have a clue what to do next, but I told him not to panic because Kaars does!*

## CHAPTER 16

## *Amstelveen, Tamara's house, later*

Checking his rear-view mirror once again, Van den Bergen wasn't sure if his early morning dyspepsia was to blame for his growing sense of unease, or if he was right in thinking that the Jaguar that had been behind him for the last few miles was actually following him.

'Don't be such a berk,' he told himself, now unable to distinguish the Jag's round headlights from the other cars that had subsequently overtaken it. 'You're letting things get on top of you. You need to get to the allotment.'

Pulling into Tamara's street in the leafy Elsrijk area of Amstelveen, he reminded the tree outside her terraced house that this was an area where nothing ever happened. Parking up, he told the orderly hedgerow that he needed a holiday – or perhaps an entire career change. Maybe Maarten Minks *should* offer him early retirement and a nice, fat payout. Locking his car, he approached the mid-century, not-quite-starter home. It had generously sized picture windows that overlooked the canal – just about – and a loft conversion that he'd taken on a loan to fund. He told this place, which was beginning to feel like a second home, that he had tried to shoulder too many responsibilities all at once. George was right. The part-time parenting of a baby at his age was an impractical arrangement for a chief inspector with a heavy caseload. And yet…

Craning his neck to see the car that had flashed by at the end of Oud Mijl – the utterly uneventful street that Tamara and Numb-Nuts called home – he could have sworn it was the Jaguar. With the early morning sun now beginning to rise in earnest, he had even caught a glimpse of the colour: British Racing Green. He made a mental note to look out for it again before he pressed the bell.

Numb-Nuts answered with Eva on his hip, crying and covered in snot. A ridiculous grin on his son-in-law's unkempt mess of a face, though.

'Morning, Pops.'

His baby granddaughter turned to him with outstretched arms and fat tears in her eyes. Van den Bergen plucked her from Numb-Nuts's grasp. 'I'm not your Pops, Willem, so don't call me that. Why haven't you wiped her face, you feckless arsehole?'

If there was any animosity simmering beneath the surface of his son-in-law's Prozac-happy expression, he wasn't able to detect it. 'We were just having breakfast, weren't we, little honeybee-bee?'

'Hi, Dad!' Tamara called from upstairs.

As Van den Bergen swiped the wet wipes from the console table in the narrow hall and tried to tug one loose with his free hand, he saw a blur of grey as his daughter marched across the landing at the top of the stairs, tucking her blouse into her skirt.

'I don't understand why Willem couldn't have—'

'Thanks so much for this. You really are the best opa in the world.' There was the sound of brisk footsteps and drawers slamming as she hurried to get ready. 'I'm *praying* I get this job. Honestly, if I don't, we're in big trouble.' Her voice became muffled as she closed a door somewhere upstairs.

119

Where the hell was Numb-Nuts now? Heading out the door with his guitar on his back. At 6 a.m. The lazy turd wasn't usually even awake until Tamara left for work at eight thirty.

'Wait a minute!' he shouted, feeling like the last rat left aboard a sinking ship.

But the front door slammed in his face, leaving him with a fractious baby who smelled suspiciously of dirty nappy. Where was the changing bag?

'Tamara!' Standing at the bottom of the stairs, he imagined he could hear George's castigatory told-you-so's cutting through even the shrill protestations of his crotchety grand-daughter. 'Is she running a temperature?' The back of his hand on the baby's chest and a generous wipe of snotty nose all over his clean shirt gave him the answer. 'And why couldn't Daddy have looked after her? You do realise I'm a busy, busy man?'

But there was no response. Moments later, Tamara thun-dered down the stairs in stockinged feet. She kissed him fleetingly and disappeared into the living room. Re-emerged, carrying a crocodile clip for her hair.

'You're a star, Dad. Honestly. I wish Mum was more hands-on, like you. Mummy wishes Oma was more useful, like Opa, doesn't she, Eva? Yeees! Who's a lovely little sugar-puff, then? Oh, my little smelly baby bum-bum.' Talking gobbledegook at Eva, Tamara's attention was immediately snatched away by an alarm bleeping somewhere in the house. 'Shit. I'm gonna be late. I'll miss the train. Where's my phone? Where's my phone? Where are my goddamn shoes?' Her fumbling fingers had somehow pushed her hair into the clip and now she was pressing her feet into unpolished, worn-down shoes that Van den Bergen was sure would make George itchy.

What was the point in protesting? His daughter was so blind with travel-panic and lack of sleep, she wouldn't notice her father's look of harried concern for his own health and schedule. She didn't have time to stand still for a moment and really take note of him. He resolved to let her go, un-grilled.

With the house quiet and empty of shirking new parents, Van den Bergen first ventured into the untidy kitchen, which was strewn with dirty pots, baby bottles and unopened post. First, he dosed his florid-faced baby granddaughter with liquid paracetamol. Then, he took her up to her nursery and set her down on the changing station. As he started to change her stinking nappy, he wondered if anybody had ever thought to manufacture changing stations with adjustable height for the extra tall and the extra short. Perhaps when Minks fired him, he would create just such a thing, saving a raft of stay-at-home Dutch fathers from backache. Hell, the Scandinavians were tall and into all that progressive daddy-day-care crap too, weren't they?

'What a lovely, clean-smelling girl you are, my little darling!'

Kissing the top of the baby's head, Van den Bergen strolled over to her window, resisting the temptation to put her in the cot whilst he tidied up. Fuck it, if he was going to do the jobs that Numb-Nuts was supposed to.

Feeling that he was being observed from some unknown vantage point by some shadowy Jag-driver, perhaps from the other side of the canal, Van den Bergen jumped when his phone rang. Elvis.

'Van den Bergen. Speak.'

'Last night, boss.'

'What about it?' He closed the Venetian blind, leaving the slats partially open so he could look out without being seen. If there was somebody lurking, they would surely reveal themselves if he stood there for long enough.

Elvis sneezed.

'Don't tell me you're not coming into work.'

There was an awkward silence, followed by another deafening sneeze. 'I was in damp clothes for hours, boss. Don't worry. I'll be in. But listen. Den Bosch is definitely up to no good. He collected rent from about five run-down houses full of illegals. Then, guess what?'

Van den Bergen nuzzled the soft hair of Eva's head. 'He donated the cash to a cancer charity? Bought puppy dogs?'

'Handed it over to some neo-Nazi who seemed to be at the epicentre of a big rally outside the mosque last night.'

Did Van den Bergen spy a man, dressed in a tailored coat and trilby, standing outside one of the houses on the far side of the canal, staring straight into the baby's room? He blinked hard. Shook his head and kissed Eva's little fingers, which were exploring the deep grooves that arced either side of his mouth. As he scanned the suburban morning that was unfolding beyond the blinds, he saw nobody there. He was just an elastic band stretched to its limit. One dead trafficked girl, four dead nonagenarians, an angry George and an apoplectic digestive system – what a combination.

'No surprises there, though, eh?' he said. 'George and I already got the impression that Frederik den Bosch is no charmer.'

'You should see the display cabinet in his office. There are some choice exhibits.'

'I hope you got photos.'

Another hurricane of a sneeze had Van den Bergen holding his phone away from his ear.

'Don't worry, boss. Marie's going to show them to you when you get in, unless you want her to email them now?'

'I'll be in! If Minks asks, though, I've gone to question the trafficked survivors or something. Don't, whatever you do, tell him I'm at Tamara's.' He decided not to give Elvis time to respond. Didn't want to hear it, if his subordinate member of staff wasn't prepared to lie for him. Well … it was less of a lie and more of a fib. 'What I want to know is what a fascist is doing letting his houses to foreigners. Surely the last thing he wants to do is facilitate a load of illegal immigrants living on his doorstep. And yet he's funding neo-Nazi activity with the cash.'

'Boss! He slipped away from the rally. Guess where he went.'

'Get on with it, for Christ's sake!'

'The mosque. The imam let him in.'

Absently watching a red car cruise to the end of the street, Van den Bergen mulled over the prospect of a right-winger like Den Bosch fraternising with his enemy. His agitated guts roiled with painful bubbles of gas. He remembered that he hadn't yet eaten. Tablets on an empty stomach. Not good. He didn't clock the green Jaguar as it appeared at the head of the street, rolling slowly forward.

'Get over to the mosque. Better still, research this imam and we'll go over there together when I've finished. I'm going to do what I can to find out about Hendrik van Eden while I'm babysitting. We've got hardly anything on him. And don't tell Minks. Not about me. Not about the Force of Five. No updates on Den Bosch either. He can wait.'

It was only when he rang off that he spotted the Jaguar. Ordinarily, his instinct would be to confront the bastard and ask what his business was. But right then, with no service weapon to hand and a baby to care for, he realised he was vulnerable.

He placed Eva on her changing mat once again, hurriedly putting warmer clothes on her. Oblivious to what was going on, she kicked her legs freely, making gurgling noises. At least her temperature had come down.

'Opa's taking you for a walk,' he said in jolly tones.

Fumbling with the stiff fingers of a man just past his prime, he put her into her padded *Sesamstraat* romper suit and snapped the press studs shut. The goggle-eyed characters were gawping out at him from their velvet appliquéd vantage point. Their stares were accusatory. How dare he be a grandfather with such a dangerous job? What the hell was he thinking?

Where the fuck was Numb-Nuts when he needed him? Fathering was *his* responsibility. Van den Bergen was no longer fit for this young man's crap.

Breathing raggedly as his heart raced to keep up with his imagination, he marched down the stairs, setting up the buggy with one shaking hand. 'Yes,' he said, keeping the levity in his voice. 'We're going to have a lovely time in the park and watch all the birdies.' He snatched the only bottle in the steamer that was clean and poured boiled water from the kettle into it. Scalding himself in his haste. It would cool. Not quite enough for a decent drink, but it was better than nothing.

Glancing back, he saw a tall figure standing at the end of the path. The frosted glazing revealed no detail, but Van den Bergen was certain this was the man in the trilby he had glimpsed from Eva's room.

'Okay, lady. Let's go.' He was careful to pick up the changing bag and shove a dummy in her mouth – an unwelcome gift he'd bought when she was born. Tamara wouldn't approve, but Eva sucked greedily on it. More to the point, she fell absolutely silent but for the click, click, click sound of her chomping on the soother.

They slipped out of the back door and made their way stealthily to the end of the garden. Van den Bergen prayed that Eva would keep sucking on the dummy, and that her continued silence would enable them to slip away from the watchful man in the green Jaguar.

Still, how likely was it that somebody would ring him at the exact moment of his escape? Before he could undo the lock on the rotten back gate, Van den Bergen's phone rang shrilly on maximum volume.

# CHAPTER 17

# The practice of Dr André Baumgartner, Oud Zuid, later

'Jesus. I don't know how you do this all day,' George said, sitting in the dark, cramped waiting room. She ran her finger-tips over the arms of the armchair, exquisitely upholstered in velvet jacquard fabric, but uncomfortable as hell. A rich old fart's chair. 'All this waiting around for people. This lot has got more attitude than most ghetto gangsta wannabes, to keep the cops sitting around.'

Marie threw down the magazine she had been flicking through, a heavy, glossy tome on the interiors and gardens of the wealthy. 'You get used to it.' She yawned and stretched her arms upwards, revealing dark stains below her armpits.

George grimaced, turning her attention instead to the horrible oil painting of a Friesian cow that hung on the wall. Nineteenth century, no doubt. George hated all that gilt-framed, ye-olde crap. She thought wistfully of the temple to mid-century chic that would one day be hers. If only Van den Bergen would shit or get off the pot. If only she hadn't lost her sodding job in the UK. *Shelve it, George. You're on the payroll here, now.*

She was just about to ask what excuse Marie had given to

Minks for her absence from the office when the main door to the private consulting rooms slammed shut, further inside the converted apartment.

'Oh, you're back. Good,' came the secretary's voice. 'There are two young ladies waiting for you. Police. One's a doctor. Not a medical doctor.'

Ignoring the pointed remark about her PhD, which was de rigueur among the pretentious, whether they were London SW3's 'finest' or the upper crust of the Oud Zuid, George listened to the deep croak of an older man. Leaned back to catch sight of him before he could come in with a prepared smile on his face. Caught a glimpse through the crack in the door of a slim old guy in a dapper grey suit.

She heard low voices as they continued to whisper.

Then: 'Yes. Pass your hat and coat to me, Dr Baumgartner. I'll hang them up for you. Don't worry. And your post is on your desk.' The secretary's voice was back to normal pitch. She was gabbling as though this was the most excitement she had seen in years. 'The ladies are through there. Shall I send them into your office? I'll bring through a tray. Coffee?'

Finally, George and Marie were ushered by the secretary into Baumgartner's office. It was similar in décor and feel to the waiting room. Old money. Baumgartner looked more sprightly than his croaking voice had suggested. His posture was impeccable. He presided like a lord over this mini fiefdom, spreading his hands in an open gesture across his rosewood desk. Rose to greet them. Shook their hands.

'Officers! Welcome. How nice to have such charming young ladies in my consulting rooms.'

George took a seat on yet another bloody uncomfortable chair, wondering if the rich were prone to piles as a result of their furniture choices. 'It's Doctor and Detective, actually, but we'll let you off.'

She gave the old duffer a winning grin. Just like the Life

Fellows at Cambridge, this one. At her side, Marie's cheeks flushed scarlet.

'How may I help?' Baumgartner directed his enquiry to Marie, failing to make eye contact with George.

Marie leaned forward, opening her pad at a new page. She hooked her red hair behind her ear. It was reasonably clean today, for a change, but a duller hue at the still-lank roots than it should have been. Fixing Baumgartner with a steely gaze, she clicked her pen into action. 'We're investigating four suspicious deaths of patients at the surgery you own.'

Baumgartner laced his fingers together and cocked his head to the side, a convincing look of surprise on his face. 'Oh? Suspicious? Suspicious in what way? This is the first I've heard of it.'

'It's not yet a *formal* murder investigation,' Marie explained. 'But it's come to the police's attention that four elderly gentlemen recently died in almost identical circumstances. They were all patients of Dr Saif Abadi, your employee. We wanted to speak to you about him.'

Baumgartner's bushy grey eyebrows scudded upwards. 'Who are the gentlemen in question, may I ask?'

Marie gave the identities of the old men.

'Oh dear. What a pity they've passed. A good age though. Fitting for such fine, upstanding fellows.' Baumgartner's expression had softened.

George caught sight of a tall figure in the corner of her eye. Looked round to see it was only Baumgartner's dark overcoat and hat, hanging on a peg in the consulting room beyond. She wondered if she was spending too much time around Van den Bergen's natural paranoia, and reading Rivka Zemel's suffocating tale of being backed into a corner of history that nobody enjoyed remembering.

'Did you know them?' she asked him. 'Personally, I mean? Could you tell me what sort of men they were?'

Shaking his head, Baumgartner treated George to a sympathetic half-smile. 'I'm afraid not.'

'You spoke as though you knew them.'

'No. I'm afraid you misunderstand. I wasn't acquainted with them. But everybody of a certain age knows of them. They were quite the war heroes in their day.'

Carefully observing his body language for signs that he knew more than he was letting on, George nodded slowly. Never taking her eyes off his, skilled as she was in spotting a bullshitter's tell. Baumgartner was Abadi's boss, and he owned the practice where the dead men had been registered for medical care. Perhaps he was hiding something or someone. 'Coincidence that they should all die of heart attacks within weeks of each other though.'

'That's coincidence for you,' Baumgartner said, completely deadpan. 'But you often find that couples or close friends die one after the other, especially when they're very old. It's like they just give up. A strange phenomenon, but I have absolute faith it's just a coincidence.' He cocked his head to the side again. Was that a patronising expression on his well-groomed face? 'What did the post-mortem reports record?' he asked Marie.

'Death by natural causes.'

'Then why are we having this conversation, ladies?' He chuckled, craning his head forward like a tolerant schoolteacher.

George wanted to punch him. Though he was seventy, he looked healthy enough to warrant a punch. It definitely wouldn't class as elder abuse. 'Because three of them left money to Abadi,' she said. 'Another coincidence. And they all had been prescribed dangerous doses of medication known to bring on heart attacks in certain circumstances. More coincidence. There comes a point when a series of amazing coincidences starts to look like a pattern of planned criminal activity.' She examined her fingernails, waiting for her challenge to sink in with a man who almost certainly wasn't used to such confrontation – especially coming from a 'young lady'. 'So … Abadi. What's he like?'

Almost theatrically, Baumgartner stroked his chin and looked up to the large Flemish chandelier that hung from the ceiling. The bright light reflected in his pale green eyes, giving him a twinkle that made him seem ten, maybe twenty years younger. Here was a man who hadn't surrendered to age. George thought of Sally Wright, coughing her smoker's blackened guts up in a cold, damp, medieval room in St John's, mitigating the shakes of ill health with hot toddies made from pilfered college cooking whisky and not-quite-boiled water from her tea urn. Or Letitia, not yet fifty, but wheezing thanks to obesity, too many Lambert & Butlers and her 'shocking bloody pulmonaries'. Baumgartner's visible robustness was something George only saw in the Dutch. A product of bike rides, simple meals, uncomplicated thinking and never having to endure the inherited angst of a persecuted people. It was genetics. She closed her duffel coat against those green eyes, now locked onto her, as if to hide her own shoddy genetic makeup.

'Dr Abadi is an excellent physician,' Baumgartner said. 'Excellent. He's worked for me for many, many years now, and I've never once had anything but outstanding feedback about his performance as a family doctor. He's trustworthy, bright, diligent …' He pursed his lips and frowned. 'I admit, he does come across as a little odd. Eccentric, perhaps. Sometimes he's even somewhat jumpy, though I'd always put it down to his ethnic background. Different cultures. You know?'

Just as George was about to come back at him with a sharp retort, Marie shot her a silencing glance.

'So, you trust him, then?' Marie asked, scribbling in her pad. She poked her tongue out of the corner of her mouth in concentration.

'I trust him as head of my practice, yes. And by implication, I trust him with a good chunk of my money and my reputation, too.' Baumgartner pointedly checked the time on his gold watch: a discreet vintage Swiss number, by the looks of it. Money – another reason to look so damned virile in your dotage.

Carefully, George withdrew from her satchel several photos of the dead men's medication and laid them in a row on the desk, facing Baumgartner. 'Do you recognise these?'

'Well, I know what the tablets are. But what do you mean?'

'The pharmacy labels, for a start. Titiaans Apotheek.'

Baumgartner shook his head. Smoothed the silk of the pale grey handkerchief that poked out of his jacket's top pocket. 'Not the pharmacy that the practice's patients use.'

'Titiaanstraat is not far from here, though, is it?' George watched closely for a reaction, wondering. Just wondering...

'There are a number of pharmacies in this area, Miss McKenzie.'

'Dr McKenzie.'

'Have you asked the pharmacy you believe to have dispensed these tablets if they still have the prescription dockets on file?' He sucked in his cheeks. Donned a pair of bifocals, looking every inch the formidable pillar of society that various prestigious medical societies lauded him as being. A man with an impressive online presence. An arrogant dick.

'Yes,' Marie said. 'They didn't. They didn't have any CCTV footage either. It's an old-fashioned outfit in a good neighbourhood where all the houses and apartments are rigged up with security like Area 51, so they don't have to. And why would they? The Bijlmer methadone junkies are hardly queuing to steal extra gear from there.'

'So you've drawn a blank on these mystery deaths that don't seem to me to be terribly mysterious at all.'

'There's still the question of the high doses,' George said.

'Who might have prescribed these tablets, if Saif Abadi didn't?'

Baumgartner stood, making it clear the meeting was at an end. 'My dear, there are countless practices across this city alone. And then there's the internet, where any old fool can buy what he hopes will be the key to a few more years in pill form. If these poor gentlemen finally met their end because they refused to take Dr Abadi's measured advice and sought false hope elsewhere, then I'm afraid that was down to them. Free choice, as individuals.'

George collected up the photos, put them in her bag and rose from the chair. Pins and needles in her bottom would have her hobbling back to the smelly old pool car. She forced herself not to grimace with the pain. 'Tell me, Dr Baumgartner. What services do you offer in these fine rooms?'

'I'm a psychiatrist. I help the genuinely mentally ill as well as the terminally deluded. Tell me, Dr McKenzie, what kind of "doctor" are you?'

He actually did the quotation marks with his fingers. George clasped her hands together tightly, so tempted was she to pull his fucking fingers off.

'Criminology, Dr Baumgartner. It's my job to know criminals. And I don't need to be a "shrink"' – she did the fingers back at him – 'with a fancy office and an extortionate hourly fee to know if their behaviour is down to mental illness or terminal delusion.' She snorted gleefully and pointed at her nose. 'I can smell bullshit a mile off.'

To her chagrin, Baumgartner placed his hand on her shoulder as though they were long-lost friends or close colleagues. 'Ah, a bullshit doctor,' he said, chuckling. Walked her to the door, holding it open for her like the charming old bastard he was. 'I haven't met one of those before. Be careful though, Dr McKenzie. Shit sticks.'

# CHAPTER 18

## *Amstelveen, Tamara's house, then the mosque near Bijlmer, later*

'Come on, sweetie,' Van den Bergen said, pushing the buggy containing his granddaughter at speed through the anonymous identi-streets of Amstelveen. 'Let's see if we can shake off this weirdo and maybe even find your arsehole of a daddy.'

He estimated that they had been going for a good ten minutes. Pausing by a thick bush that bordered an alleyway, he peered into the adjacent road. Nobody there. The sense of being watched had abated. Good.

'Thank God your daddy can't be bothered to do the garden,' he told a gurgling Eva, who was entirely unaware of the strange set of circumstances in which she was embroiled. 'Thanks to his lazy-arsed ways, all that wilderness swallowed the sound of my ringtone completely!'

Taking out his phone, he dialled Elvis. Careful to check the volume was no longer on max. Elvis answered after five irritatingly long rings that had Van den Bergen swallowing down a glob of stomach acid.

'Boss. What's up? Are you coming to see the imam with me?'

'Shortly. Listen. I'm in a bit of a pickle and need to find

someone. He's not answering my call. It's my dick of a son-in-law. He's supposed to have gone to help a friend out in a café, but he left carrying his guitar and didn't look dressed for any kind of work I know. Do me a favour. See if you can get one of the guys to triangulate his phone signal, pronto.'

On the other end of the line, Elvis barked with laughter. 'Really?!'

Van den Bergen growled, realising the ridiculousness of the situation. Minks would have his balls nailed to the noticeboard in HQ's reception if he found out his chief inspector was using official resources to track down his errant son-in-law. Bad enough he was using work time to babysit. Maybe George was right. The thought rankled.

'Forget it. I'll text you as soon as I've …'

He ended the call, flushed hot with embarrassment. Should he call Tamara? No. He didn't want to interrupt her job interview, which had seen her take a train to Utrecht at the crack of dawn for a 'breakfast' slot. That would be unfair. Could he take the baby to the mosque? Absurd! Any imam who was getting into bed with a funder of neo-Nazis was not a bona fide imam. He was an unknown quantity. And unknown quantities were bad news.

'Damn it!'

He tried Andrea. Nothing but an earful of abuse from her for him having called her while she was at work. Like his job – hunting traffickers and serial murderers – didn't bloody matter!

When his granddaughter started to cry, throwing her dummy from the buggy, he plucked her from her straps and held her close to his chest. Cradled her delicate little head inside his large hand and kissed the fluff that sprouted from her glorious-smelling scalp. She was hot again.

'Sh-sh-shh, little darling!' he said softly. 'Opa's left holding the baby, but he doesn't mind one bit.'

As they hastened back in the direction of Tamara's house, he wondered if he could go through all this again at his age and in his condition. Broken nights. Changing nappies. He'd have to retire and let George take the breadwinner-reins, of course. No way would he force her to ruin her burgeoning career when his was in slow decline anyway. Wasn't this why she was so grumpy? She'd finally realised that, nearing thirty, her clock was starting to tick. Perhaps this was the commitment she sought. A child. But his granddaughter was not his child. She was Numb-Nuts's.

When he returned to Oud Mijl, the sleepy street showed no sign of a green Jaguar or the mystery man who had trailed him there. He stopped dead outside a house four doors down from Tamara's, staring at a scene that had caught his attention.

'I'm sure that's the back of his head,' he muttered, contemplating the contours of a scruffy bastard who was sitting at a table full of middle-aged women and one old man, playing cards.

Opening the gate, he pushed the buggy up the path to get a closer look. The bright light shining overhead illuminated every detail of the motley group's activity. Van den Bergen welcomed the surge of indignant rage when he saw the pile of cash in the middle of the table. Every player had their eyes down, concentrating on their cards. Until Numb-Nuts threw something onto the table. He'd folded.

Van den Bergen thumped on the window. Numb-Nuts turned round when the others pointed out their irate audience. The stricken look on his pale face said everything.

'Got you, you cheeky little fucker!'

The memory of Numb-Nuts begging for forgiveness in that kiddy-detritus-strewn kitchen buoyed Van den Bergen all the way back to HQ to pick up Elvis. His son-in-law's pleading resounded merrily in his ears, as though it played on a joyous loop on the car stereo, all the way to the mosque:

'Please don't tell Tamara. Please. For our daughter's sake. If she found out that's why there's no money left in the account, she'd divorce me. Really, Paul. She would.'

The lying, scabby-faced toad had had crocodile tears in his eyes. He had actually clutched his hands together in supplication. A ruin of a workshy, faux-hippy turd, who in sucking dry the family finances with his gambling addiction had relinquished any remaining vestiges of manly moral fibre that might have kept his spine together.

'I don't like you,' Van den Bergen had said, cuddling his granddaughter, stepping from one foot to another in a bid to soothe her. 'I never have. I don't think you're fit to lick my Tamara's shoes clean. You're a sponger. I knew it the moment I met you, Mr Trainee Bloody Rockstar.'

Numb-Nut's face had blanched to a satisfying shade of grey. 'I'm so sorry.' Big words said in a small voice.

Now, though, Elvis encroached on Van den Bergen's memories.

'How are we going to play this, boss?'

'How do you think? The guy lets extremist clerics in to poison the minds of his young flock, if the papers are to be believed. I'm not pandering to the ego of some pro-terror shit-stirrer who's happy to have people's children brainwashed and sent to early graves. We play it straight!'

Manoeuvring his Mercedes into a miserly parking space with the deftness and confidence of a man whose morning had taken a turn for the triumphant, Van den Bergen privately acknowledged that being tailed by some oddball in a Jaguar would require further consideration, but right now he had to shelve his concerns and focus on Abdullah al Haq.

As they entered the foyer of the mosque, Van den Bergen removed his size thirteen loafers.

'Exactly how may I help you?' the imam asked, examining his card with interest. He stroked his beard, but otherwise there was no reaction – no obvious guilty conscience. Cool as a cucumber.

'I believe you know Frederik den Bosch,' Van den Bergen said.

'Do I?'

Elvis stepped forward. Held out a grainy photo of the two men's apparently clandestine meeting that had taken place the previous evening.

'You'd better follow me.'

At that time of day, in between prayers, the mosque was empty, echoing and vast. Van den Bergen caught a glimpse through an open fire door of a vaulted white space that could no doubt accommodate thousands. It was impressive. In contrast, the imam's office was a riot of colour and clutter – floor-to-ceiling shelves were filled with books, the spines of which glittered with gold-leaf Arabic lettering, and on the floor lay a patchwork of glorious Persian rugs. The imam took a seat behind an incongruous plain IKEA desk. He sat with his hands laced together on his lap. Looked at them expectantly.

'Tell us about your relationship with Den Bosch,' Van den Bergen said.

'I barely know the man.'

Elvis tapped a bitten fingernail on the photo, which he'd placed in front of the imam. 'You two seemed on very familiar terms last night. I took this photo and I saw you with my own eyes. So don't try to pass off your meeting as some chance encounter.'

The imam shrugged. 'I know many people. I'm a cultural leader in a cosmopolitan city.'

'Why are you fraternising with a neo-Nazi?' Van den Bergen asked. 'What would your flock think about that?'

'Den Bosch is merely a business acquaintance. I'm not his keeper,' the imam said.

Van den Bergen noticed the man's left lower eyelid beginning to flicker. But, otherwise, his earnest expression remained immutable.

'Business? What kind of business?' Van den Bergen started to draw Eva's chubby little hand in his notebook, carefully crosshatching the contours of her palm with his biro.

'He supplies my Islamic centre directly with vegetables at a cut price. You'd be surprised how much food we need to cook up for various Eid celebrations.'

'Did you know he's a practising fascist?' Elvis asked. 'Or that he's a slum landlord? I'll bet a few of his tenants attend this mosque. How many Syrians come here? Or Afghans?'

The imam folded his arms defensively, as Van den Bergen had seen him do on television, when quizzed about the radicalisation of young men inside the city's mosques. This was a man used to dodging confrontational media bullets. It appeared he had clicked into that mode now.

'I told you, what Mr Den Bosch does in his spare time has never been the subject of discussion,' the imam said, closing his eyes, as if lecturing a naive student. 'The price of his produce has, however. I have a community to lead and feed. That said, I thank you for bringing his beliefs to my attention. I will seek a supplier elsewhere. The rally outside my mosque last night was blasphemy.' He looked heavenwards and shook his head. Turned his focus back to Van den Bergen. 'But I resent the implication that I pimp my community out to ruthless landlords.' He raised an eyebrow. That lower eyelid was still pulsating.

'Did you know a Den Bosch truck is at the centre of a trafficking investigation?' Van den Bergen asked. 'A twelve-year-old Syrian girl is dead and the other passengers who were crammed like produce into the back of that truck are fighting for their lives in hospital. We're thinking maybe Mr Den Bosch is transporting more than tomatoes in his fleet of heavy goods vehicles. Maybe he's trafficking people from some war-torn location in the Arab world to Amsterdam. Swelling the ranks of *your* congregation.'

The imam swallowed hard. He scratched beneath his pristine crocheted mosque hat and sniffed hard. Sweat stains were blossoming beneath his arms, turning the fabric of his tunic a dark brown. 'What a terribly racist suggestion,' he said. 'I'm offended. Do you think all Muslims are terrorists?'

Flustered, Van den Bergen lifted his pen from the paper. 'I wasn't talking about terrorism. And I can't possibly see how I've offended you. I was talking about people trafficking.'

'You're implying I'm involved somehow. But no matter.' Seemingly calm, the imam opened a notepad that lay in his in-tray and took the lid off a Mont Blanc fountain pen. 'Can I have the name of your superior officer, please?' He set the pen down, never taking his eyes from Van den Bergen's. 'Oh no. Hang on. No need. I know the chief of police personally. I'm sure he'll be intrigued to hear about two of his subordinates bringing thinly disguised racial harassment and defamation to my door.'

Van den Bergen's biro ran through the sketch of Eva's hand, puncturing the thick paper. He felt every muscle in his face stiffen. Suddenly, the spectre of the Jaguar driver outside Tamara's door cast a shadow on the imam's office, and the imam himself seemed to suck all of the heat from the room, leaving him shivering beneath his slightly sicked-on work suit.

'Thank you for your time,' he told the imam.

He marched back to the foyer as quickly as his stockinged feet would take him and reclaimed his shoes.

Outside, Asian men were scrubbing at the pavement with buckets full of hot, soapy water and stiff yard brushes, trying to remove the blood from the slaughtered pigs. Van den Bergen wrapped his arms around himself and strode to the car, wondering if he'd caught his granddaughter's virus in record time. Was it even possible?

'Get in the car,' he told Elvis. 'Then we'll talk.'

Squealing away from the place in the comfort of his Mercedes, with his heated seat on full whack, Van den Bergen exhaled deeply.

'Well?' Elvis asked, then immediately sneezed with gusto, leaving a shower of spittle on the dashboard.

'For God's sake, Elvis! Use a damned handkerchief or open the bloody window. You're like a fucked trumpet.'

'Sorry, boss. But what did you think of the imam? His story about the cheap veg?'

'He's a goddamn liar,' Van den Bergen said, speeding back towards HQ and the generous supply of ibuprofen in his desk drawer. 'Get surveillance on that place, on him and on Den Bosch. Twenty-four hours. I want to know exactly what those two are up to. And when we get in, I want to see Abadi. I'm going to have to let the asshole go, but first I've got a proposition for him.'

# CHAPTER 19

## *Amstelveen, Tamara's house, later*

'For God's sake, Dad!' Tamara whispered down the phone. 'You ruined my job interview completely. I had to leave halfway through because Willem wouldn't stop calling me. It was so embarrassing, the way they looked at me. I won't hear from them again. That's it! An opportunity buggered. The first job interview in a month, too!' She remembered the disapproving looks that the interview panel had exchanged with each other as her phone rang, time after time. If only she'd switched the thing off. But then if anything had happened to Eva while she'd been out ... 'And then you land this bombshell on me! Thanks a fucking bundle.'

'Calm down! You're shooting the messenger. *I* didn't gamble away your life savings. *My* damned life savings. But we'll sort this. We will. *I* will.'

'You're a bastard. Bastard, bastard, bastard! Why the hell didn't you warn me?'

Tamara didn't really know why she was calling her father, half shouting at him in vitriolic whispers down the phone. None of this was his fault. Deep down, she knew that.

'Take a deep breath. You don't mean that. How am I a bastard, precisely? I've done nothing but indulge you from the minute you met that workshy prick with his misplaced musical ambitions. Didn't I tell you when you brought him back to mine for lunch that he was a waste of space? Didn't I? But you told me to butt out and keep my opinions to myself. And God knows, Tamara, I've bloody well tried. The times I've bitten my tongue …'

He was right, of course. He'd seen through Willem immediately, where she had been blinded by what she thought was love but had really just been relief that someone fancied her enough to stick around for more than a month or two. Willem, with his cool hair and ethno-tat clothing and ballads he'd said were about her, performed in her mother's kitchen to rapturous applause from everyone but her father. Hadn't Dad just sat there, bouncing his enormous right foot on his left knee, grimacing and checking his phone or watch, like a harbinger of romantic doom on a time limit?

Tamara stroked Eva's brow as she lay in her cot, finally off to sleep. A miracle, since the argument had sent her spiralling into near hysteria. Mummy and Daddy screaming hard enough to shake the house on its sturdy foundations.

A single tear fell onto her daughter's hand, causing the baby girl to jerk suddenly in her sleep.

Allowing grief to envelop her like a damp, rough blanket, Tamara backed away from the nursery and padded downstairs. In the kitchen, she could let some of the pain leach out without disturbing her daughter's rest.

'Why, Dad? Why?'

On the other end of the phone, her father's no-nonsense, gruff rumble softened to the vocal equivalent of the warm *stroopwafels* he'd placated her with as a child when she worked herself into a frenzy during some parental meltdown or other: Mum, throwing crockery at Dad just because she could; Dad, glowering in the corner – his silence just as deafening as Mum's apoplectic shrieking. Now, Dad's cinnamon-caramel words of solace poured over her.

'Willem's a dick, sweetheart. I always said it. Listen, we all make mistakes.'

'History repeating itself, you mean? Except Mum married an artist and you turned out to be a rock.' She couldn't keep the stutter and heave out of her voice. She was seven years old again, but with the responsibilities of an adult, bringing up a baby and an overgrown man-child. 'How could I have been so blind?' Her shoulders shook as the hiccoughs kicked in and the sobs really took hold.

'Where is he now? I presume he's not there.'

Tamara moved through to the living room at the front of the house, peering through the Venetian blinds at the quiet scene of the suburban street. The rest of the neighbourhood was oblivious to her strife. Apart from that bitch a few doors down who had facilitated all this. 'God knows. He took his guitar and stormed out, saying I'd driven him to it.' She gulped down a mixture of rage and disappointment. 'I'm so worried about him, Dad. What if he's thrown himself in the canal?'

On the other end of the phone, her father's hollow laugh said it all. 'That bastard is too self-interested to do us all that particular favour. Don't you worry about him. I bet he's already playing poker in some other old crone's house, or throwing your hard-earned euros into a slot machine at the casino to cheer himself up. He's an addict, Tamara. Get rid of the cheating bastard.'

A small part of her brain registered the man who was standing on the opposite side of the road, staring straight into the living room. But the greater portion was too overwhelmed by the realisation that her marriage might be at an end. She backed away from the window.

'He's never cheated on me,' she sobbed. Her wedding photo caught her eye. She strode over to the sideboard and picked up the heavy frame. Willem looked so handsome, wearing an embroidered kaftan with garlands of flowers around his neck.

It hadn't been her idea to have a faux Hindu-style ceremony after their sober civil union. She'd have preferred a traditional party. But still, the sari had suited her, though she'd felt a fraud and a little stupid in front of all those conservative bores on her mother's side of the family. Nobody but George on her dad's. And now … 'I'm going to lose him, aren't I?'

'Good riddance! The sooner he's out the door, the better, darling. I'll help you. We can do this together. I'm sure your mother will give her support, too. You're far better off on your own. You're young enough to start again. Let's face it, you're the breadwinner! You've always been the one to do all the hard graft of putting a home together and looking after the baby. What in God's name has he ever done apart from chip away at your confidence and spend all your cash?'

The doorbell rang. Should she answer it in this state?

'Dad, there's somebody at the—'

'And if he's lied about the gambling, what else has he lied about, eh? How do you know he's not been unfaithful? I'm sorry to say it, Tamara. I know it must hurt like hell. But you need to wake up! Don't let this using bastard take you for a fool any longer. If you're going to live a pauper's life, make sure you're saving the money for Eva, not letting that wanker fritter it away on illegal games of bridge. Bridge! Who the hell gets hooked on bloody bridge?'

Again, the doorbell rang. Upstairs, the baby started to stir. Damn it.

'Dad, I've got to go.'

'No! Wait!' he said. 'Didn't I tell you about that guy in the green—?'

'Dad, I'm going. Come over when your shift ends.'

Ending the call, Tamara wiped her eyes on the sleeve of her blouse and opened the door to this unexpected and insistent visitor.

# CHAPTER 20

## *Police headquarters, later still*

'Get in here, both of you! And close the door.'

With a growling stomach, George reluctantly followed Van den Bergen into Minks's office. It was the first time she'd ever been roped into one of Van den Bergen's bollockings, and she didn't like it one bit. Minks wasn't even her boss, for God's sake!

'Can we do this after lunch?' she offered, treating the commissioner to a winning smile. 'Only, I could eat a scabby horse on toast and I can barely hear you for my—'

'Sit down, McKenzie!' Minks barked. 'This involves you too. And for the record, scabby horse on toast is not a phrase in Dutch.'

George sucked her teeth at Minks. *Cheeky. Fucking. Arsehole.* So tempted was she to give him a dressing-down – her hand on her hip, getting right up in his grill and giving him some proper South East London attitude, complete with pointing and a well-placed snap of the fingers in his doughy face – that she realised she was mouthing the words, her head sliding indignantly from side to side as, in her imagination, she told him how linguistic *humour* works, and how her Dutch is spot on, *thank you*, and how *he* might be a pissy graduate but *she* was a fucking *doctor* and research fellow of St John's College,

144

Cambridge (ex-research fellow, now that Sally Wright had had her tenure rescinded, but still ...). *Massive* wanker.

At her side, Van den Bergen folded himself into a chair and folded his arms across his body – bracing himself for impact. It was strange to see her lover in this subordinate position. So, this was what happened to the outspoken, the honest, the borderline antisocial. They thought they had reached the peaks of their careers, only to discover they were still only halfway up the mountain because they'd not been allocated a seat on the gravy train by the slick-veneered and honey-mouthed who were destined for the top. This was her future. Of that, she had no doubt.

'Maarten,' Van den Bergen began. 'I really don't see why Georgina—'

'Can it, Van den Bergen.' Minks ran his fingers up and down his silk tie. Up and down. Up and down. Struggling to deal with Van den Bergen, a loose cannon with far more experience than him, George assessed. 'You're in deep shit – and *she's* been dragging you deeper.'

Leaning back in her chair, as if she were merely waiting for a bus, George raised an eyebrow. 'How do you work that one out? I'm a freelance specialist consultant, working on a trafficking case. And Van den Bergen's doing his job. Do you know what time he gets up in the morning to start work?'

Smiling at her with a piranha grin, Minks carefully lifted a printout from his in-tray. Laid it in front of him on the table and started to toy with his mother-of-pearl cufflinks. A frat boy drunk on his own political potency. 'Does he work at his daughter's house in Amstelveen? Because the tracker on his vehicle ...' He leaned towards Van den Bergen, fixing him with a hard stare. 'Need I remind you that your very nice Mercedes is owned by the police force and intended for police business use only? The tracker says you were there for most of this morning.'

'I thought you approved of me taking time out to reflect on cases,' Van den Bergen said. 'I've got the best clearance rate of any senior officer in the building. And it's because of my methods.'

Minks laced his fingers together and nodded, a beatified grin on his face now. What was this Jekyll and Hyde nonsense? 'It's true. I admire your legendary trips to the allotment for thinking time enormously. It was genius management on Kamphuis's part to allow you to do that. But I think you and I know that's not what you've been doing recently. Now that you're a *grandfather*. What with your daughter living in Amstelveen and all.' Wink, wink. Chummy tosser.

'Kamphuis was corrupt. He's also dead. I wouldn't use him as a shining example of how to be a commissioner, Commissioner Minks.' George took out some dental floss and pulled out a long piece. Started to give her molars a thorough going over, enjoying the look of consternation on Minks's face. She wondered how much force and skill it would take to flick her excavations onto that silk tie of his.

'Stop that, please.'

'Nah,' she answered in English. She needed the work, but she didn't need to take Minks's crap. 'Dental hygiene's very important, innit? And I'm preparing for my scabby horse.' Back to Dutch. 'Why are we here?'

He pointed at Van den Bergen. '*You're* slacking. And when you are working, you're agitating notorious troublemaking imams who threaten to go to the papers, and you're harassing respectable businessmen who pay their taxes. You may catch the bad guys, Paul, but you've got as much subtlety as a bucket of sick. These are tricky times. The Ministry of Justice and Security is caught between a rock and a hard place.' He held his palms wide, like some wannabe Jesus in a Hugo Boss suit. 'The immigrant community on one side and the conservative majority on the other. We have to tread carefully.'

Van den Bergen's face crumpled into a glare that could strip the finish from Minks's gleaming desk. 'How am I supposed to do my job properly if I can't interrogate suspects, for Christ's sake? You want me to solve the trafficking case, so I'm working the case! Dirk followed Den Bosch to the mosque. There's collusion between a neo-Nazi and an imam who's reputed to be less than above board. Remember when *he was accused by de Volkskrant* for allowing Daesh recruiters and extremist clerics into the mosque? The guy's dirty.'

'Well, if you're so diligently going about the trafficking case, why the hell have you got her' – he flicked his thumb dismissively in George's direction – 'and Marie haranguing a respected physician over some Syrian family doctor you've got in custody? It's not even in connection with the Den Bosch case. Marie told me you're investigating the deaths of four old men. I mean, what the hell, Paul?'

'It became apparent—'

'Became apparent nothing.' Minks held his hands up as if in surrender. 'You're off the trafficking case as of today.'

'What do you mean?' Van den Bergen's lightly tanned complexion paled to a sickly grey.

George saw her bank balance winding back from sweet FA to absolute zero and then into the red. No case meant no freelance work. No money coming in meant she was doomed to a life in the UK spent sleeping cheek-by-jowl with her cousins in Aunty Sharon's cramped council house, having to intervene in the ferocious arguments between Letitia the Dragon and whoever was within shrieking distance. If her Cambridge career somehow recovered from Sally Wright's machinations, her life would be spent forevermore renting low-grade college accommodation with a bunch of idiot undergraduates who smoked weed and drank until the early hours, audible through the thin walls as they crapped on loudly about Nietzsche. The bastards never cleaned the shower and inevitable hairy plughole either.

And if Van den Bergen ever committed to her properly and agreed to get their own place together...

'Why are you doing this?' she asked Minks. 'Paul's a brilliant investigator and team manager. His staff adore him. He gets the job done. He should have had your job, if we're being honest.'

Minks's glower soured yet further. 'Your boyfriend doesn't have the diplomatic skills required of a commissioner. That's why he's been overlooked for the post *twice*.'

Van den Bergen placed a hand on George's shoulder. She was so agitated on his behalf, and panicked at the prospect of unemployment, that she wasn't sure whether she was comforted by his touch or annoyed by it. Her default reaction was to shrug him off.

'You're making a big mistake,' she told Minks. 'We're making excellent inroads into—'

'Who are you bringing in?' Van den Bergen asked.

'Roel de Vries.' Minks pursed his lips, clearly expecting a reaction.

'That prick? Seriously? He's such a bad detective, they had to move him to head up traffic.' Van den Bergen shook his head. 'You're making a big mistake. Den Bosch and the imam are in cahoots. A lot of the city's Muslim illegals will belong to that mosque. Den Bosch is a slum landlord, housing recent immigrants – that's a fact. And a pile of trafficked Syrians were found in his truck. A little more digging, and I'm fairly certain I'll be able to see the full picture. We're onto something with those two. I can feel it.'

'Then you can hand over what you've got and let Roel and his team get on with the matter of finding the trafficker behind that girl's death. He's a good guy. I went to school with him. An old friend of the family. *You* are on the brink of burnout, Van den Bergen.' He was pointing – a slender finger on a manicured hand, complete with some kind of chunky gold fraternity ring on his pinkie. 'And *I*, as your caring superior officer, am going to give you the respite you need. You'll thank me for it.'

George was poised to protest, but then came a knock at the door. A grinning face peered through the window into the office. Nose pressed against the glass like a kid. A thumbs up to Minks. George got a glimpse of Roel de Vries' Homer Simpson tie and had the measure of him immediately.

'Jesus,' Van den Bergen said, exchanging a desperate glance with George. He lowered his voice to speak in English, talking quickly while Minks and de Vries exchanged overly friendly backslaps and a fist bump. 'This guy can't find his ass with both hands. We need to get out of here. I can't take it anymore.'

Van den Bergen stood, towering some ten inches above the interloper. They shook hands formally. Absolutely no fist bumps.

'Hey, big man!' Roel enthused, patting Van den Bergen's forearm. 'You look knackered. Grandfatherhood taking its toll? I hear you're being put on my traffic detail. Sometimes it's good to change things up. Recharges the batteries.'

*What a patronising tosspot*, George thought, biting her tongue. *Shiny arse on those trousers, too. Bet he gets his shitty clobber from C&A. How old is this numpty? Thirty? Fifty? I can't even tell. Dick.*

Minks sat back down in his captain's chair, showing de Vries into George's now vacated seat. In less than six months, the new commissioner had changed from an ever-impressed Van den Bergen fanboy to this point-scoring autocrat who only wanted to fill the spaces around his table with sycophants.

'I know you're going to bring a fresh perspective to this terrible case, Roel. Any resources you need will be at your disposal. I'm sure Van den Bergen won't mind you making use of Marie and Elvis, either.'

'Oh, brilliant.' Roel beamed. 'More hands on deck. We're

going to grill the hell out of the refugees from the truck. See if we can put pressure on them to blab.'

'A good chunk of them are still critically ill in hospital,' Van den Bergen said, closing his eyes. 'And the ones who aren't are refusing to speak. George had an excellent idea to use Abadi—'

But Minks wasn't listening. He rubbed his hands together and leaned back, stretching towards the small desk that contained his printer and a coffee maker, which he switched on. 'Don't let me and Roel keep you, Paul. You can wheel your desk chair down to traffic if the one there doesn't suit your height. I know you're funny about that and I take staff welfare *very* seriously, as you know.'

Biting back barbed sentiments, George gathered up her bag and duffel coat. She was almost doubled up, thanks to the sucker punch Minks had given them both. Another black mark on her CV. At her side, the tendons in Van den Bergen's lean face flinched. His grey, hooded eyes were charged with ferocity. But he said nothing. Merely ground his molars.

In the doorway, poised to make their getaway, Van den Bergen turned back to Minks. 'One thing, Roel. You're not having Marie or Dirk. If either of you have a problem with that, take it up with the chief of police, because I intend to.'

He strode so quickly away from Minks's office that George had to jog alongside him to keep up. She needed a cigarette – and fast.

'Where are you going?' she asked.

'To the allotment. I need time out before I burst into flames.' He rubbed his stomach and winced.

'Great. Can I come with you? Shall we grab something to eat on the way?'

Van den Bergen stopped dead outside the photocopier room. He appeared to be contemplating something; sizing her proposition up, perhaps. George searched his inscrutable expression for a sign of how he might be feeling. Was he angry? Bereft? Glad she was there?

'No,' he said. 'I need to speak to Elvis and Marie, but before I do that, I've got to nip over to Tamara's. Check on her and the baby.'

Check on Tamara. Of course he needed to check on fucking Tamara.

As her ageing lover stalked hastily away from her, disappearing off towards the lifts, George balled her fists tightly, reluctantly allowing tears of frustration to leak onto her cheeks. The pain of rejection and disappointment seared inside her, far worse than her griping hunger pangs. Almost on a par with grief. It bit deeply, opening old wounds. Memories resurfacing of the times in her life when she had been jettisoned, used, considered insignificant in the minds of those she'd loved deeply.

'Cunt,' she said, almost inaudibly. 'You and me are so over.'

# CHAPTER 21

# *Hoek van Holland, Stena Line ferry,*
# *that evening*

'Boarding pass and passports open at the photo page, please,' the steward on the Stena Line ferry said in a monotonous voice, wearing a fixed smile on her face.

George shuffled forward with the other plebs on the dreaded overnighter to Harwich. The weather reports had predicted they'd be sailing in the tail end of some hurricane that had hit the East Coast of America and the Caribbean a few days ago. *This is gonna be a bloody riot*, she thought as she handed her documentation over, elbowing out of the way the backpack of some rainbow-jumper-clad travelling wanker who reeked of weed.

Relieved and outraged in equal measure that she was ushered through a damn sight quicker than the young Asian lads in front of her, who were siphoned to the side for questioning, George followed the herd of passengers to the upper decks, feeling like she was involved in some disappointing gold rush where the only land she'd be able to claim would be an uncomfortable seat for those who couldn't afford cabins. Already, the ferry was surging from side to side, heralding the bumpy ride back to the UK.

'Story of my life,' she said, counting her euros to see if she could afford a gin and tonic from the bar.

As the ferry chugged out into the North Sea, George watched the passengers who rolled into the duty-free shop, already half pissed. They rolled out again carrying clanking bags of spirits and packets of ciggies. She already had a 200-box of Silk Cut, which Van den Bergen would certainly disapprove of. Well, fuck him.

Leaving her bag on her seat to be guarded by the kind-looking Aruban woman next to her, George took the dregs of her gin and a packet of cigarettes to be alone at the back of the ship with the other smokers. She needed to process all that had come to pass in the last four hours.

After several failed attempts in the stiff North Sea wind, with the shoreline of the Hoek van Holland growing small and insignificant in the distance, George lit her cigarette and watched the foaming wake that trailed behind the ferry, hoping to cast her regrets into the sea and look only ahead to the future. Van den Bergen was a dick and had chosen his adult daughter over his long-term girlfriend, sacrificing the happiness in his own life to service that of a child who had a life of her own and who wouldn't thank him for it.

As she had hastily packed sufficient clothes to last her a week or so, he had called for a fleeting two minutes to tell her how concerned he was that some guy had delivered a complimentary organic veg box to Tamara, and how he was convinced it was some kind of threat. Crapping on about how he feared for his daughter's safety, as if malformed carrots and unwashed potatoes were calling cards for death.

'Paranoid old bastard,' George said, flicking her ash over the railing, though the treacherous wind whipped the ash back onto her, covering her nearly new duffel in smudges of shitty grey. 'Best part of ten years.' She exhaled heavily, annoyed when hiccoughs sucked the air out of her lungs and put paid to her smoking attempts, as though Van den Bergen had somehow foiled her from across the waves. 'All that time and sod all to show for it.'

'Talking to yourself, pet?'

She turned to her right and drank in the sight of an over-sized Geordie who looked, judging by the plaster on his workmen's boots, as though he had been working over the water and had just finished a shift. He reeked of stale alcohol and unwashed arse.

George wrinkled her nose and put her cigarettes and lighter in her pocket. 'Only time I get a sensible answer, innit?'

'I thought you were trying to chat us up, like. Fancy a top-up on your disco-lemonade? You look as though you could use it.'

Jesus. He was hitting on her. George flushed hot, suddenly feeling claustrophobic in the wide-open space. More so when she noticed the three other men behind him, similarly dressed, whose red noses and whisky breath attested to rather more than the effects of the sea breeze on a cold autumnal evening.

'No, ta.'

She clutched her coat tighter to her, taking a step towards the door. The warmth of the ferry's stuffy interior beckoned. Except, as she pulled the door open, she felt a hand grab at the back of her coat.

'Come on, pet. Let's have some fun, eh? You look like a girl who likes to enjoy herself.'

'Get fucked!' George said, feeling the red mist descend as she caught sight of the oversized Geordie's guffawing travel companions. She tried to wrench herself free, but her captor wouldn't let go. 'You fancy a fishy on a little dishy, twat-boy, just carry on. 'Cos the way I'm feeling right now, it wouldn't take much for me to tip you over that fucking railing into the sea, big as you are. Do you get me?'

He relinquished his grip as a hatched-faced older woman

emerged onto the outer deck, clutching a packet of Superkings. George took the opportunity to scoot back down to the main lounge, but her ridiculed pursuer was following her, jeering, letting her know at the top of his croaking smoker's voice that she was a cheeky black slag and that he'd give her fucking fishy on a dishy when he got hold of her.

With her breath coming short, George hastened towards the grand staircase, stumbling down the steps. No sign of a steward. Down, down, down she descended into the cabin decks, until she had lost sight of the persistent prick.

'Thank Christ for that,' she said, holding her knees and panting. She looked from side to side along the cramped corridor, which sported uniform, anonymous cabin doors on one side. The air was stale as hell down here, causing her to sneeze. Stumbling as the ferry started to lurch in earnest now that they had reached the open sea, George realised she was lost. She steadied herself against the utilitarian plastic walls and made her way carefully to the far end of the corridor, in search of a map. Squeezed past a man with a giant beer gut who emerged from one of the cabins, tucking his shirt into his trousers. Catching a glimpse of his tiny cabin interior before he shut his door, she realised these rooms were below deck. She had come down further than she'd thought. Seeing the dark stain on the crotch of the man's trousers, she opted not to ask him which deck they were on or which way the main lounge lay. Sod that.

With a thudding heart, George realised that she might have inadvertently cut herself off from safety down here, given how silent it was but for the distant thrum of the ferry's engine rooms. Deserted too, now that the man with the gut had gone. Pitching and rolling, she reached a narrow, uncarpeted staircase. In the harsh artificial light, she spotted a map just below. Carefully, she climbed down the stairs, clinging tightly to the metal handrail.

'Shitting Nora,' she said, spying row after row of cars, all parked bumper to bumper. 'The bloody car deck.'

The ferry heaved violently on the waves. Feeling nausea sweep over her, George swallowed down a lump of gin-flavoured regurgitation. She was about to climb the perilous steps back up when she heard whimpering from the car deck. What the hell was that? An abandoned dog? Surely not. But then she heard a child's voice quite clearly above the tinnitus hum of the ferry's bowels, crying and shouting in a small voice. Speaking a language she didn't at first recognise, but then realised was an Arabic dialect.

'Hello! Who's there?' she called out in Arabic. She wasn't fluent, but she'd picked up enough to get by over the years – always handy in the wilds of multi-ethnic South East London, and especially so now that her life revolved around research into trafficking, where a good proportion of the victims, often from the Middle East and Central Asia, spoke little English, if any.

From between the gleaming bonnets of the BMWs and Audis and Citroëns, a small child crawled towards her. He couldn't have been more than six or seven, George assessed, though she was fairly hopeless as far as children were concerned.

'What's your name?' she asked, extending a hand to him whilst clinging to the bottom of the handrail. 'Come on. Don't be scared.'

The little boy was dressed in filthy jeans and a hoodie. Tears poured from huge, sorrowful brown eyes, streaking his dusty skin with clean furrows. His lip trembled.

George didn't understand much of his response, but she did pick out the word 'Ummi'. He was looking for his mother. Where the hell had he come from?

'What are you doing on the car deck, kiddo?' she asked, knowing the child couldn't understand her. But, of course, she was fairly certain she knew what a dishevelled, lost kid on the lower decks of the Stena Line ferry from the Netherlands to Harwich might feasibly be doing.

Enveloping the small sobbing boy in her arms, she stroked his thick black hair and shushed him until he began to calm. Two broken hearts in one day on one ferry. But George suspected there were rather more, hidden somewhere among the stationary vehicles on some lower deck. This boy's mother, for one, no doubt anguished at the disappearance of her son. She had a decision to make: alert the authorities now, or let the boy lead her to the vehicle in question and then raise the alarm? Her common sense screamed at her to find a steward.

'Take me to Ummi,' she told the boy. 'Are you in a car?'

Hadn't she cast her common sense aside already, when she'd phoned her father and asked him to pick her up from Harwich in the morning in Aunty Sharon's old VW Polo? Bollocks to it. George wasn't about to hand this boy back to his captors, but she at least wanted to get a good look at who'd had him, and still possibly had the rest of his family – perhaps concealed under some blankets in a boot or in the back of a van.

Scanning the deck they were currently on, she thought it unlikely a people trafficker would own a family saloon or premium estate car.

'Did you climb steps?' she asked in Arabic, using her walking fingers as supplementary explanation.

He nodded, and made to wipe the glistening string of snot from his upper lip with his sleeve. George whipped out a tissue and cleaned his nose. Her senses quickened as they climbed further into the belly of the vessel, feeling their way along the dark places where the light didn't reach, holding on to whatever they could as the ferry fought against the pitch and roll of the stormy seas. They crept low, avoiding the scrutiny of whoever might be down there.

Suddenly, the boy yelped, and pulled her back with some

force. George placed her hand firmly over his mouth and shushed him.

'Where?' she asked.

But she needn't have asked. In the far corner of the lowest deck, she spotted an almost familiar livery on a long-wheel-based van.

'BBT,' she whispered. 'Bosch, Boom & Tuin Bloemen.' Forest, Tree and Garden. She imagined desperate people being smuggled from war-torn parts of the world amongst unseasonal tulips, roses and amaryllis bulbs, en route from the glasshouses of Western Europe's breadbasket to the crappy small-town florists of Beckenham, Blackpool or Bridgend. It was so very reminiscent of Groenten Den Bosch; even the van's logo was written in an identical font. Similar. But not the same.

Getting close enough to make a note of the van's number plate would be impossible without putting her and the boy at risk, even if they continued to crawl along at tyre height. His mother would certainly raise the alarm when she realised he was missing, wouldn't she? Or perhaps Ummi was dead beneath some bombed-out masonry in Aleppo. It was impossible to know; her Arabic was so unreliable and the boy was shaking with fear.

'Ummi!' he whimpered, pointing at the van.

It was time to get the authorities involved, George decided. She was in an enclosed, deserted space with no way to defend herself, and in charge of someone else's precious son. No. She had seen enough. But at least from this distance, she might get a quick snapshot of the van's livery to send to Marie.

Raising her index finger to her mouth, willing the boy to remain silent, she took out her phone. Fumbling fingers failed to bring up the photo function. The ferry tipped violently. The boy wailed, falling into the side of a car.

'Hey, you!' A gruff voice in Dutch resounded throughout the industrial vastness of the lower deck.

George looked up from her phone to see a brick wall of a man, dressed in a high-vis jacket and jeans. The van door was open. This was the driver, no doubt. A scream from the boy rent the still air.

Clambering to her feet, George snatched the boy up. She glanced behind. The stairs weren't far. She could make a run for it with the kid, couldn't she?

The driver took something from his pocket. Was it a gun? She had time neither for fear nor recrimination nor understanding of what in fresh hell was going on. He held the black thing in his hand up. A phone. He pointed it at her – *click* – and winked.

As George sprinted with her trafficked charge to the safety of the stairs, she realised two things: if she raised the alarm, she would be putting the trafficked cargo in that van in mortal danger. It took only a moment to shoot someone or cut their throat, and she'd heard often enough of how expendable these refugees were to their traffickers, if they thought their necks were on the line. But perhaps most worryingly of all, the driver had taken her photo. His boss would know who she was. And nowadays, she wasn't that hard to find.

# CHAPTER 22

## *Harwich International Port, then Cambridge, 19 October*

'Oh, thank God you're here,' George said, throwing her bag onto the back seat of Aunty Sharon's VW Polo.

Looking round furtively, she checked that there were no customs officials marching towards her, no transport police and, most importantly, no trafficker the size of a brick outhouse. She kissed her father. He smelled of the same deodorant as Van den Bergen. Shuddering, she slapped the dashboard. 'Go! Come on!' she said in Spanish. 'Let's get as far away from here as possible.'

'What's wrong, *cara mia*? You seem on edge.' Her father negotiated the snake of traffic queuing to leave the port, looking at her askance when she ducked, curling up in her seat with her head almost between her knees.

George looked up at him, praying she wouldn't vomit in the pristine interior of the car. But seasickness had kicked in in earnest, and the seat beneath her felt as though it were rising and falling, like she was still being tossed around on board the ferry. 'You wouldn't believe the journey I've had. I've just left a little boy with the authorities and given them a tip-off about some people-trafficking arsehole I came up against on the car deck.'

'What were you doing down there?'

'Long story,' she said. 'Jesus. How can I live with what I've just done? I've separated a small child from his mother and possibly put a load of illegal immigrants in mortal danger. I'm some kind of proper class-A shithouse.'

Peering over the top of the dashboard, she saw that the Bosch, Boom & Tuin Bloemen truck was being ushered by a gang of port authority police and customs officials into a special bay. She said a silent prayer to the universe, hoping that the driver had been taken by surprise. Perhaps he'd thought that George was some random weirdo, snooping around a lower deck, hoping to break into a car. That was the most hopeful scenario. She remembered the little boy's bewildered expression and apologised to him in her mind's eye.

Finally sitting up in the passenger seat, she cast an appraising glance at her father. 'You look well,' she said. 'It's only been a couple of weeks, but you've put on weight. You look relaxed. You've got good colour.'

They turned onto the motorway. Her father shot her a mischievous grin. 'Your mother's in Spain. I'm in England. The house is empty. It's bliss.' He was speaking in English now.

George laughed at his pronunciation of 'bliss' as 'blees'. All those long years without her father in her life, and now here he was, finally playing Dad Taxi and being the shoulder she so desperately needed to cry on.

'Enjoy it while you can. They're back tomorrow – Letitia in all her glory, weighted down with duty free and a donkey piñata.' She swallowed hard, pushing down the pain that threatened to surface along with the contents of her stomach. 'I've left Paul.'

'What? You've been together for nearly ten years, haven't you?'

'Long enough. After you came back, I asked him if he wanted to get a place with me. Properly commit. Either in London or Amsterdam. Maybe even Cambridge. I'm sick of this rootless, flitting-back-and-forth, long-distance crap.'

'And he wouldn't?'

'He was always commitment-phobic, but since his grand-daughter came along, he's been using that silly cow – his daughter – as an excuse to push me away.'

'Self-sabotage,' her father said. 'Your mother did the same to us when you were little. She picked and picked at me, at our relationship, until we fell apart at the seams.' He patted her hand. 'She's intolerable though. I could never have stayed with her. She would have driven me crazy.' The car whizzed under the sign that told them Cambridge was only ten miles away. 'But you two … I thought he was The One. You guys have something really special.'

George wiped the slightly steamy passenger window with her sleeve. Looked out at the flat, brown expanse of the tilled East Anglian countryside. So much like the Netherlands and yet … not. 'Do we? You can't know what goes on between two people behind closed doors, Dad. I'm not letting him treat me like this. He needs to shit or get off the pot. If he wants to abandon his happiness by the roadside of middle age, I ain't going on that journey with him. Life's too short … or too long, depending on how many years you get given.'

Checking the side mirror to see that her hair still passed muster, George balked as she caught sight again of a car that had been following them since Harwich. A coincidence. Britain's roads were full of silver Mondeos. Weren't they? Suddenly, anguished thoughts of her stagnating love life were displaced by the fear that she was being trailed by some face-less thug in cahoots with the driver from the ferry. Bosch, Boom & Tuin. Forest, Tree and Garden. The name struck a chord deep in the complexity of her subconscious, and not because Bosch put her in mind of Den Bosch. Den Bosch was, after all, just an abbreviation of 's-Hertogenbosch, which was a town in the middle of the Netherlands. There was something about the combination of those three words, though, that made perfect sense for a wholesaler of florist supplies.

As Cambridge came into view, George scrolled past the unread emails and missed call notifications on her phone from Van den Bergen, who had finally worked out that she had left the country – and him. She picked up a text thread between her and Marie. Thumbed out a message.

```
'Can u look into Den Bosch's records
2 see if involvement in a co. called
Bosch, Boom & Tuin Bloemen?'
```

Parking up in Cambridge was, as ever, nothing short of a nightmare, so her father dropped her at the side entrance to St John's and arranged a rendezvous some thirty minutes later, beyond the backs by the University Library.

George marched through the courtyards, stepping back through time architecturally from the early twentieth century to Henry VIII's time, until she reached the staircase that led up to Sally Wright's set of rooms. Her breath steamed on the autumnal air, but she had no time to soak up the beauty of Cambridge dressed in its fiery October finery, nor did she have the inclination to marvel at the extreme youth of the freshers who were wandering round in their smart, washed-by-Mum jeans and new trainers, still looking pristine; still looking like they couldn't quite believe they'd left home and gone to heaven.

Pride was an unpalatable repast, but George had determined to swallow hers. Didn't the recognition that bending over was sometimes necessary come with maturity? Dragging her wobbly, seasick legs up a staircase that had been worn smooth and shiny over the centuries, she found the Vice Chancellor's door, knocked once and burst in.

'You want an apology, you've got it,' she simply said.

Professor Sally Wright was sitting with her ski-sock-clad feet up on her desk. She was smoking a cigarette and had been mid bollocking when George had interrupted. A fresher was sitting in the much lower seat on the other side of the desk – a narrow-shouldered lad dressed in a red Adidas top and skinny jeans, whose milky complexion was so hairless that his skin shone as though his gyp-lady had polished him with beeswax. He looked as though he had been hammered further into the seat pad with every word that issued forth from Sally's nicotine-laced mouth. Drug misdemeanour? Skiving? Puking in the library?

Feeling only slightly stupid, George cleared her throat and awaited a response. Arms folded. Itchy with discomfort. Apologies chafed against the very fibre of her being.

Sally took her feet off the table and narrowed her eyes at George. She stuck her cigarette between her brown-stained teeth, turned to the boy and clapped her hands together. 'I'll deal with you later. Go!'

Just the two of them, now. George swayed from side to side, feeling sick as a dog. This was the last thing she'd wanted to do, straight off the red-eye from the Hoek van Holland, but it was a festering boil that needed to be lanced. She needed the money.

'Well, well, well,' Sally said, offering her a cigarette.

George felt certain the apology had worked, then, though Sally would still make her endure squeamish words of rebuke. She took a cigarette and lit up in silence. Offered a placatory shit-eating grin – the kind she swore she'd never wear.

'Your aunt spoke down to me like I was some smart-mouthed child, lecturing me about how unfairly treated you are – as though I'm some great, white oppressor! She forgets

I'm the one who allowed you to climb this ivory tower, leaving the filth of the gutter beneath you. I'm your boss, George. And yet you saw fit to flout my advice and go disappearing off in the midst of our book launch. All so you could engage in some kind of wild goose chase after ghastly parents who never gave a hoot about you!' Sally glared at her, breathing heavily through flared nostrils.

Biting her tongue until the pain lanced through her mouth, George remained silent. A decade earlier, she would have given as good as she got. *Let the old bag have her say and burn herself out. Fuck your hurt sensibilities. You need this job or the future's bleak. No career. No mortgage. No home.*

But Sally Wright was clearly nowhere near finished. Her pruned mouth, paused mid rant, twitched back into life. 'When you finally do deign to come back from a bout of unsanctioned globetrotting and playing happy families, you give me some impertinent lecture about blood being thicker than water, getting on your high horse about how I'm profiteering from your labour and dead Dobkin's research.' Her voice reached a thunderous pitch. 'Who do you think you are? And what makes you think you can just walk back into your old life with a half-arsed apology like that?'

Considering her words carefully, George mulled over her approach. Flattery was going to happen over her dead body. The truth might get her thrown out and back to square one. Something in between, then. She kept her voice uncharacteristically small.

'Look. I belong here. You and me go way back. It seemed daft. And I reckon I might be back for good. In the UK, I mean.'

The woman who had plucked her from prison, where she'd been on remand, and had offered her a fresh start raised a finely plucked, steel-grey eyebrow. Looked down at George over the top of her red cat's-eye glasses. Stubbed out her cigarette.

'What a sorry sight you are with your tail between your legs, Georgina McKenzie. And what a fucking cheek you've got, bursting into my rooms with a bullshit "soz" when there's not a shred of remorse on your disingenuous face.' She lit another cigarette. 'Kindly Foxtrot Oscar and don't let the door smack you on the way out, dear.'

Perhaps the apology hadn't worked as well as George had hoped. The seasickness was exacerbated by the curdling feeling in her gut that told her this chapter of her life might not have quite the happy ending she'd hoped for. She'd jettisoned everyone and everything that had ever meant anything to her. She couldn't go forwards if she couldn't go back. She was finished.

What the hell had she done?

'Let's get to London as fast as we can,' George said, buckling up in the Polo. She wished the passenger seat would swallow her whole, so that she no longer had to eat the crap that the universe had served up to her.

'Well, what did she say? It can't have been that bad.' Her father averted his gaze from the road ahead, shooting her a bemused glance.

'You were kidnapped by a cartel and forced to work as a slave for years, and now you're having to live under the same roof as my mother. And you tell me things can't be that bad?'

Visualising the walk of shame she'd inevitably have to take to the dole office or Jobcentre or wherever the hell it was people signed on, George acknowledged her feelings of rising panic. For the first time in her entire adult life, she wasn't gainfully employed or self-employed. Aunty Sharon was the only breadwinner left in the small council-estate terrace that housed her extended family.

'Papa, you're looking for work, right?'

He nodded. Sighed. 'Looking. And looking. It seems nobody

wants to employ a Spanish guy with PTSD and skills that are years out of date. There's not a massive demand from the UK's engineering firms for drug-smuggling semi-submersibles. And therapy's not exactly a talking point in a job interview.' He laughed heartily, though George detected the disappointment that underpinned the gesture.

As they chugged along the M11 towards London, George's thoughts turned back to the van driver and little trafficked boy on the ferry. Concern that the guy had taken her photograph had abated now, but she considered the Den Bosch case, wondering if tackling it from a different angle might put that prick Van den Bergen back in Minks's good books and her back on the payroll.

'Are there any asylum seekers at your therapy sessions?' she asked.

Her father frowned. 'Yes. Come to think of it, there are. Three Somalis. A couple of Syrian refugees … We all get put in the same group therapy because we're dirty, traumatised foreigners.' He turned to her and winked.

'Do you know what transit country they came into the UK from?'

'No. Sorry.'

She visualised the Bosch, Boom & Tuin van; the Den Bosch heavy goods vehicle. There was more than one way to skin this cat. 'Any chance you can get me in front of them?'

# CHAPTER 23

# *Amsterdam, Van den Bergen's apartment, then the Sloterdijkermeer allotments, then the Drie Goudene Honden pub, later*

Creeping out of the apartment, leaving Tamara and the baby sleeping in his and George's bedroom, Van den Bergen drove down to the Sloterdijkermeer allotment complex. Stiff from two nights spent in the rather too short guest bed, he had been only too happy throw the towel in at 4.30 a.m. and start the day. Besides, there was much to think about: George was refusing to take his calls and had merely texted a curt 'London' in response to his querying her whereabouts. Perhaps there had been a family emergency. No surprises there if that was the case. He'd never known such a bunch of melodramatic lunatics. As if that wasn't bad enough, Roel de Vries was already rubbing everybody up the wrong way over the Den Bosch case.

As he parked the Mercedes in front of the allotment gates, he imagined de Vries' bungling traffic prats interviewing those poor bastards in the hospital, demanding to know who they'd paid to ship them to the UK via the Netherlands, when they were rather more concerned with recovering from oxygen deprivation and dysentery. As if he and Elvis hadn't already made discreet enquiries and come up with zilch. Thanks to George's suggestion that a Syrian-born doctor might have a better chance than a white Dutch policeman of gaining the trust of Syrian recent refugees, Abadi was the last card he had up his sleeve. But that was to be played later.

Right now, Van den Bergen unlocked the gate, closing it carefully behind him. In the half-light of a dawn that was but a yellow-grey smudge on the horizon, he made his way along the path, past the other sheds and summer houses, drinking in the good smell of earth and newly rotting leaves that had fallen from the surrounding deciduous trees in a shower of October gold. It was too early to deadhead his giant cosmos or to check how the last of his dahlias were faring in the colder mornings.

*Click, click, click.*

Van den Bergen stopped, some twenty metres from his own plot. Was that someone else's footfalls on the path? At this time of the morning? Surely not. Gripping his large tartan flask tightly, he turned around.

'Who's there?'

The boom of his voice was swallowed by the tall trees. There was nothing to hear beyond the flutter of leaves and the banging of an unsecured shed door, opening and closing in the early morning wind.

'Silly old fart.'

Van den Bergen continued to his cabin, checking around him. He inserted the key into the stiff, giant padlock. No sign of intrusion. Good. No more imagined footsteps. Better. After Tamara had received the unsolicited box of organic vegetables the same morning that he had been trailed by some weirdo in a green Jag, it paid to be vigilant.

Making a mental note to upgrade his security arrangements so that he could lock himself into the cabin, as well as secure it from the outside, he switched on the light, squinting in the glare of a bare bulb that buzzed in protest at this pre-dawn abuse. He swept the fine layer of compost off the rickety chair and onto the floor. Pushed up the tray of seedlings so that he could set his flask down. Even though he was dressed in his winter thermals, with his denim dungarees and old fleece, it was cold in here. His toes were numb inside his giant mud-encrusted wellies.

He glanced up at Debbie Harry, who clung to the damp wooden wall by just one functioning piece of sellotape, her feet curled up to her thighs now, but otherwise still infusing his cold heart of glass with a little nostalgic warmth.

'Right,' he told Debbie. 'I've had enough of Numb-Nuts to last me a lifetime. George is sulking but I'm damned if I know why. Fanboy Minks hates my guts. All I've got left is police work. If I can't officially work on the Den Bosch case, the least I can do is try to find out what happened to those hapless old farts in the Force of Five. First, Hendrik van Eden. Let's see what we can find out about him, shall we?'

Sipping the vile, scalding coffee from his plastic thermos cup, Van den Bergen donned his reading glasses and started to leaf through the file of information that Marie had gathered on Hendrik, the elderly victim that he knew least about.

'Okay, what have we got here? Death certificate.'

Cause of death had been listed as a heart attack, of course. Nobody was listed as being his next of kin.

'No wife. No kids. No siblings. Nothing but a solicitor. Poor old bastard. Nobody gave a shit about you, did they, Mr Resistance Fighter Hero?'

As the stomach acid spurted up onto his tongue in protest at the coffee, he contemplated how easily he might be in the same position had Andrea not fallen pregnant with Tamara. But then, had he not failed dismally to take precautions as a spotty-faced student, who was merely amazed that he had

170

managed to get laid at all given his string-bean physique and embarrassing size-thirteen clown feet, he might by now have been the toast of the art world, painting portraits of the royal family. Perhaps he'd have fathered five children to a much nicer woman, all clamouring to be named on his death certificate because they gave an enormous shit that their father had died.

'God help me.' Memories of his own dying father gnawed away at the back of his troubled mind. 'What else? Come on, Hendrik. There must be somebody I can bloody follow up with.'

Several pages in, beyond Abadi's neatly written medical records for the nonagenarian, Van den Bergen found the deeds to a pub by the Singel in the centre, registered as having been bought by a Gustav van Eden in 1941, but with Hendrik van Eden's name on the licence.

'A landlord, eh? Maybe the new owner knows who was close to this guy apart from his GP.' He closed the file, determining to visit Hendrik van Eden's apartment and one-time pub. This man had mattered enough to *someone* that they should want to kill him. In the silence of his cabin, the only words Van den Bergen could hear resonating inside his overtired brain were 'Ed Sijpesteijn' – the only member of the Force of Five who hadn't been recently killed by a heart attack. The only member of the Force of Five who was ostensibly still alive, and who might be holding a grudge…

Knocking up the landlord of the Drie Goudene Honden – the Three Golden Dogs – made Van den Bergen deeply unpopular with the entire locale. At 5.20 a.m., the middle-class home-owners who lived above the smart bars thought nothing of hanging out of their windows, threatening to call the police at best, and take legal action at worst.

'I *am* the police,' Van den Bergen said, flashing his badge and a mirthless grin at one particularly confrontational arsehole –

almost certainly an entitled American frat boy on an exchange year, paid for by Mom and Dad. 'And this is a murder investigation. Get your head back in your apartment and mind your own business. This is Amsterdam, son. You can't call your lawyer every time someone disturbs your beauty sleep.'

Finally the new landlord appeared, bleary-eyed. 'Jesus. I only went to bed three hours ago. We don't open till 10 a.m.'

'Better get the coffee on, then.'

In the living quarters above an old bar that stank of the 1970s – stale cigars, spilled brandy and bad drains – and which showed no evidence of golden dogs whatsoever, unless Van den Bergen counted the giant, drooling golden retriever that snored gently in its dog basket by a yellowed radiator, the new owner of Drie Goudene Honden filled his kettle and took a seat at a battered kitchen table. He scratched at his baggy pants and rubbed a hairy hand over his grubby vest.

'This isn't a sociable hour for landlords, you know.' The landlord looked down at Van den Bergen's giant boots. 'Jesus. Are you in porn?'

Still wearing his gardening gear, Van den Bergen took a seat opposite him and took his notebook out of the vest pocket of his dungarees. 'I'm in law enforcement. I was too big for porn. Now. Hendrik van Eden. You bought the business from him ten years ago. What can you tell me about him?'

The landlord rubbed his bulbous, red-veined nose and blinked hard. 'He was old. Eighty-odd. He wanted to retire. The old fucker drove me into the ground on a deal though.' He lit a cigarette. Brushed back his greasy hair with nicotine-stained fingers. 'Still had all his marbles, I can tell you. He ran a tight ship. Only thing wrong with this place when I bought it was a slipped tile on the roof. Oh, and the concrete in the yard's a pile of shit. Tree roots from a beech on the boundary, Van Eden reckoned. I had the thing chopped down and my concrete's still breaking up like a bastard.'

'There's a smell of drains. Maybe you've got a cracked drain.'

'I'm not going looking for trouble, pal. Drains cost. Old buildings, you see?'

'Was the place in profit? Did he have friends? Enemies? Anything you can tell me about him. Anything.'

Nodding, pouring the coffee from an oily-looking percolator jug, the landlord scratched his backside and smirked. 'Everyone was scared of Van Eden. He was an old war hero, you know. Still came in here to drink, even after I bought the pub from him. Drank like Richard Burton. Quite a man. Quite a temper.'

Van den Bergen looked at the mug the landlord was pouring the coffee into. Realised there were pink lipstick marks around the rim. George would never drink from that cup. He opted not to either. 'So, not popular then?'

'Oh, popular when he was in a good mood. But if you got on the wrong side of him …' He raised a shaggy eyebrow. Coughed. His breath smelled of Marlboros and stale whisky. 'He was one of those wiry old guys who never lost his potency, you know? If he hadn't been running a pub, he'd have run marathons. It takes some mettle to throw the drunks and stoners out when they misbehave. Especially the stag parties from the UK and Germany. They're utter wankers. But Van Eden had big balls and charisma. He spun a cracking war yarn. Talked about his old girlfriend, Ava or Anna or some shit. Anna Groen. That's right. Some wartime chanteuse who was all tits and tambourines. Said he had his heart broken. Talked about a son.'

Van den Bergen shifted his position in the uncomfortable seat. 'A son?'

The landlord nodded slowly, as if his storytelling was still fuelled by single malt. 'Apparently. Don't know the details, though. Maybe he had a kid with the songstress.' He shrugged. Toyed with the curling chest hair that poked through a hole in his vest. 'He certainly didn't have a wife. Jesus. I'm only

173

forty and I don't have a wife! Good women are hard to come by.'

Questioning the landlord's response, Van den Bergen looked pointedly at the lipstick on the cup.

'I have a friend who visits,' he said by way of explanation. 'She's got rubber boots and she's too big for porn, as well. You two should meet.'

'Van Eden ever mention another old war hero called Ed Sijpesteijn?' Van den Bergen asked, ignoring the comment. Feverishly making notes in his diary.

'No. Never heard of him.'

The reception he received at Van Eden's former home was less revealing than the pub. At 7.13 a.m., he arrived at the small mid-century apartment in Bos en Lommer to the west of the city. The door was opened by a bearded man in his mid twenties, who looked the type who did something boring for the council but dabbled in hand-crafted pottery at the weekend.

'Are you related to Hendrik van Eden?' he asked hopefully, curling his lip only slightly at the cool young man's bare feet, stuffed into Birkenstocks. There was a fleeting glimpse of a woman who peered out from the doorway leading to another room and immediately retreated.

Birkenstocks looked Van den Bergen up and down, wiping cereal thoughtfully from his moustache. 'I'm the new tenant. I moved in a fortnight ago.'

Van den Bergen took a step over the threshold.

'Jan!' he heard the woman call out. 'Don't let him in with those boots on, for Christ's sake. Make him take them off at the door. No boots!'

Retreating back onto the coir doormat, Van den Bergen realised suddenly that he had been stripped of his authority. What the hell was he doing there, investigating unofficial murders, wearing his gardening gear like some yokel from the

174

country? Minks had taken his caseload away, and Van den Bergen had inadvertently started to act like some wet-behind-the-ears junior detective: apologetic; placatory. An ageing chief inspector dreading the hulking presence of retirement on the horizon. A grandfather, fearing for his family. A weak man, cowed by the whims of the strong women around him.

'Tell your girl I'll arrest her for obstructing justice if she doesn't shut up about my boots. Okay? Enough about the goddamned boots!'

Birkenstocks swallowed hard. 'Look, man. We're tenants. We didn't know Van Eden. He was some old guy who croaked in the supermarket. That's it.'

'Who's the landlord?'

'Some doctor guy.'

'Abadi?' Van den Bergen's pulse quickened. Had Abadi been stringing him a line? Was his connection with the old men more significant than he had let on?

'No. Something German-sounding. Gartner, maybe. I'd have to dig out my tenancy agreement. We went through a letting agent.'

He jotted the name in his notebook, nodding. 'Who cleared the flat out?'

'His grandson.'

# CHAPTER 24

# London, a sandwich shop in New Cross, then Aunty Sharon's house in Catford, 20 October

'Hendrik van Eden led a secret life.
Why won't you take my calls? Px'

George read Van den Bergen's text and threw her phone back into her bag in disgust. Shivering, she pulled her thick cardigan tighter around her, feeling aches in her muscles that heralded the onset of a crappy virus. Typical. The moment she downed tools, she got ill. But sickness would have to wait.

'Are you Georgina?'

Registering the hand on her shoulder, George turned around to find a young woman standing over her. The woman wore a hijab but was otherwise dressed like any other girl of her age – skinny jeans, a clinging long-sleeved top and a fashionable mohair coat. Behind her stood a girl who looked to be in her late teens. She too wore a hijab on her head, but was clad in the full-length, loose-fitting black smock that was typical of ultra-devout Muslim women. Her face looked tiny, surrounded by the swathes of black fabric, George thought.

'Yes. Thanks for coming.'

'I'm Qamar,' she said. Her South East London accent was tinged with a hint of Middle Eastern intonation. 'I've come to interpret for Ishtar, here. Your father says you're a Cambridge academic.'

George swallowed hard, remembering the fury and disgust etched into Sally Wright's face as she'd been summarily dismissed from her rooms. At that moment, George was an academic with no fixed abode. But she wasn't about to reveal her shameful fall from grace to a stranger. 'Yep. That's me. I've published studies on women in prison and inmates' mental health. I co-wrote a book about trafficking, too.' She lowered her voice and spoke quickly, as though the words burned her tongue. 'A *Sunday Times* non-fiction bestseller. I doubt you've heard of it.'

With Ishtar seated opposite her, furtively looking at anyone who entered the near-deserted sandwich shop on a quiet New Cross side street, George wondered if this impromptu interview would bear fruit.

'I'm trying to get an understanding of your journey from Syria to London, Ishtar.'

George smiled as warmly as possible while Qamar translated. She took the opportunity to knock back two ibuprofen that she found in the bottom of her bag, willing them to kick in swiftly as she swallowed them down with cheap instant coffee.

Ishtar spoke haltingly, between sips of Fanta. George received the translation in bursts from the girl's companion.

'My family's from Aleppo,' she said. 'My father was an academic too – that's why I agreed to speak to you, I suppose. He was a brilliant mathematician, working at the university. We made the mistake of living in a part of the city that was overtaken by rebels. I guess my father should have been quicker to get us out. The fighting was already dreadful, bombs exploding on a regular basis. My mother reminisced about a peaceful, beautiful city – an Aleppo I just didn't recognise.' Ishtar looked at the bubbles rising to the surface of her drink. 'I wish we could have left before it got really bad.' A single tear broke free, betraying her apparent stoicism. 'But my parents were afraid to move my brother because of his illness.'

The diary of Rivka Zemel immediately sprang to mind. George recalled the reluctance of Rivka's father to secure passage to Britain or America because of Shmuel's delicate health. Prisoners of fortune, caught between the conquering devil and a deep North Sea. 'What's wrong with your brother?'

Wiping her face with a trembling right hand, Ishtar looked down at her lap. Toyed with the fabric of her robe. 'He had cerebral palsy.'

'Had?'

She looked up to a damp patch on the sandwich shop's ceiling and inhaled deeply. 'Assad denied dropping a bomb containing Sarin gas. The rebels swore he was behind it. The Russians had another story.' Tugging violently at a frayed patch on her left sleeve, her chin dimpled. 'The dead were mostly children. You can't smell Sarin gas. But if you inhale it, the choking starts quickly. Then comes vomiting. Foaming at the mouth. And the eyes ...' She said something to Qamar that George didn't catch, and which the interpreter didn't translate. Drank from her Fanta, regaining her composure. 'My mother and my brother died. My father and I had nothing to stay for except a half-bombed house and a lifetime of bad memories.'

'I'm so sorry,' George said, wondering how it would feel when Letitia eventually succumbed to her 'fucked pulmonaries' and her 'sickle-cell anaemics' – if the cigarettes didn't get her first. But Letitia was in the midst of a war only with herself. Silly cow. 'So, how did you get out?'

Ishtar shook her head. 'We spent all the money we had left. We were lucky. Most people just try to get to the refugee camp in Turkey. I've heard it's a waking nightmare. Anyway, there's this man. I don't know how my father managed to find out about him, but, as you can imagine, there's no shortage of people trying to flee the war.'

'A Syrian?'

'Yes. But he has contacts in the Netherlands.'

George sat up straight. 'Contacts? You mean there's more than one? Do you know their names?'

Chewing her lip, Ishtar spoke again to her companion without being translated.

Looking questioningly at Qamar, George tried to keep her excitement to herself, though her breathing quickened. *Come on! Come on! Say it's Den Bosch, for God's sake. Then order will be restored in the bloody galaxy and we can all pay our bills.* 'What's she saying?'

The two continued what sounded like a heated exchange for several minutes, much to George's frustration. Finally, Qamar turned to her. 'She won't give you the names. They're dangerous men.'

'Jesus!' George said, slapping the table so her cup rattled in its saucer. Apologising profusely when the Syrian girls both jumped. 'Seriously, though. What are you both worried about now? You're here! You're safe! This is New Cross, not Aleppo. You're more likely to get chronic earache from Stormzy than suffer retribution from Assad or some Dutch nutcases. Whoever the main man is, he's had your money. He's long gone.'

Ishtar shook her head and began to speak, as Qamar translated. 'There's no guarantee I'll get to stay, if my asylum case fails. I'll be deported. The trafficker in Syria isn't someone I want to mess with. And the Dutchman has people working for him everywhere. In the Netherlands. Over here. In the Muslim community.' She studied George's face cautiously. Narrowed her eyes. 'Why do you want a name? I thought this was all anonymous, that it was for an academic study.'

Taking her napkin and polishing her unused cutlery until it shone, George realised this vulnerable girl deserved the truth. So she told her about the truck found in the Port of Amsterdam and the scores of people who had almost lost their lives in amongst the greenhouse-grown courgettes and red peppers bound for Britain. 'One dead girl, Ishtar. Isn't one dead girl one too many? What if more had died? I hear a couple of the men have been left with brain damage because of oxygen deprivation. Men like your dad. Women like your mum. They all trusted this guy and he took their money and piled them into an unventilated truck like cattle.'

But the girl remained steadfastly silent.

'Was he called Frederik Den Bosch? The Dutch trafficker, I mean. Did you travel over in one of his lorries?'

George watched her interviewee's eyes for the smallest tell. Dilated pupils. A surfeit of blinking. But there was nothing beyond a subtle paling of her olive complexion. 'What about Bosch, Boom & Tuin? Forest, Tree and Garden? It's a florists' supplier.'

Ishtar bit the inside of her cheek. Qamar nudged her in the ribs discreetly. There it was. The same company name had cropped up again.

'Please give me a name,' George asked. She reached out, hoping to take Ishtar's left hand as a gesture of solidarity.

The young woman looked at George's hand in horror. Glanced down at her frayed sleeve. Her eyes hardened. Defiantly, she wrenched up the fabric to show a stump where her arm had been severed just above the elbow. 'See why I don't want to take chances?' There was barely restrained anger in her voice. 'If I get deported, I get more of this. Blown up by Assad or the Russians. Shot or defiled by Daesh. If I talk about my trafficker ...' She looked over at the woman behind the counter, who was busy mashing boiled eggs and blithely singing along to Whitney Houston on Radio 2, then glanced back to Qamar for corroboration. 'My father and I could be killed in our beds. I just want to lie low and get through this. Get permission to stay in the UK.' She fixed her eyes on George; eyes that had seen too much devastation. 'Nobody will ever marry a one-armed girl, but it's better than being dead, Georgina McKenzie.'

The two Syrian women started to talk in their native tongue, with Qamar seemingly disagreeing with Ishtar. Repeatedly, George heard the Arabic word for doctor come up in their exchange.

'Doctor? What doctor?'

But though she pressed them for an explanation, none was forthcoming. In a billowing cloud of black fabric, Ishtar stood and the two of them left.

Aunty Sharon's house felt like it had been sucked dry of its soul with only her in it. Lying in Tinesha's bed, feeling like she had been trampled underfoot by a herd of angry bulls, George mulled over her interview. Forest, Tree and Garden. There was something in the name. And the mention of a doctor. Had they been discussing her academic prowess, or was a doctor somehow involved with the trafficking enterprise? How wide was the network's reach, if it had tentacles in Syria, the Netherlands and the UK?

'Knock knock. Do you want to come down and watch the TV?' Her father had suddenly appeared in the doorway to the bedroom, carrying a cup of something steaming hot. He made his way to the battered bedside cabinet, covered in One Direction stickers and other hallmarks of her cousin's peak teen years. Set the cup down on a coaster. He felt her forehead with the back of his hand. 'You've got a temperature.'

'I feel like shit,' George said, sitting up, feeling like an over-grown child in her winceyette pyjamas. Her teeth clacked. Fucking flu. Great.

181

'I'm just downstairs if you want me. There's this reality show on where a bunch of engineers have to build an escape vehicle out of crash-site bits.'

'Coals to Newcastle for you. Knock yourself out, Papa. I'm going to sit up here and feel sorry for myself while I still can.'

'They're all back tomorrow.' He wore a look of weary resignation on his face. His posture bowed at the neck and shoulders. Life with Letitia the Dragon was clearly burdensome. He'd exchanged one marauding captor for another, except Letitia specialised in pillaging the spirit, rather than the flesh.

'God help us all.'

With her father gone, George opened Rivka Zemel's diary, picking up where she had left off. The menfolk in the Zemel household had been ordered to register for 'work'. But as they suspected, and history had borne out, 'work' had more sinister connotations.

*15 August 1942*
*We left everything in the middle of the night. Papa allowed us to carry only one suitcase each, containing the bare essentials – clothes, a book each, Mama's Sabbath candlesticks and a handful of old photos: my grandparents on their wedding day; my father in his prayer shawl at his bar mitzvah; Mama and Papa holding Shmuel as a baby; me in a darling knitted hat, skating on the frozen Keizersgracht, holding Mama's hand. Kaars had given us clear instructions not to tell a soul as to our intentions. We couldn't even say goodbye to our neighbours. None of that mattered, however, as the Verhagens were risking everything to ensure our safety. The 'oproeping' – the call-up for work – is not a risk worth taking, given the fate of Jews further east, under Nazi occupation. We know we're not wanted in the Fatherland and its annexed territory.*

*As I sit here, writing this diary entry in the same patch of space where I've been bedding down now for almost a month, it now feels unremarkable. I suppose we're comfortable enough. I recall, however, that on the first night in our little sanctuary I felt terribly claustrophobic and frightened. Though I've worked in this house as a domestic for years, I'd never slept here. It smells different to home. The boards creak differently to those in our house. But worst, that night, was the anticipation of what might come ... By morning, it would be clear to all that we had absconded. The Germans are meticulous record-keepers and it was hardly likely they would just give up on looking for us. Had anybody seen us leave or followed us here? Would some visitor to the Verhagen house realise that four Jewish fugitives lived in their midst?*

*I needn't have worried, though, because Mr Verhagen had constructed a space of such genius and cunning that it would take a determined sleuth a good long while to work out that there was a hiding place between the grand salon at the front of the house and the dining room at the back: the room between the rooms, masquerading as a chimney breast. The first few weeks were a trial, as we got used to having no privacy beyond a blanket that Mama had strung up around the toilet bucket and the separate ablutions bucket. How perfectly horrid for Kaars to have to empty the waste bucket every morning! The embarrassment was intense, and I have to admit that I felt as though I were no better than a beast when he first carried it out, covered in newspaper. I wonder that Famke does not challenge him. Apparently, they have told her I've left through necessity and won't be coming back.*

*But beyond discomfort, rather more of a challenge is to survive in this cramped, windowless space without going insane. Dear diary, we are cooped up in nothing more than* a cupboard with no respite from the mood swings and terrible habits of one another. Shmuel coughs constantly. His asthma seems worse in this poorly ventilated space. Papa is ill-tempered much of the time and Mama has withdrawn into herself, becoming terribly quiet. She embroiders all day long, using the thread that Mrs Verhagen sourced for her. At least it keeps her occupied. I have encouraged them all to spend at least fifteen minutes each day, walking on the spot. We all get unbearably stiff.

Kaars and the other members of the Force of Five do visit, however. These are the highlights of our otherwise identically long, long days. The boys bring newspapers, telling of the further segregation of the Jews in the city. So many Jewish Amsterdamers have been transported elsewhere, perhaps never to return. Those who remain are all wearing the yellow stars emblazoned with 'Jew' in black lettering that is supposed to resemble Hebrew. But spirits remain high. There is talk of the Allied forces gaining in strength. The Nazis continue to take a battering on the Eastern Front. Surely our situation cannot last indefinitely.

For my part, Ed's visits are the most welcome. He brings news of the Force of Five's exploits. They have been tearing down Nazi propaganda posters around town and helping other Jewish families and some homosexuals to find refuge among sympathetic families. I was so desperate to feel the sun on my face and the wind in my hair and to walk in the park, hand in hand with my love, that when Anna Groen came by with Hendrik and offered, once again, to bleach my hair, I agreed.

Through some act of great stealth and cunning, Hendrik has managed to procure falsified papers for me. When I asked him how, he tapped his nose and winked. I didn't dare press him on the matter. So, last night, Anna and I crept up to the Verhagens' bathroom and bleached my hair.

*It was such a joy to have a bath and to wash my hair properly after spending an age relying on a good strip-wash in a bucket and nothing more. It's a wonder Ed hasn't abandoned me for smelling like a dead cat!*

*In the middle of the night, despite Mama and Papa's protestations, my beau and I left the Verhagen house in as stealthy a fashion as we could muster and went for a walk. It was there, beneath the great oak in the Vondelpark, that Ed swore we would marry after the war. But he made me an unexpected offer. He told me that he feared for the future, despite what he'd said in front of the others about the Allied forces' hopeful prospects. He said that I should trust nobody save him and Kaars. Then, he asked if I wanted to be smuggled out of the Netherlands to America.*

Feeling the painkillers kick in, making her drowsy, George closed the diary and shut her eyes momentarily. Her thoughts wandered to the subject of trafficking, and how traffickers provided a much-needed service where the state failed desperate people. The only difference between the likes of Ed Sijpesteijn, with his offer to smuggle Rivka onto a ship to the US, and those who ran trafficking services out of Syria to the UK, was that modern-day traffickers were in it purely for gain and usually exploited their customers. But there was a definite grey area around trafficking – a blurred distinction between rebellious heroism and criminality.

Having drifted off, George was jolted awake a while later by her phone buzzing with a text. It was from Marie.

```
'Den Bosch owns Bosch, Boom & Tuin
— a subsidiary of Groenten Den Bosch.
André Baumgartner is listed as a
company director.'
```

How had she missed it? Boom – tree, and tuin – garden were Baum and Garten in German. Baumgartner. Dr Baumgartner.

'Oh, George. You thick, thick bastard,' she told her reflection in Tinesha's dressing-table mirror.

But as she tried to make sense of the connection between the respected old psychiatrist and a neo-Nazi farmer half his age, her reflection in the mirror wobbled at the same time as she heard a loud crash from below.

'Papa!'

## CHAPTER 25

# *The Den Bosch farm near Nieuw-Vennep, then houses in De Pijp, later*

'Why did you deliver a veg box to my daughter, you weirdo?' Van den Bergen had Den Bosch by the collar and was pulling him up to eye level. No mean feat, given Den Bosch was built like a side of beef.

Investigating Hendrik van Eden's bloodline on the side could wait. After a morning of dealing with urban congestion woes and dangerous drivers in his tedious new role as senior traffic hump, Van den Bergen had used his lunch break to speed out to Den Bosch's farm and confront the tattooed, shifty, gold-toothed prick about Tamara's gift. The irony of his committing a traffic offence or two en route was not lost on him. George would laugh. But George wasn't there. Angry Opa was flying solo.

'Answer me!' He bent Den Bosch backwards over his desk, but Den Bosch was strong and quickly pushed him off.

'Police brutality, eh? Over a veg box? Groenten Den Bosch is a wholesaler, you fucking idiot. I don't give out sampler boxes to private households. I supply British supermarkets. Is your daughter Tesco? Is she?' He brushed himself down with some drama and much obvious contempt. 'You're jumping to ridiculous conclusions because you can't solve your case. It's not my fault some little Arab cow died in the back of one of my *stolen* trucks.'

'Show some respect for the dead, you pig!' Van den Bergen noticed florid red scratches on his cheek. Pointed to them. 'Where did you get those?'

'I'm a farmer. I run a farm with mature hedging that's just been cut back hard for the winter. Have you never got scratched to shit by hawthorn?' Den Bosch touched his cheek absently and scowled. Dirt beneath his fingernails attested to a working life spent with his hands in the earth. 'You're a gardener, aren't you?'

Observing Den Bosch through narrowed eyes, Van den Bergen advanced towards him again. But his quarry was too quick and had already repositioned himself with the bulk of the desk between them. 'What the hell do you know about my hobbies? Was that you or one of your men at the allotment this morning? I know someone was following me. I'm not bloody stupid.'

Den Bosch's secretary walked in at that moment, carrying a stack of lever-arch folders. She was a stout, well-scrubbed woman of advanced years. The most excitement she ever saw was probably a cake sale at church.

'Oh, sorry, Frederik. I didn't realise you had company.'

'Chief Inspector Van den Bergen was just leaving, weren't you?'

Van den Bergen tried and failed to stifle a low growl. 'I haven't finished with you,' he said. 'You're up to something. I know you are. You and that imam.' He squeezed his index finger and thumb together. 'I'm this close to having enough evidence for it all to stand up in court.'

Den Bosch folded his arms, revealing those carefully executed Nazi tattoos as his shirtsleeves rode up. He flashed a smile that would have the owner of a cash-for-gold branch peeing with excitement. 'If you've got a warrant, arrest me.' He chuckled smugly. 'Except you're not on this case anymore, are you? A little birdy called Roel de Vries told me that you got your bony arse kicked off it.' With his secretary bearing witness to this confrontation, Den Bosch moved back around the desk. Ushered Van den Bergen to the door as though he were a guest who had merely come to the end of a sanctioned visit. 'Know what I'd do, Paul?'

'Paul? Do you think this is some kind of joke?' Van den Bergen straightened up, hoping to use his height to gain an advantage over this chump.

But this particular farmer was not easily intimidated, slapping the policeman on the back as if they were old pals. 'Paul, with your cabin at Sloterdijkermeer, and your apartment with the nice French doors onto the balcony where McKenzie likes to have a sly smoke, and your daughter, Tamara, who may or may not enjoy organic courgettes in the safety of her nice Amstelveen starter-home … My dear Paul, I'd keep my nose out of respectable businessmen's private lives, if I were you. You never know what terrible fate might befall you and yours. I believe the darkies call it karma. I'd call it common sense.'

With Den Bosch's unsavoury words leaving a foul taste in his mouth, Van den Bergen hastened away from the flat expanses of the countryside, where he felt naked and exposed, back towards the relative normality of the city and the enclosed safety of police headquarters, swallowing down a veritable eruption of stomach acid.

'Cheeky bastard,' he told the roadworks, conjuring in his mind's eye an image of Den Bosch, with his tattooed arms and that smug expression on his face. 'I'm going to bring you down, you disrespectful, exploitative son of a bitch.'

He called his home number on his car phone. Tamara picked up.

'What is it, Dad?' The baby was crying in the background.

'Do me a favour. Don't open the door to anybody. Stay in. It's wet anyway.'

'But I've got to get some bits from the house. I've run out of—'

'Text me a list. I'll go to the shop. Stay away from the windows.'

'Dad! That's ridiculous.'

'Just do it, will you?'

He hung up. Agitated, he parked badly in a space that was too tight for his E-Class. Jogged from the car park into the Elandsgracht building, acutely aware that he was late and that his tardiness wouldn't go unnoticed. As he flung his coat onto his chair, Marie and Elvis looked at him quizzically, but he shook his head. He dialled George. Straight to voicemail.

'George. It's me. I know you're in the UK but please, please be vigilant. I've just had a run-in with that prick Den Bosch and he knew too much about our lives for comfort. We're being watched.'

Behind him, a man cleared his throat. 'Being watched, are you?'

Van den Bergen turned to find Roel de Vries, standing with his hands behind his back, scowling.

'You.'

'Yes. Me. Are you harassing my witness during lunch, Paul? I hope not.'

Van den Bergen grabbed his lesser colleague by the forearms. 'Get a warrant for his arrest. For Christ's sake, Roel. He's as dirty as they come.'

Slowly, de Vries shook his head and tutted. 'I'm not about to engage in such slipshod police work. Especially when my interviews with the victims of the Port of Amsterdam debacle yielded not a single halal sausage. Den Bosch is clean. You've been looking in the wrong place. But there's an ex-con from Utrecht who recently got out for drug smuggling and car theft that my team is looking into. Bobby de Wit. His father was a Manchester United supporter and called him after Bobby Charlton. That's grounds for suspicion right there.' His scowl evaporated as he bellowed with laughter at his own joke. 'Oh, I think we have our man. He fits the bill. He was even spotted in Amsterdam the night the Den Bosch truck got stolen.' He slapped Van den Bergen on the back. 'Sometimes, all you need is a fresh outlook.' His breath smelled of eggs and cigars. 'Now, how are you getting on with our great city's highways and byways?'

'What do you want, Roel?'

'Marie. I've come to claim your lovely IT girl as my own. Minks approved it.'

Van den Bergen studied his colleague's wind-burnt face, with that absurd greasy comb-over he wore and the joke tie. Garfield, today. 'No way. Tell Minks it's over my dead body. You've got your own team. Get your own IT expert to research Bobby bloody Charlton.'

Roel's expression soured again. 'It might well be over your dead body if you keep aggravating taxpayers without solid grounds.'

Marie stood up abruptly, her face flushed bright red. A blotchy rash crawled up her neck. 'I'm not coming with you, Inspector de Vries. I'm sorry. My place is here with Chief Inspector Van den Bergen or at home in bed.'

Holding his hand out, Van den Bergen shook his head. 'No, Marie. That's really kind, but you mustn't jeopardise your—'

'I'm not coming. I have a *very* contagious skin complaint.' She scratched at the two ripe spots on her chin that Van den Bergen had been careful not to look at until now. '*Very* contagious. In fact, I should be off sick at home. So, it's your choice. I either go home right now, or I spread my skin disease among your team. Dirk, here and Van den Bergen have immunity, you see.'

Roel de Vries paled visibly. 'What is your … er … complaint?'

'Emblisticised hepititoid nodules. Very painful and can cause impotence in men.' She smiled sincerely, ran her hand through the greasy folds of her red-brown hair and sat back down, as though she knew there would be no further challenge.

'Oh. Is that the time?' Roel said, glancing down at his watch. Wiping his upper lip and adjusting his tie at the neck. 'I'll be in touch.' With a disconcerted half-smile plastered across his waxy face, he strode off down the corridor.

'What's happened to Abadi?' Van den Bergen shouted after him.

'I'm cutting him loose.'

'Bobby Charlton, my arse,' Van den Bergen said to Elvis and Marie. He trudged over to the coffee machine and made each of his junior detectives an almost drinkable cup of coffee. 'I've got to nail Den Bosch,' he said, returning with the mugs.

'Boss. You love me. All these years, and you never said a word.' Elvis looked into the beaker of grey frothy liquid with an eyebrow raised.

Van den Bergen cleared his throat of acid and belched in response. 'That was a brave thing you did there, Marie. Thanks. You didn't have to.'

The red blotches on Marie's neck crawled northwards to meet the flushed skin of her face. She dropped her gaze to her keyboard, fingers tapping away as if he hadn't just paid her a compliment. 'Thanks for the coffee. Do you mind if I frame it, rather than drink it, boss?'

But Van den Bergen didn't register the playful jibe. He was thinking about Saif Abadi, no doubt collecting his shoelaces and belt at that very moment, as Roel de Vries checked him out of his two-star, high-security accommodation and booted him back onto the street. If he was quick, he could corner the doctor, whom they didn't have enough evidence against to detain, before he left the building.

'Elvis. Fancy a little door to door?'

When Marie shouted after him – 'Oh I meant to tell you. Den Bosch has a subsidiary company called Bosch, Boom & Tuin. He co-owns it with Baumgartner' – Van den Bergen was too engrossed in explaining his plan to Elvis to hear her.

'Ah, Dr Abadi,' he said, relieved to see they'd caught him before he'd had the chance to hail a cab or be picked up.

The doctor was looking rather more dishevelled than he had at the time of his arrest. Days without a shave had given the dark-haired man a beaten-down air. The scruffy clothes didn't help. Van den Bergen registered a twinge of guilt coming from a place deep within him. It never sat well with him to arrest the wrong man, and his policeman's gut instinct told him this doctor was no criminal – merely caught up in somebody else's chicanery. He offered his hand by way of apology.

Abadi merely looked down at his oversized palm and turned away, clutching his effects in a clear bag. 'I've got nothing to say to you.'

'Please. I need your help. This is nothing to do with your patients' deaths. It's about another case – a dead twelve-year-old Syrian girl who was treated like a side of beef in the back of a heavy goods vehicle, along with fifty-three of her countrymen. Two sustained brain damage on a journey that should have been a fresh start, no matter how illegal. Please. First, do no harm, right?'

As the Syrian doctor scrutinised him, evident animosity in his weary-looking black eyes, Van den Bergen forced a conciliatory smile onto his face. Realised he must look such a fake to this wronged man. Where the hell was George when he needed her? She was so much better at connecting with anyone who wasn't white. She'd find it so easy to explain to the Syrian doctor how his shared cultural heritage meant he had a far better chance than Van den Bergen at getting Den Bosch's tenants to open up about their landlord and their journey to the Netherlands. And she wouldn't make it sound like the doctor was being used.

'What are the magic words?' Abadi asked, pulling his jacket on, studying Van den Bergen's face so intently that he started to squirm.

'We were just following a line of enquiry.'

'You jumped to conclusions. I understand the case had never even been officially opened and now any investigation has been dropped at the say-so of your superior. My solicitor has told me to sue. So, again, what are the magic words?'

'Sorry. I'm sorry.'

At the addresses Elvis had noted as being Den Bosch-owned houses, rented to immigrants, Abadi was welcomed inside while Van den Bergen was told to wait in the hallway like an unwelcome door-to-door salesman. The interiors were as grim as the exteriors – run-down, dirty, smelling strongly of damp beneath the wholesome cooking smells. He exchanged glances with Elvis, sneezing repeatedly as mildew and black mould stung in his nostrils.

'Jesus. This is such a waste of time. I don't know why George thought Abadi could help.'

'I know. These are the people who slammed doors in our faces already, boss. They're not stupid. Even if they trust him, if they know he's representing us, they'll keep schtum.'

Van den Bergen nodded. Sat down on the bottom step of an uncarpeted staircase, wishing he could understand the conversation that was taking place over coffee in the kitchen – the only room in the house that wasn't being used as a bedroom. Arabic, or something. It was the fourth house they'd been inside. Abadi reported that the others had revealed little other than a story of travel west in a variety of trucks and the odd train – a slick yarn that had been worn smooth in the retelling. But no names.

Finally, Abadi emerged from the kitchen.

'You look like you've seen a ghost,' Van den Bergen said, eyeing his pallor and blank stare with excitement, feeling certain there had been a revelation worth hearing inside that kitchen.

'I'm going home,' Abadi said, pushing past them. 'I should never have got involved.'

Outside, the rain fell in slanting rods, blackening the already grimy facades of the houses, as though a demon had breathed on them, marking them out as the hellish places where the damned lived.

Abadi hastened down the street towards the tram, not looking back at Van den Bergen.

'Wait!' Elvis shouted, jogging to catch up.

But Abadi merely glanced up at the black squares of the overlooking windows, apprehension evident in his eyes even from this angle. Van den Bergen sped up. Pulled alongside.

'What the hell went on in there?'

'You never saw me today. I came out of the holding cells and went straight home to my family.' His hands were stuffed deeply into the pockets of his suit jacket. His hair had flattened to his skull in the rain. It was hard to tell if the water on his cheeks was rain or fearful tears.

Van den Bergen grabbed him by the shoulder. 'They gave you names, didn't they? Who is it, Saif? Tell me and I can make sure nobody else dies needlessly.'

Still walking at a pace Van den Bergen wouldn't have thought possible in a man much smaller than him, Abadi ploughed on, only slowing as he approached the tram tracks.

'Names! For God's sake. Give me names!'

The doctor stopped abruptly. His voice was low and his words staccato. 'Look. There's an imam involved.'

'Yeah. We already know,' Elvis said. 'Abdullah al Haq. He's the one who's always mouthing off on the TV. Runs the big mosque in—'

'You don't understand. This guy is dangerous. He has clerics coming to the mosque to recruit for Daesh. People like me – moderate Muslims – are risking life and limb to leave Syria. But there are scores of young men and women from well-established, settled families, converts from privileged Calvinist backgrounds, who are queuing up to go there and fight for the Islamic State.' He tapped the side of his head. 'Kids who are vulnerable. Mentally ill. Easily influenced and violent as hell. That's the sort of army of thugs this imam has at his disposal. He's going to hear that I've been digging. Speaking to you. He'll send some lunatic after me and my beheading will be on YouTube by Monday morning.'

'So al Haq is a people trafficker? But he's not got a ready supply of heavy goods vehicles. He's in cahoots.' Van den Bergen pushed his drenched hair from his forehead and wiped the freezing rainwater from his eyes. A tram was approaching, rattling towards them at speed. He had to get the other names from Abadi before he boarded the tram home. With a fast-beating heart, Van den Bergen sensed that this was his only chance.

'Tell me who else. Den Bosch is running the show, isn't he? Tell me.'

Abadi shook his head. 'It's far worse than that.' There was a haunted look in his eyes.

The beleaguered Syrian doctor stepped in front of the tram before the driver had a chance to slam on his brakes. The collision was a violent end. Saif Abadi was carried by momentum within feet of the tram stop, but when his body fell to the ground, he was unequivocally dead.

# CHAPTER 26

## *The house of Kaars Verhagen,*
## *Oud Zuid, much later*

'Please let me in,' Van den Bergen asked Cornelia Verhagen.
'I have some difficult questions that need answering.'

Kaars Verhagen's daughter looked flustered. With one arm
in the sleeve of her coat, it was clear he had caught her at a
bad time.

'I'm sorry, Chief Inspector. I'm in a hurry. I've got an
appointment at an auctioneer's. I'm selling Dad's art collection.
He had some absolute beauties – worth a small fortune. I
desperately need the money to finish this building work. You
can't sell a house half-renovated.'

After the time Van den Bergen had had, being hauled over
the coals by Minks for roping Abadi into an unsanctioned
interrogation of Den Bosch's tenants, a move that had resulted
in the doctor's suicide, he couldn't bear the thought that his
day might end like this – being thwarted by Cornelia Verhagen
at a point where the case needed desperately to be cracked
wide open. *Suspended, pending investigation*. Words he'd never
hoped to hear, and yet they were ringing in his ears. His career
was over. Unless he could finish what he'd started.

'Ms Verhagen. Please. I've just seen your father's family doctor leap in front of a tram at the mention of someone implicated in a trafficking case. I've got a truckload of dead and dying Syrian refugees and four murdered old men. The common denominator is whoever Abadi was trying to escape through death. Call it a policeman's intuition, but I feel sure there's a people-smuggling killer out there, and I need to find him or her and put a stop to them.'

A neighbour poked her head out of her doorway, shooting a glance at them both, neck craned and ears almost visibly pricked, like some overweight meerkat. She began to sweep her already spotless step.

'Can we go inside?' Van den Bergen asked. 'I'm sure you can reschedule with the auctioneer. If there's good money to be made, they'll be bending over backwards to please you.'

He could see Cornelia Verhagen's resolve crumbling as she removed her coat and held the door open, beckoning him inside.

Over milky coffee and stroopwafels that would cause a veritable fountain of stomach acid later, Van den Bergen started to quiz her.

'I need to know more about Hendrik van Eden. Arnold van Blanken's children knew everything about their father, even down to what he had for dinner the night before he died. They were a very close-knit family. Brechtus Bruin's son, Eric, let us rummage through all his dad's belongings in the garage. His life story seems straightforward and well documented. But there are two I know little about. Ed, your father's cousin, for one …'

Cornelia Verhagen ran her finger around the rim of the coffee cup, eyes flitting to the clock on the wall. 'I never knew Ed. He and Dad were like brothers, but he went missing suddenly during the war. I already told you this. The SS were shooting suspected resistance members. Dad and the others just assumed Ed had been unlucky.'

'But his body was never found.'

'No.' Her eyes moved to the clock yet again. Clearly, her thoughts were on the auctioneer and not the case.

Van den Bergen was tempted to slap his hand on the rough oak table to get her attention. But then he remembered how he'd struggled for money when his own father had died. The old man had left a string of unpaid bills and eye-watering debt for a Dutchman. Clearly hadn't got the memo: '*Zuinigheid is een deugd*' – No. Sadly, the old Dutch insistence that 'Thriftiness is a virtue' had meant nothing to Van den Bergen senior. Profligate old sod.

'Look, I know it's tough when a parent dies and leaves you in the lurch financially. But please, try to remember everything you can. Dr Abadi threw himself in front of a tram because he was scared to death – literally. Maybe he was frightened of whoever killed the Force of Five. Can you think of anything odd about your father around the time of his death? Anyone he was being intimidated by, or who cropped up just once too often in his life?'

Sighing, Cornelia picked up another stroopwafel and bent the syrupy cookie until it broke in two. She pointed a fragment of it at Van den Bergen.

'Dad became obsessive about something just before he died. He was …' She frowned, searching for the right words. 'Furtive. Excitable.'

'Oh?' Van den Bergen sat up straighter.

'He said he was involved in "historical research". That's what he called it. I thought it was something to do with his art collection. But whenever I tried to quiz him on it, he clammed up. Honestly, I've never known him so tight-lipped. Arnold and Brechtus came round and I could hear them talking in low whispers. They shooed me out of the living room as though it was top secret! Or maybe Dad was getting dementia.' She shrugged and raised an eyebrow. 'Maybe they all were. At that age, they're forgetful at the best of times, though my dad kept his marbles until he got into his early nineties. But you know, a few years makes a lot of difference when you're heading for one hundred. They start talking gibberish sometimes, especially if they're ill. Dad was often rough after his chemo, of course. It leaves them very susceptible to infection.'

'I know.' Memories flickered in Van den Bergen's mind of the times he'd rushed his father to hospital in the car, because it had been quicker than calling an ambulance. His old man with a raging temperature in the passenger seat. He'd spent sixteen months living in the shadow of death, preparing for the end on an almost fortnightly basis. In the hospital. Out of the hospital. All those memories were coming back.

This case was killing him. But it had also lit a fire within him that wasn't just down to his hiatus hernia.

'So, your father gets a bee in his bonnet about something historical. Possibly something in his past?'

'I hadn't thought of it like that. Yes. Maybe.'

'Okay.' Van den Bergen started to scribble notes into his notebook, beneath the sketch of George he'd been doing from memory. Disconcerting. He'd forgotten the line of her lips and she'd only been gone a couple of days. 'Now. Hendrik. He's the one I just can't find out anything of substance about. No wife, no siblings, no children – though I've had one person say he had a son and one person mention a grandson. I thought you, of all people, would be the most clued up, since your father's house acted as a hub for the friends.'

He looked around the kitchen, through the doorway of the dining room to the hall beyond, visualising the room within the rooms and wondering what George had found out from Rivka Zemel's diaries. Surely she would have been in touch if she had happened upon a significant detail. Thinking wistfully of her, he drank in the smell of unfinished timber studwork and the mustiness of exposed bricks. He imagined the old men sitting around the little kitchen table mid building work, chewing over nine decades of secrets with false teeth.

'Funnily enough, Hendrik didn't come round when Dad had Brechtus and Arnold over. I don't think he was privy to Dad's "historic research". But then, if it was about the art collection, Hendrik just wasn't that kind of guy. He was brusque and practical.' She smiled. 'Very dry. Everyone had him down as a rare wit and charismatic. But Hendrik always scared me a bit, if I'm honest. A very private man. The rest lived in each other's pockets for as long as I can remember, I guess because they'd socialised as families once wives and children came onto the scene. Hendrik dipped in and out. I don't think he ever got over losing Anna Groen.'

'What happened there?' Van den Bergen asked. His coffee had gone cold and so had this line of enquiry, it seemed.

'She ran off with another man. That's all I know.'

'And Rivka Zemel. Did she die?'

Cornelia looked blankly at Van den Bergen. 'I have no idea if she's living or dead.' Her expression was suddenly stony. 'You snatched those diaries off me. You should know. Now, if you don't mind, I've got paintings to sell.'

Advancing down the cold hallway, Van den Bergen caught a glimpse of large paintings in ornate gilt frames, stacked in the living room against the wall. A room he hadn't been in before. On the walls themselves hung breathtakingly beautiful oil portraits. One depicted a rabbi, carrying the sacred Torah scrolls of the Jews. Without waiting to be invited, he entered to get a closer look.

'The door's this way, Chief Inspector.' Cornelia Verhagen's tone was no longer one of patient indulgence.

Van den Bergen took a sharp intake of breath as he examined an impressionist painting behind the door. 'Is this a Monet?' He stared at the signature in disbelief.

'Well, I might find out if you go.'

'But these are exquisite.' Leafing through the stack, he was certain he spotted a Kandinsky. Turned back to the portrait of the rabbi. 'Is this an Isidor Kaufmann?'

'Goodbye, Chief Inspector.'

Her phone rang. She answered the call, holding the door open for Van den Bergen. 'Dr Verhagen speaking. Yes. I'm on my way.' She shooed him off the step and slammed the door behind him.

Doctor. Van den Bergen had called her Ms, and she hadn't corrected him this time. As he made his way back to his car, he toyed with a theory that caused more of a dyspeptic eruption than the stroopwafels. He texted George.

'Please come back. I miss your lips. Also, think Kaars Verhagen stole art from the Jews in the war. Could Cornelia Verhagen be our murderer? Must check wills again. Px'

# CHAPTER 27

## *South East London, Aunty Sharon's house, 21 October*

*2 March 1943*
*The last few weeks have been intolerable. Word has come through to us that the SS are shooting any freedom fighters they find. Every member of the Force of Five is really worried that their subterfuge will be discovered. Brechtus and Arnold were particularly agitated when they came to the Verhagen house last night. Shmuel has an infection and is struggling to breathe, so the boys didn't come into our little secret room – Papa insisted everyone keep away. I did, however, listen through the wall to their conversation. It was tricky, as Kaars's father had the secret partitions constructed of almost soundproof material, but when I cracked the door a little, I heard enough.*

*Brechtus and Arnold had been arrested earlier in the week and questioned by the SS. They complained that they'd been beaten and held in cells. The SS had somehow got wind that they had constructed some kind of radio device and were contacting the British (which of course, they had). I suspect the boys have been doing this not only to pass on information about our dreaded German invaders but* also to make contact with willing people in England who will help smuggle Jews out of the country.

Ed has begged me to accept his offer of a safe passage to England or America, but Papa insists Shmuel is absolutely too sick to move. The stifling, stuffy air in this beastly little room doesn't help. I'm the lucky one. I can still sneak out at night with my falsified papers. I pressed Hendrik on where he got hold of them, but he merely tapped the side of his nose and winked. Perhaps Anna's singing engagements in the restaurants frequented by the Nazi officers have paved the way for a deal with someone in administration. The Nazis can't all be bad. There must be one or more among them who aren't happy with the way the Jews are being carted off to labour camps on cramped trains. I think there's hardly a Jew left in the city!

Anyway, Brechtus and Arnold were eventually released when their family homes were searched and the transmitting equipment couldn't be found. Fortunately, both of their fathers are wealthy business owners. Brechtus's owns a printing company that the Nazis use to print their propaganda (what irony that Brechtus tears those posters down!) and Arnold's has been co-opted into manufacturing parachutes for the German army. No business owner has wanted to say no to the Germans – even if they were able to – because there's a fortune to be made from the war. I'm sure Papa's old business partner is sitting on a mountain of Nazi gold now!

Anyway, I have no doubt it would have caused problems if the SS had simply flung the boys into prison on an unproven suspicion. Money talks, now more than ever. I have no doubt that the Jewish families that are making good their escape to America are wealthy. There are many diamond merchants in Amsterdam, after all...

Papa doesn't seem to realise that we're fortunate to have

*a little band of heroic fellows who are willing to whisk us to safety for absolutely nothing at all. (Just as well, for our family now has absolutely nothing at all, apart from my parents' wedding rings and a pinkie ring that Papa has allowed me to give to Ed as a betrothal of sorts. Ed has given me a tiny diamond ring in return.)*

*Though Shmuel is sick and we're uncomfortable here – Mama cries herself to sleep at night thanks to her back pain and the feverish torment of being cooped up in a cramped space – we rely on the loyalty and discretion of the Force of Five to stay safe and alive. I can't imagine if one of the boys or one of the Verhagen household…*

George sneezed, putting her compelling read down. Memories of the previous day flooded back: the deafening bang that had shaken the whole house; haring downstairs to find that a brick that had been lobbed through Aunty Sharon's living room window, only narrowly missed hitting Papa; calling the council's emergency board-up service. Had the van driver from the ferry tracked her down? Had the brick been his warning for her to keep her big mouth shut, or simply some kids cutting their teeth on a life of urban terrorism and gangsta-grime? George had to assume the latter, since no violent encore had followed, thankfully. Now, Rivka Zemel's words sucked George back into the wartime world of the diary. Her own woes seemed like child's play compared to the peril that the young Jewish maid had had to endure.

Blowing her nose, she skipped ahead to the following entry. Here was some drama that surpassed all the vandalism and people traffickers that South East London could throw at George, as the Verhagen house was searched by the Nazis…

*I have never been so terrified in all my life. Through the walls, we could hear them shouting at Mr Verhagen and*

*Kaars, though we couldn't make out what was being said.*
*A shot was fired! Had somebody been killed? We held our*
*breath as long as we could, but Shmuel started to cough*
*uncontrollably. Surely the Nazis would be able to hear that.*
*Had I left the door cracked to let in a little air?*

Biting her lip, George found she was holding her own breath.
But though she desperately wanted to carry on reading, the
sudden cacophony of angry voices coming from the hallway
forced her to abandon Rivka's diary and throw off the sweaty
bedclothes.

'Jesus. Here we go,' she muttered.

Below, Letitia's dulcet tones almost made the windows rattle
in their frames.

'Hey. Don't you be defending him, for fuck's sake! He drove
like a nutcase, innit? Them taxi drivers get their licences out
of a lucky bag. Know what I mean?'

Aunty Sharon: 'You're a tight bastard, Letitia. All you had
to do was tip him fifty pence. Fifty bleeding pence, yeah? That's
the difference between you being a greedy cow and a good
person.'

Now, Letitia's voice ascended an octave, and George paused
before opening Tinesha's bedroom door, lest her eardrums
burst or dogs come running from the neighbouring two streets.

'I'm a greedy cow? Is that so? Is that fucking so? Hey. Don't
you be lecturing me about being a good person, when you got
a job and money coming out of your fat arse, lady love! I paid
for the cab, didn't I? Eh?'

'I paid the one going. You want a medal for paying your
way? Who bought that rum for the room?'

Patrice's low voice sounded once, almost certainly in a bid
to intervene in this sisterly set-to. But he was dismissed.

'Less interfering, bwoy,' Aunty Sharon said. 'This ain't your
beef. Go and get the kettle on.'

George stood at the top of the landing, staring at the two overweight, middle-aged black women on the brink of fisticuffs in a narrow hallway that could barely accommodate them. Pointing. Pointing. Hands on hips. Hands waving aggressively as though they added more weight to whatever bullshit argument her mother was coming out with for failing to bung the driver a tip.

'You better watch it, Letitia, or you'll be poking Aunty Shaz's eye out with those nails.'

Suddenly, her aunty was all smiles with outstretched arms. Letitia made do with a grimace that could have stripped paint.

'How are you, my favourite niece? Come and have a cup of tea and we'll tell you all about our holiday, won't we, Letitia?'

'Why you here?' Her mother was less enthusiastic, glowering at George's fluffy slippers.

George bumped fists with Patrice and hugged Tinesha. Ignored her mother. Silly cow. Mustered all the strength she could to drag her fluey body into the kitchen behind them all.

They sat around Aunty Sharon's kitchen table, sipping tea, with her father and Patrice leaning against the kitchen worktop, saying as little as possible, and Tinesha already texting her boyfriend and mates on Snapchat, in a world of her own. George allowed herself to be regaled with tales of how Letitia had started an argument with the maître d' in the hotel dining room because they kept serving up 'well shitty fruit for afters', and how Letitia had given 'them fucking presuming German bastards what-for for nicking my sun lounger at 5 a.m.'. Aunty Sharon corroborated that Letitia, much to the party's minor embarrassment and chagrin, had on three occasions lifted the towel, lilo, dry clothing and beach bag off the purloined sunbeds and tipped them into the pool.

'That's right!' Letitia the Dragon proclaimed, waving her cigarette hand around in an almost perfect figure of eight so that she was surrounded by her own cloud of blue smoke. 'I showed 'em how it be done in the UK, yeah? I says to this fella in Speedos with a gut the size of Deptford hanging over this tiny cock … I says, "Listen, waga waga German wanker! I suh mi duh mi ting."' She stood with hands on hips, reconstructing the scene like a Kingstonian *Crimewatch*, where the victim always wins with a killer put-down to rival any bullet. 'Like it or lump it, man. We didn't win no World War Two for nuffink. Didn't I say that, Shaz?'

'Yeah, George.' A reluctant-sounding titter turned into a hearty guffaw, as though sibling rivalry wasn't even a baby elephant in that small, well-scrubbed room. 'She definitely did. That pimple-dicked German geezer and his Hausfrau didn't know what hit them when we landed.' Aunty Shaz turned serious. 'But in fairness, they had shoved Patrice's towel off in the first place, 'cos he put one across five beds for us when he came back from the club with Tin at 4.30 a.m. First come, first served, right?'

Within five minutes of their overly loud regaling of the Tale of Torremolinos, George's head was pounding. Her paracetamol had started to wear off and the shakes had begun anew.

'Ew. You ill?' Letitia asked, treating her to a look of disgust that could have stripped her nail varnish off. ''Cos I can't be around no invalid with my sickle-cell anaemics. You'd better get a cab and fuck off back up the motorway to Cambridge, 'cos I ain't ready to trade in my extra legroom on TUI for no crappy lickle hole in Bromley Hill cemetery, cheers all the same.'

'What's the matter with you, George? I thought you was working some case in Amsterdam?'

Aunty Sharon had joined in the interrogation, now, and soon George had no option but to reveal that she had decided to leave her long-term lover until he grew a pair. And that she had flu from the stress of his unappreciative behaviour and that whole thing of losing her book deal *and* her tenure *and* her contract work for the police. Or possibly the flu was just down to the air con on the ferry over to the UK. Oh, and that the driver for a dangerous Dutch people trafficker had possibly put a brick through the front window.

'Serious? Oh my days!' Aunty Sharon hastened into the living room and shouted through to the kitchen. 'How come I never noticed this when we was getting out of the cab? Jesus Christ on a bike! Didn't you think to call the emergency glazing? Michael! I left you in charge, man.'

'Don't worry, George,' her father said, oblivious to Sharon's complaint. He placed warm, comforting hands on her shoulder. Smelled of Marlboro cigarettes, strong soap and sandalwood, just like he had when she'd been a little girl. 'You're strong. You can get through this. Get yourself better and fight back! I'll get the *Guardian* tomorrow. You can look for a new job. You know I'll always help.'

'It's not that easy, Papa.' George reached back to place her hand on his, savouring the contact.

It was the spark that lit Letitia's perennially short fuse.

'Oh, I see how this has been playing while we've been away, Shaz,' she shouted, standing up suddenly, reaching over the table and swiping George across the face.

George's cheek stung. Dumbfounded, she stared at her mother as the smouldering fury of the dragon became an inferno. 'What the fuck did you do that for, you mad cow?'

'You looked at me funny. You and him.' She was pointing to George's father with the glowing tip of her cigarette as though it were a smoking gun. '"You know *I'll* help you, George." And you're lapping it up, girl, ain't you? My clever Spanish daddy. That's where I got my brains from. Not my poor old mum. Not this mug who's spent the last thirty years bringing you up right while he was off gallivanting in fucking South America like Crocodile bastard Dundee with extra chorizo.'

Aunty Sharon walked in on the scene, phone already pressed to her ear, wearing a thunderous expression. She covered the mouthpiece. 'Shut it. I'm on the phone to the glazing.'

Patrice sucked his teeth and pushed his way out of the kitchen, opting for the solitude of his bedroom instead. Tinesha clapped her hands over her ears, absently reading the copy of the *Evening Standard* that lay on the table. But now, it was George's turn to ignite.

'*You*? Bringing me up? Are you having a laugh? Seriously, woman. You left me rotting on remand in prison after you'd set me up to be a grass and it all went tits up. To save your arse, 'cos you'd been nicking. My God.' She sucked her teeth long and low, eyeing her mother's vindictive, narrow-eyed expression. 'Snakes make better mothers than you. And you've got the cheek to have a pop at Papa, when he spent the last three years in Mexico with a gun to his head! What. The. Hell. Is. Wrong. With. You?' She folded her arms, sweating profusely as her aching body cried out for analgesics. 'In fact, I'll tell you what's wrong. You're a frigging sociopath. A narcissist. Yep. That's it. In a nutshell. Remind me again why I came back from Holland.'

At that moment, as the argument escalated to a pitch even she hadn't thought possible, George reflected fleetingly on Rivka Zemel, cooped up in a space that had been ten feet by ten with her ailing brother, short-tempered father and with-drawn mother. How intolerable that must have been, and for over a year. How bitterly they must have hated one another by the end – whatever that end may have been. Had Rivka resented not being able to get on that boat or plane to the States for fear of upsetting her family or seemingly skipping out on them?

'Do you know …' George muttered to herself, as a bitter war of words raged between her mother and father, with Aunty Sharon trying to placate both but succeeding with neither. 'I'm flitting like a nomad between London and Amsterdam and neither feels like home. This is fucked up.'

Downing two ibuprofen with a glass of brackish tap water, George battled through the kitchen-based family tempest and dragged her feverish body upstairs. Unsure what to do. Dismayed at the realisation she was crying. She checked her phone. Found a text from Van den Bergen and felt a sudden pang of longing for the peace of his apartment, regardless of his inattentiveness and the nebulous nature of their relationship and living arrangements. Her finger hovered over the button. She was the ball in a video game of Pong, destined to bat back and forth over the battle line drawn between two opposing camps for the rest of her days. Nobody ever won that volley.

Should she call?

# CHAPTER 28

## *Amsterdam, the house of Kaars Verhagen, 23 October*

'Are you going to up your game then?' George asked as they stood side by side, waiting for the sound of footsteps and for a light to be switched on in the hall.

'What do you mean? I don't even know why you disappeared off without so much as a goodbye.' Van den Bergen pressed the doorbell again. It rang merrily for the fifth time. He knocked on the stained glass. 'She's not in, is she?' He peered through the glass to no avail.

They stood facing each other, there on Kaars Verhagen's doorstep. Van den Bergen reached out to trace his index finger along the line of her lips, then leaned in to kiss her. George felt her pulse quicken and her cheeks flush. Was it relief, desire or her temperature kicking back in? She looked away and sneezed violently onto the door. Blew her nose noisily on one of the tissues Aunty Sharon had insisted she take in her bag.

'I mean, you need to make more of an effort, Paul.' She sighed. What was the bloody point if she had to spell it out to him? 'I feel like an afterthought since you became a grand-father. Action bloody Opa. It's ridiculous. I'm not going to take crumbs from the table anymore. Right? You make a proper commitment to our relationship or we're done. I mean it.' There. She felt better for saying it, though she realised his response might be the last thing she'd want to hear.

He hammered yet again on the door. But George could tell it was just his way of trying to avoid confrontation.

'I sent you money for the plane ticket, didn't I?'

Processing what he'd said, George slapped her thighs in frustration. 'Jesus, Paul. Thanks for the money. Obviously. But don't think a Ryanair ticket is a valid alternative to moving in together.'

'You already stay at mine all the time.' As he looked down at her, with a perplexed look on his face, George could tell he still didn't get it.

'I mean … Jesus!' She slapped his shoulder with force, only just about staying on the right side of violent. 'Dossing at yours when I'm over doesn't mean I have a home with you. I need a home, Paul. Make your damned choice. Either here or in the UK. Your English is good enough, so don't use that as an excuse. You could easily get a job.'

'At my age? Ha.' He checked his watch. Took several steps back.

'Can I help you?'

The nosy neighbour. Of course, George thought. Hadn't she seen the curtains twitch as they'd parked up? She stifled a sneeze.

'Is Cornelia Verhagen in? Have you seen her?' she asked.

The neighbour ignored George but smiled coquettishly at Van den Bergen. 'Ooh, you're a big lad, aren't you? I can see you eat your vla every day!'

Van den Bergen produced a card from his wallet. 'Chief Inspector Paul van den Bergen. I've been to Dr Verhagen's home and she wasn't in. I presumed she'd be here, cleaning her father's place out. I called her phone, but she's not picking up, and I urgently need to talk to her. Any ideas where she might be, Mevrouw … ?'

'De Jong. But you can call me Renate.' The policeman-fancying pensioner treated Van den Bergen to a radiant show of dentures.

'Very well, Renate. Have you seen her lately?'

Renate stuffed her duster into the waistband of her old-fashioned apron. 'I miss Kaars. It's such a shame he's gone. She didn't do him in for her inheritance, did she? Ha ha.'

George caught herself looking heavenwards. Realised that would be counterproductive, so opted for standing with her arms folded while Renate undressed Van den Bergen with eyes that were starting to turn milky with cataracts. She could see a handsome man well enough, though, the cheeky old cow. *Chill out, George. Stop behaving like a jealous weirdo.*

When Van den Bergen didn't respond, the admiring smile slid from Renate de Jong's puffy-cheeked face. 'I saw Cornelia earlier. Some fellow with tattoos all over his arms turned up.' Suddenly, her face flushed, as though the beginning of a good yarn had suffused her with warmth. She spoke with the conspiratorial air of a woman with sleuthing aptitude and nothing better to do than spy on her neighbours. 'They were shouting. Bashing about in there.'

'Were you concerned for Cornelia's safety?'

The neighbour shrugged. 'It died down after a bit. I wondered if it was a boyfriend or something. I don't like that Cornelia. Never did. She used to give me backchat when she was a teenager, and many a time I copped her smoking by the canal and drinking beer with some very unsavoury-looking youngsters. Her father had his hands full, I can tell you. In fact …' The cloudiness in her eyes seemed to have all but gone. Her cheeks were bright red now. 'She killed her mother. Of that, I'm certain.'

'Killed? As in murdered?' George asked.

Renate de Jong laughed, as though George had said the most stupid thing in the world. 'No, no, no! The aggravation. The stress of bringing up a snotty little madam like that sent Maartje to an early grave. You mark my words. And now Kaars has popped his clogs too.'

'He was ninety-five,' George said, wanting to shove a big spanner in the grinding wheel of this judgemental old battle-axe's gossip mill. 'You've got to go at some point.'

'Tell me about the tattooed man,' Van den Bergen said, shooting a castigatory glance at George. 'Did he leave?'

'I didn't see. Like I said, it all went quiet.'

Nodding, Van den Bergen described Den Bosch to the neighbour, beyond his tattoos.

'That's right. Sounds like him. Maybe it's her boyfriend. I wouldn't be surprised.' She curled her lip. 'That doctorate she's got isn't even proper. She does something useless with history. Writes books, that sort of thing. Couldn't prescribe you a plaster if you cut yourself! Ha.'

George bit her tongue, but fantasised about wrapping Renate de Jong's fat head in her apron and pulling the ties tight.

'Maybe she's still in there.' Renate's eyes widened at the possible intrigue. 'Maybe he's done her in! Hardly surprising. She's always been full of it, Mrs Pretend Doctor. Just the type to hang around with dead wrong'uns.'

'Pretend doctor?' No more biting her tongue. George had fought hard to become Dr McKenzie and she was sick and tired of hearing people ridicule those with a PhD, just because they didn't wear a white coat and sit behind a desk, doling out antibiotics. She bodily ushered the nosy neighbour back into her house and pulled the door shut with some force. 'I'm one of those "pretend doctors", you wanky old bag,' she shouted in English through the letterbox. 'So, stuff your intellectual snobbery up your fat arse!' She turned to Van den Bergen. 'We going to do what I think we're going to do?'

He nodded. 'Best if we go in through the back where Mrs Nose won't be able to see us. If there's even a glimmer of a possibility that Cornelia Verhagen is in trouble inside and unable to raise the alarm, it won't hurt to give this place another quick once-over. If not, we'd better pay Den Bosch another visit.'

As they scaled the back garden wall behind the Verhagen house, Van den Bergen whispered, 'Oh, and by the way. When we get back to mine, we'll have to bunk up in the single guest bed, because Tamara and Eva are staying in the master.'

'You are taking the piss.'

How tempted George was to push her lover over the wall.


George had never struggled with breaking and entering houses. Van den Bergen knew not to ask her how she'd become so adept at it or where she'd got the skeleton keys from. Relics of her past, not quite forgotten. As the five-lever mortise on the glazed back door clicked open, she grinned.

'Life skills,' she said, winking.

Van den Bergen gave her a wry smile, saying nothing more. Hardly surprising, given they were now operating outside of the law. But what did they have to lose? Nothing, George decided.

'We're doing our civic duty,' she whispered, stepping inside. She was trembling, but now from adrenalin, not ill health. Her flu was forgotten.

The cramped, old-fashioned kitchen smelled of stale frying and decades of baking, with base notes of damp and cigarette smoke in the walls. Feeling for his service weapon, holstered against his body, Van den Bergen motioned that she should follow, not lead. As if that was going to happen! George ignored him, grabbing a carving knife from the block on the sticky yellowed worktop. She crept past the Formica kitchen table with its vintage vinyl chairs: a scene from the 1950s, frozen in time. Small wonder Kaars Verhagen had been planning to renovate the place. The room was barely wide enough to accommodate a wheelchair.

Somewhere closer to the front of the house, there was a loud bang. Perhaps a door slamming.

'For God's sake,' Van den Bergen whispered. 'Let me go first.'

George relented, wincing as the bare board beneath her feet creaked. Further into the house, the air was heavy with dusty plaster and the smell of bricks. She stifled a sneeze with her sleeve.

Scanning the bedroom-cum-dining room, Van den Bergen looked back at her and shook his head. They moved forward to the living room. The stacks of paintings were there, just as they had been the previous day. The study and downstairs toilet were also empty. Their footsteps echoed around the old house.

'I'm going upstairs,' he whispered.

George nodded, still clutching the knife tightly. Could the nosy old bag from next door hear their footsteps? Van den Bergen's large feet clattered on the uncarpeted staircase. Everything was too loud. If Den Bosch was there, they could hardly rely on the element of surprise. She stood at the foot of the staircase, watching Van den Bergen navigate the galleried landing and disappear into the master bedroom. Glancing at the front door, she could hear her own breath coming ragged and quick. *If Cornelia Verhagen puts her key in the door right now, we'll have a lot of explaining to do. Come on, Paul! Hurry up!*

Realising there was no rushing the search of a four-storey house of this size, George finally followed him up, advancing ahead of him to the second floor. Every room was empty. Then she heard another loud bang. It was coming from the attic. Steeling herself to climb the now narrow and steep stairs to the very top,

George's hand was slick with sweat. If she was forced to defend herself, she was certain the knife would slip from her grip like a wet bar of soap.

As she entered the low-ceilinged room, it all became clear. A window had been left wide open, presumably to get rid of the strong smell of damp up there. The door to the inner, windowless attic room was slamming shut and blowing open. She exhaled, only then realising that she'd been holding her breath. It was a far cry from the attic room above the Cracked Pot Coffee Shop that she'd lived in when she'd spent that first year in Amsterdam as an Erasmus student, revelling in the colour and craziness of living in the red light district. This one was freezing cold, for a start, and strung with dusty old cobwebs. She wanted to get out of there, fast.

Back on the first floor, Van den Bergen looked at her expectantly. 'Anything?'

'No. Maybe she went out. Maybe Den Bosch is her friend and they're in it together.' George ran her finger thoughtfully over the blade of the carving knife. It was blunt anyway. 'I could ride all the way to Margate and back on this,' she said in English, smiling. 'Do you really think she might have bumped her dad for the estate?'

'He was cash poor and asset rich. It's possible, if she's got money trouble. Though it doesn't explain the deaths of the other old men. Why would she prescribe them all the wrong thing? The lovely neighbour, Mevrouw de Jong, reckons she's a PhD, not a medical doctor. Unless she's got the wrong end of the stick …'

'And there was me thinking André Baumgartner might somehow be in the frame,' George said. 'Especially when the Syrian girls I spoke to in London kept mentioning a doctor in Arabic.'

Van den Bergen had begun his descent to the ground floor. He paused, knuckles white as his hand enclosed tightly around the banister. 'André Baumgartner? What?'

'Didn't Marie tell you? About Bosch, Boom & Tuin?'

Those soulful grey eyes narrowed. 'No.' He cocked his head to the side, studying her intently.

'There was this van on the ferry. The name put me in mind of Den Bosch, obviously, and the same font had been used for the van's livery as Groenten Den Bosch. I found a little kid roaming the lower car deck, purely by accident. I'd been chased down there by this drunken prat. Got lost. Long story. Anyway, my gut instinct told me the boy had been trafficked.' She related a potted version of her brush with the sinister-looking driver who had taken her photo, and the brick that he may or may not have thrown through Aunty Sharon's living room window. 'Then again, it's South East London, isn't it? It's more likely to have been kids, I guess. But Den Bosch co-owns the Bosch, Boom & Tuin subsidiary company with none other than the owner of the practice where Saif Abadi works.'

'Worked, you mean. Abadi threw himself in front of the tram because he was petrified of someone in his life who would find out he'd been helping the police. I'd assumed it was the imam – al Haq. But it wasn't, was it? We've been putting two and two together and completely missing the right answer.'

George grabbed her lover and kissed him hard on the mouth. 'Den Bosch is in bed with Baumgartner. Baumgartner's the link between the old men's deaths and the trafficking case. We've got the bastards! How did I not see that straightaway?'

Pressing his hand to her forehead, he gave her one of those patronising, almost fatherly looks. 'There is the small matter of you being ill. You're burning up. You shouldn't be here.'

'Like you give a shit, Action Opa,' George said, pushing his hand away. Ignoring the hangdog expression he was now wearing. Manipulative old bastard. This was precisely how he'd got away with not changing one iota in all the years they'd been together. 'Den Bosch and Baumgartner. How do those two come to be working together? I haven't come across a connection, but obviously there must be one.'

'Why are you shutting me out?' Van den Bergen asked, clearing his throat as though he couldn't quite believe he'd said something so emotionally confrontational.

*No, no, no, old man. I'm not playing on your terms. Not here. Not while I feel so shitty.* The adrenalin had all but gone now. The virus had her in its grip again. 'One place we haven't checked,' she said, 'is the room between the rooms.'

Finding the secret door, which was now entirely exposed, George switched on the light. Nothing.

'The bulb's gone,' Van den Bergen said. 'Has the light gone out on our love, Georgina?'

'Pack it in, will you? Making corny, guilt-tripping puns! What the hell has got into you?' She took her lighter out of her coat pocket. Went back into the kitchen and picked up the old newspaper on the side. It was dated two months ago, with a headline about a Jewish-owned Rembrandt, stolen during the war, having been discovered in the attic of a house near the Vondelpark. She rolled the newspaper up and lit it.

'Torch. See? I feel like *Indiana Jones in the Temple of Incontinence.*'

'Jesus. Be careful with that thing.'

She waved the torch near his face, not revealing that the flames made her nervous and reminded her rather too well of being petrol-bombed as a teen. 'One last look. Since we're here anyway. This was where the Verhagens' biggest secrets were kept. Stands to reason we might have missed something.'

Treading on every single board, checking for loose fixings, they moved from one side of the room to the other. Van den Bergen took up the board beneath which they had found Rivka Zemel's diary.

'Bring the light closer,' he said. 'Mind my hair, though.' He donned his glasses, grunting as he bent over to peer into the dark, musty cavity.

'Anything?'

'No.'

'Shit,' George said, feeling the blazing heat burn closer to her unprotected hand. By now, sparks of charred, still-glowing newspaper were starting to shower down onto the wooden boards. She was just about to hasten to the kitchen to fling her impromptu torch into the sink when it occurred to her that they hadn't checked everywhere. 'Hang on. The skirting boards.'

Van den Bergen scanned the edging around the floor. 'Looks solid enough. There's a good seventy years' worth of dust on them, for a start.'

'Don't fancy bending over, Action Opa?' George asked, rolling her eyes. 'Feeling a bit stiff? Tamara had you changing one shitty nappy too many?'

'That's low,' Van den Bergen said.

'No. I'm telling the truth of it. This is why I went to England. I'm sick and tired of playing second fiddle to your "girls", like they're *real* family and I'm just some worthless bolt-on, like an irritating tagnut on your arse that won't wash off but doesn't really bother you either.'

He was open-mouthed. Then his lips started to move without sound, like a guppy gasping for air. Frowning. Clearly processing.

'Is that what this is all about? You're jealous?'

The urge to kick him in the shins was intense. 'No! Don't switch this so it's my issue. You're taking our relationship for granted. You've stopped making an effort. Your head is only ever in work or your daughter's shit. I've saved a deposit for a flat, and like a dick, I'm willing to stick my money into the pot with you. But you want to stay in your shitty thrift shop of an apartment because it's yours and you want to keep all the control.'

221

'Is that what you think?'

'That's how it is! Jesus. Hold this!' She thrust the torch into his hand and knelt down. Felt her way along the skirting boards, shuddering as her nails dipped into the copious amounts of dark grey fluff. 'Kaars's dad built this well. Can't believe he put skirts on! Maybe it was originally meant to be his red room of pain, but old Mrs Verhagen found out.' She laughed at her own joke. Towering over her, Van den Bergen said nothing. 'Follow me round, and stop bloody sulking.'

'I'm not sulking. I'm thinking. Look ... can we not argue? Any minute, Cornelia Verhagen could walk through that door and come down on us like a ton of bricks for breaking and entering. No warrant, George. Minks will fry us both alive.'

Moving methodically along each wall in the half-light, George almost yelped with excitement when she realised that, among the decades-old grime, there was a piece carefully cut out of the wooden strip, along with white streaks that attested to some of the filth recently having been disturbed. 'Bingo!' She took the blunt-as-hell carving knife from her coat pocket and used it to prise the piece of board away from the wall. It came away easily – another indication that it couldn't have been long since the board had been last removed.

'What can you see?' Van den Bergen asked, bringing the torch close enough that George could feel its heat on her cheek.

She coughed as the dust was dislodged. Gagged as she plunged her hand inside the hidey-hole.

'I'm going to have to scrub my hands in hot bleach water for a whole week,' she said, switching to English. 'This is some bare skanky shit, man.' Her fingers made out firm, straight edges. 'It's a box. A box!' Thrusting her arms in as far as they would go, she grabbed hold of the container and manoeuvred it out slowly.

'Ow. Come on, George! My fingers are burning off. Bring it into the kitchen.'

Knowing their trespass might be discovered at any minute, George set the box on the battered kitchen table and removed the lid. 'The box itself isn't dusty at all.'

Together they peered inside at the contents: fat sheaves of invoices, receipts and correspondence, dated from 1942 to 1944.

'This is all in German,' George said. She fingered the letter-head at the top of the receipts – an iconic black art-deco-style eagle, clutching the swastika in a laurel wreath. Beneath it was written, in German gothic script, 'Deutches Reich'. 'Shit a brick. What the hell was Kaars Verhagen into?'

# CHAPTER 29

## *En route to Van den Bergen's apartment, later*

'I'm sure we're being followed,' George said, glancing over her shoulder to look through the rear window of Van den Bergen's Mercedes.

'What kind of car?' Van den Bergen swallowed hard, peering in his rear-view mirror to catch a glimpse of whatever she thought she had seen. There was nothing untoward, as far as he could ascertain. A truck. A police van. A mini. An estate car.

She shrugged. 'Maybe I'm mistaken. There was a saloon, but I can't see it now. Maybe my imagination's gone into overdrive because of all this.' Patting the box, her attention returned to their find from Kaars Verhagen's room between the rooms.

Listening to George's attempts at translating the German documents as they drove back through heavy traffic towards his apartment, Van den Bergen weighed up the evidence they had so far gathered. Was it enough to make an arrest? Enough to make a conviction stick?

'We know the van on the ferry belonged to Den Bosch,' he said. 'And we know Den Bosch has Baumgartner as a partner.

The old men were patients at Baumgartner's practice but he wasn't their family doctor. Are you sure British port police pulled the van over?'

'Yes. I saw them do it as I was leaving. And I've been calling to find out what happed to the little boy I rescued. I must have left four messages, but I'm still none the wiser.' George held up a photo and started to scrutinise it. 'This is a picture of the Force of Five. All of them. And some others besides.' She turned the yellowed photo over. 'It says it was taken in 1943.' He could hear the smile in her voice. 'Do you know what? I think Rivka Zemel and her family are in this.' She chuckled quietly to herself as she leafed through yet more paper. 'Hey! I think it's Anna Groen. Wow. She was quite a showstopper. From 1943 as well. And there's another few photos of Hendrik here. Says so on the back. Hendrik and Anna, posing hand in hand in the park. More Hendrik and Anna. Anna showing off her engagement ring. Good God, that was a rock and a half! Ooh. Anna in her bra and knickers! Ha. Dirty sod. Sexting, 1940s stylee.'

Van den Bergen caught sight of Anna Groen in her underwear, perched on the end of an iron bedstead, her curvaceous body arranged in a coquettish pose. 'What the hell is Kaars Verhagen doing with a box of photos of Hendrik and his fiancée? Or the Zemels, for that matter?'

'Christ knows. You must surely know someone at the Harwich port who can help me find out about more about the little boy and what happened to whoever was in that van.'

Absent-mindedly nodding, he pulled into the parking area of his apartment complex, irritated that next door's son had parked his Opel in his space, yet again. Little bag of bollocks. He pulled the Mercedes across the back of the Opel. If the idiot wanted to get out, he'd have to come up to the flat, and Van den Bergen could give him what for. Then again, it wouldn't do the baby any good to be around any kind of strife.

Having second thoughts, he swung the car into the disabled space and shrugged. 'A hiatus hernia counts as a disability, doesn't it?'

Carrying the box, allowing George to unlock the door, he was greeted by the sounds of his infant granddaughter screeching angrily and Tamara talking too fast into the phone. She wafted into view, baby on her hip and the phone wedged between her chin and shoulder. A harried expression on her face. Poor thing looked as far from a city-slick lawyer as it was possible to be: velour tracksuit covered in what smelled like baby sick, hair in a greasy ponytail and George's slippers on her feet. Oh God. Had George noticed? That wouldn't go down at all well.

'Are you wearing my slippers?' George asked, staring at Tamara's feet. 'Get them off. Now.'

Tamara stared at her, a vague look of disgust on her face. The baby continued to scream, her little face bright red and blotchy from the effort. Van den Bergen set the box onto the kitchen table and took Eva from his daughter.

'Come to Opa, my little darling.' He started to sing a lullaby – 'Slaap, kindje, slaap' – to her in the hope that she might indeed sleep, but to no avail. The baby continued to shriek. She definitely had her grandmother's lungs.

Tamara had ended her call.

'Is she ill?' he asked.

'What do you think?' Tamara held her hands out to take her daughter back, a stricken look on her face. 'That was the doctor. I wondered if I should take her to A & E. She's been crying for hours and sicked up all over me.' Tears started to fall. Her voice was suddenly small and tremulous. 'Maybe she's got meningitis.'

'What did the doctor say?'

'Virus. He told me to give her liquid paracetamol and lots of water. Keep her cool. If she's still bad by this evening, I've got to take her to hospital.'

Van den Bergen looked carefully at the little girl. Checked her chest for a temperature. None. Checked the back of her neck for a rash. No sign. Observed her as he held her near the light. 'She's fine.' He used his fingers to feel her gums. Peered inside her mouth. The gums were so fiery red, they all but glowed. He could feel a little bump just beneath the surface. 'Teething,' he said. 'Give her some ice cream.'

'No, Dad!' Tamara shouted. 'She's ill. I'm telling you. It's meningitis or some dreadful infection. She's been sick!'

Sitting on the sofa, Van den Bergen started to bounce Eva on his knee. The crying abated slightly. George appeared from the kitchen, holding a pot of Häagen-Dazs and a teaspoon.

'You can't give her that!' Tamara shouted, clutching the sides of her head.

George sneezed, wiping her nose on her shoulder.

'And *she's* ill! Why have you brought her here?'

'I could ask the same of you,' George said. 'I've got flu and I live here. What's your excuse?'

'Not now, you two,' he said, willing these two firebrands to shelve their differences. His eyes were on the box they'd found hidden behind the skirting board. His German was rudimentary but he felt they were on the cusp of a breakthrough, here. If he solved the case, Roel de Vries and Minks could go to hell. Paul van den Bergen's reputation would be unimpeachable, and any suggestion of being suspended would be forgotten.

Staring blankly into his granddaughter's angry eyes, he spooned the vanilla ice cream into her little rosebud mouth. Made a mental note to get Marie and Elvis to bring Baumgartner in for questioning, somehow. Perhaps on a trumped-up traffic charge, since the link to the Stena Line traffickers was tenuous, at best, until George's allegations had been corroborated by police in the UK. Yes. That was it. A fudged speeding ticket. The old bastard had better have a driving licence.

'See? She's calmed down now.' He smiled at the baby. Rubbed noses with her as her mood changed entirely from apoplexy to joy. She grabbed the teaspoon and rammed it into her mouth, chomping merrily on the cold metal, dribbling as though there were a switched-on drool-tap in her inflamed mouth. 'Teething. Opa's no stranger to babies, is he, schatje?' He spoke in babyish tones to the tiny girl. His little treasure. She had his grey eyes. He silently prayed that she would see far lovelier things through those Van den Bergen eyes than murder and mayhem and existential disappointment.

'You shouldn't have *her* here with the flu. Eva has no immunity. I can't cope with being kept up at night.'

'Where do you think I caught the flu from in the first place? Do me a favour and piss off, Tamara,' George said in English, only just about audible enough to hear. 'Fucking prima donna. Thinks she's the first woman in the world to shit a kid out.' Pausing in her search through the German documents, she looked up from the kitchen table, shooting daggers at Tamara. 'Haven't you got a home to go to? And a husband?'

'Fine,' Tamara said. 'I know where I'm not wanted. All Eva's medicines are at my place, anyway.' She turned to Van den Bergen, accusation in her voice. 'I'm out of nappies, out of clean Babygros and there's nothing in the fridge for dinner. Not so much as a chunk of cheese. I've got that veg box on the side. Shame to let it go to waste. I reckon it was just a neighbourhood free trial and you panicked for nothing. You'll watch the baby, won't you, Dad?'

Van den Bergen recalled the sinister figure on the other side of the obscured glass of his daughter's front door. The green Jaguar. The sense that he was being watched or followed. He could feel the panic infecting and warping his very bones. 'I'll go. You put the baby down for a nap. She'll be exhausted after all this crying.'

Feeling no small degree of relief as he sat in the quiet, fine-smelling elegance of his Mercedes, Van den Bergen drove over to Amstelveen, praying as he sang along to Placebo on the car's stereo, that the two women wouldn't kill one another while he was gone.

He called Elvis and gave the order to bring Baumgartner in, then he tried Cornelia Verhagen. Still no answer. He rang his old contact in Berlin – Hakan Güngör – who would surely make short shrift of translating the Nazi documentation, if George's Collins English–German dictionary didn't quite cut the mustard.

On the quiet Amstelveen street, there was no sign of anything out of the ordinary. No Jag. No stalkers. Not even the card-playing neighbour who had led Numb-Nuts astray. It was as if the whole world was out at work.

Using Tamara's key, he unlocked the door. The house smelled stale, the windows not having been opened for several days. There was no sign that Numb-Nuts had been back. It was exactly as Tamara had left it when he'd picked her up in a panic.

Half-whistling, half-singing Placebo's *Pure Morning*, feeling suddenly chipper – the glorious buzz he got when he felt jigsaw pieces finally slotting into place – Van den Bergen went to the kitchen cupboard and piled Eva's medicines into a HEMA bag. He climbed the stairs to the nursery and found a giant pack of unbleached eco-nappies. He gathered the clean clothing together. Piled everything into the boot of his car. He was so preoccupied with fantasies of seeing Den Bosch being slayed by a top prosecutor in front of a judge and a jury full of right-eous, bloodthirsty, ethnically diverse citizens, that when he went back in to pick up the veg box, he didn't notice the company livery on the side: Bosch, Boom & Tuin.

The drive back felt like a sign that soon, the clouds would part and the sun would come out for him and George. There was no traffic. He even remembered to avoid the roadworks. And on his return to his apartment complex, he found that the spotty little turd had moved his Opel. Van den Bergen manoeuvred into his space with a degree of satisfaction that felt like a warm blanket, almost quelling the constant spring of his stomach acid.

Taking Tamara's baby stuff and the vegetables out of the car was a struggle, but he managed it, even climbing the stairs two at a time, though he was laden down. He kicked the door three times – no hand free to press the bell or retrieve his key.

George answered. Didn't even look him in the eye. She was poring over her English–German pocket dictionary.

'Jesus. German's hard! I can't make head or tail of these bloody papers. I'm looking words up that must have fallen out of use decades ago, or else it's nouns rammed together to make a new word and I just can't fathom it. It's nothing like Dutch or Spanish. And the verbs! The verbs are fucking ridiculous. Auf. Aus. An. A million damned prepositions. This is going to take forever.'

Van den Bergen leaned in to kiss her but his lips met with fresh air. She'd already retreated to the kitchen. Setting medicine bag and nappies down, he plonked the veg on the kitchen worktop, eyed the soil-covered potatoes and nodded approvingly. The carrots looked good too.

'I've got your stuff, Tamara. Willem's not been back, I don't think.'

'Save your breath,' George said.

'Whoever grew these veggies must have some incredible compost. This potato's as big as my head!' He lifted out the potato in question, grinning at the prizewinner, then picked up a big bunch of carrots by their long, leafy foliage. For the first time, he noticed the veg box's provenance, now that it was no longer obscured by the carrot leaves.

He felt the blood drain from his face. 'Oh my God. Tamara?'

George stretched and yawned. 'She's gone. Oh, and thinking about it, the car I thought was following us was green.'

'Gone? What do you mean "gone"? Gone where?' His hunch had been correct. The room was spinning, his breathing shallow and quick.

George shrugged. 'No idea. A walk? The newsagent? Who cares? She's a grown-up.'

'Where's the baby?!'

## CHAPTER 30

# *Van den Bergen's apartment, minutes later*

'Answer your phone, damn it!'

George observed Van den Bergen as he paced the hall, waiting for his daughter to pick up. He stopped at the doorway to his bedroom. The floor creaked beneath him as he took several paces inside, checking that Eva was still asleep in her cot.

'She'll be fine,' George said, loud enough for him to hear, but not so loud that the baby might wake. 'She was only going to the shop for some chocolate and milk. Honestly, Paul—'

'Tamara. This is Dad again. Please call me and let me know you're safe.' Van den Bergen stalked back down the hall towards George, his normally strong, gravelly voice breathy and cracking with fear.

Throwing his phone down onto the kitchen table, he rubbed his face and made a howling sound like an animal, suffering and in pain.

'Are you crying? Seriously?' George rubbed his arm, baffled by the overreaction. 'She's gone to the shops in broad daylight in the most boring suburb of the most laid-back city in the world, for God's sake. What do you think's going to happen?'

He removed his hands, revealing red, watery eyes filled with sorrow. 'Den Bosch. Or Baumgartner. Two dangerous, heart-less traffickers. That's what's going to happen.'

George flung a stack of Deutsches Reich papers towards him. 'It's your anxiety. You're fast-forwarding to the apocalypse. Stop it.'

But he was up on his feet, already donning his raincoat. 'I'm going after her.'

He was just about to step through the front door when his phone rang.

'Oh, thank God,' Van den Bergen said, the relief audible. 'Please come back as quick as you can. I was worried.'

'See?' George said, smiling as he peeled his outer layer off and took a seat opposite her. 'No drama necessary. A grown adult woman goes out to buy chocolate. That's not headline news, Paul.' She switched to English. 'You need to calm down.'

He nodded. Popped a chewable antacid onto his tongue and chased it down with a couple of painkillers and a swig of cranberry juice. 'We're going on holiday when all this is over.'

'Mexico?' George winked at him.

'Maybe not.' Finally, the utter desolation in that melancholy face left him and was replaced by a smile.

Methodically, he began to photograph the Nazi paperwork, emailing the images over to Hakan in Berlin.

'Hang on,' George said. She picked up a sizeable pile of letters, all from late 1942 to 1944, bound with string, and almost all addressed to Hendrik. Freeing one or two from their yellowed envelopes, she glanced at the contents and realised they were personal letters. 'Hey. Guess who these are from.'

Van den Bergen looked up, his eyes like saucers behind the smudged lenses of his reading glasses. No response beyond a blank look.

'SS Obersturmführer Bruno *Baumgartner*!'

'Really?' He stood and came round to her side of the table, peering over her shoulder.

'Yep. You want to get these snapped and pinged over to Hakan first. I really want to know what they say. I wish to God my German was better.' She ran her finger over the indents in the page where the typewriter keys had bashed against the heavy, parchment-like paper. An SS livery at the top with an Amsterdam address. 'This guy must have been important,' she said. 'He gets his own letterhead.'

Van den Bergen spread the first couple of letters out and started to photograph them. 'Let's see what Hakan says.'

He made a call to his Berlin-based ally, with whom he had joined forces in a previous case of missing children. Made it clear that this was by no means part of an official police investigation but that the translation was urgently required. 'If you can just give me the gist, that would be great. We need to know what we're dealing with here.'

George could hear Hakan talking on the other end of the phone. The words were indistinct, but she could make out his German intonation. Her cheeks flushed hot as she remembered standing in her hotel room in her bath towel, flirting with the Turkish-born, violin-playing German who was so very easy on the eye and who had been so deeply flustered by the encounter. *Concentrate, George.* She wondered if he was still single. Lovely Hakan. *Stop it, you silly cow.*

Van den Bergen turned to speak to her, distracting her from lascivious thoughts about a man who wasn't her partner. He put his hand over the mouthpiece and whispered, 'He can't get to them until this evening. He's having his car serviced.' He rolled his eyes at what he clearly deemed to be a terrible excuse.

High-pitched wailing from down the hall brought the call to a swift end.

'I feel like shit,' George said. 'I'm going to get some reading done.'

Unwilling to face watching Van den Bergen turn into an

entirely different man with Eva in his arms, George repaired to the guest bedroom and closed the door. She took out Rivka Zemel's diary, thumbing through the pages. There couldn't be more than two or three entries left. Trying to focus, though the tempest that was little Eva raged on only feet away, on the other side of the door, George read. Fully expecting the diary to end abruptly, where Rivka would almost certainly be carted off by the Nazis to some gas chamber at the end of a fateful train journey, she swallowed hard, inhaled deeply and picked up where she'd left off…

*Imagine my surprise when the front door slammed. All that while we'd been crouched in our room between the rooms, expecting the German soldiers to burst in on us at any moment. There had been screaming after the shot had been fired. I recognised Famke's voice as she'd shrieked for them to let her go, telling them that she was just the housekeeper and knew nothing. But despite the commotion, the first face to appear in our secret doorway, flooding the pitch-black place with light once again, was Kaars's.*

*He told us that they'd gone, and wasn't it lucky that the officer had only fired his gun into the ceiling through sheer frustration that he hadn't been able to find anything? Shmuel was finally able to indulge in a violent coughing fit that saw him bring up blood. Poor, poor Shmuel. I fear that this secret little room may be the death of my brother. He has grown so weak.*

*Once again, I begged Papa that we take Ed up on his offer to arrange a safe passage to England – there are Jewish communities, established during the time of the Russian pogroms, in London, Liverpool, Manchester and Leeds. Ideally though, I long to go to New York.*

*Anna Groen – soon to be Mevrouw Hendrik van Eden (how romantic and exciting!) – has been showing me photos* that her uncle sent from the glittering city that was once called New Amsterdam. He owns an import-export business there that brings everything from Far Eastern silks to rare Dutch tulip bulbs all the way to America. Everyone in his photographs, including him, looked terribly dashing, as though they had just walked off set in one of the Hollywood studios. Though the Americans are hard at war with the Japanese, and I hear that many have been stationed in England, too, in order to boost the British air force's bombing power, life over there looks a good deal better than it does here, in our tiny windowless space in the Verhagen house.

Kaars and Ed have managed so far to spirit as many as forty families out of the country on merchant ships destined for all sorts of wonderful destinations where the Germans and their filthy allies have no jurisdiction. Obviously, they've been doing this out of the goodness of their hearts – that is the purpose of the Force of Five. Brechtus and Arnold have forged contacts at the docks, mainly with shipping companies and civilians who own boats. It has apparently been surprising how willing some are to help the Jews, merely from a deep-seated need to right some of the Nazis' wrongs. What has happened as a result, however, is that the grateful Jewish families have been giving Kaars gifts of paintings that they cannot take with them and which they do not want Hitler's thugs to seize.

At first, I didn't believe that people could give away such treasures so willingly, but I did witness the extremely well-off Cohen family give him a Dutch School still life and a small Vermeer. Imagine that! They said diamonds were easy to conceal on their persons but a gilt-framed masterpiece was not so easy. Papa should realise that we have no such luck as to own assets that can be used to barter

*with or simply given as tokens of gratitude. We desperately*
*need to go.*

*In fact, as I write this, there is an insistent knock at the*
*door yet again. I have only moments before Mama turns*
*the light off and plunges us all into darkness. It is them,*
*though. Kaars has banged three times on the wall as a*
*warning. Please God, we will...*

George opened her eyes, sat up, plumped her pillows and blew
her streaming nose on a long piece of toilet roll. She was
surprised to see Van den Bergen standing in the doorway. He
had a harried look about him, clutching a now-sleeping Eva
against his chest and shoulder. His lower eyelid was flickering,
the way it did occasionally when he was under extreme pressure.

'Tamara's still not back, George.'

She looked at the clock, but it had stopped. 'How long has
she been gone?'

'An hour.'

'Jesus. I must have fallen asleep.' She rubbed her eyes. 'Have
you phoned her?'

'Three times. She's not picking up. I need to go and look
for her.'

'Yep. Put the baby in her cot and go. I'll watch Eva.'

Feeling certain that Van den Bergen was overreacting and
that Tamara was in all likelihood sitting in the local café with
some old acquaintance she had bumped into, George yawned
and stretched. She was foggy-headed, thanks to a deep afternoon sleep and the effects of the Lemsip she'd brought from
London. As she sought the place in Rivka's diary where she'd
left off, it occurred to her that Van den Bergen's panic wasn't
entirely unfounded. It was strange for a mother to leave her
baby for an hour without pre-arrangement. Perhaps Tamara
was suffering from postnatal stress.

Resolving not to add to her lover's mounting hysteria, she read on.

*Please God we will remain undiscovered.*

Nothing more was written on that page. George wondered for a moment if this was the end of young Rivka's story. But no. She turned the page to find another entry. It was the last, however.

*27 April 1943*
*Dear diary, earlier today Ed arrived at the Verhagen house carrying a box. He was terribly flustered – his blond hair was dishevelled, his skin flushed red and with a thin veil of sweat. Normally, he's such a composed chap. I soon understood why, however. He asked that I conceal the box inside our cunning room between rooms, suggesting that we put it in the cavity behind the skirting board, which he knew was hollow as he had been privy to Mr Verhagen's construction methods when there was first a plan to hide my family. When he said it was extremely important that the box remain secret and that it contained evidence of dastardly doings within, we all agreed. Papa was concerned that if the Nazis succeeded in finding us after two failed attempts, then it would do us no good to be harbouring incriminating objects.*

*Ed would tell us nothing more other than the dire news that somebody within the Force of Five had turned and that we must neither try to open the box and view its contents nor must we breathe a word of its existence to anyone – even Kaars. When Papa pushed him on what he meant by 'turned', Ed just said that one of his fellow freedom fighters and lifelong friends was in league with the SS and was giving up Jews in return for cash. As we enjoyed a swift parting embrace – and oh, that had such a melancholy finality to it – he told us that he had found a new safe location. He made a promise that he would be moving us as well as dealing with the box tonight.*

*As I sit here writing by the flickering light of my lamp, it must be the early hours of the morning. Ed has not returned and I am so, so fearful for his safety. I am trying to conjure his handsome, strong face and joyful blue eyes in my imagination, but I find myself so overwhelmed by dark thoughts that I can only visualise the composite parts of the face of the man I intend to marry, and not the whole.*

*Dear Ed, please come back to me and move us to safety. The war will surely be over in a week or two. Hitler is buckling under the pressure exerted by the Soviets on the Eastern Front. The allies are growing in confidence. We Zemels, however, are still in fear for our lives and the Nazis are getting even more aggressive and extreme in their violent bully-boy tactics, like fighting dogs backed down a dead end.*

*I must put out the candle. There is knocking at the door. Could it be Ed? There are footsteps upstairs as the rest of the household wakes. Now, a man is speaking to someone. It must be Mr Verhagen. Now, there is German being shouted. 'Raus! Raus! Wir wissen wo die Juden sind!'*

*They know where the Jews are. Us! They're coming inside. Please God, no! I fear we cannot evade capture again.*

The diary entries ended abruptly and George was surprised to find she was crying. What had happened to Rivka and her family? Ed had found the rotten apple in the barrel. But what terrible fate had befallen the clandestine couple?

Van den Bergen's key was in the lock. She threw back the covers, expecting him to walk in with Tamara, who had almost certainly just taken liberties with her old man's free babysitting service. Except Van den Bergen was alone. All the colour had leached from his face, leaving even his lips a ghostly off-white.

'She wasn't there. Nobody in the shops has seen her.'

## CHAPTER 31

# *Van den Bergen's apartment,*
# *then an Uber taxi, later*

'Get your lazy arse over here and parent your daughter,' George shouted down the phone to Numb-Nuts.

On the other end of the line, Tamara's wanker of a husband was making some kind of lame excuse about a fungal infection in his foot and needing to be at his parents' place. 'And besides, Tamara's made it pretty clear she doesn't want to see me.'

With his raincoat half on, half off, Van den Bergen grabbed George's phone and barked at his son-in-law. 'She's gone missing, you prick. I'm going to try to find her. If you're not over here in twenty minutes to take Eva, I'm going to strangle the life out of you with my bare hands. Have you seen the size of my hands, Willem? Because they're very big, extremely strong gardener's hands, and I've had a hell of a lot of theoretical practice over the years, fantasising about choking the living daylights out of you with these very big hands. Do you understand?'

He thrust the phone back at George. 'I cut him off,' Van den Bergen said, pulling on his coat properly. 'He'll be here, if he knows what's good for him.'

'I wish you'd call the station and get them to send a couple of uniforms out to the farm, instead of going yourself.' George folded her arms, watching Eva sitting merrily in her inflatable ring, chewing on the pages of a fabric baby book. Left holding the baby, and she wasn't even hers. Nice. 'It's dangerous to go alone. It's getting dark. You don't know the lay of the land. It'll be pitch black out—'

But Van den Bergen shook his head and snatched his car keys from the side. 'I'm suspended, remember? Persona non grata. And she's only been gone just over an hour. She doesn't qualify as a missing person yet. There's no way they'll send a squad car out into the country on my hunch.'

'They've got a point.' She searched his eyes to see if there was any indication he was actually listening to her. 'She didn't answer her phone at first, did she?'

'There's a veg box from Bosch, Boom & Tuin on the side. That tells me everything I need to know. Den Bosch has had eyes on her, George. I've felt like someone has been watching me of late. I'm sure I was followed to the allotments the other morning. The guy threatened me in person, didn't he? He basically said that I need to butt out, or else. Well, this is the "or else".'

'Don't go alone, Paul. At least wait for Numb-Nuts, so I can come with!'

She knew she'd lost him when he opened the front door. 'Nappies and wipes are in a bag by my nightstand. Change her on a mat on the floor, not the bed. She's starting to really roll around now.'

And he was gone.

Silly bastard. George wasn't sure how to feel. Frightened that something dreadful would befall him? It wouldn't be the first time. Van den Bergen's best trick was ignoring everyone's advice and getting into tight corners. But then, was she any different? Didn't that come with the territory?

Calling Marie, she tapped her knee with her biro until she

picked up. 'Any joy finding Baumgartner?'

'None,' Marie said. 'Me and Elvis both went round to his surgery but the secretary said he's gone on holiday to visit family. He won't be back for a week. She wouldn't give us contact details.'

'What? Isn't that obstruction of justice?'

'She said she didn't have a number or anything. There was no room for manoeuvre, given we're not in a position to arrest him or Den Bosch until we've had confirmation from the UK police that the Bosch, Boom & Tuin van from your ferry was actually found to have trafficked people on board.'

'When do you hope to hear back from them?'

Eva gurgled loudly, grabbing at her two-handled cup and sucking at the spout. Water gushed in rivulets onto her sleepsuit.

'Say that again,' George said, frowning at the happy little girl who understood none of the gravity of the situation and was high as a kite on liquid paracetamol and ice cream.

'End of play today,' Marie said. 'And I've asked one of the traffic lads here to check the ANPR cameras on every motorway to track Baumgartner down.'

George remembered the car that had been following them on the way to Van den Bergen's apartment. 'What does Baumgartner drive?'

'A green S-Type Jaguar.'

'Jesus.' She swallowed hard. Felt in the very marrow of her bones that Baumgartner had kidnapped Tamara. She had to warn Van den Bergen that he was walking into a deadly trap. 'Marie, the silly old fart's gone out to Den Bosch's farm. As soon as his son-in-law picks up his daughter, I'm going to get a cab there myself. Please, please, please get as many bodies as you can over there ASAP. You, Elvis, as many uniforms as you can muster. I've got a really nasty feeling that this is going to end badly. Van den Bergen will try to take these two bastards on single-handedly; you know what he's like.'

'Yes,' Marie said, falling momentarily silent. 'I know. I'm on it.'

Standing on the balcony, staring at the screen of her phone, George lit a cigarette, careful to blow the smoke out into the open. Van den Bergen wasn't there to enforce the no-smoking rule and her nerves were shot. Screw it. She'd already called him twice to warn him, but the old fart wasn't picking up.

She had put on a DVD of *In the Night Garden* that she had brought over from the UK for Eva. The tiny girl was occupied and poo-free for now, but that wouldn't last for long.

'Come on! Come on!'

Where the fuck was Numb-Nuts? Five minutes into the wait, it was still too early to expect his arrival. Silently, she cursed Eva's parents for being such flaky wankers and for abusing Van den Bergen's generous nature. She considered her own mother. No, it definitely wasn't entirely Van den Bergen's fault. You couldn't pick your relatives.

She called Cornelia Verhagen. Straight to voicemail.

Fidgeted. Thought about Rivka Zemel and Ed Sijpesteijn as she played This Little Piggy with Eva, wondering what could have happened to the ill-fated young couple. How little the world had changed over the decades: families were still being torn apart by war; people were still handing over everything they owned to secure a passage – albeit potentially fraught with danger – to a new homeland and better life; the most deep-rooted, truest love in the world could still be destroyed by the vagaries of everyday life and the violence of men.

Still no Numb-Nuts.

'Come on, you twat!' She checked her watch. Ten minutes. Van den Bergen wouldn't even be on the motorway yet. He was safe … for now.

Her phone pinged. An email. She was delighted to see Hakan had copied her in on his translations so far:

Dear Paul,

Thanks for emailing over photos of the old documents. Translation is a time-consuming thing, so I have only made a small dent in the box's contents so far.

I can tell you that the invoices are from Hendrik van Eden to SS Obersturmführer Bruno Baumgartner for 'services rendered to the Deutsches Reich'. When I match the invoices to the receipts – the Germans were sticklers for administrative precision, so it is easy to tie everything together, thanks to a system of accounting reference numbers – it is clear that Hendrik was selling information on the Dutch Resistance to the Nazis, with Baumgartner being his main contact.

One receipt clarifies that Hendrik had informed the Nazis that the Verhagens were hiding a Jewish family – the Zemels – in their house. He also sold information concerning the whereabouts of the Meijers family, the Stern family, the Liebermans, the Levys, the Rosenthals, the Herzbergs, the Wolffs and the Lipschitzes. In total, seventy-six Jews from those families alone were transported to Treblinka, including children as young as two years old. There are still scores of invoices left, which I haven't even looked at.

Hendrik sent letters detailing the personal lives of many of his friends, including Kaars Verhagen, Ed Sijpesteijn, Arnold van Blanken and Brechtus Bruin. He tells Baumgartner in one letter that he suspects Van Blanken and Bruin are homosexuals in a relationship, and that Bruin's grandmother is of Roma or Sinti origin. He recommends highly that both Van Blanken and Bruin be arrested as a result. It is strange that letters addressed to Baumgartner are in this box, but the ink is a little messy and has a slight purple hue to it. I think they look like carbon copies, and they all have receipts and payment slips attached. Again, it seems that this is Baumgartner and Van Eden's fastidious accounting procedure. Perhaps all of their correspondence was typed or written up in duplicate and both men had copies of everything.

The tone of all of Hendrik's letters that I have so far read is friendly. I can tell that he and Baumgartner mixed socially, as Hendrik mentions 'seeing you at the club, where Anna was delighted you were sitting in the front row, applauding her performance. I swear, if she wasn't my darling fiancée, I might think she was sweet on you, Bruno.'

'Hendrik van Eden, you duplicitous old bastard. Your secret's out. So, this is what Ed found out about you. You were rumbled, mate.' George checked her watch again. Numb-Nuts should be knocking on the door at any moment, provided his indulgent fool of a mother was dropping him off in the car, rather than making him come on a tram across town. 'Hurry up, arsehole.' She wondered how Van den Bergen was faring.

She turned her attentions back to Hakan's email…

The letter that you asked me to focus my translation efforts on was in a sealed envelope, you say. Well, you already know that it was addressed to Bruno Baumgartner, intended to be sent to his home address in Teniersstraat in Amsterdam's Museum Quarter. (I've googled it. What a whopper of a mansion house! I spoke to my friend in the Bundesarchiv – the archive that holds military records. Much was destroyed during the war, but still, many documents remain. Baumgartner's grand house had been requisitioned by the SS from a wealthy Jewish merchant, Avram Solomon, and his family.)

Here is the letter, word for word, written by hand by Hendrik and translated to the best of my abilities. His penmanship is somewhat shaky in this missive, and when you read on, you'll understand why:

Just as George was about to read a letter that she felt might hold the key to this curious mystery, the doorbell sounded.

'At last!'

Struggling to don her duffel coat whilst carrying Eva on her hip, she opened the door to see a perplexed-looking Numb-Nuts on the step.

'Jesus. Couldn't you have got here any quicker?'

'Where's Paul?'

'Not here. And neither should I be. Nappies and whatnot are in the changing bag. She needs feeding.'

'Can't I come in? I thought Paul wanted to speak to me. I thought it was something to do with Tamara. Has she forgiven me? Is she here?' His face was illuminated by an electric smile that was powered purely by self-delusion, clearly.

'No to all of that. Now, why are you standing there like a turd? Take your daughter!'

His smile faltered and sputtered out, as though somebody had pulled the switch. He put his trainer-clad foot over the threshold, onto the clean wooden floor in the hall.

'Off,' George said. 'That's clean space. Your shoes are dirty.'

'They're not dirty. I didn't step in anything.'

'You've been outside. Where do dogs, cats, foxes, birds and tramps piss, Willem?'

'Outside. But—'

'Can you see dried-in dog piss?'

'No.'

'Then your shoes are dirty. And I've got heroic shit to do for your wife. Out!'

Handing Eva over, planting a hasty kiss on the baby's forehead, George pushed her left arm into her coat, stepped into her boots, whipped her handbag from the console table in the hall and slammed the door in Willem's face. Left him standing at the top of the stairs like the feckless, hapless tagnut he was. She waved to the baby and blew her another kiss. Poor little Eva didn't deserve the bullshit she'd been served up. And who knew? By the end of the night, it was entirely possible the kid's mother would be dead. She'd be left to Numb-Nuts.

Shaking her head at the imagined tragic scenario, George's pinging phone told her the Uber was outside.

'Groenten Den Bosch farm and fast, please. It's a matter of life or death.'

The driver looked nonplussed. 'Postcode? The postcode I am given is not work.'

Using Google as her guide, she gave him directions good enough to get him within striking distance. He was clearly discombobulated at having to drive her to the middle of nowhere in the failing light, so George took her last twenty euros out of her purse and waved them in his face.

'Step on it.'

'Like in cop films,' he said, grinning at her through the rear-view mirror. He sounded like a Somali. She spotted his ID dangling from his sun visor.

'Yes, Ibrahim. Exactly like in a cop film. Hurry!'

Ordinarily, she would have loved nothing more than to chat to this taxi driver and ask him how he came to be driving an Uber in Amsterdam. Perhaps he'd been a pirate or in the militia. Perhaps he'd been trafficked himself. But George didn't have time. She was heading to the edge of the cliff. But first, before she fell, she wanted to read the letter to Baumgartner. Even if she was going to her death at the hand of a tattooed psycho-path and his debonair old sidekick, she wanted to solve the riddle.

*Dear Bruno,*

*I write this letter with no small degree of anger in my heart. You have betrayed me. At a point when I felt that you and I were akin to brothers in our trusting bond and friendship, I realise all this while you had been plotting to take what was mine and cast me aside. Anna didn't need to tell me, though she confessed when I confronted her. You and she have been having an affair behind my back for a year. A year! You, Bruno Baumgartner, are a lying, cheating cad. I do not care if you have me arrested on some kind of trumped-up charge of treachery. Have me shot! You may as well kill me, for I am already dead inside.*

*Did we not do great work together, rounding up the Jews who had gone into hiding so that Amsterdam would be cleansed of its problem for good, leaving only Aryans behind? The Führer wished it, and we made his dream come true, albeit in a small way. I betrayed my own coun-trymen to help the Deutsches Reich maintain stable control in the Netherlands, thinking that German governance would benefit us a good deal more than a weak liberal Dutch leadership that would pander to the British and the Americans, or else buckle at the first sign of the Soviets on our doorstep. Yet all of that seems to count for nothing.*

*You never wanted my support or friendship. You wanted Anna – the gorgeous girl on my arm – forgetting that she is the love of my life and that we are to be married. Or, should I say, were. I know she is carrying your child, Baumgartner. It sickens me to think that you have planted your rotten German seed in fertile ground that belonged to me. When you do die, I hope death will come to you*

*not from a bullet but from the weight of guilt as it pain-
fully crushes your heart, for you have crushed mine.*

*I wish a plague of hellfire on your head, Bruno
Baumgartner. I wish I had never met you, and when the
Nazis fall to the Soviets and the communists come to cut
off your balls and string you up in Dam Square outside
the palace, I shall deny ever having had any dealings with
you whatsoever. I wish for what's left of your pathetic life
to be a wasteland of pain and misery.*

*Hendrik van Eden*

Baumgartner had had a son with Anna Groen. Surely that was
André Baumgartner. The ages were right. Had the septuage-
narian doctor killed his father's love rival and all his friends
in some fit of revenge, decades after the war had ended? And
where did Den Bosch come into this story?

With many questions still unanswered, George was irritated
to see that the cab was bouncing up a country lane she didn't
recognise. But surely she was almost there. The blood was
rushing in her ears. *I'm coming, Van den Bergen,* she thought.
*Wait for me!*

But hang on. Hadn't they driven past this farm shop a few
minutes ago?

'Are we going round in circles?' she asked the taxi driver,
panic engulfing her in an icy deluge of cortisol.

He shrugged. Pointed to the satnav mounted on his dashboard. 'Address not here. Lost.'

# CHAPTER 32

## *En route to the Den Bosch farm, later*

'I feel sick as a dog,' Marie said, as Elvis took the curve of the slip road too fast in a pool car that couldn't handle his boy-racer cornering. 'Drive like a normal person, will you?'

With the dongle connected to her laptop, she was determined to get the information George needed, if only the damned signal stayed strong.

'I'm doing the best I can. This thing starts to shake like the spin cycle on my mum's old washing machine the minute you get it up to a hundred kilometres an hour. But if we're going to get to the Den Bosch farm in time for a showdown, I need to floor it.' Elvis's Adam's apple lurched up and down, as though it too felt sick.

In truth, Elvis looked peaky in the glow of the motorway lights, the shadows accentuating his newfound cheekbones. Too thin to put up much of a fight against that beefcake Frederik Den Bosch, Marie assessed, despite years of training on the job. The Rotterdam Silencer had turned Elvis from an aspiring tiger into a house cat. Their odds weren't good.

Struggling to hit the keys reliably, Marie logged into the register of births, deaths and marriages to find the entry for André Baumgartner.

'He's got to be here somewhere,' she said. 'Seventy-five years old ...' She calculated the years in which he might have been born, depending on whether he was a winter or summer baby. 'Damn it! This connection's terrible. And I'm going dizzy. Ugh.'

'Try not to get travel-sick,' Elvis said. 'You'll need to get out fighting at the other end, knowing Van den Bergen.' He flashed a dawdling BMW in the fast lane to get the hell out of his way. 'Bloody old men in their souped-up cars. Why do they bother if they're going to trundle along at sixty kilometres an hour?' He glanced over at her. 'Do you really have to do that now? Can't it wait?'

'Don't you want some answers? The boss has risked his career on these two cases, and they're connected. Knowledge is power, Dirk.' Marie could see a sheen of sweat glistening on his forehead and upper lip. His hair was flattening out with sweat. 'Now, worry less about what I'm doing and take it easy, for Christ's sake. I'd like to get there alive.'

The dongle's light showed green one moment and orange the next, telling her that the connection was dipping in and out. Hardly surprising, this far into the countryside. As night descended, all she could see out here were the flat, black expanses of the polders, punctuated by the odd dyke, its water glistening in the fledgling moonlight like a strip of mother of pearl in a black lacquered tabletop. Giant wind turbines were spinning slowly; brooding giants, seeming to stride through an otherwise pristine agricultural horizon. No phone masts though, and hardly any Wi-Fi signal.

Marie thought about her slide into accidental traffic duty thanks to Van den Bergen's fall from grace. Since her son had died, all she had was work. Her life had disintegrated into so much meaningless dust. This was her chance to help put things right. Bring back the only light that remained in her life apart from the odd Skype session with an overweight German whom she'd never quite managed to date – the intrigue of solving murders.

'Did you check your service weapon?' Elvis asked, indicating to pull off the motorway.

'Twice. Fully loaded and in working order.'

'I wish we could have got uniformed backup. I feel bad that we're as good as it gets.'

The dongle was glowing green. The page she required was starting to load on her laptop. Good. 'If Minks gets wind of Van den Bergen going vigilante on a murder case that was taken off him, when he's meant to be suspended, his career will definitely be over. Our careers will be finished too. It's a gamble, but—'

'If he's got the wrong end of the stick, and there's nothing going on at the farm …'

'Aha!' Marie punched the air as the photographed entries of the birth register from over seventy years ago were displayed clearly, in scrolling, copperplate writing, typical of the mid 1940s. 'There we have it. The birth of André Baumgartner. Daddy was SS Obersturmführer Bruno Baumgartner. And guess who Mummy was? Anna Groen! Didn't George say Hendrik van Eden was engaged to Anna Groen? But hang on, Groen is listed as Mejuffrouw – Miss. She didn't marry her SS officer. Cooee. That must have caused quite a bit of gossip after the war. I wouldn't have liked to be in Anna Groen's shoes if she stayed in the Netherlands and they found out her illegitimate son had a Nazi for a father. Nice.'

'What about Den Bosch?' Elvis asked, navigating his way along a country lane, full-beamed headlamps on the car picking out the hedgerows in triangular white shafts of light. 'He's about the right age to be Baumgartner's son. Neo-Nazi grandson of a Nazi. Not sure if that would count as a case of nature or nurture, but sounds about right.'

She typed Frederik den Bosch into the search engine but

there were no results. 'Nothing. According to the registry of births, deaths and marriages, Frederik den Bosch doesn't exist.' She frowned at her screen. 'He's using a false name. How the hell has he managed to set up businesses and pay taxes with a false name? Unless!' She clicked her fingers. Pointed. 'Unless he's taken his mother's name.'

She searched for details of André Baumgartner's marriage, not knowing if he'd been married at all. 'Aha! Baumgartner junior did get hitched, in 1967, to a woman called Sofie Jansen.' She read on through the entry, struggling to decipher the loops of the registrar's fountain pen. 'No. Wait a minute. I've got it! Maybe the wife came from 's-Hertogenbosch. Nope. Shit. She was an Amsterdamer. I'm stumped. And the fucking signal's gone.' She thumped the dash.

'Calm down, sweary!' Elvis's wavering voice sounded anything but composed. He was hyped up to the eyeballs on adrenalin, clearly. 'We're here.'

He parked the pool car just outside the entrance to the Den Bosch farm, killing the headlights. The large wooden gate was standing open and the gravel courtyard looked empty, but for a small Den Bosch van parked beneath a solitary security light.

'No sign of Van den Bergen's Mercedes. That's weird. There's no way we could have beaten him to it.'

'It's a big site,' Marie said. 'Acres of fields and greenhouses. If there's another entrance, it's not on the map. I wouldn't know, though. I've never been out this way. The boss came with George to do the first interview – I've texted him but the signal's gone again.'

'Which means we could be the first and only officers on the scene, investigating a kidnapping by a dangerous trafficker. Christ, I wish I'd had something nicer than stamppot with instant mash for dinner, seeing as it might be my last.' He ran a shaking hand through stylish hair that no longer qualified him for the 'Elvis' moniker. No more mutton chops either.

Nowadays, he was like a tree stripped of its bark and rendered vulnerable.

Marie studied him, wondering if he was up to this night-time adventure. Realised she had no option but to give him the benefit of the doubt. It was hardly like they were rookies anymore. And they had to evade the scrutiny of both Roel de Vries and Minks.

Slamming her laptop shut, she shook her head. 'He must have changed his surname by law. It's not difficult to do. You just need to file a request with the Dienst Justis and the Ministry for Justice. I wish I'd had time to find out the name of André Baumgartner's child, or children, if he had them.'

'Maybe they're just business partners, Marie. Maybe they're both right-wingers and met at some rally. We might get to ask him in person.'

'And I still haven't managed to get a copy of Hendrik van Eden's will.' She felt the truth niggling at her, taunting her, but she couldn't quite grasp it. 'He's the only one out of the Force of Five that we can't get good information on. His solicitor's been playing arseholes all along. Damn it! This is so frustrating. My whole job revolves around detailed research and solving puzzles. I feel like I've found every piece of the bloody jigsaw apart from the one I need to see the picture.'

'Forget it, Marie. Tamara's life is at stake. Maybe the boss's too. Let's do this.'

Checking her gun was in its holster and her shoelaces were tied tightly, Marie stashed her beloved laptop in the passenger footwell of the car. She stepped out just as a clapped-out Skoda swung into the courtyard. The huge sticker on the side showed it was an Uber taxi. The passenger, with her mane of wild black curls, could only be one person.

'It's George! Come on!'

There was the slam of the Skoda's door and an audible utterance of 'Get a fucking map, dickhead!' followed by the crunch of gravel underfoot as George hastened across the yard.

Marie motioned that she and Elvis should follow, but they were stalled at the entrance as the reversing taxi driver slowed, looking left, right and totally flustered. She knocked on the window, flashing her badge, gesticulating that he should move on immediately.

By the time she and Elvis stood by the marks indented into the gravel by the taxi, there was no sign of George whatsoever.

# CHAPTER 33

## *Den Bosch's house, De Pijp, then the Den Bosch farm near Nieuw-Vennep, at the same time*

Deciding where to begin his search had been fraught. As he had turned over the engine of his Mercedes in his parking space, he'd realised that time was the commodity he had in shortest supply. He had seen what had happened to Elvis at the hands of traffickers in a matter of hours – from being a captive dragged off the street to being garrotted and shoved into a body bag in three easy moves. Knowing how vast the farm was and how it might easily take hours to search it on his own, Van den Bergen had decided to first scope out the closest and smallest location where Tamara might be being held – the trafficker's house.

He had floored the car over to De Pijp, using his blues and twos when the traffic had bunched up. Kicking the back door in, flashing his chief inspector's badge at the only neighbour who dared challenge him over the garden fence, it hadn't taken long to search the house from attic to basement. Nothing. But then his phone had vibrated in his pocket. With a thundering heart, he'd checked the screen to see who was calling, daring to hope it was his daughter.

```
Tamara calling.
Accept. Decline with a message. Decline.
```

Pawing frantically at the 'accept' button, he'd pressed the phone to his ear. Grinning and hopeful.

'Where the hell—?'

His words had been drowned out by a blood-curdling scream. Then, silence.

'Tamara! Where are you?'

'Help,' she'd whimpered.

The line had gone dead.

Parental anguish had cut deeper than any blade. Van den Bergen had dropped to his knees in Den Bosch's nightmarish basement, surrounded by macabre mannequins that stood to attention in rows – a private battalion primed and ready for some modern-day race war, dressed in the uniforms of various Nazi ranks. Wehrmacht infantry, SS officers, Luftwaffe. Clutching his phone to his belly, he'd let out a searing howl. But he'd realised instantly that falling to pieces on the wrong side of town would do Tamara no good.

Replaying the call in his imagination, he had been certain he'd heard the rumble of a diesel engine and the crunch of loose stones.

'The farm. He's taking her to the farm in a truck. What the hell am I doing here? I've wasted precious time, goddammit!'

With cracking knees, Van den Bergen had forced himself to stand. The bones in his legs had seemed to liquefy, corroded by the fear of what might be. He'd raced back to his car, becoming snarled up in traffic as Amsterdam's workers hastened home to where their loved ones were waiting, safe from murderous monsters with intimidation and violence on their minds.

'Get out of the way, you dickheads!'

He'd beeped the horn, ready to switch on his sirens and

258

lights, but the opposite lane had been blocked by a broken-down bus. Eventually, he'd manoeuvred his way to the front of the queue, speeding off into the path of an oncoming tram. It had rung its bell, the driver glaring at him through the windscreen, shouting something Van den Bergen hadn't been able to hear. Closer. Closer. The perpendicular lines of the metal tram tracks had shone in the headlights of the tram like glow-in-the-dark barriers, warning Van den Bergen that he mustn't play chicken with thirty-eight tons of steel travelling towards him at fifty kilometres per hour. Not its top speed, but fast enough to turn his E-Class into a concertina of leather upholstery, mangled steel and aluminium. He'd assessed that the likelihood of death on impact would have been around seventy or eighty per cent.

But Van den Bergen had been in the mood for flouting probability. Though the tram's horn had been blaring and the brakes had squealed like pigs at an abattoir, he'd merely treated the tram driver to the finger. Ten years with George hadn't been lost on him.

'No you don't, bastard!'

Flooring the car, he'd shot over the slippery, damp tracks, missing the tram by only two or three feet. Still alive. *I'm coming, Tamara.*

Having had no real plan of what he might do once he arrived, beyond finding his daughter and neutralising her captors by any means necessary, when he did pull in to the Den Bosch farm's courtyard, he realised how precarious his situation was.

'Gun. Where's my … ?' For a fleeting moment, he had visions of having left his service weapon on top of the fridge-freezer, high up where Eva couldn't get at it. But no. The Sig Sauer was strapped beneath his armpit. 'Oh, thank God.'

Bypassing the Den Bosch transit van parked beneath the security light, he drove the Mercedes slowly round to the back of the main reception building and parked in the long shadows, by the bins, next to the green Jaguar and Den Bosch's Jeep. Knowing the farm was vast, he took a moment to consider what he might do with a hostage on such a site. No lights shone in the windows of the first building, but what about the other outbuildings? Yes. Perhaps he would take a person there. But what was Den Bosch hoping to achieve by taking his daughter? Spilling the blood of a chief inspector's child would bring the weight of the entire Dutch police force crashing down on Den Bosch. For a criminal who presumably wanted to make dirty money in peace, killing Tamara, of all people, would be a poor choice.

'Damn it,' Van den Bergen said, unfastening his seatbelt and checking again that the gun was loaded. 'Guys like Den Bosch don't follow rules.' He took a swig of some liquid antacid from the emergency bottle in his glove box and stepped out of the car.

The outbuildings stood in darkness, like giant tombs. Van den Bergen shivered – as much from the prospect of what he might find as the cold. Every crunched step on the gravel sounded too loud. Was Den Bosch watching him, savouring the sight of him walking into a trap?

Breathing too quickly, feeling light-headed, he tried the door to the first outbuilding. Locked. No lights on. The other three were identical, but it wouldn't do any harm to check round the back. He crept along the miserly space between the buildings in total blackness until he felt the air freshen. Acres and acres of planted fields beyond. He could smell the good earth, calling to him in the dark. The plants would be stretching up towards the stars in the firmament. Out here, there was no rose-pink light pollution to snuff out Venus and her band of dedicated followers.

When he spotted a light burning in the upper storey of the neighbouring building, his heart was a spooked horse setting off at a gallop. Holding his gun before him with the safety off, he found that the heavy iron door was open just a crack. He crept inside. Climbed a damp stone staircase. The place had a mouldy, organic smell to it. Unheated. Freezing cold. He imagined moss growing in corners that never dried out. As he approached the room upstairs from where the light emanated, he caught sight of his breath steaming on the air. He listened outside for a few moments but heard nothing. Not even the sound of a cigarette being inhaled, or of someone struggling against their bonds. He was certain his heart would give out at any moment; convinced he could feel it flipping dangerously against the left side of his ribcage. If he got out of this alive, he determined to get his cholesterol re-checked.

*I'm coming, darling*, he thought, picturing his girl beyond the door. Aware that it was too silent and that maybe, just maybe, they were waiting for him with pistols cocked, ready to shoot.

Nose of the Sig Sauer first, he pushed his way in quickly, checking forward, right, left, up, forward again. Clear. He advanced further into a room that had clearly been in use not so long ago. A half-drunk cup of coffee was warm to the touch. There was a clean patch in an otherwise dusty floor, where someone had been sitting. A roll of duct tape on an old wooden school chair. An ashtray with the embers of a spent cigarette, still glowing.

Advancing forward, he wondered if they were hidden in the shadows beyond the next threshold. He took five long strides across the space, until he was on the edge of more darkness. He listened again, but could hear only his own tinnitus. Feeling for a switch on his right and flipping it, the room filled with glaring light. There was nothing there but a walk-in deep freeze.

'Jesus. No.'

The porthole window to the freezer was fogged up. Frost

scattered in white lace flowers over the glass. The temperature gauge said minus thirty-seven. Could she be in there, pale blue-grey and frozen solid, still wearing her final expression?

He steeled himself to look through the window. Empty but for rack upon rack of green beans and Brussels sprouts, waiting to be clothed in Tesco or Albert Heijn bags, perhaps.

'Thank you, God.'

Backtracking, facing the great outdoors, he realised that Tamara's final moments could be far, far worse than enduring the excruciating pins and needles that came with freezing to death.

Scanning the black fields, he realised he might be too late. As his eyes adjusted to the dark, he made out a path that led out among the maze of polytunnels, rippling in the wind. Tried to remember what it had all looked like during the daytime, but couldn't. On his own in that desolate place, with the wind turbines whining in the background as they churned the night sky, he imagined Den Bosch's men watching his every move; sentries waiting in the shadows, guns cocked. Was it possible George would send help?

Forging his way through the first field, he soon spotted a white glowing light in the distance, off to his right. It shone from crystalline structures on the horizon.

'Greenhouses!'

Sinking to the ground, unable to make out anything of note, he traced careful fingers over the makeshift path spread out before him. Felt parallel furrows in the flattened soil. 'A trolley. They've taken her to the greenhouse on a trolley.'

He started to run, panting and tiring more quickly than he would have hoped. He had once chased like a prize greyhound after serial killers, thieves and drug dealers. But he was older now. Bearing the scars of his difficult forties, he was no longer quite as fit. If Tamara died tonight and he was unlucky enough to live, he didn't mind if Minks kicked him off the force. It was time, he decided. There, in the middle of a field of cabbages, he realised he was finished.

*Crack.*

The gunshot ripped through the cold air, bursting his heavy, choking bubble of self-doubt and nihilism. The wind whipped around his head, awakening his senses. There had been a flash of light from the direction of the greenhouses as the bullet had been discharged.

*Crack.* Another. This time, it hit. He was sent flying backwards, the breath knocked out of him as he hit the deck.

*I've been shot in the fucking head! But I'm still alive. Get up, you shitty old bastard.*

Then, grunting and squealing. What the hell was this? He could feel the ground beneath him reverberate as at least two heavy creatures pounded their way towards him. Pigs? Or boars? Jesus. Now he was in real trouble. Above him, the moon emerged suddenly from behind thick cloud and he caught a glimpse of the bone-coloured scimitars that were the boars' tusks. They were giants. What kind of screwed-up lunatic kept boars for security? What did that even make them? Guard pigs? It was absurd.

Scrambling to his feet, he started running towards the creatures, keeping them in his line of sight. If he missed, he knew they would gore him to death within minutes and devour him like a sinewy canapé. The larger of the two was a fully grown male, the size of a small elephant. *The bastard must be over three hundred kilos. Shit. I'm a goner.*

He knew he had to shoot straight. Yelling as he neared them, he let off bullet after bullet until the chamber of his gun was empty and his ears rang painfully. In that light, it was hard to see if his aim had been true. The squealing hit an even higher octave. One of the creatures seemed to have peeled off to the left and was now cantering away from him, between tall rows of sprouts. The large male was still coming for him, though, its snout bloodied and its gait drunken. Was a wounded boar more dangerous?

Touching his head as he sprinted, he realised the graze from the bullet was bleeding heavily. No time to worry, for the boar was upon him. It thundered up on small, rapid legs, barrelling into him, sending him flying into the sprout plants.

*Crack.*

Another gunshot fired. But where was the damned boar? It had rounded on him and was coming back for more.

Van den Bergen fumbled in his coat for a second magazine of bullets to slide into his gun. Fingertips slippery from the blood couldn't get a grip. And here came the elephantine alpha, brandishing its tusks like a warrior, intent on finishing what it had started.

'Not on my watch, you bastard. This is one pig you won't dominate. I'll see you in a sandwich first.'

Finally, the magazine clip slid into the Sig Sauer. Lying on his back, lifting his shoulders up to see ahead, he had an excellent low vantage point. He squeezed the trigger four times in rapid succession. The boar howled. Skidded towards him in the mud on legs that were buckling. Collapsed onto Van den Bergen's lower half, pinning him to the ground beneath its tremendous bulk.

Its body still rose and fell. Alive, but only just. The creature's hot blood seeped into his clothing.

Van den Bergen struggled to move beneath the weight of the beast, feeling his circulation failing him as his feet became numb. Had it broken his shin bones? Shouldn't he feel pain? Pushing with all his might, he tried to heave the thing off him.

In the distance, towards the greenhouses, he heard men's voices. They grew closer.

'He's on the path. Get him and bring him to me.'

Den Bosch. He'd recognise that oaf anywhere.

But further away, back towards the entrance to the farm, he heard another voice, carried to him on the wind. A familiar voice. Unexpected.

'Get a fucking map, dickhead!'

George. He'd never been so glad in his life to hear her voice. And he'd never been so terrified. George had come to save him, but if he were killed, who the hell would save her and Tamara?

# CHAPTER 34

## *The Den Bosch farm, at the same time*

Already riled, thanks to the taxi journey from hell, George didn't so much feel the red mist descending. She was already surrounded by her own personal fog of the stuff, still annoyed with Numb-Nuts and Tamara for putting Van den Bergen in this position at all, the selfish, entitled kidults.

Traversing the courtyard, disoriented by the long shadows cast from the one solitary security light, not really knowing where the hell she was going, she heard men's voices a way off, carried to her on the wind. Shouting. She glanced around at the outbuildings. A light burned in the second storey of one of them.

She flinched at the sound of a gunshot, though it wasn't sharp and immediate. There was a slight delay as the sound rippled in waves over some distance, she assessed. She froze so that she might judge where the shots had come from. The fields. A shaft of light in the distance punctured the black night sky. Greenhouses. George could make out their boxy shapes as the source of the glow. No time to waste.

She was unarmed, however. So frantic had she been to leave Van den Bergen's apartment that she had turned up to a gunfight with a satchel containing nothing more sinister than

Rivka Zemel's diary, her cigarettes, lighter and vaping stick, two sanitary towels, a fresh pack of industrial-strength Compeed blister plasters, roll-on deodorant, flight socks, one steroidal anal suppository in case Van den Bergen had a haemorrhoid emergency and, finally, a telescopic umbrella. By the time she had come across the dead boar in the middle of the muddy path that led to the greenhouse complex, she had devised several uses for the contents of her bag in a combat situation.

She tripped on the boar's snout, falling headlong into the spires of sprouts to her left.

'Jesus. What the *fuck* is that?'

Getting to her feet, she stood over the dead creature. It was the size of a small elephant. Its mouth lolled open, exposing those ferocious tusks. The bullet holes in its head told her the likely sequence of events.

'He killed you, didn't he? They set a boar on him. Christ. These people are mental. And now my new Docs are muddy and covered in blood because of you, you big hairy bastard.' She was tempted to kick the boar but heard the squealing of what was unmistakeably a second some way off among the militarily precise rows of vegetables. Realised a sanitary towel probably wouldn't do much against an angry boar.

George started to run. Sprinting towards the light, praying she wouldn't turn her ankle in that treacherous soft ground that was rutted with trolley tracks, hoof prints and perhaps drag marks from Van den Bergen's shoes. The tightness in her chest where her heart was breaking and the flaming ball of anger in her stomach almost sucked all the air out of her. But she ran through the pain.

'Come on, you bastards!' she shouted in English. If she drew them away from Van den Bergen, perhaps he'd have a chance to break free. If he were still alive. 'I know you're there. Come and fucking try it with me, if you're hard enough.'

Fumbling in her satchel, she put the brand-new roll-on deodorant – mercifully a weighty little glass bottle – inside one of the flight socks. She swung it at her side, ready to challenge whoever was first to step forwards. David stepping up to Goliath.

But nobody came.

The dazzling brightness of the first greenhouse made her squint. It was enormous – the size of a warehouse. The interior was lush and green, full of unseasonal tomato plants growing tall and strong, with clusters of young fruit hanging like magical balls of jade near the bases, a canopy of leaves on high. As she stepped inside, she was hit by the warm, damp air. Further in were red, yellow and green capsicums growing fat and shiny – jewels hidden in among giant plants with large, almond-shaped leaves that drooped as if they were tired out by merely growing. Their water was supplied by a complicated rig-up of tubing that snaked along the ground and sprinklers that had been planted in perfect rows like soldiers on parade. Above were more nozzles – for additional watering or perhaps to spray the crops against pests. They hung from a criss-cross web of large steel girders, suspended from the glazed roof of that industrial hangar-sized space.

It was so silent in there, all George could hear beyond her thudding heart was the air con system, or whatever it was that Den Bosch used to keep the heat and humidity high. She unbuttoned her duffel coat, keeping a watchful eye out for some useful discarded tool or one of Den Bosch's men, hiding in plain sight amongst the greenery.

'Where are you, Paul?' she whispered under her breath. The ache in her chest was still there. The deodorant-in-sock weapon in her hand felt ridiculously makeshift and inadequate. Would there ever be a time when she didn't have to be brave? *Silly question.*

It was an eerie space. The pungent, metallic stink of the

tomato plants made her want to sneeze. The lights were so bright, the green of the plants so unbroken and the black night sky above her so dense that she knew she was a walking target for any chump who could point a gun. Black girls in tartan duffels didn't exactly blend in.

'This is a fucking nightmare.'

Gingerly, reluctantly, she entered the next greenhouse. In here was a sea of purple-pink chrysanthemums. Ironic that Van den Bergen would have bloody loved a guided tour of the gardening mecca, under very different circumstances. But she wasn't loving this at all. She glanced down at her muddy boots.

'Aw, thems is fuckeroonied, man.' She sucked her teeth.

A sound, suddenly, on the far side of this greenhouse. Low voices, talking. George strained her eyes to see who was there. She clutched her flight-sock tightly. Stooped a little, wishing the chrysanths were as tall as the tomatoes and peppers. Dropping to the ground, she started to crawl, commando style, towards the voices. Men. She could hear the sound of shovels scraping at the earth. Or was she imagining it? The voices were suddenly more alert. She craned her neck to see what had changed. Eyes were staring straight at her.

Den Bosch.

His tattooed arms and glinting gold teeth were unmistakable.

It happened so quickly. The four men in the corner of the greenhouse sprinted towards the far exit. The overhead sprinklers started to hiss, emitting something unseen. Not water. Was it crop spray?

George was suddenly tired. Sluggish. Barely able to shuffle forward on her elbows and knees.

'I'm coming, old man.'

She thought she'd said the words, but had she? Her thoughts were cloudy. That red mist had been replaced by a mental pea-souper. The idea that sedative – perhaps something akin to ether – was being pumped through the overhead irrigation system inveigled its way into what remained of her salient thought. 'Fucksticks. Come on, George.'

Getting to her knees was no mean feat; standing up, even more of a challenge. She started to totter towards the exit, yawning, stumbling into the plants, like a drunk in a nightclub trying to weave their way to the bar for a glass of water that would come six pints too late.

'What are you lot up to in that corner?'

Hearing her own speech, slurring and clumsy, George shook her head in a bid to clear it. Felt sleep wrapping its tentacles around her, pulling her down to the ground. She had covered the distance to the corner where Den Bosch and his henchmen had been busy. A shovel was standing proud where it had been wedged vertically into the earth.

'What am I doing?' Drifting in and out of sleep as the gas pumped from the overhead jets, George willed herself to move. But she could no longer tell the difference between wakefulness and dreams.

She was lying sprawled on her side, staring into the face of a deathly pale Tamara, half submerged in the soil. Only her head, one shoulder and arm poked above ground, as though quicksand had tried to swallow her but had stalled halfway through its carnivorous meal. The ground around her was disturbed. Dirt beneath her fingernails. Blood dried on her temple.

In this dreamlike state, George saw Tamara blink. A bead of blood tracked down from her temple onto her cheek and into the corner of her mouth. Her lips parted.

'Help.'

The slightest of sounds. What a strange dream George was having.

'Help me.'

Except it wasn't a dream.

270

Forcing herself to take everything she saw as reality, rather than a drugged fantasy, George reached out to touch Tamara's face. She felt strangely distanced from her. Knew she had to get them both into the fresh air.

'Where's Paul? Your dad. Where is he?'

Tamara stared at her blankly. 'Gone. They're going to kill us all.'

Her speech was laboured and barely audible.

*Come on, George. Snap out of it. Find the switch to shut off the sprinklers.*

Crawling past Tamara, George was dimly aware of a mound of earth, roughly six feet long, beside her. No time for that though. She had to find the switch.

Beyond the shovel, she saw a control panel festooned with switches and a flashing light. She guessed there would be a canister of gas nearby, connected up to the pipework. George realised she had to disconnect the canister or switch the delivery system off. Hitting the panel clumsily, water started to come through the sprinklers. But she couldn't be sure the gas wasn't still being piped through. Tripping, she realised she'd walked into a barrel. On the side, there was a hazard label.

'Fluothane – halothane vapour. Warning. Causes drowsiness. Do not operate machinery.'

A pipe had been rigged up, feeding from the gas barrel to the sprinkler system. Searching for a cap or a bung to seal the barrel once she'd wrenched the pipe free, George drew a blank. But then she remembered the sanitary towel in her bag. A giant pad for night-time. Taking it out and unfurling it, she held it under the nearest sprinkler until it was puffy and sodden. She rolled it up, pulled out the pipe and plugged the Fluothane barrel with the soggy towel. It would buy them time. Stumbling to the door, she flung it open to let the fresh air in. The biting wind blasted inside, immediately blowing away some of the narcotic cobwebs that the gas had spun around her.

'Help!' Tamara shouted weakly.

'I'm coming.'

Clawing at the loose earth around her, George worked as much of Tamara free as she could. There was soil in her hair, her ears. Even her eyelashes.

'Were they burying you?'

Tugging at Tamara's arm almost dislocated her own. She was a dead weight.

'You've got to help me, here, for Christ's sake! Try to push any way you can. Hurry up. I've got to go after your dad.'

George yanked the shovel from its anchorage and started to dig around her to loosen the compacted earth. She took a step back onto the low mound beside Tamara's burial ground but felt something give beneath her feet.

'Oh, you're joking. This can't be happening.'

Feeling the contents of her stomach rising in her throat, George backed off hastily, flinging the shovel to the ground. She started to claw at the mound, shunting the topsoil away to see what lay beneath.

'Jesus. No.'

Her careful fingers exposed the unmistakable tip of a nose. Excavating further, she traced the line of a forehead, chin, cheekbones. She swept the earth aside, revealing the grey death mask of someone she had last seen mere hours ago.

'Cornelia Verhagen. Oh my God. You poor sod.'

'Is she dead?'

George felt for a pulse, but the alabaster cold of the dead woman's skin said it all. 'Very.' She choked back an angry sob, and started to claw again at the earth that still had Tamara in its grip, wanting to free her from this macabre burial ground.

With a little more effort, Tamara was free. She scrambled to her feet, her clothes dishevelled and covered in soil. Shaking from head to toe, teeth chattering. Her colour was bad; a blue tinge to her lips.

Hastily taking off her duffel, George felt the sedative fog lifting in earnest. She wrapped her coat around Tamara's shoulders, led her to the path and pointed to the door through which she had entered. 'Go back to the first greenhouse. Hide in the tomato plants until I come for you.'

'But Dad's that way.' She pointed to the door that led on to the unknown.

'You're not coming with me. You'll slow me down. With a bit of luck, more police should arrive at any minute.'

'And if they don't?' Tamara's eyes were filled with tears. 'And if you don't come back for me?'

'I've got Compeed, cigs and Nivea forty-eight-hour deodorant,' George said. 'I'm fucking unstoppable.'

## CHAPTER 35

# *The Den Bosch farm, at the same time*

'How could you?' Van den Bergen asked, unashamedly weeping. 'Why? Just tell me why!'

The pain in his legs was intense. He couldn't move them without excruciating bolts shooting up to his groin. Despite his best efforts to move them, they lay on the flatbed trolley as though they were no longer part of him. Broken from the weight of the hog. Already swelling. But it was nothing compared to the agony of having seen Tamara on the cusp of death and all but buried in the ground.

'She'll be dead by now,' Den Bosch said, checking his watch as though the killing of a young woman required precision timing, of which he was a master. 'That gas we've just pumped in there should finish off your daughter and that cunt, your girlfriend, within minutes. If it hasn't …' He slapped the nose of his pistol in his hand. Grinned at Baumgartner, who merely sat imperiously on a camping stool, framed by a forest of giant oriental tree lilies. 'One bullet each should do it.' Winking, he licked his lips lasciviously, flashing that intimidating grille of gold teeth. 'Mind you, I'll wait until I've had a little fun with that girlfriend of yours first. I don't mind a bit of dark meat on the side, as long as we're purely talking recreation.'

Though the misery threatened to engulf him, Van den Bergen clung to the raft of his wrath. 'If it's me you want to punish, why the hell did you pick on the women in my life? Aren't you man enough to square up to me in person? You've got to have your bully boys do it for you, you Nazi limp-dick?'

He could see the sneer forming on Den Bosch's weather-beaten face, though beneath it, the punctured pride was obvious. Good. He had nothing left to lose. He'd been anticipating death for many, many years, and now, surrounded by five armed men, stripped of his Sig Sauer and unable to move his legs, he felt finally that the end was upon him.

Den Bosch approached and squatted beside him. He pushed Van den Bergen's chin up roughly, using the nose of his handgun. A Smith & Wesson semi-automatic.

'You stuck your big hooter into my business and you didn't heed my warning. I don't make idle threats, Chief Inspector. You take a swing at me, I'll hit you where it hurts the most.' His breath reeked of Jack Daniel's and cigarettes, pronounced even above the pungent aroma of the giant fragrant lilies. Those normally hard eyes were somewhat unfocused. 'Cornelia Verhagen made the mistake of tangling with me and my father.' He looked over his shoulder at Baumgartner. 'Bet she's fucking regretting it now she's in a shallow grave. I'm not sure if I should let her rot or feed her *and* your daughter to my surviving boar. Punishment for killing my stud.' He forced the gun harder beneath Van den Bergen's chin so that his neck was bent painfully backwards. 'I make a lot of money from breeding those babies. We have some good fights. You know how much I can make in a night with a big boar and a dog in the ring? A hundred thousand. More. And you shot my best boy. Wanker.'

His face was twisted with hatred; those wind-burned cheeks beetroot red with anger and alcohol. But Van den Bergen pushed the pain of two broken shin bones aside to focus on what was before him. First, it was clear Baumgartner was indeed Den

Bosch's father. Secondly, if Den Bosch loosed a bullet at that angle into Van den Bergen's head, it would guarantee a frontal lobotomy but, in all probability, not death. The arsehole didn't know one end of a gun from another. At least ten shots had been fired from the greenhouses into the field, but not one had definitively found its mark. The graze to the head had almost certainly been a lucky accident. Perhaps, even from this vantage point, there was a way he could disarm the bastard and take out Baumgartner and the three other men before they could even let a round off. Finally, Van den Bergen reminded himself that all was not lost. Far from it. While Tamara and George might well be dying in the adjacent greenhouse, they were not yet dead. He had everything to fight for. And he was damned if he would leave little Eva to Numb-Nuts with nobody competent to oversee that shitbird's parenting attempts.

Scanning his immediate surroundings, he could see that the three farm hands were big brutes. They didn't look overly bright though, and he suspected they were half cut on spirits too. Baumgartner was the one to watch. Even at seventy-five, Van den Bergen spied a dangerously sharp intellect behind those calculating eyes. The elderly psychiatrist held a shotgun across his lap. Something in the way he held it spelled ex-military. And this was a man who knew how to manipulate and render a victim emotionally defenceless with just a few words.

'If you're going to kill me and feed me to the lilies, then you might as well tell me ...' He focused on Baumgartner. 'Why did you murder the members of the Force of Five?'

Baumgartner stood, eyebrow raised, and took a few steps towards Van den Bergen. He poked at his leg with the barrel of his shotgun. 'All that length of leg. Not much use to you now, is it?'

Van den Bergen bit hard on his tongue. It was all he could do to stifle a scream. He wasn't about to given Baumgartner that satisfaction. He gasped. 'You prescribed those old men the wrong medication, didn't you? You killed them.'

The psychiatrist took a seat on the end of the horticultural trolley on which Van den Bergen lay. 'Ah, dear Chief Inspector Van den Bergen. I've been watching you these past few weeks. And your daughter, of course.' He smiled benignly, but a monster in a fine suit with a convincing smile was still a monster. 'And your granddaughter. How lovely she is.'

*Don't react. Don't react.*

'I'll fucking kill you if you lay a hand on her,' Van den Bergen said, mustering all the strength he had in those shot-to-bits stomach muscles of his and propelling himself upwards to sitting position. Trying to take a swing at Baumgartner. Except his hands were tied behind him with gardening twine that bit into his wrists.

Den Bosch intervened, pushing Van den Bergen back down hard so that his head hit the thick plywood pallet. Lights popped like sparks in his field of vision.

'Not so fast, Van den Bergen. This is not the time for you to be getting cocky. It's over for you. You're the only reason why I'm still under police scrutiny.'

'The British police are on to you. One of your vans got pulled over coming off a passenger ferry from the Hoek van Holland.'

Den Bosch grinned. Took his phone out of the breast pocket of his soiled denim shirt and deftly thumbed through several screens with only his left hand – gun still in the right, now pressed against Van den Bergen's temple. He turned the screen to Van den Bergen. There was a picture of George on the lower deck of the Stena Line passenger ferry, looking as though she'd been cornered.

'You think you're clever, don't you? You police types. Think you're a cut above a simple businessman like me. But you're wrong there, pal. What you fail to understand is that I've been doing my job – as a farmer and as a trafficker – for twenty years. I learned from the master ...' Phone in hand, he saluted his father. A Nazi Sieg Heil, of course. 'And he learned from not one, but two masters.'

'Two?'

Den Bosch looked at him as if he didn't understand such a simplistic question. 'Why do you think I killed Cornelia Verhagen? Because she and her interfering, judgemental old bastard of a father started a witch hunt against—'

'Frederik!' Baumgartner raised his voice. Not so gentlemanly now.

'Why not tell him? I'm going to put a bullet in his head anyway.' Den Bosch turned back to Van den Bergen. 'Just because port police pull over a suspicious-looking van or truck doesn't mean they're going to find the cargo inside. Know what I mean? You lot only found those Syrians because my driver totally fucked up. He'd been on the marching powder. He was unreliable. But normally ... How else do you think I've been bolstering Amsterdam's illegal immigrant population for all these years?' He turned to his horticultural cronies for support. 'When that El Al plane flew into the Bijlmer apartment block back in '92, only forty-three fatalities were reported. But I can tell you, mate ...' Phone away now, he poked himself in the chest. Slow movements. Definitely under the influence. 'There were *hundreds* more, thanks to me. I'd just done my first shipment. Twenty, I was. Tender twenty. And I got paid a king's ransom to bring a load of illegals in from whatever war-torn shithole was big in the news at the time. Sierra Leone, was it? Or Rwanda.'

'Yugoslavia,' Baumgartner offered. 'Rwanda was in '94. Remember? That was a good year. Genocide always pays well.'

Den Bosch withdrew a hip flask, taking a swig. Clearly enjoying himself, he waved his father away, focusing his attention on Van den Bergen. 'Anyway. You've got fuck all on me, my friend. And now you're a dead man walking. Except you're not walking. And I'm going to split the hips on that black bitch you live with. Maybe I'll have a go on your daughter, too. Do you think if I leave my seed in her dead body and she turns to compost that there'll be a crop of Den Bosch plants?' He started to laugh maniacally.

*This guy's completely crackers*, Van den Bergen thought, trying to keep the despair at bay. *Men like him make mistakes. You've got this, Paul. Ignore the taunts. He's sick, but he's not invincible.*

His less heroic alter-ego had other ideas, however.

*Jesus Christ. It's not enough he's going to kill me and everyone I ever gave a damn about. He's going to defile them as well. I wish I could die now. I've had enough. Please let me go, God. If you're up there, just let me die right now, so I don't have to see or hear anything else.*

He held his breath. He didn't die. He wanted the truth. And he needed to give George time to switch off the noxious gas in the adjacent greenhouse. If she was still breathing.

Turning to Baumgartner to avoid Den Bosch's taunts, he asked, 'The Force of Five. They all left money to Abadi. Was that it? Did you want their money? Abadi threw himself in front of a tram because he was so petrified that someone in his life would find out he was helping the police to gather information about your son and his trafficking exploits. It was you, wasn't it? He was frightened of you. You were a major influence in all of their lives. Kaars Verhagen, Arnold van Blanken, Brechtus Bruin.'

'Of course.' Baumgartner folded his hands primly over his shotgun.

'But Ed Sijpesteijn's missing and I know that Hendrik van Eden was somehow involved with a Nazi officer called Bruno Baumgartner.'

Recognition in the psychiatrist's eyes. 'How do you know that?' He wore a wry smile.

'Cornelia Verhagen knew about the box of letters and invoices, didn't she? That's why you killed her. But I don't understand why it mattered. Hendrik van Eden wasn't your father. Bruno Baumgartner must have been. You have his name.'

André Baumgartner stood. 'I've had enough of this cross-examination. If I wanted to tell the police all my bloody business, I'd have answered their queries and turned myself in.' He picked up a hoe that was stuck into the earth and raised it above his head with naked determination in his eyes. Staring straight at Van den Bergen.

The last thing Van den Bergen saw before the blade of the hoe came down on his head was the glimmer of movement in the furthest corner of his peripheral vision. Reflected in the glass of the greenhouse, he was certain he spied George. Big hair. Furious expression. Doc Marten boots, creeping closer, closer—

# CHAPTER 36

# The Den Bosch farm, at the same time

George covered her mouth when the hoe made contact with Van den Bergen's head. She blinked back tears, heart in free fall at the thought that the man she truly loved had been killed. The blood drained from her limbs and she started to slide, slide, slide down the glass wall of the giant greenhouse.

Thanks to the cover of the five-foot-tall lily trees, they hadn't noticed her arrival. She could hear them talking and laughing. Lighting cigarettes and swigging from Den Bosch's hip flask. Baumgartner's voice was the most commanding. The others fell silent when he spoke.

'A good night's work, boys. That's the way we deal with threats. We give them short shrift. The police can't put you behind bars if all the witnesses are under the sod or in a boar's belly.'

He was sitting on the end of the horticultural trolley with his back to her. Van den Bergen's body lying on the pallet at an awkward angle. Head skewed improbably. Hands tied behind his back. George was put in mind of the C. S. Lewis book she had devoured over and over again as a child, *The Lion, the Witch and the Wardrobe*. Van den Bergen was Aslan, lying shaved of his mane, cold and inanimate on the stone table, while Jadis, the White Witch who made it always winter and never Christmas, celebrated with her foul and pestilent cronies. A nightmarish scene from a fairy tale. Except this was reality. And George was no Lucy Pevensie.

'I thought you were going to tell him about Hendrik,' Den Bosch said, swaying slightly. 'I nearly did. I had to bite my tongue, there.'

'You need to watch the drink,' Baumgartner said, wagging a castigatory finger in his direction. 'If he'd somehow escaped … and you'd let slip that Hendrik was my biological father, I wouldn't have been pleased.'

'What difference would it make?' one of the farm workers asked.

Baumgartner grunted as he stood. 'It's complicated. Bruno Baumgartner was my father, as far as I'm concerned, even though we were largely estranged. It was my mother, Anna, who brought me up. What a woman she was. A beauty, certainly.' He squeezed Den Bosch's shoulder affectionately. 'You have her eyes. ' Turned back to his captive audience of farm workers. 'My poor Mama endured years of being ostracised. Hendrik van Eden hounded her out of Amsterdam. He publicly shamed her as a Nazi collaborator, telling anyone who'd listen that *she* betrayed Jews to the German SS in return for fine silk dresses and trips to the Berghof in Bavaria, hobnobbing with Hitler and Eva Braun. He was jealous, you see. Bitter that Bruno had wooed her away from him. She had to run away to 's-Hertogenbosch with me – only a baby. That's where Frederik takes his name from.'

'They know, Dad.'

'Ach, my mother brought me up to believe my German Papi was a hero of epic proportions, despite being branded a war criminal and being packed off to prison. Even when the locals shaved her head to shame her for collaborating, she still held a candle for him.' His shoulders sagged. A consummate actor, enjoying delivering this performance.

'Listen how he finds out Hendrik is his father,' Den Bosch said, slapping his thigh as though some excellent joke were about to be cracked. Just a normal telling of tall tales around the campfire, except Van den Bergen lay dead on that damned trolley and Cornelia Verhagen's body was already starting to spoil in the adjoining greenhouse. 'This bit will kill you.'

'It's not that bloody amusing.' Baumgartner's jubilant expression curdled. 'I lost a kidney. That's no walk in the park, you know. My remaining one was already scarred to hell. I needed a transplant. Mama wasn't a match. Turned out my SS hero father wasn't either. I was only thirty at the time. I thought I was going to die. When you were thirty, young man, you were living high off the hog with not a care in the world, apart from the danger of the police catching up with you. You've never known suffering.'

Den Bosch looked suddenly contrite. George watched his clumsy body language, thinking about how she might feasibly take him out with a limited cache of makeshift weapons at her disposal. She was definitely going to kill the bastard tonight, though. No matter what.

'So let me guess,' the farm worker said, taking a hit from the hip flask. 'You tracked down Hendrik and hey presto! There's a match.'

Baumgartner nodded. 'Exactly. Turns out he was my biological father all along. We hit it off from the word go, and I decided his betrayal of my mother was water under the bridge.'

'Your mother was a bit of a slag,' the farm worker said. 'Was she fit?'

The seventy-five-year-old psychiatrist was up and at his throat like a greyhound bursting from its starting gate to catch the rabbit. 'What did you say, you piece of shit peasant?'

Suddenly, it was mayhem. The two other farm workers were trying to pull Baumgartner off their friend. Den Bosch joined in the fray, raining down punches, not caring where they might land.

'Don't you dare insult my family!' he yelled.

Father and son fought against employees on the payroll. Nobody paid the slightest heed to George creeping forward to lift a hefty bag of compost.

As George swung the bag into Den Bosch, the men scattered. Caught by surprise at the sight of a mere woman coming back from the dead. Den Bosch's knees gave way. George whipped out the Compeed she'd stowed in her pocked, deftly plastering them onto his eyes. He tried to peel off the super-adhesive blister plasters.

'I'm blind!' he screamed. 'My eyes!'

The farm workers were fumbling for their guns with shaky bourbon hands. Too slow. Like Charles Bronson with premenstrual tension and her own *Death Wish* to match, George spun her makeshift deodorant in its stocking. It whistled through the air, hitting the worker who had insulted Anna Groen on the temple with such speed and ferocity that he sank to the ground. Out cold. Two down, three to go. George fumbled with her umbrella but it refused to be reassembled into a decent weapon. She was out of ideas.

André Baumgartner's sudden presence behind her took her by surprise; the sharp scratch of a syringe against her neck even more so.

'Hands in the air, Dr McKenzie, or I'll pump a nice air bubble straight into your carotid artery.'

## CHAPTER 37

## *The Den Bosch farm, at the same time*

'You're going to kill me anyway,' George said, glancing down at Van den Bergen. Certain she could feel her heart breaking. Though he appeared to be out cold, his colour was still good. 'Aren't you?'

'Shut your mouth and walk,' Baumgartner said.

He pushed her further in amongst the ranks of tall lily trees, where the scent was so pungent that George felt almost intoxicated. Her legs felt leaden, but her mind whirred into action.

*Keep him talking. Marie and Elvis are bound to be on their way. They'd better have brought the fucking cavalry with them.*

'If Hendrik was your father, then why did you kill him and his friends?'

'Move it. And less talk, you interfering little cow.'

The needle stung as it dug into her. He'd almost certainly punctured the skin. Any deeper and she'd be in real trouble. 'I just want to know what turns an intelligent man into a cold-blooded killer, Dr Baumgartner. You took an oath to first do no harm. But you killed your own father. Was it revenge for your mother? All that ridicule she endured after the war?'

Ahead, she could see a clearing had been prepared. Two men, clearly of South-Eastern European or Middle Eastern

285

origin, wearing filthy clothes, were leaning on spades. Just beyond them, she glimpsed a grave. They spoke to one another in Arabic, inclining their heads towards her.

'Help me!' she said in their tongue. As the adrenalin coursed through her, vocabulary she had learned years ago and forgotten started to come back to her. Synapses flaring with ideas. Do or die. 'The police are coming. I will make sure you get free of this bastard and get Dutch citizenship. But you'll need to help me.'

These filthy, skinny, frightened-looking men were the only secret weapon she had left. If they had any loyalty to Den Bosch, it was game over. But if she was right and they were trafficked slave labour, trying to win their loyalty with the promise of a visa was worth a punt.

Two sets of desperate brown eyes turned to her. Had one nodded imperceptibly? Had Baumgartner noticed?

'What are you saying to them, you sneaky little bitch?'

'I told them you're a shit doctor and that I wouldn't come to you if I had an itchy arsehole.'

He jabbed the needle further into her neck. Warm blood spilling in fat beads, seeping into the collar of her top. 'I'm an outstanding psychiatrist, missy. And my father died of natural causes, if you must know.'

'Don't try to tell me that Arnold van Blanken, Kaars Verhagen and Brechtus Bruin all coincidentally died of heart attacks.' She did her damnedest to slow his pace. Buying time while the workers exchanged glances.

'Kaars Verhagen is to blame. You want a culprit? He's your man. He had to go and find a box full of correspondence between my German father and Hendrik. Verhagen threatened to expose Hendrik as a Nazi collaborator.'

'It wouldn't have bothered you! Have you seen the state of your son? And why would his grandfather be getting his tits in a tangle over something that happened seventy-odd years ago?'

'Hendrik van Eden spent his entire adult life being celebrated as one of Amsterdam's most beloved sons,' Baumgartner said. 'He practically had the keys to the city. Why do you think he died of a heart attack?' There was fury in his voice. 'Kaars found invoices for Hendrik's trafficking endeavours. Him and those other busybodies threatened to expose him to the national press. Can you imagine the embarrassment that would have caused? The shame? The stress was enough to kill Hendrik. And I vowed I'd get my revenge. I was with him as he breathed his last on a sticky supermarket floor, squinting beneath the god-awful fluorescent lighting. I swore to him that I'd take out every last one of those interfering, do-gooding sons of bitches. Hendrik's heart had given up, so I'd make sure theirs would too. And I did. And I hope it damn well hurt like hell at the end.'

'They trusted you with their healthcare and you betrayed that trust. You're a snake.'

At the edge of the grave, they came to a halt. With the panic constricting her throat, she wondered if she'd even be able to scream. Arms encircled her from behind. Den Bosch?

'Before you go, I'm going to have a little fun with you. I did promise Van den Bergen I would.'

George could feel his erection pressing into her back.

*If you're on the premises, Marie and Elvis, now's the time to fucking step it up, guys.*

She tried to wriggle loose. 'Get off me, you fascist monster! If you're going to kill me, get on with it. But don't think you're sticking your crappy excuse for a dick anywhere near me.'

Mouthing the word 'Now!' in Arabic at the workers, she hooked her Doc-Marten-clad foot around Den Bosch's ankle, trying to destabilise him. They scuffled, and she edged him towards the deep hole that was intended as her final resting place. It only seemed to fuel Den Bosch's ardour.

'I love it when you lot struggle. You're so primitive.' He grabbed her breasts from behind.

'Fucking pervert. Can you Nazis only get it on when you're being watched by your parents and you're sticking it in black women? Bet you wish you were hung like a black guy, don't you? Sorry, but my genetic superiority's not going to rub off on you, pal.'

Mustering all the strength she had, she wrong-footed Den Bosch, treated him to a ferocious backwards kick from the heel of her boot that was worthy of a mule and hauled him over her shoulder. He was dead weight, but she was so buoyed by fury that he toppled over like a ragdoll. Falling, falling, to land broken and screaming at the bottom of the grave.

'My leg! You've broken my leg, you bitch!'

'Diddums,' George said. 'An eye for an eye, and a leg for a leg. Twat.'

As she spat on him in the grave, Baumgartner and Den Bosch's cronies, who had been watching, rapt, as though their struggle had been particularly good daytime TV, suddenly sprang into action. Baumgartner plunged his syringe into George's shoulder.

But he was too late.

The trafficked gravediggers fell upon the remaining three men with their spades. Baumgartner's arm was the first casualty. The syringe flew through the air, though the needle remained sticking out of George's flesh like a hellish splinter. The spade followed through to Baumgartner's face, heaved with all the resentful vitriol that dwelled inside that modern-day slave. There was a sickening crack as the psychiatrist's nose and cheekbone fractured simultaneously. Blood spattered onto his mouth and chin. His eyes rolled back in his head as he dropped to the ground.

The remaining two henchmen were younger and stronger. One grabbed the second trafficked man's spade out of the air and sent him flying sideways into a copse of lily trees, leaping after him with the spade raised high, clearly with the intention of pulverising him with his own gardening implement. But the fighting and the noise provided distraction enough for George to scramble for the shotgun that Baumgartner had dropped.

'No, you don't!' Baumgartner snatched at the barrel of his weapon, only inches from his reach as he sprawled on the ground.

But George had the upper hand. She stamped on his wrist, pinning him to the floor. 'Yes, I fucking well do.' She snatched up the shotgun, aiming it at his head. It was heavy enough to make the muscles in her hand scream with the effort of holding it steady, but she made every effort not to let her discomfort show. With her free left hand, she plucked the needle from her shoulder as though it were a mere inconvenience. Tossed it aside. 'Hands on your head. It's over.'

With the gun in her hands, George was optimistic that she could bring the situation under control, at least temporarily. Except, she hadn't accounted for Den Bosch climbing out of the grave when she had been looking the other way. And she hadn't reckoned with the farm workers easily overpowering the half-starved gravediggers. Suddenly, George found the weapon wrenched out of her hands. She felt herself falling. The air was knocked out of her as she fell into the grave. Earth began to fall on her in gritty clods.

'No!' she cried.

The soil filled her mouth as a manic, grinning Den Bosch dropped spade after spade of crumbly earth onto her head. She shook herself free of it. Got onto her knees and tried to claw her way up the sheer sides of the grave. When the two consecutive gunshots rang through the air, George wondered if she'd been wounded. As the two trafficked workers plummeted into the hole, lifeless and with dark red bloodstains blossoming across their chests, she was forced to acknowledge that she'd been outsmarted and outnumbered. Now, she was trapped beneath their weight.

'Let me out! Marie! Elvis!' She screamed, using every ounce of strength that she could muster. Praying that this wouldn't be the end.

'Lie down and accept what's happening to you,' Baumgartner said. 'Being buried alive is very stressful and you're making it worse.' He grinned, as his beast of a son and his two men shovelled earth into the grave at an alarming rate.

The smell of death threatened to overpower George as the trafficked men's bodies bled out onto her. Her muscles burned with the effort of trying to push them off, but in that deep, claustrophobic space, the more she struggled, the more she found herself trapped. Within moments, her body was pinned in place by the soil. It rose like water, until her chin was submerged, then her mouth. Only her nose remained uncovered. She kept shaking her head to loosen the grip of the earth, but still, they shovelled, as though she was a rose bush they intended to plant.

She shook her head free like a weak swimmer bobbing above water one last time, before the undertow of a freezing lake claimed them for good. 'Help! Help me!'

George used all that remained of her energy to scream before her mouth and nose were inundated again. They were working too hard and too fast. The soil was blocking her airways. Too heavy to shrug off.

She was covered.

She was hidden.

It was over.

# CHAPTER 38

## *The Den Bosch farm,*
## *several minutes earlier*

'They've definitely gone that way,' Marie said, pointing towards the greenhouses. 'That's where the noise is coming from. That's where the damn light is coming from.'

'I think we should check this outbuilding first.' Elvis stared up at the brightly lit window above them. His voice was a mere whisper. 'I don't want to go haring down a pitch-black dirt track and find some neo-Nazi thug creeping up behind me.'

Frustrated by her colleague, Marie set off at a brisk pace into the fields. Glancing behind her. 'Do what you like. I'm not wasting precious time.'

Elvis was standing by the heavy door, which was ajar, a crestfallen look on his face. She knew he was fighting the demons that still possessed him; understood that every time he was faced with a chase, he would only ever be able to see the inside of a body bag. Ploughing on through the field, she made a mental note to recommend her therapist to him.

*Van den Bergen would bollock you for steaming off into a hostage situation without backup,* she thought. But then she remembered Van den Bergen had put them in this position in the first place, and that nobody realised quite how much Marie was capable of. *They think I'm just an IT house cat. Let them think that. They don't know a thing.*

She stepped lightly over the dead boar, relishing the excitement of the danger she faced and the weight of the gun in her hand. Savouring the potential to avenge the Syrian girl – to get revenge on behalf of another mother who had lost her child needlessly.

'Wait! Wait for me!'

She heard footsteps behind her as Elvis jogged down the rutted path.

'Look, if you're not ready for this, go back.'

He stared down at the dead boar. Shook his head. 'I'm a cop. Of course I'm ready.'

They crept amid the sprouts and cabbages until they came to the first cathedral of glass and light.

'Jesus. This place is enormous. It's like an aircraft hangar.' Elvis gazed up at the greenhouse in wonder.

'Let's go.'

Her senses were sharp as she led them inside. Tomato plants towered above her. The smell reminded her of her childhood, when her mother had grown tomatoes in the garden, tasking a ten-year-old Marie with pollinating them with a feather. She was just musing on the industrial-scale beauty of the place when a grey-faced body tumbled out of the tall foliage and fell onto them.

They both let out a shriek.

'Tamara!' Elvis caught her, manoeuvring her carefully to the ground.

'Is she alive?' Marie asked, transfixed by the sight of the limp form of Van den Bergen's only child, her eyes rolled back in her head, mouth open, covered in soil.

Elvis felt for a pulse in her neck, cradling her head on his knees. 'Weak pulse, but yes.' He patted her face. 'Tamara.'

She moaned, blinked. Licked her lips. There was recognition in her eyes as she registered Elvis's face. 'Thank God. Get Dad.'

'What should we do?' Elvis asked, looking to Marie for guidance.

'Take her to the pool car. Call an ambulance.'

'What about De Vries? We need backup, Marie. This is too much for two of us to take on.'

Marie looked to the far side of the greenhouse. Spied another giant structure beyond. 'George is in here somewhere. And Van den Bergen. We're not alone.' Elvis was right, of course. They were in over their heads. But if that grubby, duplicitous little tit, Roel de Vries, descended on the place with his team of bumbling homicide wannabes, she knew the boss and their little unit would end up being beaten with the shitty end of the stick. 'Leave that to me. You sort out Tamara with an ambulance. I'll deal with backup.'

She feigned dialling HQ on her phone. No signal, of course. Elvis said nothing. Either he was complicit or too overwhelmed to realise that she was stringing him a line.

'Oh, and give me your gun. I might need a second gun.'

'No way. What if we're ambushed on the way out?'

'Just give me the flipping gun, Dirk. The party's in the greenhouses. Not back there.'

As he passed the weapon to her, Marie sensed her colleague had symbolically handed his badge in. She could see it in his eyes. Burnout. Elvis's days as a cop on active duty were over. He looked relieved. Even mustered a weak smile.

Now she was alone but for two Sig Sauers and the delicious feeling that anything was possible. Jogging forward through the tall plants, clutching a gun in each hand, she felt like Lara Croft in *Tomb Raider*. No longer stinky Marie that everyone took the piss out of – a woman who spent her days in the IT suite, trawling through snuff videos and paedo porn sites and the dregs of the darknet in the hope of catching the bad guys, and who spent her nights gaming in the dark at home to block out the pain of being alone. Now, she was a heroine. She could be more like George.

At the end of the greenhouse, she came across the partially excavated shallow grave of Cornelia Verhagen. Felt warmed by her fury and the sense that she was so very alive next to this cold, dead woman.

She passed through to the second greenhouse, almost tripping headlong over the horticultural trolley that was scudding across her path at pace, seemingly driven by Van den Bergen.

She dropped to a crouch.

'Boss. What the hell is going on? What are you doing?'

He lay on the trolley, belly down, but was walking his hands forward on the ground to propel himself along. Blood still dripped from a head wound that had clearly been pouring not long ago. Red beads seeped from a claret-coloured crust the size of a fist onto black soil that had been flattened by many feet. His wrists were bloodied too. Telltale streaks of vermillion along the metal edge of the trolley showed where he had probably cut himself free of his bonds.

'You see that boar back there? Well, my legs are bust thanks to him, and these fuckers bashed my head in with a hoe. Then left me for dead.' He grimaced. 'But I put a bullet right between the pig's eyes and now I'm going to sneak up on these bastards. They killed my Tamara.' He let out a dry, racking sob that abated suddenly. 'And I'm going to kill them. There's about five of them. Marie … they've got George.' His speech was laboured; his eyes unfocused.

'Stay there, boss. You're a danger to yourself.'

'And send you in to fight five murderers on your own? No way. Where the fuck is Elvis?'

'Tamara's alive, boss. Elvis has taken her to the car. He's getting an ambulance.'

Van den Bergen vomited explosively on the base of a tall pink lily tree.

'Stay here, for Christ's sake,' Marie said.

She was the only one who had nothing whatsoever to lose. Her son was gone. She had no love in her life. She only had the festering disappointment and simmering wrath of the wrongfully bereaved.

The sound of men's laughter some way off punctured the silence of the dense, humid air. With a gun in both hands, Marie marched forward, adoring the heady feeling of invincibility, no matter how fleeting her moment of triumph may be. For now, she was the mousy IT girl gone rogue – an unknown quantity.

Den Bosch, Baumgartner and their men were so preoccupied by a large hip flask and raucous high-fiving that they didn't notice her step through the lily trees into the clearing.

'Drop your weapons. On the floor. Hands above your heads.'

But it was as though she hadn't spoken at all. They were bellowing with laughter as they turned towards her.

Baumgartner said something in German to Den Bosch that Marie didn't quite catch. Before she had time to work out what had been said, before she had time to let a single shot off, Baumgartner had blown holes in her both of her kneecaps with his shotgun. Her downfall came to pass as if in slow motion. She fell to the ground, screaming, arms flailing dramatically in the air as she couldn't help but let go of her guns. Hitting the deck hard.

'No!' She gasped.

The pain was excruciating. At that moment, she wished more than anything that she was unconscious. This case had been the undoing of them all. Amid the crippling agony, Marie looked just beyond where she had fallen and spied a deep pit. A grave. Jesus. Would they roll her in? Would this be the end of IT Marie? Was this some karmic payback for what she had done to Kamphuis?

'Is that all of them?' Den Bosch asked. 'Have we managed to take out half of the Dutch police force?' He wheezed with mirth, as though he'd cracked the funniest joke in the world. Swaying above Marie, he lunged to kick her in the upper thigh. 'This one looks like she never washes her hair. Lads? Anyone want a go?'

Marie felt a still-smouldering cigarette butt fizz against her skin. She rolled away from it, desperately trying to spot the discarded guns. One, she'd somehow tossed behind her. The other must have fallen into the grave.

'Nah. She stinks of onions. And it's late. Let's go. She'll have bled out by the morning.'

Another man: 'We can dig another deep one tomorrow and shove them all in. It'll be like nothing ever happened.'

'The plants will be amazing,' said Den Bosch. 'Nothing like a dead body for excellent fertiliser.' It was as though they were on a simple shopping trip to a garden centre.

The men were collecting up their tools. Clanking. Chatting. Drunk, but otherwise seeming as though they'd merely reached the end of a hard day's work, whilst Marie writhed in agony, too weak to speak. She felt her consciousness slipping away, leaving only bottomless pain in place of humanity. Had Baumgartner punctured a major blood vessel? Was this it? If so, she'd failed. Damn it.

Marie's thoughts became befuddled. She started to dream of her baby son, as though he were still alive and she were cradling him in her arms. How beautiful he was, staring up at her with shining blue eyes and the perfect rose blush of a baby's cheeks. Strawberry-blond fluff for hair. He was perfect. The end was nigh and it was everything she wanted. She had come home to her son. Even the pain was abating. Death wasn't so bad, after all.

'Fucking wankers.' It was George McKenzie.

How did this fit with her final dream?

The sound of gunshot. Marie was wrenched from her glorious exit from this world back into the here and now. She opened her eyes to see George emerge from the deep, deep grave. The pistol in her hand – Marie's service weapon – was smoking. Three shots had been fired. Inclining her head with the energy she had left, Marie spied Den Bosch and his men on the ground. Bloodied. Writhing. Clutching the places where they'd been wounded. One was out cold – perhaps dead. Only Baumgartner was still standing, loading the shotgun.

'Keep still, you old Nazi bastard, I'm trying to kill you.' George let off three further rounds. One found its home in the shoulder of an already prone Den Bosch. The other two kicked up dust by Baumgartner's feet. The gun clicked uselessly as George tried to fire anew. Either an empty magazine or jammed. She tossed the weapon aside. Started to climb out, scowling and grunting at the gargantuan effort of scaling the wall of such a deep pit.

'Silly English bitch. You've shot my boy!'

Baumgartner hastened towards her, standing on her hand. He aimed the shotgun point-blank at the top of George's head. If he pulled the trigger, it would be an instant and messy death.

But more deafening shots rang out from somewhere close to Marie. She turned to the side to see Van den Bergen lying on the ground next to her, his legs at an awkward angle, his arms stretched out before him, holding Elvis's gun, poised to shoot again.

The target – Baumgartner – sank to his knees. His back was peppered with holes that bloomed dark red. He dropped his shotgun. Fell forward into the hole.

'Is he dead?' Van den Bergen asked.

George looked down into the pit beneath her.

'With five holes in his back? He looks a bit rough at best, I'd say.'

# CHAPTER 39

## *Amsterdam, the Onze Lieve Vrouwehospitaal, 24 October*

'Aw, get something to eat down you, darling. You look thin,' Aunty Sharon said, pulling a package wrapped in tinfoil from her shopping bag. 'I baked some bun yesterday. We only had a couple of slices out of it. Get a bit down you. That'll put hairs on your chest.'

George waved the offering away. 'I'm all right, Aunty Shaz. I'm not hungry. They gave me toast.' She took a gulp of the oxygen-enriched air from the mask that she was supposed to be wearing. Though she was glad to see her family by her hospital bedside, she was exhausted from her ordeal. All she really wanted to do was sit quietly and try to make sense of what had come to pass. She needed to figure out what she could have done better. Fathom how she was feeling about Van den Bergen.

'My daughter saved old lanky twat's girl,' Letitia pronounced from the bedside chair that she sat on as though it were a throne. 'She gets her hero genes from me, innit? Remember how I survived being captivated by that Rotterdam Silencer for ages?' She folded her arms, looking like a novelty Christmas decoration in some shining chenille number with an appliqué dog on the front. Even at 9.30 a.m., it apparently was not too early for eyelash extensions and the flowing ombré Beyoncé hairdo. 'Bravery. That's what we got in spades in the Williams-May family.' Letitia cast a disparaging look towards George's father, who stood on the other side of the bed, opening his mouth to get a word in edgeways and failing. 'Give us that bun, Shaz. If she ain't gonna eat it, it's a shame to let it go to waste.'

But Aunty Sharon had already put the foil-wrapped Jamaican fruitcake in the bedside locker. 'Nah, man. You ain't the one laid up with breathing difficulties and dehydration. This is for my niece, 'cos she been fighting off trafficking Nazi rarseclarts. Not for you.'

'Hey! Cheeky cow.' Letitia was up and out of her vinyl throne, clicking her fingers and sucking her teeth. 'I was the one who got us all sat together on fucking Ryanair.' She poked herself in the chest with a chubby finger topped with a blue nail extension. 'Never mind Nazis. Them fucking seating regulations is like something out of the Nazis. And I managed to nick free peanuts off the snack trolley without getting copped. More than you did, eh?'

It was all George could do to sit helplessly on her bed, revisiting the horrific memory of discovering Cornelia Verhagen's death mask of a face, just beneath the soil, the feeling of the two trafficked slave-workers tumbling into that grave on top of her. Dead weight.

She turned to her father, holding out her hand. Amid this chaos, George needed an anchor. They exchanged a knowing look. His eyes were smiling as he squeezed her hand. She could tell that Michael Carlos Isquierdo Moreno knew what she was going through, at least.

With great tenderness, he placed the oxygen mask over her face. 'Pretend to be asleep,' he said to her in Spanish. 'I'll get them out of here. We can come back later, when you've had a chance to rest.'

She closed her eyes, complicit. Thankful to have the calming influence of her father in her life to mitigate the petulance and unpredictability of her mother. With the love of her Aunty Sharon, George felt at that moment, despite the bickering sisters, that she was the luckiest woman alive.

Later, the doctor allowed her to wander along the corridor to the room where Tamara lay. She found her hooked up to an array of medical kit: drips fed fluid into her dehydrated body; monitoring apparatus binged and bonged, singing a song of recovery and hope. At her side, Numb-Nuts was snoring, his head bent at an awkward angle. He was wearing a papoose, and baby Eva slept, snuggled into his chest. The only wakeful, watchful person in the room was Tamara herself.

'I owe you,' she said, breaking into a violent coughing fit. Whatever she had inhaled in that greenhouse rumbled ominously in her chest.

Numb-Nuts and the baby slept on.

'No you don't. I did what any normal person would do.'

'Normal people don't barge into the midst of a hostage situation armed with plasters and deodorant. You're in a different league, George. I can see what Dad loves so much about you.'

George pressed her lips together. Saw Van den Bergen in the sharp angles of Tamara's face. 'I'm not sure how much your dad loves me at all, actually. But anyway.' She felt sadness wrapping itself around her chest, heavy and suffocating like phlegm. She tightened the knot of her dressing gown and clenched her toes together inside her slippers. 'I'm going to see him in a minute. I want to be the first to sign the casts on his legs.' George patted Tamara's hand. 'You'd better get back on your feet quickly. Your dad is going to be a nightmare to look after if he's on crutches for weeks and weeks.'

She felt resentment lodge in her throat. A ball of acidic

words that she couldn't allow to escape. Not under these circumstances. *If you had stayed put like your dad asked. If you and your dick of a husband weren't such fucking liabilities. If…*

'I can't believe you did all this for me,' Tamara said. 'I never thought—'

'I didn't do it for you,' George said, sighing. 'I did it for your father, because doting, easily manipulated fools rush in where more selfish, sensible bastards fear to tread. I did it for the twelve-year-old girl who ended up in the morgue because of Den Bosch and Baumgartner. Nobody's around to avenge her death. But I was. And I did. I got revenge for that girl, and all the others like her, whose parents can't or whose parents won't. Me and Marie and Elvis and Van den Bergen. We closed that trafficking ring down because that's how we roll. So, I'm sorry to disappoint you, Tamara, dear.' She switched to English. 'But sometimes shit just ain't all about you.'

Her next stop was Marie's room.

The unassuming redhead lay in bed with both knees raised above her, encased in plaster. At her side, a fully stocked drip stand stood guard: a bag of blood running dark red into the fat cannula in her arm; a clear bag of saline drip-dripping moisture back into her system; and yet another bag, containing who knew what. When George shuffled towards the bedside in her fluffy slippers, they shared a satisfied grin. She raised a hand to high five Marie, only remembering Marie's propensity for soap dodging once she had committed to the gesture. *Don't be a cow, for Christ's sake. They're bound to have given her a good bed bath. You can always alcohol-rub your hands afterwards.*

'That was quite some double act we pulled there.'

Marie slapped her palm in answer, grimacing as her legs moved along with her body. 'The morphine's wearing off.' She gestured up at the unidentified bag and raised an oversized syringe as an explanation. 'They've told me I can self-administer, but I don't want to overdo it. I want to stay alert.'

George shook her head and sat gingerly on the guest chair. 'I'd take all the drugs I could get if it was me. What have they said? Will you walk again?'

Shrugging, Marie said, 'Do you know how long they had me in surgery last night? Four hours. Four bloody hours. Baumgartner nicked an artery in the left one. I'm lucky I didn't bleed to death.'

Staring up at the bag of blood, George realised that she had got off lucky being buried alive. 'Do you feel better for the transfusion?'

Marie managed a smile. 'Lots. They've replaced both knees but I'm going to have to have quite a few operations over the next year. I need new ligaments. All sorts.'

'If they give you a wheelchair, can I call you Ironside?'

'Wrong profession.'

'Works for me.'

Though Marie's face was pale from loss of blood, her eyes shone. The blue irises were sharp, as though the experience had somehow polished up Marie's spirit where previously it had been dulled by a burdensome, repetitive life. 'I love it. Ironside it is. It's not fair Dirk should get the only decent nickname on the team.'

'If you'd not have dropped that gun onto my chest …' George fluffed up hair that needed washing; remnants of soil still clung stubbornly to her curls. She craned her neck to see that it was a sunny day outside, in an Amsterdam that they had made safer. 'This would all have ended very differently. But I'm sorry about your knees. I'm sorry I didn't shoot sooner. The poor sods who fell on top of me and all that soil …'

Shaking her head and closing her eyes, Marie made a harrumphing sound. 'No need to explain. I played it wrong.

I should have worried less about getting a bollocking from Minks and called it in properly. I fancied myself as bloody Angelina Jolie, didn't I? I wanted to save the day, instead of being stuck behind a desk with every pervy wank-fantasy known to humanity and a pile of boring data.' She sipped from a glass of water, looking suddenly crestfallen. Pink in her cheeks and a florid rash on her neck. 'I screwed up. I deserve these knees and whatever else fate has in store for me.'

'No. You helped put a trafficking gang out of action. If De Vries had bumbled onto the scene, there would have been more needless deaths than Cornelia Verhagen.' George looked over at the giant 'Get Well Soon!' card, wanting to change the subject. 'Who's that from?'

Marie grinned. 'Minks. He's utterly pissed off with Van den Bergen, apparently, but has decided me and Elvis are heroes of the day. Fancy that!'

'What the hell can he say? It was Minks who insisted we ease off Den Bosch. He was the one who wheeled some toady in to take over the case. De Vries never had a clue. No way would he have solved a case this complex. And nobody apart from Van den Bergen acknowledged that the deaths of the four old men were pertinent.' George dabbed at the site on her arm where she had pulled her own cannula out. It was no longer bleeding, but it was sore and itchy.

She grabbed the card and started to read it, deciphering signatures from everyone in HQ who had ever had dealings with Marie, and plenty who hadn't. An overly long and gushing message from Minks took pride of place in the middle. 'Minks could get done for obstruction of justice, the way he behaved. He hasn't got a leg to stand on.'

Marie laughed. 'Neither have I!'

George patted her on the shoulder. 'You did good, Ironside. You're what we English call "nails". Listen, I've got somewhere to be. I'll catch you later.'

She'd left him until last, unsure how to feel. Having already made enquiries as soon as her paramedics had wheeled her from the ambulance into the hospital, she knew that Van den Bergen had suffered no more than a concussion and two fractured tibiae, thanks to the dead weight of what had appeared to be a half-ton pig landing on him awkwardly. She knew that the round he'd emptied into Baumgartner's back had saved her life; that if he hadn't dragged himself in agony that hundred metres or so from where Den Bosch and Baumgartner had left him for dead, crippled and with a head wound, there would be no triumph. They would all be turning to compost in the middle of an industrial greenhouse, situated in a complex of greenhouses that was too vast to properly excavate.

The real hero in this story was Van den Bergen.

But George had already determined to leave her inattentive, distracted man. She had resolved to commit that most selfish of crimes – to break a lover's heart in a bid to free her own.

'Ah, there you are. Thank God.' Van den Bergen was awake. He held his hand out, beckoning her to draw close. Like Marie, both his legs were in plaster and raised high. On his head was taped a thick wad of dressing.

'That's going to hurt like hell when they take it off,' George said, wincing at the thought of all the white hair that would come out with the adhesive. 'How do you feel, old man? Got a headache?'

His expression was one of pained stoicism. 'Like you wouldn't believe. And weeks of public transport ahead of me.' He pulled her hand to his lips and kissed the back. Held her palm to his stubbled face. 'I thought I'd lost you both there.' He choked on a sob. A solitary tear fell onto his cheek and tracked its way along the sunken furrow beneath his cheekbone. 'My girls.'

My girls. She swallowed his words, but they sank, heavy and indigestible, to the pit of her stomach. When had she become lumped in with Tamara on every fucking occasion so that there was barely a distinction between his daughter and his partner anymore? *Stop being churlish,* she thought. *You know he doesn't mean it as a slight.*

'I love you, George. Don't ever pull a stunt like that again.'

Studying that familiar face, George felt a surge of emotion threaten to overwhelm her. She still loved this stubborn idiot of a man, with all his health anxieties and quirks and his bad cooking. 'I could say the same of you. You're not a superhero, Paul. You're breakable. I wish you'd accept that, or one of these days I'm going to lose you. And where you go, I always follow. It's not fair on either of us.' She was sorely tempted to bring up, yet again, the possibility of his taking retirement and moving to the UK, where he could easily get some consultancy job or other. They could make a life that revolved around them, for a change, instead of his work and the antics of Amsterdam's underbelly. *Don't say it. Don't nag. Not while his legs are in plaster. Bite your damned tongue, George.*

'If Baumgartner had killed you, I wouldn't have wanted to live. I'm nothing without you, George.' His voice cracked, his mouth turned down at the corners. Those melancholy grey eyes were awash with sorrow. 'Don't ever leave me.'

She made the decision there and then, examining the scabbed wounds on his palms, that ending this lunacy they called a relationship could wait. A non-committal roll of her eyes and shake of her head would suffice in answer to his demand … for now.

'You'd better get yourself well, old man,' she said. 'We've got loose ends that need tying up and Minks is overdue a big slice of humble pie. I want to be there when you force-feed it to the slippery little shithouse.'

'Sign my cast?'

He grabbed a felt-tip pen from his nightstand and held it out to her.

Though George knew he was probably expecting her to write some kind of 'Roses are red, violets are blue' love limerick, under the circumstances, she could think only of one thing.

'A cock and balls?' The disappointment in his voice was more than apparent.

'It's good enough for Banksy.'

'Banksy never drew a cock and balls. Certainly not on my bloody plaster cast.'

She signed her tiny work of art: 'Wanksy'.

'Yeah he did. Look!' She pointed at her handiwork.

'That says, Wanksy, not Banksy.'

'Speech impediment, innit?'

There was a smile. For now, they had a workable truce.

# CHAPTER 40

# *Amsterdam, police headquarters,*
# *31 October*

'Oh, here he is,' Roel de Vries said. 'Hopalong Cassidy's back.'

The jumped-up little shit looked as though somebody had pricked him with a needle, and now all the hot air and bullshit was leaching out like a wet fart. Van den Bergen kept that thought to himself as he swung his crutches ahead of him, dragging his heavy casts along until he had reached his old desk. Everything De Vries owned was in a box. Van den Bergen pointedly started to hum the Beyoncé song he'd heard George singing whenever they'd had an argument.

'I see your box is *to the left* …'

But the reference was completely lost on Mr Joke Tie.

'Boss!'

He recognised that voice immediately, craning his neck to see Elvis pushing Marie's wheelchair down the corridor towards him.

Roel de Vries started to clap slowly. Sarcastically. 'The war heroes all return. Look at this. It looks like Christmas at the pensioner's club.'

'Shut your trap, de Vries,' Van den Bergen said, his consonants snapping like slingshots against the man who had been brought in to usurp him. 'Get your box, get your team of idle, grinning traffic humps and get the hell out of my department. We do proper police work in here.'

De Vries fingered today's joke tie – *South Park* from the 1990s, shiny from over-ironing. 'You may have solved the case, but your arrogance won't stand you in any kind of stead with Minks. He wanted a man beneath him who knows what "team" means.'

Propping himself on one crutch, Van den Bergen yanked the typing chair from behind De Vries and lowered himself into it. 'Minks retracted my suspension and issued an apology, willingly. At the end of the day, Roel, what matters to the commissioner is solve rates, not the quality of tonguing his arse gets in briefings. Now, if you don't mind …'

The man who had tried and failed to step briefly into his size thirteens picked up his belongings, opening and closing his mouth, clearly searching for a witty response. He found none.

With his department back under his jurisdiction, Van den Bergen called a meeting in Marie's IT suite, which smelled of lavender air freshener and new carpet.

'I don't know what the hell they think they've been doing in here,' Marie said, wrinkling her nose. 'It's a disgrace.' She gestured to Elvis that he should pass over her embroidered barrel bag. She took out a family-sized bag of cheese-and-onion crisps, grinned mischievously and opened the foul-smelling snack. 'Better.' She took out the photo of her son and set it next to the various oversized computer monitors. 'That's more like it.'

'I paid the taxi driver.' George's voice made them all turn. She was standing in the doorway, waving a receipt. Smiling.

He was so relieved to see her fully recovered – physically, at least, though he sensed a blockage in their communication since the ordeal. Perhaps, like his tibia bones, any rift would heal with time.

With his legs resting on a chair, Van den Bergen closed his eyes and steepled his fingers together, savouring triumph for thirty seconds. 'Now. We've still got work to do. We know that Cornelia Verhagen discovered the box of incriminating evidence on Hendrik's collusion with the Nazis when her father died.'

'And that resulted in her death,' Elvis offered.

Van den Bergen nodded. 'George heard Baumgartner say that Kaars Verhagen was the one to find the box most recently, and that set off the chain of events leading to the old men's deaths. They'd threatened to expose Hendrik. He'd had a heart attack with the worry. Baumgartner took it upon himself to avenge his biological father. Fine. But I still want to know what happened to Ed Sijpesteijn and Rivka Zemel. If we can find out …'

'I sent an email to Hakan Güngör,' George said. 'I was hoping he'd be able to find some Nazi record of their deaths. He's come up with sod all so far.'

Something nagged at the back of Van den Bergen's mind. He had given little thought to the case during his time off. It had been a carousel of hospital appointments, pain wearing off thanks to codeine, pain flaring up without, visits from Tamara and Eva, now that Tamara was fully recovered and reunited with that infernal arse-pimple, Numb-Nuts. He'd spent hours worrying about George's low mood and what she could possibly be saying during her long Skype sessions with her Aunty Sharon and her father. He had whiled away a few days painting an oil portrait of Tamara holding Eva, reminiscent of medieval Dutch masters' depictions of the Virgin Mary with Jesus as an infant, complete with gold skies. Why not? He'd fancied experimenting, though George had sneered at it, pronouncing it as a 'tacky pastiche that screams Oedipal issues'. But now, for the first time in a while, ideas took shape inside the policeman's part of his brain.

'Cracked concrete,' he said, looking at George.

'Where?'

'Hendrik van Eden's old pub. The new landlord clearly spends nothing whatsoever on maintenance and said the concrete in the yard had always been cracked. When did Van Eden buy that pub?' He looked at Marie, who logged into her computer and brought the scans of the deeds up on the monitor.

'1941,' she said. 'He'd bought it a couple of years before Ed went missing. In fact, his father had bought it for him as a going concern, but Hendrik had always been down as the landlord and inherited it when old man Van Eden died in the Sixties.'

Slapping the desk, marvelling at how restorative it felt to be back on the job, he pointed to Elvis. 'We need to get that yard up. I'll be damned if we don't find something of interest under that concrete.'

'Okay, boss. It's worth a try.'

Two days later, Van den Bergen stood and watched as a mini digger started to rip up the uppermost slab of concrete from the back yard of the Drie Goudene Honden pub. At his side, George stood, dragging hard on her vaping stick.

'Do you think we'll find anything?' she asked.

He leaned on her, stealing a surreptitious kiss on the side of her head while the ground-worker and the landlord weren't watching. 'I've got a tingling feeling.'

George looked at his crotch and raised her eyebrows. 'I'm not sure here is either the time or the place. But if you order in pizza tonight, you might get lucky.'

Their light-hearted exchange was brought to an abrupt halt as the digger's engine fell silent.

'What is it?' Van den Bergen asked, swinging himself forward on his crutches.

The ground-worker was out of his cab, standing at the edge of the newly dug hole, not more than four feet or so deep.

'See for yourself,' he said, taking a cigarette out of the pocket of his high-vis jacket and lighting up with shaking hands. 'There's your cracking and drainage problem. How old do you reckon that is?'

Van den Bergen looked down at the muddied, grinning skeleton. There was no trace of clothing but for leather shoes, still on the feet, a watch around its wrist and the glint of a gold pinkie ring on the thin bones of the little finger of the skeleton's right hand. He could see large chips had been hacked out of the skull. Next to the skeleton, though the handle was still buried in unexcavated earth, he spied the unmistakable blade of a hatchet.

'Oh, I think our friend has been sleeping here fitfully since 1943.' He felt tears prick the backs of his eyes, certain that this was Ed Sijpesteijn and that the ring on his finger had been given to him by Rivka Zemel. 'I think it's time we found this young fellow a proper resting place.'

## CHAPTER 41

# Amsterdam, Schiphol airport, then police headquarters, 8 November

Picturing the Facebook profile photo Marie had shown her only days earlier, George wondered if she would be able to spot the elderly lady as she emerged from baggage reclaim. The flight to Amsterdam's Schiphol airport from New York had landed a good forty minutes earlier. She yawned, holding the plaque aloft, clearly inscribed in thick black felt tip with the traveller's name: Rivka Levy.

'Come on. Come on.'

A grey-haired woman, clearly in her late eighties or early nineties, came towards her, walking slowly, spine bent as though she suffered badly with osteoporosis, wheeling a suit-case that was almost as big as she was. George's heart started to race as she prepared to meet the author of the diary that she had found so captivating. But the elderly woman walked straight past George towards three middle-aged women who waved and stretched out their arms to greet this weary traveller.

Considering all that Marie had found out, George didn't know what to expect. It was hard to tell from a profile photo, which had obviously been taken a good twenty years earlier, how the woman would look now. The friend list of Rivka Levy, née Zemel, had revealed hundreds upon hundreds of men and women, most of whom who had presumably been taught by her at one stage. Rivka Zemel, retired high school history teacher. It made sense that somebody who had played such a fascinating role in such a key time in recent history should teach younger generations about the perils of national arrogance, militarised rule and institutionalised hatred. George smiled at the thought, hoping she would like the only surviving cast member of the Verhagen drama when she emerged through those automatic doors.

There was a tap on her shoulder. 'Are you looking for me?'

George did a double take at the sprightly, beautiful old woman who stood before her. Her hair was cut in a short, platinum-blonde bob. She wore a fur-trimmed parka, the funkiest jeans George had seen in a while and gold sneakers. If this was what the bleakest phase of life's winter looked like, George resolved not to dread it quite so much.

Rivka Levy took off her Dior shades to reveal almost smooth eyes, which had most likely seen the surgeon's knife.

'Are you Marie from Facebook, sweetie?' She spoke with a thick New York accent. 'Are you the Dutch cop?'

'No.' George clasped Rivka Zemel's liver-spotted hands inside hers and started to gabble excitedly. 'I'm Dr McKenzie. A criminologist. Please, call me Georgina. George. I work with Marie and Chief Inspector Van den Bergen. I'm the one who found your war diary in the Verhagen house. I read it cover to cover.' Inexplicably, George found it was all she could do to hold back a sob. 'I never thought—'

Rivka Zemel wrenched her hand free and patted George's arm. 'That's nice. I gotta pee, honey. Where's the restroom? At my age, a nine-hour flight plays havoc on my bladder like you wouldn't believe.'

She was nothing like the woman she'd been expecting. George realised that life may have stopped for Ed Sijpesteijn in 1943, but it had moved on by some seven decades for this one-time fugitive. She smiled at the thought.

Van den Bergen was waiting in the pickup area in the Mercedes, Elvis at the wheel. He introduced himself formally, reaching behind to shake Rivka's hand. 'We're so glad to have found you, Mrs Levy. You're the final piece in our puzzle.'

Rivka was eyeing the casts on Van den Bergen's legs. 'What kind of puzzle leaves you in such bad shape? Have you been playing extreme Twister or something? Looks like you do things differently in Amsterdam these days.' She laughed heartily but it was clear from the tightness around her eyes that she was dreading what was to come.

George tried to imagine what it must feel like to have to travel halfway around the world to finally lay to rest the one-time love of your life.

'Have you been back since the war?' she asked.

But Rivka was not listening. She stared out of the window of the Mercedes at the surrounding countryside as they sped away from the airport. Miles and miles of flat green, punctuated only by giant wind turbines.

'It hasn't changed that much,' the old woman said, dabbing at her eyes. When she caught Van den Bergen looking back at her, she hastily donned her sunglasses and treated him to a curt smile.

At the station, Marie rolled up in her wheelchair to greet the woman who had proven so tricky to track down.

Sitting around the oversized table in the meeting room, Rivka Zemel nursed a scalding, barely drinkable coffee that Elvis had made.

'I'm sorry to have brought you back under such tragic circumstances, Mrs Levy,' Van den Bergen began.

'How do I know it's him, after all this time?' She turned to Marie. 'You said there were items on his person that survived. Can I see them?'

Van den Bergen placed the watch and the pinkie ring carefully on the table. All eyes were on the elderly woman who, if their assumptions were correct, had not seen these pieces since they were last worn by a living, breathing Ed Sijpesteijn.

Spreading her wrinkled hands on the table, she slowly reached out to stroke the watch. Speaking in her native Dutch tongue, she sounded more like the Rivka who had written those diaries. 'His father gave that to him on his eighteenth birthday,' she said. Removing her glasses, she started to weep freely, clutching the watch to her chest. Next, she picked up the ring and gasped. 'I gave this to him.' Nodding. 'It was Papa's. We exchanged rings as a betrothal of sorts. Mama and Papa hadn't wanted me to marry out of the faith. Before the war, they'd hoped they'd find a nice Jewish man for me to settle down with. Start a family. It meant a lot to them because I think they realised Shmuel was never going to enjoy a full life. He was just so delicate. All their hopes were pinned on me. But when we were cooped up in Kaars's house and Ed was such a gentleman – so doting and thoughtful … Such a mensch.' The words caught in her throat. She took a sip of coffee. 'Oy.' She looked over at Elvis and spoke as a New Yorker. 'As a barista, you make a good street-sweeper. Don't give up being a cop.'

'Please …' Van den Bergen popped a painkiller onto his tongue. Swallowed some of his own drink, grimacing. 'Go on.'

Rivka took out a stiffened envelope from her handbag. From inside, she produced an old black and white photo in almost pristine condition. It was of a young couple with their arms around each other, beaming into the lens of the camera. They were standing on a path in a park, where the trees were in leaf. A horse chestnut bloomed behind them, garlanded with upright clusters of pale flowers that seemed to glow against the canvas of dark foliage, even during the daytime.

'Me and Ed. Look! Weren't we young?' She patted her chest gently, then sniffed and tutted. 'Kaars took this of us both. It was one of those days when I'd snuck out. Hendrik's girlfriend, Anna, had dyed my hair blonde, you see, and I was lucky enough to have falsified papers.'

'Hendrik had got those from Bruno Baumgartner,' George said. 'We found a reference to them in a box that you mentioned in your diary. Do you remember? The last time you saw Ed, he told you to keep the box safe, and you hid it behind the skirting board in the room between rooms, didn't you?'

Rivka's face took on a faraway expression. 'It's like it was only yesterday. He came running in, red in the face, and told me someone in the Force of Five had turned. I never got to see what was in that box because the Nazis came that night. Ed had promised to move us, but I never saw him after that last visit with the box. Papa said he'd run away to avoid capture, but I knew Ed would never abandon us like that. He had the heart of a lion. And he loved me.' She locked eyes with George, as if she sought corroboration. 'He did.'

'What happened to you and your family that night?' George asked, desperate to know how the blank pages of the diary might have been filled had young Rivka continued to write. 'After the Nazis took you? Did the rest of your family escape? What happened to the Verhagens?'

'The Verhagens were lined up against the wall at gunpoint as we were dragged from our hiding place.' Her voice cracked. 'Shmuel was so ill by that stage that he could barely walk.' She inclined her head so that George could no longer see her face clearly. Fat tears dropped onto her jeans, spotting the denim with dark patches. 'They shot him dead before he reached the train and left his body in the street. I don't know— I …' She held her hands up in a gesture of despair. 'Poor Shmuel deserved so much better. And Mama and Papa …'

George leaned over, placing a hand on Rivka's heaving shoulder as she quaked with grief. 'Go on. If you can.'

'We were piled onto a train to a transit camp in Westerbork but we were ultimately destined for Auschwitz. I knew it would be the end for Mama and Papa. Papa was stiff from so long spent in the hiding place. Mama's mental health was in ruins. They weren't strong.' She lifted her face. Even more than seventy years on, she was a woman racked with guilt.

'Did you all survive the war?' Van den Bergen asked, peering down at the photo of her and Ed Sijpesteijn through his reading glasses. Holding it with obvious reverence.

'As far as I know, my parents, may they rest in peace, met their end in Auschwitz. The train was packed like a cattle truck, so who knows? Maybe they died en route. I hope so. I hope they were spared the horrors of the gas chambers. I'll never know, because I managed to escape, of course.'

George leaned forward. 'How?'

'I worked away at some rotten planks in the carriage. Another girl from Utrecht helped. The Nazis took everything from me, including the little ring Ed had given me. But the girl's father had polio and they'd missed his leg irons completely. We stripped his leg of the supports to dig into the wood. It was so riddled with rot that it didn't take us long to open up a hole we could drop through.'

'While the train was moving?' Elvis asked, wide-eyed. He scratched at his shoulders, disbelief in his horrified expression.

Rivka shrugged. 'What choice did we have? We had to risk death on the tracks or face the gas chambers in Auschwitz.'

'Weren't you frightened?' Marie asked.

'Of course. I seem to remember peeing my pants. But Papi more or less pushed me through the hole when the train slowed near a junction. His final words to me were …' She seemed to peer into the past as though through a patch of thick fog. 'Do you know? I can't remember them. Oh, that is sad.' Staring into her unpalatable coffee, she raised an eyebrow, wiped a tear away and swallowed the brew whole. 'A lifetime ago, now.

But I remember how my parents felt in my arms as we hugged for the last time. I was so young, so unlucky to lose them, but luckier than six million that I survived.'

She closed her eyes and lifted her head as though she were having a private exchange with the spirits of her mother, father and brother. 'It was a miracle that me and Hannah, the girl from Utrecht, made it out alive. We just dropped down and lay still until the train passed over us. It was dark, luckily. Then, we ran and ran into a forest until we thought our lungs would burst. God must have been watching over us because we came across members of the resistance in that forest. They smuggled us both onto a cargo ship bound for the States. Hannah said she had plans to go to California. I'd had enough of travelling, so I made a new life for myself in New York. Met my husband, Harold, when I was training to be a teacher.' She smiled wistfully. 'I've had a good life. A different life than the one I'd hoped for, though. If you'd told me when I was in the room between rooms that I'd spend most of my adulthood on a different continent with a man other than Ed, I'd have laughed at you. My plan was always to wait the war out in that stinking hidey-hole. All that time, we hid patiently. But the SS found us in the end. We were betrayed.'

From the box, George produced a piece of paper, stamped with the Deutches Reich insignia. A receipt made out to Hendrik van Eden, signed by Bruno Baumgartner.

'Hendrik van Eden sold you out for a fist full of guilders.'

Rivka took the document and snorted. 'I saw him, you know. As we were being dragged out of the house. He was standing under a tree, watching. I could just about make him out in the streetlight. For years, I wondered if I'd been mistaken, but I should have known. Of course it was him. The others were beyond reproach. Ed said one of the group was a turncoat. I knew it was Hendrik. And you say his son and grandson were behind a trafficking ring? The apple didn't fall far from the tree, then.'

Van den Bergen cleared his throat. 'Precisely. André Baumgartner – Hendrik and Anna Groen's biological son, despite the confusion over the name – was the mastermind behind the operation. He's dead now. Frederik Den Bosch is behind bars, awaiting trial, but we've got a raft of slave labourers and slum tenants that he'd trafficked—'

'And an actual truckload of recovering refugees,' George added.

'Yes. They're all willing to testify against Den Bosch now that he's off the streets. We've also arrested an imam in conjunction with the case. He was supplying them with willing customers in Syria and other parts of the Islamic world that have refugee crises. It's ironic that a known fascist should bring immigrants into the country, but where there's big piles of cash to be made and free labour to be exploited ... Like the Jews during the war, people will happily give everything they own to secure a safe passage to a new life.'

'Ed and Kaars were doing it for free. Any gifts they were given were just that. Gifts.' There was a defensive tone to Rivka's voice.

'The reputations of Kaars Verhagen and Ed Sijpesteijn are absolutely not in question, Mrs Levy. Marie here has corroborated that the artwork in Verhagen's house was not stolen. There are no Verhagen grandchildren, so we're repatriating the paintings to the descendants of the Jewish families that owned them originally, where possible. The rest will go to the Rijksmuseum. I believe that four of the Force of Five genuine heroes. Hendrik, though ... he was a snake in the grass – and a murderer.'

In silence, Rivka dabbed at her eyes. 'How did it happen? How did my Ed die?'

Van den Bergen folded his arms and sighed. 'Perhaps it's best you don't know.'

'No. I need to.'

'We'll never know the exact circumstances, but forensic evidence points to Ed having been killed by multiple head wounds. It was a frenzied attack. I'm so sorry.'

'And Hendrik was the culprit? You're sure of that?'

'He had motive to kill Ed. With that box, Ed had enough evidence to shame Hendrik in his little social circle of freedom fighters. Hendrik was the landlord of the pub where Ed was presumably killed, and then buried, along with the murder weapon. The concrete covering dates from the mid Forties, according to our forensic archaeologist. We don't have paperwork showing that Hendrik paid for that yard to be resurfaced once Ed had been buried there, but I'd put money on it that he did. I'm fairly certain that Hendrik murdered Ed to silence him and then had you and your family arrested. His betrayal remained undiscovered for decades because nobody knew a thing about that Pandora's box until Kaars happened upon it recently during building work.'

Rubbing her gnarled hands over her mouth, Rivka sighed deeply. 'At least now we can lay my Ed to rest. I've already buried one husband in this lifetime. Now, it's time to say farewell to the man who was meant to be my first.'

# CHAPTER 42

## *Van den Bergen's apartment, 30 November*

'You need to decide if you're gonna start living *your* life or if you're gonna keep on living *his*.' Letitia's words had been her parting gift as she'd left George's bedside in the hospital. Now, it was the oft-repeated nugget of wisdom that she bludgeoned her with during every single Skype session. Worse still, Aunty Shaz and her father agreed.

Throwing clean underwear into the suitcase, George decided that she couldn't bear the mess. She took everything out, refolded it and set it back in its proper place. Better. As she packed the stack of well-worn T-shirts, her attention was diverted away from the suitcase to the letter. It sat crisply on the duvet of the guest bed.

Dear Dr McKenzie,
Thank you for coming to be interviewed last week. It is with great pleasure that I am offering you the role of Senior Lecturer in Goldsmiths Sociology Department...

This was it. Her chance to start living her own life, back in London. Not Sally Wright's. Not Letitia the Dragon's. Not Van den Bergen's. The post carried with it a salary decent enough to raise something of a mortgage. She had a good chunk of cash already saved towards a deposit. Her father was suing the Rotterdam Silencer for damages with marvellous prospects, according to his solicitor. He had promised to help financially if he got a decent payout. But even if that never came to fruition, in accepting this post, there would be fresh opportunity to attract funding for her research projects. And on top of that, her failed book deal was seemingly back on.

'Messages from the universe, George. Messages from the universe.'

Closing the suitcase, she felt like she had ended the final chapter of a long story and was finally closing the book. Her heart weighed a little more inside her recovered body, but she forced a smile onto her face as Van den Bergen cleared his throat behind her. His eyes were red from late nights of talking and regretful tears.

'It doesn't have to be this way, you know.'

She turned around to face him. Free of the casts on his legs now, he looked almost back to normal but for the few extra pounds he carried thanks to weeks of being almost immobile. 'No, you're right. It doesn't. I've told you. You can come to England and start a life with me. We put down roots together. Or I can try to get a job here and we get a place.'

He sighed deeply. Groaned. 'I can't just walk away from my family, George.'

*Bastard.* George yanked the zip closed and fastened her padlock. 'I'm asking you to commit to putting your name next to mine on a mortgage deed. I wasn't even asking you to leave Amsterdam. Just to start again properly with me. A little permanence. And I'm not asking you to walk away from anything. But if I stayed, it would be with the understanding that you stop putting our life together as a couple on the backburner so you can go running to Tamara every time she farts wrong. You've changed, Paul.'

'I'm trying to be a good grandfather.' He folded his arms tightly, his handsome face set into a frown.

'No. You're overcompensating for the absent father that you were to Tamara by usurping Numb-Nuts's role with Eva. It's not on. You were the one who told me expressly that you didn't want more children, but now, here you are parenting someone else's. Between the job and the baby, there's nothing left of you for me.'

'Jesus. That's selfish.'

'Is it? You're asking me to stay here in this flat in this stasis; to join you in your line of work now you're finally back in Minks's good books and the funds are flowing to the department again. What about *my* family? My family is in London, not Amsterdam. I've got a couple of years left with my mother, maybe, and a father I've still got to get to know. And my job isn't in the police. I'm a criminologist. Remember? An academic and a specialist in trafficking. You brought me in on the Den Bosch case because of that, not because I needed to be thrown a charitable bone. Fuck it, Paul. I don't want to be a spare punctuation mark at the end of somebody else's sentence. Don't do that to me. Don't treat me as an afterthought. I won't let you.'

She'd forced herself to be as calm – as reasoned and articulate as possible. She'd focused on her breathing throughout the speech she'd rehearsed over and over. Tried not to ball her fists and thump the stubborn bastard in the chest.

'Don't you love me anymore?' He took a step towards her. Held out his hand.

'Don't insult my intelligence.' She ignored his placatory gesture. Looked away to check her baggage tag. 'You can keep that guilt-tripping shit for Tamara and Numb-Nuts when they decide they're getting bored of Opa and give you the order of the boot.'

'I don't know why you're breaking us up like this, George.

I don't know why what we have isn't enough anymore.' He tried to wrestle the case from her. 'Stay, for Christ's sake.'

She slapped him away. 'What we have isn't what we had, Paul. Can't you see that? Get off my fucking bag. I'm going. I've got a future to pursue where that poor little girl from the back of the Den Bosch truck had hers stolen from her.'

He grabbed her and pulled her to him, planting a hard kiss on her mouth. 'I love you, you bloody woman. Stop using the case as an excuse for leaving me. You're all I want.' He kissed her again.

Against her better judgement, she reciprocated, savouring the feel of his tongue entwined with hers and his torso pressed against her breasts. Freshly showered, he smelled of that sport deodorant she loved and hot, clean skin. But this was not the time for resentful sex and a half-arsed reunion that would disintegrate within days.

She broke free, panting. Pushed him away, stifling the mischievous grin that was trying desperately to displace her 'I mean business' face.

'The ball's in your court, Chief Inspector,' she said, waving her University of London offer letter in his face. 'You can come to London and start fresh. It's hardly expensive to shuttle back and forth on a budget airline to see Eva, is it? And Tamara can bring her over to visit you. You'd find a job in five minutes in the UK with your languages and skill set.'

'What? As a security guard at Tesco?'

'Don't give me that bullshit.' Her arms betrayed her mind and wrapped themselves around his middle. She found herself stroking the line of his triangular nose, his lips, his freshly shaven chin. She poked him in the slight dimple. 'This doesn't have to be the end, Paul. But it's your call. You know where I am if you think what we have is worth building something solid on.'

Outside, a horn beeped. Her taxi.

Extracting herself from her obstinate lover's embrace, George lifted the small case from the bed, stuffed her job offer letter, e-ticket and passport into her bag and headed for the door.

'Don't go,' he said, his sorrowful voice sounding uncharacteristically thin in the hallway. 'I don't want to be without you.'

George turned back to Van den Bergen, aware that her heart was thudding fast enough to break, sapping her resolve. 'Then grow some balls and make a choice, for God's sake. Come on, Paul. Does our story end here, or do you want it continue?'

He opened and closed his mouth, his eyebrows bunching together quizzically.

'Oh, bloody forget it,' George said as she opened the front door and stepped out into a world that was all her own.

# Acknowledgements

This series has been going for five books, now. George McKenzie has a wonderfully loyal following, which I'm exceedingly proud of and grateful for. So far, though, George and Van den Bergen's adventures have only been available digitally, despite being award-winning best-sellers. As all five books are finally becoming published in paperback to celebrate the publication of *The Girl Who Got Revenge*, my thankyous feel even more important than ever, so please do take the time to read them. If nothing else, it gives you a little insight into how many other people work hard behind the scenes to bring you books like this.

As always, my heartfelt thanks go first and foremost to my children, Natalie and Adam, who make me want to be a better woman and to write better stories that they will eventually be old enough to read!

Thanks to Christian, for his unfaltering child-wrangling skills and encouraging words. He's always the first to read the finished, published article and I can't wait to see what he makes of this!

All of the thanks to Special Agent, Caspian Dennis, without whom none of *my* words would be words *you* could read in a book or on kindle. Not only is he the best partner in crime-fiction I could ask for, but his lustrous beard has magical power. Fact.

Thanks to the rest of the team at Abner Stein, whose professional shit-hotness make me proud and relieved to be among the agency's stable of stellar names – especially Sandy, Ben, Ray and Felicity.

Many many thanks to the brilliant team at Avon for their unfaltering support of the George McKenzie series and my writing. They are dynamism personified. Special thanks to Victoria Oundjian and Phoebe Morgan for their excellent editorial support … also to Sabah Khan for her PR wizardry, Elke Desanghere for her marketing nouse and to all on the fabulous sales team.

A huge thanks to the Cockblankets for services to humanity, to my many other close friends who lend me a sympathetic ear when I'm stressed off my tits and a MASSIVE thanks to those who put me up when I'm down in London doing bookish shit! I'll name and shame them: Wendy Storer, Steph Williams, Martin de Mello, Ed James, Paulette Geelan, Sarah Stephens-Smith, Steph Broadribb, Louise Voss, Alex Watson and of course, Doris' human, the amazing Tammy Cohen.

Enormous thanks to the many, many bloggers who read tirelessly and give their support to my writing, never asking for anything in return. You guys share the title of Heroes of the Book World only with my readers! My readers really are my diamonds and rubies in this publishing world of ever-shifting fortunes.

Last but certainly not least, I owe the inspiration for this book, yet again, to Louise Owen. Thanks, Weez, for giving me that old Dutch memoir. Without it, *The Girl Who Got Revenge* would have been an entirely different story. I owe you a massive booze on our next lady-date-night.

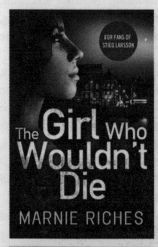
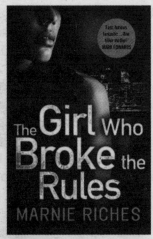
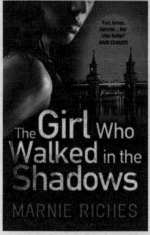